IT'S THE EPIC BATTLE OF BRAINS AGAINST MANES. WHICH SIDE ARE YOU ON?

TEAM UNICORN

EDITED BY HOLLY BLACK

KATHLEEN DUEY

MEG CABOT

GARTH NIX

MARGO LANAGAN

NAOMI NOVIK

DIANA PETERFREUND

TEAM ZOMBIE

EDITED BY JUSTINE LARBALESTIER

LIBBA BRAY

ALAYA DAWN JOHNSON

CASSANDRA CLARE

MAUREEN JOHNSON

SCOTT WESTERFELD

CARRIE RYAN

PRAISE FOR
ZOMBIES VS. UNICORNS

★"Zombies or unicorns? There's no clear
winner, unless it's readers."

—*Publishers Weekly*, starred review

"Who is the victor in this epic
smackdown? Readers, of course!"

—*Kirkus Reviews*

"A hilarious, absurdly quirky book
that takes readers somewhere
no reader has ever gone before."

—*New York Review of Books*

★"A must-have."

—*SLJ*, starred review

JUSTINE LARBALESTIER

ZOMBIES vs.

vs. HOLLY BLACK

UNICORNS

SAGA PRESS

LONDON SYDNEY NEW YORK TORONTO NEW DELHI

SAGA PRESS
AN IMPRINT OF SIMON & SCHUSTER, INC.
1230 AVENUE OF THE AMERICAS, NEW YORK, NEW YORK 10020

For Scott Westerfeld, because there's no one
I'd rather spend the zombie apocalypse with
—J. L.

For Justine, who dragged me into this,
and to whom I am so grateful
—H. B.

Contents

ix   Introduction

1   The Highest Justice
by

19   Love Will Tear Us Apart
by

49   Purity Test
by

69   Bougainvillea
by

109   A Thousand Flowers
by MARGO LANAGAN

145   The Children of the Revolution
by **MAUREEN JOHNSON**

179   The Care and Feeding of Your Baby
Killer Unicorn
by *Diana Peterfreund*

237   Inoculata
by *Scott Westerfeld*

273   Princess Prettypants
by **MEG CABOT**

323   Cold Hands
by **CASSANDRA CLARE**

349   The Third Virgin
by *Kathleen Duey*

383   Prom Night
by **LIBBA BRAY**

Introduction

Since the dawn of time one question has dominated all others:
Zombies or Unicorns?

Well, okay, maybe not since the dawn of time, but definitely since February 2007. That was the day Holly Black and Justine Larbalestier began a heated exchange about the creatures' relative merits on Justine's blog. Since then the question has become an unstoppable Internet meme, crowding comment threads and even making it to YouTube.

Here in the real world Holly and Justine are often called upon to defend, respectively, unicorns and zombies. The whole thing has gotten so out of hand that the only remedy is . . .

Zombies vs. Unicorns. The anthology.

That's right, you have in your hands the book that will settle the debate once and for all.

For Justine it is a question of metaphors: Which creature better symbolizes the human condition? The answer is obviously zombies, which can be used to comment on almost any aspect of our existence. They are walking entropy. They are the dissolute wreck of consumerism. They are the eventual death that faces us all. They are a metaphor for slavery, conformity, and oblivion. What are unicorns? Fluffy, monochrome, sticky tedium.

For Holly, however, unicorns are majestic beasts that are at once symbols of healing and fierce killers with long pointy objects attached to their heads. They were hunted by mythical kings, their image emblazoned on standards by noble families. And they continue to fascinate people today (often in sticker-and-rainbow form, she admits). Besides, between a unicorn and a zombie, which would you rather be trapped down a mine shaft with?

They spend a lot of time having arguments like this one:

Holly: Seriously, you don't like unicorns? What kind of person doesn't like unicorns?

Justine: What kind of a person doesn't like zombies? What have zombies ever done to you?

Holly: Zombies shamble. I disapprove of shambling. And they have bits that fall off. You never see a unicorn behaving that way.

Justine: I shamble. Bits fall off me all the time: hair, skin cells. Are you saying you disapprove of me?

Cherie Priest: But Holly, if you ask nicely, a zombie will give you a piggyback ride even if you are not a virgin. And that is why zombies win.

Justine: See, Holly? No one holds with your zombie-hating ways.

Holly: But the horn of a unicorn can cure diseases! Possibly the diseases you might get from accepting a piggyback ride from a zombie.

Justine: Oh, I see, so you're all for the use of unicorn products. Are you thinking about having a unicorn coat made for yourself as well? I wonder how PETA feels about your unicorn-exploiting ways. . . . Not to mention that zombies don't *have* diseases. I'm appalled that you would spread lies about them.

Clearly, we had to gather the finest minds in our field to answer this urgent question.

Team Zombie, led by **JUSTINE LARBALESTIER**, consists of:

LIBBA BRAY, who has dated only zombies since high school.

Cassandra Clare, who was a nonpracticing zombie until anthology stress made her fall off the brains wagon.

ALAYA DAWN JOHNSON, who has been a zombie lover ever since a pack of them took out all her high school enemies.

MAUREEN JOHNSON (also known as Subject M), who can be subdued by being given her computer, whereupon she will spend hours typing out "brains brains brains brains" on Twitter.

DIANA PETERFREUND, who founded the Southern Zombie Refuge and is still in possession of almost all her limbs.

Scott Westerfeld, who holds numerous patents in flame-thrower technology and is the inventor of the zombie-proof cravat.

HOLLY BLACK's Team Unicorn members are:

MEG CABOT, who has ridden in the unicorn rodeo since she was knee-high to a grasshopper.

Kathleen Duey, who was brought up on a unicorn farm, and learned as a girl that you can't trust them. You really can't.

MARGO LANAGAN, who likes unicorns even more than she likes bears, elephants, langur monkeys, and naked mole rats.

Garth Nix, who distills frightful eau-de-vie from the tears of scorned unicorns.

Naomi Novik, whose unprecedented career as a land pirate could not have been achieved without her unicorn-drawn pirate ship.

Diana Peterfreund, who earned a PhD in Unicorn Studies from Yale for her dissertation on the limits of parthenophobic behavior in the lesser species of *Monoceros monoceros.*

Because Holly can't stand to read about zombies and Justine would rather eat her own eyeballs than read about unicorns, we have kindly ensured that each story is marked by a zombie or unicorn icon. No unwary zombie fan will accidentally start reading a unicorn story or vice versa.

We can all rest easy.

Especially those among us who love to read about zombies *and* unicorns, who now have a book crowded with stories about both creatures by the best talent in the field.

If you're strong enough to read all the stories, you will know by the end of this anthology which is better: zombies or unicorns!

Justine: ZOMBIES!!!! (I win.)

"The Highest Justice"

Holly: Legends of unicorns occur all over the world throughout recorded history. From a unicorn in Persia, described in the fourth century as having a long white horn tipped in crimson, to the German unicorn whose single horn broke into branches like a stag, to the fierce Indian unicorn, black-horned and too dangerous to be taken alive. There's the kirin in Japan, with a deerlike body, a single horn, and a head like a lion or wolf. And there's the medieval European unicorn, with the beard of a goat and cloven hooves.

No matter the origin, the unicorn is usually thought to be a solitary creature whose very body possesses the power to heal. The legends describe it as elusive and beautiful, fierce and strange.

In fact, such is the mysterious draw of the unicorn that originally the story that follows was meant to be a zombie story. Somehow the power of the unicorn caused the story itself to switch sides.

Garth Nix's "The Highest Justice" draws on the association between unicorns and kings. The Chinese qilin presaged the death of Emperors. The heraldic unicorn shows up on coats of arms, including the Royal Arms of Scotland and England. And in "The Highest Justice," a unicorn takes an even more direct interest in a royal family.

Justine: That is so unconvincing. Emperors and kings. Noble families. You're just saying unicorns are stuck-up snobs. Zombies are the proleteriat. Long live the workers!

Also, your global list of genetic experiments gone wrong (deer with the head of a lion? Talk about top heavy!) prove nothing about unicorn variation. Everyone knows unicorns are all-white or rainbow-colored. Ewww. Zombies come in all races. There is nothing more democratic than zombies!

It's an outright lie that the power of the unicorn caused the story to switch sides. Garth Nix has always been a unicorn lover! He was supposed to write a zombie-unicorn story. But he messed it up, didn't he? (Dear Readers, you will notice much messing up from Team Unicorn throughout this anthology.)

Holly: Zombies represent the workers? A seething mass out to get us all, eh? That doesn't seem so egalitarian.

The Highest Justice
By Garth Nix

The girl did not ride the unicorn, because no one ever did. She rode a nervous oat-colored palfrey that had no name, and led the second horse, a blind and almost deaf ancient who long ago had been called Rinaldo and was now simply Rin. The unicorn sometimes paced next to the palfrey, and sometimes not.

Rin bore the dead Queen on his back, barely noticing her twitches and mumbles and the cloying stench of decaying flesh that seeped out through the honey- and spice-soaked bandages. She was tied to the saddle, but could have snapped those bonds if she had thought to do so. She had become monstrously strong since her death three days before, and the intervention by her daughter that had returned her to a semblance of life.

Not that Princess Jess was a witch or necromancer. She knew no more magic than any other young woman. But she was fifteen years old, a virgin, and she believed the old tale of the kingdom's founding: that the unicorn who had aided the legendary Queen Jessibelle the First was still alive and would honor the compact made so long ago, to come in the time of the kingdom's need.

The unicorn's secret name was Elibet. Jess had called this name to the waxing moon at midnight from the tallest tower of the castle, and had seen something ripple in answer across the surface of the earth's companion in the sky.

An hour later Elibet was in the tower. She was somewhat

like a horse with a horn, if you looked at her full on, albeit one
made of white cloud and moonshine. Looked at sideways she
was a fiercer thing, of less familiar shape, made of storm clouds
and darkness, the horn more prominent and bloody at the tip,
like the setting sun. Jess preferred to see a white horse with a
silvery horn, and so that is what she saw.

Jess had called the unicorn as her mother gasped out her final
breath. The unicorn had come too late to save the Queen, but
by then Jess had another plan. The unicorn listened and then by
the power of her horn, brought back some part of the Queen to
inhabit a body from which life had all too quickly sped.

They had then set forth, to seek the Queen's poisoner, and
mete out justice.

Jess halted her palfrey as they came to a choice of ways. The
royal forest was thick and dark in these parts, and the path was
no more than a beaten track some dozen paces wide. It forked
ahead, into two lesser, narrower paths.

"Which way?" asked Jess, speaking to the unicorn, who had
once again mysteriously appeared at her side.

The unicorn pointed her horn at the left-hand path.

"Are you sure—," Jess asked. "No, it's just that—"

"The other way looks more traveled—"

"No, I'm not losing heart—"

"I know you know—"

"Talking to yourself?" interjected a rough male voice, the
only other sound in the forest, for if the unicorn had spoken,
no one but Jess had heard her.

The palfrey shied as Jess swung around and reached for her

sword. But she was too late, as a dirty bearded ruffian held a rusty pike to her side. He grinned, and raised his eyebrows.

"Here's a tasty morsel, then," he leered. "Step down lightly, and no tricks."

"Elibet!" said Jess indignantly.

The unicorn slid out of the forest behind the outlaw, and lightly pricked him in the back of his torn leather jerkin with her horn. The man's eyebrows went up still farther and his eyes darted to the left and right.

"Ground your pike," said Jess. "My friend can strike faster than any man."

The outlaw grunted, and lowered his pike, resting its butt in the leaf litter at his feet.

"I give up," he wheezed, leaning forward as if he might escape the sharp horn. "Ease off on that spear, and take me to the sheriff. I swear—"

"Hunger," interrupted the Queen. Her voice had changed with her death. It had become gruff and leathery, and significantly less human.

The bandit glanced at the veiled figure under the broad-brimmed pilgrim's hat.

"What?" he asked hesitantly.

"Hunger," groaned the Queen. "Hunger."

She raised her right arm, and the leather cord that bound her to the saddle's high cantle snapped with a sharp crack. A bandage came loose at her wrist and dropped to the ground in a series of spinning turns, revealing the mottled blue-bruised skin beneath.

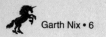

"Shoot 'em!" shouted the bandit as he dove under Jess's horse and scuttled across the path toward the safety of the trees. As he ran, an arrow flew over his head and struck the Queen in the shoulder. Another, coming behind it, went past Jess's head as she jerked herself forward and down. The third was struck out of the air by a blur of vaguely unicorn-shaped motion. There were no more arrows, but a second later there was a scream from halfway up a broad oak that loomed over the path ahead, followed by the heavy thud of a body hitting the ground.

Jess drew her sword and kicked her palfrey into a lurching charge. She caught the surviving bandit just before he managed to slip between two thorny bushes, and landed a solid blow on his head with the back of the blade. She hadn't meant to be merciful, but the sword had turned in her sweaty grasp. He fell under the horse's feet, and got trampled a little before Jess managed to turn about.

She glanced down to make sure he was at least dazed, but sure of this, spared him no more time. Her mother had broken the bonds on her left arm as well, and was ripping off the veil that hid her face.

"Hunger!" boomed the Queen, loud enough even for poor old deaf Rin to hear. He stopped eating the grass and lifted his head, time-worn nostrils almost smelling something he didn't like.

"Elibet! Please . . . ," beseeched Jess. "A little longer—we must be almost there."

The unicorn stepped out from behind a tree and looked

at her. It was the look of a stern teacher about to allow a pupil some small favor.

"One more touch, please, Elibet."

The unicorn bent her head, paced over to the dead Queen, and touched the woman lightly with her horn, briefly imbuing her with a subtle nimbus of summer sunshine, bright in the shadowed forest. Propelled by that strange light, the arrow in the Queen's shoulder popped out, the blue-black bruises on her arms faded, and her skin shone, pink and new. She stopped fumbling with the veil, slumped down in her saddle, and let out a relatively delicate and human-sounding snore.

"Thank you," said Jess.

She dismounted and went to look at the bandit. He had sat up and was trying to wipe away the blood that slowly dripped across his left eye.

"So you give up, do you?" Jess asked, and snorted.

The bandit didn't answer.

Jess pricked him with her sword, so he was forced to look at her.

"I should finish you off here and now," said Jess fiercely. "Like your friend."

"My brother," muttered the man. "But you won't finish me, will you? You're the rightful type, I can tell. Take me to the sheriff. Let him do what needs to be done."

"You're probably in league with the sheriff," said Jess.

"Makes no odds to you, anyways. Only the sheriff has the right to justice in this wood. King's wood, it is."

"I have the right to the Middle and the Low Justice, under

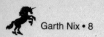

the King," said Jess, but even as she said it, she knew it was the wrong thing to say. Robbery and attempted murder in the King's wood were matters for the High Justice.

"Slip of a girl like you? Don't be daft," the bandit said, laughing. "Besides, it's the High Justice for me. I'll go willingly along to the sheriff."

"I don't have time to take you to the sheriff," said Jess. She could not help glancing back at her mother. Already there were tiny spots of darkness visible on her arm, like the first signs of mold on bread.

"Better leave me, then," said the bandit. He smiled, an expression that was part cunning and part relief beginning to appear upon his weather-beaten face.

"Leave you!" exploded Jess. "I'm not going to—What?"

She tilted her head, to look at a patch of shadow in the nearer trees.

"You have the High Justice? Really?"

"Who are you talking to?" asked the bandit nervously. The cunning look remained, but the relief was rapidly disappearing.

"Very well. I beseech you, in the King's name, to judge this man fairly. As you saw, he sought to rob me, and perhaps worse, and told his companion to shoot."

"Who are you talking to?" screamed the bandit. He staggered to his feet as Jess backed off, keeping her sword out and steady, aimed now at his guts.

"Your judge," said Jess. "Who I believe is about to announce—"

Jess stopped talking as the unicorn appeared behind the bandit, her horn already through the man's chest. The bandit walked another step, unknowing, then his mouth fell open and he looked down at the sharp whorled spike that had seemingly grown out of his heart. He lifted his hand to grasp it, but halfway there nerves and muscles failed, and his life was ended.

The unicorn tossed her head, and the bandit's corpse slid off, into the forest mulch.

Jess choked a little, and coughed. She hadn't realized she had stopped breathing. She had seen men killed before, but not by a unicorn. Elibet snorted, and wiped her horn against the trunk of a tree, like a bird sharpening its beak.

"Yes. Yes, you're right," said Jess. "I know we must hurry."

Jess quickly fastened her mother's bandages and bonds and rearranged the veil before mounting her palfrey. It shivered under her as she took up the reins, and looked back with one wild eye.

"Hup!" said Jess, and dug in her heels. She took the left-hand path, ducking under a branch.

They came to the King's hunting lodge at nightfall. It had been a simple fort once, a rectangle of earth ramparts, but the King had built a large wooden hall at its center, complete with an upper solar that had glass windows, the whole of it topped with a sharply sloped roof of dark red tiles.

Lodge and fort lay in the middle of a broad forest clearing, which was currently lit by several score of lanterns, hung from hop poles. Jess grimaced as she saw the lanterns, though it was much as she'd expected. The lodge was, after all, her father's favorite trysting place. The lanterns would be a "romantic"

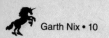

gesture from the King to his latest and most significant mistress.

The guards saw her coming, and possibly recognized the palfrey. Two came out cautiously to the forest's edge, swords drawn, while several others watched from the ramparts, their bows held ready. The King was not well-loved by his subjects, with good cause. But his guards were well-paid and, so long as they had not spent their last pay, loyal.

"Princess Jess?" asked the closer guard. "What brings you here?"

He was a new guard, who had not yet experienced enough of the King's court to be hardened by it, or so sickened that he sought leave to return to his family's estate. His name was Piers, and he was only a year or two older than Jess. She knew him as well as a Princess might know a servant, for her mother had long ago advised her to remember the names of all the guards, and make friends of them as soon as she could.

"Oh, I'm glad to see you, Piers," sighed Jess. She gestured to the cloaked and veiled figure behind. It was dark enough that the guards would not immediately see the Queen's bonds. "It is my mother. She wishes to see the King."

"Your Highness!" exclaimed Piers, and he bent his head, as did his companion, a man the other guards called Old Briars, though his name was Brian and he was not that old. "But where are your attendants? Your guards?"

"They follow," said Jess. She let her horse amble forward, so the guards had to scramble to keep alongside. "We came on ahead. My mother must see the King immediately. It is an urgent matter. She is not well."

"His Majesty the King ordered that he not be disturbed—," rumbled Old Briars.

"My mother must see His Majesty," said Jess. "Perhaps, Piers, you could run ahead and warn . . . let the King know we will soon be with him?"

"Better not, boy. You know what—," Old Briars started to say. He was interrupted by the Queen, who suddenly sat straighter and rasped out a single world.

"Edmund . . ."

Either the King's name, spoken so strangely by the Queen, or the desperate look on Jess's small, thin face made Old Briars stop talking and stand aside.

"I'll go at once," said Piers, with sudden decision. "Brian, show Their Highnesses into the *hall*."

He laid a particular stress on the last word, which Jess knew meant "Keep them out of the solar," the upper chamber that the King had undoubtedly already retired to with his latest mistress, the Lady Lieka—who, unlike Jess, actually was a witch.

They left the horses at the tumbledown stable near the gate. The king had not bothered to rebuild that. As Jess untied the Queen and helped her down, she saw Brian working hard to keep his expression stolid, to maintain the professional unseeing look all the guardsmen had long perfected. The King being what he was, the outer guards usually did not want to see anything. If they did want to watch, or even participate, they joined his inner retinue.

The Queen was mumbling and twitching again. Jess had

to breathe through her mouth to avoid the stench that was overcoming spices and scent.

"Ed-mund . . . ," rasped the Queen as Jess led her to the hall. "Ed-mund . . ."

"Yes, Mother," soothed Jess. "You will see him in a moment."

She caught a glimpse of Elibet as Brian stood aside to let them pass through the great oaken door of the hall. Piers was waiting inside, and he bowed deeply as they went in. He didn't notice the unicorn streaming in ahead, the smoke from the fire and candles eddying as she passed.

The King was seated at the high table as if he had been there all the time, though Jess could tell he had just thrown a richly furred robe of red and gold over his nightshirt. Lady Lieka, clad in a similar robe, sat on a low stool at his side, and poured a stream of dark wine into the King's jeweled goblet, as if she were some ordinary handmaiden.

None of the King's usual henchmen were with him, which suggested a very rapid descent from the solar. Jess could still hear laughter and talking above. The absence of courtiers and the inner guards could be a bad sign. The King liked an audience for his more ordinary deeds of foulness but preferred privacy when it came to mistreating his own family.

"Milady Queen and my . . . thoughtful . . . daughter," boomed out the King. "What brings you to this poor seat?"

He was very angry, Jess could tell, though his voice did not betray that anger. It was in the tightness in his eyes and the way he sat, leaning forward, ready to roar and hurl abuse.

"Ed-mund . . . ," said the Queen, the word half a growl and

half a sigh. She staggered forward. Jess ran after her, and took off her hat, the veil coming away with it.

"What is this!" exclaimed the King, rising to his feet.

"Edmund . . . ," rasped the Queen. Her face was gray and blotched, and flies clustered in the corners of her desiccated eyes, all the signs of a death three days gone returning as the unicorn's blessing faded.

"Lieka!" screamed the King.

The Queen shambled forward, her arms outstretched, the bandages unwinding behind her. Flesh peeled off her fingers as she flexed them, white bone reflecting the fire- and candlelight.

"She was poisoned!" shouted Jess angrily. She pointed accusingly at Lieka. "Poisoned by your leman! Yet even dead she loves you still!"

"No!" shrieked the King. He stood on his chair and looked wildly about. "Get her away. Lieka!"

"One kiss," mumbled the Queen. She pursed her lips, and gray-green spittle fell from her wizened mouth. "Love . . . love . . ."

"Be calm, my dove," said Lieka. She rested one almond-white hand on the King's shoulder. Under her touch he sank back down into his high-backed chair. "You—strike off her head."

She spoke to Piers. He had unsheathed his sword, but remained near the door.

"Don't, Piers!" said Jess. "Kiss her, Father, and she will be gone. That's all she wants."

"Kill it!" shrieked the King.

Piers strode across the hall, but Jess held out one beseeching hand. He stopped by her side, and went no farther. The Queen

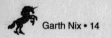

slowly shambled on, rasping and muttering as she progressed toward the raised dais, the King and Lady Lieka.

"Traitors," whined the King. "I am surrounded by traitors."

"One kiss!" shouted Jess. "You owe her that."

"Not all are traitors, Majesty," purred Lieka. She spoke in the King's ear, careless of the Queen's pathetic faltering step up onto the dais. "Shall I rid you of this relict?"

"Yes!" answered the King. "Yes!"

He turned to look the other way, shielding his face in his hands. Lieka took up a six-branched silver candelabra and whispered to it, the candle flames blazing high in answer to her call.

"Father!" screamed Jess. "One kiss! That's all she wants!"

Lieka thrust out the candelabra as the Queen finally made it onto the dais and staggered forward. The flames licked at dress and bandages, but only slowly, until Lieka made a claw with her other hand and dragged it up through the air, the flames leaping in response as if she had hauled upon their secret strings.

The Queen screeched, and ran forward with surprising speed. Lieka jumped away, but the King tripped and fell as he tried to leave his chair. Before he could get up, the Queen knelt at his side and, now completely ablaze, embraced him. The King screamed and writhed but could not break free as she bent her flame-wreathed blackened head down for a final kiss.

"Aaaahhhh!" the Queen's grateful sigh filled the hall, drowning out the final muffled choking scream of the King. She slumped over him, pushed him down into the smoldering rushes on the dais, and both were still.

Lieka gestured. The burning bodies, the smoking rushes, and the great fire in the corner pit went out. The candles and the tapers flickered, then resumed their steady light.

"A remarkable display of foolishness," the witch said to Jess, who stood staring, her face whiter than even Lieka's lead-painted visage. "What did you think to achieve?"

"Mother loved him, despite everything," whispered Jess. "And I hoped to bring the murder home to you."

"But instead you have made me Queen," said Lieka. She sat down in the King's chair. "Edmund and I were married yesterday. A full day after your mother's death."

"Then he knew . . . ," said Jess stoically. It was not a surprise, not after all this time and the King's other actions, but she had retained some small hope, now extinguished. "He knew you had poisoned her."

"He ordered it!" Lieka laughed. "But I must confess I did not dare hope that it would lead to his death in turn. I must thank you for that, girl. I am also curious how you brought the old slattern back. Or rather, who you got to do it for you. I had not thought there was another practitioner of the art who would dare to cross me."

"An old friend of the kingdom helped me," said Jess. "Someone I hope will help me again, to bring you to justice."

"Justice!" spat Lieka. "Edmund ordered me to poison your mother. I merely did as the King commanded. His own death was at the Queen's hands, or perhaps more charitably by misadventure. Besides, who can judge me now that I am the highest in the land?"

Jess looked to the darkest corner of the hall, behind the dais.

"Please," she said quietly. "Surely this is a matter for the Highest Justice of all?"

"Who are you talking to?" said Lieka. She turned in her seat and looked around, her beautiful eyes narrowed in concentration. Seeing nothing, she smiled and turned back. "You are more a fool than your mother. Guard, take her away."

Piers did not answer. He was staring at the dais. Jess watched too, as the unicorn stepped lightly to Lieka's side, and gently dipped her horn into the King's goblet.

"Take her away!" ordered Lieka again. "Lock her up somewhere dark. And summon the others from the solar. There is much to celebrate."

She raised the goblet, and took a drink. The wine stained her lips dark, and she licked them before she took another draft.

"The royal wine is swee—"

The word never quite quit Lieka's mouth. The skin on her forehead wrinkled in puzzlement, her perfectly painted face crazing over with tiny cracks. She began to turn her head toward the unicorn, and pitched forward onto the table, knocking the goblet over. The spilled wine pooled to the edge, and began to slowly drip upon the blackened feet of the Queen, who lay beneath, conjoined with her King.

"Thank you," said Jess. She slumped to the floor, raising her knees so she could make herself small and rest her head. She had never felt so tired, so totally spent, as if everything had poured out of her, all energy, emotion, and thought.

Then she felt the unicorn's horn, the side of it, not the

point. Jess raised her head, and was forced to stand up as Elibet continued to chide her, almost levering her up.

"What?" asked Jess miserably. "I said 'thank you.' It's done, now, isn't it? Justice has been served, foul murderers served their due portion. My mother even . . . even . . . got her kiss . . ."

The unicorn looked at her. Jess wiped the tears out of her eyes and listened.

"But there's my brother. He'll be old enough in a few years—well, six years—"

"I know father was a bad king, but that doesn't mean—"

"It's not fair! It's too hard! I was going to go to Aunt Maria's convent school—"

Elibet stamped her foot down, through the rushes, hard enough to make the stone flagstones beneath ring like a beaten gong. Jess swallowed her latest protest and bent her head.

"Is that a unicorn?" whispered Piers.

"You can see her?" exclaimed Jess.

Piers blushed. Jess stared at him. Evidently her father's outer guards did not take their lead from the King in all respects, or Piers was simply too new to have been forced to take part in the King's frequent bacchanalia.

"I . . . I . . . There is someone in particular . . . ," muttered Piers. He met her gaze as he spoke, not looking down as a good servant should. She noticed that his eyes were a very warm brown, and there was something about his face that made her want to look at him more closely. . . .

Then she was distracted by the unicorn, who stepped back up onto the dais and delicately plucked the simple traveling

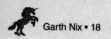

crown from the King's head with her horn. Balancing it there, she headed back to Jess.

"What's she doing?" whispered Piers.

"Dispensing justice," said Elibet. She dropped the crown onto Jess's head and tapped it in place with her horn. "I trust you will be a better judge than your father. In all respects."

"I will try," said Jess. She reached up and touched the thin gold circlet. It didn't feel real, but then nothing did. Perhaps it might in daylight, after a very long sleep.

"Do so," said Elibet. She paced around them and walked toward the door.

"Wait!" cried Jess. "Will I see you again?"

The unicorn looked back at the princess and the young guardsman at her side.

"Perhaps," said Elibet, and was gone.

ALAYA DAWN JOHNSON

"Love Will Tear Us Apart"

Justine: Hallelujah! After wading through Garth Nix's ye oldey unicorn muck you now get to read a proper zombie story. Since Holly bored you all by setting out the various different kinds of unicorns (even though we all know there are only two kinds: sickly pale or rainbow-colored) I thought I should fill you in (even though I'm sure most of you know) on the different kinds of zombies.

First, you have your voudin-inspired zombies raised from the dead (or near-dead) by magic and controlled by their masters. Then there's George Romero's reinvention of zombies that came with *Night of the Living Dead* in 1968. Romero's zombies are death itself—slow, shuffling, and inescapable. More lately there have been souped-up, running zombies, with whom I personally do not hold.

Alaya Dawn Johnson is one of my favorite writers, and this story will amply demonstrate why. Her zombies are neither voudin possessed, nor George Romero slow-shuffling brain eaters, nor are they the faster, more lethal zombies of more recent (and inferior) films. They are zombies of her own making. Zombies that can even fall in love.

That's right. You are about to read what may be the most beautiful and intense zombie romance of all time—and it is definitely one of the funniest.

Mac 'n' cheese, anyone?

Holly: What I love about this story is that it is barely a zombie story at all! No stink, no shuffling, no decay, just a *tiny* bit of brain eating. And, hey, I am all about culinary adventure. So I can pretend that it's about a revenant or ghoul or some kind of undead creature that I actually like.

Justine: See? Even Holly secretly loves zombies.

Love Will Tear Us Apart
By Alaya Dawn Johnson

1. I Bet You Look Good on the Dance Floor

Think of it like the best macaroni and cheese you've ever had. No neon yellow Velveeta and bread crumbs. I'm talking gourmet cheddar, the expensive stuff from Vermont that crackles as it melts into that crust on top. Imagine if right before you were about to tear into it, the mac and cheese starts talking to you? And it's really cool. It likes Joy Division more than New Order, and owns every Sonic Youth album, and saw you in the audience at the latest Arctic Monkeys concert, though you were too stoned to notice anything but the clearly sub-par cheesy mac you'd brought with you.

And what if he—I mean "it"—were really hot? Tall and lanky and weirdly well muscled, with bright blue eyes and ginger hair? So, he smells like the best meal you've ever eaten, but you kind of want to bone him too. Can't have it both ways. You aren't a necro. But a boy's got to eat—maybe you could just nibble a bit at the edges? A part he won't miss, and then fuck the rest of him. Eat an arm or something. He can still fuck with one arm. Not that well, though. Probably wouldn't like it. Okay, a hand. Who ever needed a left hand? Then you remember that Jack—that's his name, the mac and cheese—plays lacrosse. That's probably where he got all those yummy muscles. You need two hands for lacrosse.

A pinky? Damn, you might as well starve yourself.

And you had it all planned out. You and Jack have shared an art class for the last three weeks. You were going to admire the mobile he's been making (a twisted metal tower dangling with shattered CDs and beer tabs), look deep into his eyes, invite him back home with you to play Halo or smoke hash or whatever, and then devour him in the woods off of Route 25. Those woods are the local hunting range. You've done it at least a dozen times before, though not to your actual classmates at Edward R. Murrow High, your newest school.

Liking your meal too much to kill him? That's a first.

"Pizzicato Five?" you say, catching on to the tail end of Jack's sentence. "Who're they?"

His eyes light up. Not literally, but they get really large and you can see the blue of his irises all spangly and flecked around his dilated pupils. Bug eyes, you usually call that look.

"Dude, they're awesome," he says. "Harajuku pop. Yeah, I know, you're thinking about that Gwen Stefani crap, like, 'I totally thought Jack had better taste,' but don't worry, this is the real stuff. It's all ironic and postmodern. James Bond on a Nipponese acid trip in a bukkake club."

"Wow," you say, 'cause honestly you can only deal in monosyllables at this point.

"Hey, we can walk to my place from here. You wanna come over? I have a few of their albums."

So you don't get anywhere near Route 25. Which is good. You don't want to eat him, and you can still smell your leftovers there. The whole thing is weirding you out. You—I don't know—you like him. *Like* like him. You think you had a little sister once who would say it just like that. You don't remember eating her, but you can't be sure. And what would Jack think if he knew you were some monster who couldn't even remember if he ate his sister alive?

So you try to be engaging and charming and basically *not stupid*. You get into an argument about Belle and Sebastian.

"Sure, I like some of their stuff," he says, smiling as though he knows you don't agree. "*The Life Pursuit* has some great songs on it."

"Twee copies of the Smiths aping Jonathan Richman's airy earnestness and none of his insanity."

He laughs, and you stumble on the grass. "Hold back, Grayson," he says.

Jack gives you a long look, and there you go again, your heart beating too fast, pupils dilating, and you don't really understand it, but that smell of his? That crusty mac-and-cheese aroma? It just got about a hundred times better. When he breathes in and out, it's like he's exhaling the essence of his marrow, the rough gristle in his joints, the blood that pulses as it rushes past the tanned skin by his collarbone.

He's cutting through some woods behind the school, down an old deer path or something, and you've been too busy ogling his ass to pay much attention.

"Hey, what street do you live on again?" you ask.

"It's off of Boward. I just like to cut through here sometimes. 'I took the one less traveled by, / And that has made all the difference.'"

"Dylan?" you guess.

He stops abruptly in between two trees that still have about half their leaves. His smile is sort of sad. "Robert Frost," he says, and you don't think this is a good time to mention that you've never heard of him. Probably some emo folkie like Sufjan Stevens.

"Grayson," he says, his hands deep in his pockets. With anyone else it'd be fidgeting, but with Jack right now, the gesture is more like *Please fuck me*.

"Yeah?"

Your voice is sort of a squeak. You can smell the impending sex like it's a bum in the park.

Then Jack goes and starts laughing again, and takes his hands out of his pockets. "It's funny. Everyone thinks you're weird," he says. "But you're all right, Grayson."

"Hey, you, too."

And you think, okay, a fuck would have been better, but you sort of like the idea of listening to this Nipponese acid trip album with him. He still smells like the best meal you've never tasted.

2. Several Species of Small Furry Animals Gathered Together in a Cave and Grooving with a Pict

The sad tale of how I, Philip A. Grayson, became infected with a brain-devouring prion and was subsequently partially cured.

Part the first. I don't know who I was. I don't know how I caught it. The prion, I mean—this twisted, misshapen little bit of protein with even less autonomy than a virus, but one hell of a bigger punch. Ever heard of mad cow disease? They told me my prions are only found in bacteria that gestate at the bottom of landfills at high temperatures. It has to enter the host through the mucus membranes. That means it has to be drunk, snorted, dripped, or anally inserted. Yeah, I don't want to know what the fuck I was doing either. It's too bad, really, that I remember my name.

Part the second. I've killed a lot of people. I ate all of them, brains first. Not because I live off of gray matter or something, but because that's the best part. Don't believe me? Just ask the Fore tribe of Papua New Guinea. They loved brains so much they nearly killed themselves with this other prion: transmissible spongiform encephalopathy. They called it kuru. Laughing sickness. Talk about dying happy.

Part the third. My prion is too rare to have a name. Like kuru, it mods my behavior in a major way. Well, I don't know if you noticed, but it makes me want to eat people. Most of the time it gets rid of all of its host's higher brain functions to make the whole devouring people compulsion work better. Frontal lobes and Joy Division obsessions tend to be pretty incompatible with the sudden overpowering urge to eat your girlfriend's eyeballs.

Part the fourth. These scientists got to me before the mad proteins had a chance to do more than nibble. They gave me this drug that half-worked. My prions can't reproduce, and they can't devour my brain, but they still rattle around in there, jumping up and down on my amygdala every time I smell a human. The prions gave me these hyperactive pheromones, so I can do this thing where I lean in and smile and people go all bug-eyed and it's like they turn into zombies or something. Well, until I start to eat them. You're probably wondering why these benevolent scientists would part-cure me and then let me go into the world to seduce/eat people with my mostly intact brain functions. Don't be stupid—of course they didn't. When they figured out what had happened, they locked me in some padded cell. I ate the security guard and escaped.

The End

One last thing: About that frontal lobe the parasite didn't quite devour? I lost enough that I don't feel too bad about killing people. The way of the jungle and all that. It only bothers me sometimes. Like when they love Joy Division. Like when they laugh.

3. Behind Blue Eyes

Jack's place is a little intense. It's a stone mansion on a cul-de-sac of its own, with Pentagon-style security. One ten-digit code to get through the gate outside, a *different* twelve-digit code to get through the front door. You half-expect the knob to check his fingerprints.

"Dude," you say when the fort seems to have been breached, "this place is scary." There's not so much furniture, but every beige and mauve piece looks like it cost a fortune.

Jack shrugs, a little uncomfortable. "My dad," he says. "He's obsessed with security. His friends keep calling him about some escaped nutcase that might be in Colorado. He's gotten paranoid."

You feel sick, but try not to show it. Those scientists have tailed you for a year. What are the chances they've finally caught up now? "What's your dad do?"

"Ex-CIA," Jack says. "Shattered his hip five years ago, so now he mostly does consulting."

When you climb the staircase, you catch a whiff of gunpowder, but the only weapons you see are older—a row of antique and modern swords mounted on the wall.

"You know how to use these things?"

Jack sighs. "Sure. Dad's made me do weapons training since I could walk. Guns, swords, martial arts. So long as there's a potential for violent death, he's interested. It's all bullshit, really. Fake heroics so you can pretend you're not really killing people. 'One, two! One, two! And through and through / The vorpal blade went snicker-snack!'"

"Frost?" you say, though you know you're wrong and you can't wait for him to tell you so.

He smiles. "'The Jabberwocky.' Lewis Carroll. Dad likes that one 'cause it's all about slaying an evil beast. You know, I think he's *happy* about this nutcase on the loose? Always before it was rabid animals and no-kill tournaments and— Yeah. It's a fixation."

He looks away, holds himself too still, and you wonder what

he's not telling you about his dad's "fixation." Then he shakes his head and leads you the rest of the way up the stairs. Jack's room is like a huge middle finger up the ass of the rest of the beige-on-white medicated-Vail-yuppie house. Every inch of wall space is covered with posters. A few sports stars but mostly musicians. Pete Townshend holding up a bloody hand; Gorillaz with their animated tongues lolling; Johnny Rotten grinning like a redheaded demon pixie; all of Devo with their weird space suits and jerky, vacant expressions. There's a walk-in closet in back, and when he opens it, you see a few thousand CDs and vinyl albums lined neatly against the wall.

"I've got a few hundred gigs of MP3s, but vinyl is better, I think."

And if you weren't turned on before. "Fuck me," you say. "This is amazing."

He grins at you, awkwardness forgotten. "I'm lucky. So long as I practice, Dad tends to leave me alone."

His killer sound system includes a subwoofer about the size of your torso, so the first notes of the recording are suitably deafening. He lies down on his thick beige carpet and then looks up at you, a gesture that might be an invitation if it weren't so wary. You wonder what he thinks of you, and if you needed more evidence that something weird is happening here, that would clinch it. Part of the benefit of frontal-lobe-devouring prions is not needing to worry what the hell other people think. That's a human thing. Not whatever you've become.

You sit down next to him. He smiles a little and leans back

on his elbows, closes his eyes. You watch him. The floppy ginger hair falls over his forehead, almost concealing a long, thin scar that runs from his hairline down to his left ear. He nods in time to the screeching, childlike vocals, the swinging sixties rhythms, the psychedelic atonality.

"James Bond on a Nipponese acid trip," you say, softly.

He opens his eyes, and now they're not buggy at all. They're hard and fierce and iced. He looks like he might kill you or kiss you. You hold your too-slow breath and realize that you don't care which.

"I knew you'd like it," he says.

The air comes out in a rush. You lean back against the carpet and look at the inside of your eyelids. You see red, like always. Muscle and bone and the crunch of your oversize molars tearing through. That's what Jack would have become if he hadn't mentioned Joy Division at the end of class. And even now you can feel the heat of him beside you, the soft exhale of his pores, the smell that's a little sweat and a little detergent and some shampoo with a surprisingly girly flavor—coconut? Hibiscus? How could someone who uses hibiscus shampoo look so suddenly dangerous? He moves abruptly. You wait like you might fall on a blade.

But no, the door is opening, someone else is in the house. Slowly, too slowly, you turn around.

"Jackson," says the man who must be the father. He wears khakis the color of his furniture, and a brown polo shirt. "Your target is still clean."

If Jack was icy, his dad is absolute fucking zero. His eyebrows are so large and thick they cast his recessed eyes in deep shadow, like a pit. His mouth is pursed, not enough to be called a frown, but damn if you don't want to run straight out the window and make excuses later. Jack glances at you and then back at his dad. He turns off the CD, and the sudden silence is louder than any high-decibel subwoofer. You can hear his dad's breathing, as slow and icy as the rest of him. Ex-CIA. He was probably their go-to for those "enhanced" interrogations.

"Sorry," Jack mumbles, unrecognizable. "I was getting to it."

"I can see," says the ice man. "I've just heard from Miller again. That creature they're tracking definitely passed through here. I need you to be ready."

"Sorry," Jack says again.

The dad turns to you now, all cool speculation. You know without even trying that there's nothing your special pheromones can do to thaw this guy. He thinks you're a cockroach. He wants to stamp you out. Can he tell what you are just by looking? But no, it's impossible. If he knew, he'd shoot you on the spot and tell Jack to clean the mess.

Ice man leaves, a slight hitch in his step. Jack takes a deep, shuddering breath and slams the door shut.

You whistle. "He like that every day?"

Jack glances at you and then away. His blue eyes dilate for no reason, and blood blossoms in his cheeks like roses. You swallow.

"He's . . . you know."

You try to imagine life with someone like that. Your failure to do so feels like something broken, something sucking and desperate. Because you *know* the ice man—as only one cracked soul can recognize another.

"'But my dreams, they aren't as empty.'" You can't sing, so you just say it. But you remember the rest of the line: "'As my conscience seems to be.'"

Jack starts, like someone poked him, and then sags against the wall. He laughs, but it doesn't sound like laughter.

"My dad hates The Who," he says.

"Your dad's a dick."

For a moment you think he might take your hand.

4. Maps

I said I don't know who I was, but that's not strictly true. No invading twist of genetic code is that efficient. My hippocampus has been wiped pretty clean, but fragments remain. Hell, for all I know I remember everything, and just suppress it, like Iraq vets who can barely find Baghdad on a map. But here's what I think I know. I had a sister. She was younger than me and dumb in that dumb little sister way, which means that she'll probably grow up to be a neurochemist and invent the cure for spongiform encephalopathy. But I remember her loving *Boy Meets World* and *High School Musical* (all three) and the direct-to-DVD Olsen twins movies (in particular *Passport to Paris*). We had a dad, but I don't know what he did. No mother, as far as I can tell. Dad had a thing for banana plants. He refused to buy regular Chiquita bananas, but he'd bring home any other variety he could find: tiny brown ones, giant green ones, skinny orange ones with flesh as hard as an apple and as sour as a lime.

He had a greenhouse filled with banana plants that fruited about once every two years, and the fruit was never edible. "They're going extinct, you know," he would say to me and my sister in the supermarket, tapping the clusters of normal yellow Cavendish bananas he'd never allow in the house. "A few more years and human carelessness will have destroyed every banana plant on earth." Why? Some sort of cancer that turns them red and as hard as bricks. I know more details, but you don't want them. Same old story since Noah: Humans are lousy stewards of the earth.

I don't remember if I ate him. I don't remember much of anything until I woke up in that lab. Just snatches. Hunger slicing through my muscles like an itch that could only go away if I peeled off my own skin. Blood like steam off a lake, warm and misted in my nostrils. And meat, raw and salty, filled with bones that caught in my throat and brains that slid down like oysters. Everyone is anonymous when I pull them apart. No one has a name when I eat them. Not even my father. Not even my sister.

Not even Jack.

5. Pulling Mussels (from the Shell)

The girl two seats down from you in the bleachers thinks you're cute. You are cute—probably even before the prion problem, and certainly afterward. She has short brown hair and a nice-ish smile, though you could do without the braces. Those make nasty marks if she decides to fight back. You decide to smile after the second time she glances over her shoulder and giggles.

You have to eat sometime, after all, and the Jack situation has, in practical terms, made you go hungry. Mac-and-cheese himself is running across the field now, yelling at one of his teammates to pass him the ball as he guns for an opening in the opposing team's lines. His green jersey is drenched in sweat and clings to his muscles in a way you know makes you look as bug-eyed as the girl with braces. You've overheard enough to know that she's a good mark—here from out of town, visiting some friends. If you do this right, you might get to stay in Colorado for a few more weeks, at least. It's funny—you usually care about finding a new town as much as you used to care about finding a new supermarket. Just another place to buy meat.

On the field Jack violently checks another player. They fall to the churned-up turf while the ball sails into the net. The crowd cheers, even though Jack gets fouled. The goal is good. Jack is a lot more violent on the field than he is off of it. But then you remember that strange, fierce way he looked at you for a moment yesterday afternoon. You remember the scar on his forehead and his ice man dad.

At halftime he comes over to the bleachers, breathing hard and grinning. A few other students give him high fives. You hang back, knowing he sees you and wondering if he'll say something. It's Saturday. You've never come to a game before. The whole field smells ripe, hundreds of walking, talking, laughing Happy Meals, and even from a few feet away, Jack smells better than all of them. For a moment you contemplate leaping over the bleachers and just eating him in front of the whole crowd. You'd probably get at least a few bites in before the police come. Maybe they'd even use deadly force, seeing as how you're clearly a rabid beast, and finally solve all your problems. Saliva pools in your mouth. Jack looks up at you.

You won't eat him. No matter what.

"Grayson," he says with a half smile. He climbs the bleachers and sits next to you. "You like the game?"

You breathe very slowly. His arm brushes against yours, slick with his sweat. You have such a raging hard-on you can only hope he doesn't look down.

"Nice," you say. "You always that aggressive?"

Jack shrugs, but his grin is pleased. "If I need to be. We're winning, aren't we?"

"Guess so."

Jack looks at you quickly and then away, and once again you're enthralled by his countervailing waves of awkwardness and ferocity. "Grayson, about yesterday . . . my dad . . ."

"He's not here, is he?" you say, playing at being scared, though actually the ice man does sort of scare you.

Jack laughs. "God, I hope not. Dad barely tolerates extracurriculars. He thinks I should be training. . . . Hey, you want to go into the city with me tonight? I've got an extra ticket to Modest Mouse."

This would be marginally appealing even without the additional bonus of Jack, but you look back down at the braces girl, now chatting with her friends. Your hunger is starting to feel like that first time, a longing that cuts into your muscles and makes the world turn red. You can't go much longer without a meal.

"Sorry," you say. "Can't."

You know you ought to offer a better explanation. Homework or community service or a part-time job. But you don't want to lie to Jack.

So you hurt him instead.

"Okay," Jack says. He looks away. The game is starting again. He walks back onto the field. Deliberately, knowing he's still looking, you move so you're right behind the girl. You smile at her.

"Haven't seen you here before," you say.

She goes bug-eyed. She blushes. You can smell her blood like it's already broken the skin. "Visiting from Boulder," she says. She says other things. You can't quite hear her. Jack is staring at you from the edge of the bench. Even from here you can see the ice in those blue eyes. Like he wants to kill you.

You arrange to meet the girl—she has a name, but you try not to remember it, easier that way—in the parking lot in an hour. You tell her about some concert you have tickets to, would she like to come? In a converted farmhouse just outside the town limits. You wonder why you always get away with this routine. Like none of these girls or boys ever actually listened to a thing their guidance counselors told them about date safety. Sometimes you want to shake their shoulders and yell, "Hello? Doesn't this sound strange to you?"

Whatever. You're hungry.

The game is almost over when Jack's dad walks onto the field. His limp is more obvious now, but it doesn't make him less threatening. The referee stops the play and yells at the ice man for a few moments before deciding it's hopeless. Jack doesn't say anything, just walks off the field with his shoulders stooped. You wonder what's happened—did he forget target practice again? You wait for him to come back, but instead he grabs his gear and leaves with his father. He glances at you once. You can't see his face from so far away, but somehow you know he's afraid. *I need you to be ready*, the ice man said yesterday. Ready to kill a monster?

You're not as careful as you should be when you meet the girl after the game. You don't check if anyone sees you leave together. You don't even bother to have a conversation once she gets in the car. The doors are locked. The prions have done their job—she has entered a permanent bug-eyed state. Her pulse speeds up like old faithful when you look at her. You're pissed that you have to do this. Angry like you haven't been since you first woke up in the lab. About the normal life stripped away, at the maniac left behind. You want to be at that Modest Mouse concert with Jack so bad your stomach hurts. But you can smell the food beside you, and the urge to eat it *now*, at the intersection two blocks away from school, is almost overpowering.

It's dark by the time you get to the woods. By now even braces girl is starting to get a little worried, but you tune her out. You don't like it when they scream. Really, you don't like it when they're alive at all. Best to just knock them out and be done with it. But you hate to mess up the car, so you make up some excuse about the engine breaking down and stop in the middle of the gravel road. You know from experience that no one will find you.

"Hey," braces girl says, "I think I want to go back home. This is a little—"

"Yeah, hold on, I have to see what's wrong with the car."

She nods, nervously. You get out, pretend to look at the engine, walk back around to her side. "Something's smoking," you say. "I should probably call for a tow. Could you get out for a second? I think the number's under the seat."

She nods, reassured, though you sure as fuck don't know why. This is the worst part. The last moment they trust you, when some part of them must know they shouldn't. She opens the door.

She gets out.

6. Dirty Harry

The prudent serial killer's guide to avoiding the cool, yet bureaucratic, hand of the law.

- Move around! Superheroes call them lairs; police officers call them crime scenes.
- Blend in. In colonial Massachusetts a Quaker living alone with cats had a front-row ticket to a witch trial. In twenty-first-century America, a solitary lifestyle is still a sign of deviance. I'm about seventeen, so I go to high school. Lots of high schools. You wouldn't believe how easy it is to forge credentials, and all the teachers love a good student.
- Vary your targets. I know, the victims are supposed to be the telltale heart of serial killing. The fatal flaw: Every killer likes their type. Bad idea. I've eaten big

jocks and old ladies. I've raided funeral parlors (not recommended: formaldehyde is to corpses what the Kraft factory is to Vermont cheddar). I've even put an ad online!

And finally:

• Use your brains! Or someone else will eat them for you.

7. You Know My Name (Look Up the Number)

The girl stares at you. You stare at her. The hunger feels like knives delicately inserted into your stomach and pushed through your spine.

And then she shrugs, takes a step forward, and kisses you. Perfect opportunity. A kiss is like a non-prion version of eating someone. But you just clench your fists and return it. Why not? The braces aren't so bad. You imagine she's Jack. That's better.

"Grayson," says Jack. "Step away from her."

The girl breaks it off first, looks over your shoulder, screams. You turn around, a sudden warmth dulling the sharp edges of your hunger. Jack stands in front of the thick row of trees on the side of the gravel road. He has a gun. Despite the prion problem, you haven't had much interaction with guns in your life. This one looks big and black and shiny. Jack looks like he knows how to use it.

"Funny, I didn't peg you for the jealous type, Jack."

He grimaces, but the blush staining his neck and ears probably isn't caused by anger.

"What the hell are you doing? Are you robbing us?" The

girl's voice is so high she's nearly squeaking. She's reaching out, like she might hold you for support. But you look at Jack, his steady hand and his big black pistol, and think that might not be the best idea.

"I'm saving your life," he says.

For a moment you can't hear a thing—not your frantic pulse, not your labored breath, not even Jack as he says something to the girl and gestures with his gun.

You wish he would just shoot already. You wish he would just fucking kill you.

But the girl, trembling now, shuts the hood and opens the driver's side of your car.

"The keys are in the ignition," Jack says. "Drive home."

"But the engine . . ."

"Go."

She shuts the door. The car starts without a problem. She backs down the gravel drive, slowly at first, then so fast she nearly careens into a tree.

You and Jack are alone. He still holds the gun.

"Grayson . . . it's true? What they said about you. What you—"

"Yeah, of course it is. Why the fuck else would I be out here?" You close your eyes. "Hurry up, will you?"

"What are you doing?"

"Waiting."

"I'm putting the gun down."

"So you can stick me with your samurai sword?"

"I'm not going to kill you."

"Why the fuck not?"

"Open your damn eyes, Grayson!"

The gun is in a holster around his jeans. His hair is spiky with dried sweat, but he's changed out of his lacrosse uniform. His face is flushed red, like he might cry.

"We've got to leave. I put Dad off, but he'll be here soon."

He turns without another word and walks deeper into the woods. He's quiet, though you can't see how. When you follow him, the cracking leaves and twigs sound like an earthquake. Ten minutes later you reach his car. It's parked in the middle of a road that's little more than two ruts of packed dirt. You get in. You're not sure what else to do. He drives smoothly, carefully, and yet with the same steady fierceness you've sensed in him all along.

"Jack, if you're not going to kill me, you have to let me go."

"Dad's decided to get you on his own. He's been nuts for something like this ever since he got invalided out. It's not safe for you."

You have to laugh. "Safe? Do you really know what I am?"

There must have been something in your voice, some tremor, because Jack looks at you now for the first time since you got into the car. "Grayson . . . they said . . . ZSE is rare, but there's a few cases each year."

"ZSE?"

"Zombie Spongiform Encephalopathy."

Zombie. That's what Jack thinks you are.

"You should kill me. Your dad wants you to kill me, right? Isn't that why we're running away from him?" You don't even recognize the road signs now. He's gone far off the highway, down some long country roads bounded only by soybean fields and great tubes of hay.

"Why are you so damn interested in me killing you, Grayson?"

"Why are you giving a ride to a raving cannibal?"

"Shut up!"

"Why, it isn't true?"

"You sound just like him!"

"Then maybe he's right."

Jack abruptly slams his foot on the brake. The car skids a little on the deserted road before shuddering to a halt. When he turns to you now, he is crying, though you can tell he doesn't know it.

"I watched you decide to not kill that girl."

Is that what happened? You shrug, deliberately. "I've killed dozens of others."

"Maybe you've changed."

"Maybe I'm not that hungry. Maybe she smelled like brussels sprouts."

"I don't believe that."

You're very close to him now. Close to his long-sleeved T-shirt, his flushed cheek, his gun. "Why, Jack?"

"I don't know. 'Behind Blue Eyes' and Harajuku pop and Ian Curtis—"

Hands and lips and teeth, and you'd forgotten—no, you'd never known—this way of knowing someone, this dissolution of self, this autophagy.

His shirt rips, but you're careful with his skin.

8. Sounds of Silence

Ian Curtis killed himself on the eighteenth of May, 1980. You might think this ironic of the lead singer of a band called Joy Division, but actually their name is a reference to prostitution in Nazi concentration camps. (Which might explain why their iconic song is called "Love Will Tear Us Apart.") He hung himself, a death of slow asphyxiation, of utter helplessness for long minutes until he finally, mercifully, lost consciousness. There are certain theories of suicide that propose that the more self-loathing one feels, the more violent the method one chooses.

Elliott Smith (folksinger) stabbed himself in the heart with a kitchen knife. Nick Drake (folksinger) OD'd on antidepressants.

A qualitative difference in self-loathing? Please. When you decide to check yourself out, the difference between a gun and a rope is how long it takes to tie the knot.

9. Eat the Music

You stay in motels. And not the kind with friendly signs in primary colors and "Kids Stay Free!" deals on weekends. These motels have sputtering neon spelling "vacancy" and long rows of rooms, identical as LEGOs. The bathroom floors are coated with grime spread thin by lazy efforts to wipe it away. Sheets are haphazardly laundered. The second night, you see a bloodstain that covers half the floor. It blends well enough with the carpet and you don't tell Jack. You're hungry and you don't like to remind him of what you are.

Jack pays for the rooms, and no one asks questions. For a last-minute escape, he's managed well: a few thousand in cash, a box of emergency food supplies in the trunk, two swords, and three more of those big, black guns. You nearly vomited when he offered to let you use one. Now you just try not to look at them.

You haven't eaten human flesh in ten days. You might have snapped before now, but Jack bought a haunch of pork from a local butcher. He couldn't look you in the eye when he handed it to you. "Second thoughts about your charity case?" you asked, and felt the hollow reward of his silence.

Pork works. Not as well as warm human flesh, not even close, but at least you can keep away the worst of it, the insanity you remember from those first moments with the prion. Whatever madness you feel, whatever longings you have, are bound up in what you and Jack do late at night on scratchy sheets, and the only music you share is the hum of the hallway ice machine, the occasional rumble of pickup trucks speeding by on the country roads. During the day there are no lingering glances, tentative hand-holding, butterfly kisses. During the day you're the zombie and he's your keeper. At night he's still afraid of his father, but at least he lets you see the fear. It descends like an army. It makes him pace up and down the room, makes him cry, sometimes vomit. You hate what he won't tell you, and you hate knowing anyway.

The third night, his father calls. This is not the first time Jack's cell phone has buzzed, not the first time he's gone too still and too pale and you've wondered how much his ice man father did to him. But this time Jack picks up.

"I'm not coming back," Jack says. He's trying to sound

tough, but you can see his fears as clearly as you can see his scars in the moonlight.

"I trained you for better than this." Jack likes his speaker volume the way he likes his music: too loud. I can hear every word his father says.

"You trained me to be a monster."

His father is silent for a few seconds. "You're in room 303 of Jimmy's Truck Lodge in Osler. I'm about ten minutes away. Let me finish this, Jackson. The boys at the agency have orders to kill that creature *and* anyone with him."

"Dad, you're not—"

"You should let me finish this."

The line goes dead. You wonder for a moment what he'll do, but Jack doesn't even hesitate. He rushes you out the door. It's not hard to leave quickly—everything important is in the car. Jack is steady, so iced and cool that you wonder how much longer before he's just like his father. Maybe that's what this is really about—not loving you, not a sense of fair play, but one last, desperate ploy to not become a monster.

He gestures angrily at you. "Get in!"

"If I stay behind—"

"*And anyone with him*, remember?"

"Your dad wouldn't . . ."

"Will you bet my life on it?"

"I could bite you. Make it look authentic."

"Fuck you, Grayson."

"Why does it matter? I'm a fucking zombie! You think even this cure they gave me will last forever? What the hell is wrong with you? Let your ice man dad kill me, and you can run away somewhere and have a decent life with some decent people."

Jack isn't steady now. He punches the door—solidly, enough to hurt. "You're the only person— Fuck. You know, don't you? Get in the car. Please."

You knock him out.

It's brief and efficient, to the jaw. You know how to incapacitate people. He only has time for one wide-eyed stare before he slumps into your arms, unconscious. You carry him back into the motel room and rip his shirt. You figure the shoulder's as good a place as any. But when you look down, the light illuminates another scar, still-pink marks from stitches running across his collarbone. You swallow back bile and rip his shirt some more. Hopefully that will be enough.

Ice man is standing in the doorway when you turn around.

"So that's what this is about?" he says. Of course you couldn't fool him.

"You wondered?"

"No. Not really. I guess I never . . . I don't know what they'll do to him. Not if they think you two . . ."

"You stopped me from feeding," you say.

"That didn't look like feeding."

"What would you know about it?"

He cocks his head. Then nods. "Okay. I stopped you from feeding."

You don't think you're imagining the hint of relief in his voice, the subtle loosening of tension in his arms.

Then he shoots you in the shoulder. You just want this over

with, but Jack is moaning on the bed, and you went through way too much trouble for him to ruin this now. You rush the ice man, which surprises him enough that he falls onto the concrete outside. You run past him, feeling the blood dripping down your arm, but not much else. The prions are good about pain. A few other guests have opened their doors at the noise. The ice man lets off another shot. It misses you.

You rush to a large, empty space at the edge of the lot. You don't want to make this too obvious. It shouldn't be much work for him to hit your head from this distance. But the next shots are so wide that you can't even smell the lead.

"Come on," you mutter when the ice man just stands there.

Then he falls down.

Jack stands behind him, jaw bruised, gun smoking. There's a hole in the back of his dad's head, and you can smell it from here.

"You okay?" Jack asks, after you jog up to him. But he's the one who's shaking.

Someone shrieks. The night clerk talks rapidly into his cell phone. "I think the cops are coming," you say.

"Yeah. It'll probably take them a while."

You both look down at the corpse. Jack hauls him inside the room. "Hurry up," he says.

You only have time for the brains, but that's okay. They're the best part.

10. Shoot Out the Lights

We live in a little cottage in Mexico now, in a village so tiny that only the residents have heard of it. There's a beach with good fishing, and a market once a month an hour away. Jack spoke some Spanish before, and we're picking it up well enough. We go into town for the Internet, where Jack sells Mexican handicrafts on eBay.

I bought him a guitar for his birthday, but I ended up playing it. When I practice, he jokes about how good he's getting. I wrote him one song, and sometimes I like it. I haven't played it for him yet. Even now, it's hard for me to guess what will make him go still and icy. Sometimes I think a part of him hates me.

I know Jack will kill me if I eat again. I imagine it sometimes, when I stare too long at some plump girl in a bikini and her smell reaches back into that prion part of my brain and I can feel the old hunger tearing at my skin. I imagine him playing Joy Division, Ian Curtis's mournful voice almost scraping against the speakers, "Do you cry out in your sleep / all my failings exposed," and Jack's tears smear my lips, and I get just that last, ecstatic taste of him before the blade goes snicker-snack.

"Purity Test"

Holly: The association of the unicorn with virtue is of long origin. According to legend, a young girl would be sent ahead of unicorn-hunting parties—as shown in the famous unicorn tapestries—to lure the creature with her innocence and purity. Once the unicorn rested its head in the girl's lap, hunters would surprise the unicorn and, well, that would be that.

Some scholars have creepily suggested that unicorns are able to detect chastity, although, according to the literature, unicorns have been lured not only by women who weren't maidens, but in at least one case, by a perfumed boy dressed in women's clothes. Now, I don't think, as my coeditor will no doubt suggest, that this means unicorns are dumb, but rather they are lured by essential inner goodness.

One of the things I love most about Naomi Novik's "Purity Test" is how it takes our expectations of unicorns and maidens and turns them on their head. Plus, it's very funny.

Justine: "Purity Test" is funny because Naomi Novik is making fun of unicorns. That's right, Naomi Novik is secretly on Team Zombie. Poor Team Unicorn, in such shambles from the outset. I almost pity them. (Get it? Shambles? You know, like, zombies shambling? Never mind . . .)

Holly: "Purity Test" is funny because it makes fun of foolish zombie-loving people's *perceptions* of unicorns. She's our double agent.

Purity Test
By Naomi Novik

"Oh, stop whining," the unicorn said. "I didn't poke you that hard."

"I think I'm bleeding, my back hurts, and I'm seeing unicorns," Alison said. "I so have grounds."

She pressed the heels of her hands to her eyes and sat up slowly on the park bench. Spending her emergency train-fare-home money on margaritas in the first midtown bar that hadn't carded her had seemed like a good idea at the time. She wasn't even completely ready to give up on it yet, although the crazy hangover had been tipping the scales even before the unicorn had showed up and jabbed her.

The unicorn was extremely pretty, all long flowy silver hair and shiny hooves, indescribable grace, and a massive spiraling horn about four feet long that seemed like it should have dragged the unicorn's head down to the ground, just on basic physics. Also, it looked kind of annoyed.

"Why a unicorn?" Alison wondered at her subconscious out loud. She wasn't thirteen years old or anything. "I mean, dragons are so much cooler."

"Excuse me?" the unicorn said indignantly. "Unicorns kill dragons all the time."

"Really?" she said skeptically.

The unicorn pawed the ground a little with a forehoof.

"Okay, usually only when they're still small. But Zanzibar the Magnificent did kill Galphagor the Black in 1014."

"O-kay," Alison said. "Did you just make those names up?"

"You know what, shut up," said the unicorn. "Entertaining as it would be to spend three weeks correcting your misguided preconceptions, there's no time; the herd only gave me three days, and then that idiot Talmazan gets his turn. And if you knew him, you would understand what an unmitigated disaster that would be."

"His turn at what?"

"Finding a virgin," the unicorn said.

"Um," she said. "Maybe he'd have more luck than you. I'm not—"

"La, la, la!" the unicorn sang loudly, drowning her out. It even sang beautifully, perfectly on-key. "Have you never heard of plausible deniability?" it hissed at her, when she'd stopped trying to finish the sentence.

"Excuse me, either you don't know what 'plausible' means or I'm insulted," she said.

"Look," the unicorn said, "just be quiet a second and let me explain the situation to you."

The hangover was moving to the front and center of Alison's skull, and she was starting to get a little worried: The unicorn hallucination wasn't going away. She shut her eyes and lay back down on the bench.

The unicorn apparently took it as a sign to keep going. "Okay," it said. "So there's this wizard—"

"Wow, of course there is," Alison said.

"—and he's been grabbing baby unicorns," the unicorn said, through gritted teeth.

"You know," Alison told her subconscious, "I've got to draw the line somewhere. *Baby* unicorns is going too far."

"No kidding," the unicorn said. "You don't think I'd be wasting my time talking to a human otherwise? Anyway, wizard, baby unicorns, where was I— Oh, right. Probably he's trying to make himself immortal, which never works, except wizards never *listen* when you tell them that, and we would really prefer if he got stopped before he cuts off the babies' horns trying."

"Let me guess," Alison said. "Is his name Voldemort?"

"No, what freakish kind of name is Voldemort?" the unicorn said. "His name is Otto, Otto Penzler. He lives downtown."

"So what do you need a virgin for?"

"Do you see hands at the ends of these?" the unicorn said. Alison cracked an eye open enough to see that yes, the unicorn was still there, and it was waving a silver hoof in her face. There wasn't any dirt on the hoof, even though the unicorn was standing in the middle of a torn-up meadow.

"What does being a virgin have to do with opposable thumbs?" she said.

"Nothing!" the unicorn said. "But will anyone else in the herd listen to me? Of course not! They go off and grab the first thirteen-year-old who coos at them, and then it's all, 'Their purity will lead the way,' blah, blah, blah. Lead the way to a whole bunch of dead baby unicorns, maybe. I want a little more competence in my heroine."

"I'm drunk and sleeping on a bench in Central Park," Alison said. "That meets your criteria?"

"Hello?" The unicorn dipped its horn and lifted the dangling sleeve from her wadded-up jacket, the one she'd been using as a pillow. "U.S. Marines?"

The jacket had come out of a two-dollar bin in the army-navy store. She actually had tried to enlist, two days ago, after the last-ditch attempt to get hired at McDonald's had failed. She'd thought that the recruiters in Times Square would be hard up enough for volunteers that they wouldn't be picky about her age, but that apparently awesome idea had nearly ended with her handed over to the cops for truancy, so even if the unicorn was a hallucination, she wasn't going to let on that it was wrong.

"How do you know I wasn't dishonorably discharged?" she said.

The unicorn brightened, which Alison had to admit was something to see. "Are you a lesbian? I'm pretty sure that doesn't count toward virginity."

"I am pretty sure it *does*," Alison said, "and sorry, but no."

"Well, it was just a thought," the unicorn said. "Let's go."

"I'm not going anywhere without coffee," Alison said. She wanted a shower, too, but she had a total of nineteen dollars left, so coffee was more in reach.

The unicorn tossed its head and snorted and then whacked her on the head with its horn. "Ow! What was that for?" Alison said, and then she was wide-awake, not hungry, and felt cleaner than she had in two weeks of showering in hostels. "Oh. Okay, that's a trick."

Then she stared, because she was stone-cold sober, sitting on a bench in Central Park in the middle of the night, and there was a unicorn standing in front of her.

"Just let me do the talking if we run into any other unicorns," the unicorn said, pacing her. At four in the morning by the clock on the CNN billboard, even the streets of Manhattan were pretty quiet, but Alison would still have expected the unicorn to get at least a few double takes from the taxi drivers and the drunks going home. Nobody did more than nod to her, or at least to the uniform jacket.

"Uh-huh." She was halfheartedly trying to convince herself she really was hallucinating or still drunk, but it was a losing fight. She'd had freakish dreams before, but nothing like this, and there was something uncomfortably real about the unicorn. It was actually kind of creepy. The more she looked at it, the more it seemed like it was the *only* real thing, and the rest of the world was one of those really expensive computer games, flattened out, with too much color.

"Where did you come from, anyway? Like, Fairyland or something?"

The unicorn turned its head and gave her a blue-eyed glare. "Yes. Fairyland," it said, dripping sarcasm. "Fairyland, where the *fairies* and the *unicorns* play, and never is heard a discouraging—"

"Okay, okay, jeez," she said. "Do you want me to buy you an apple or something? Would that make you less cranky?"

The unicorn snorted and minced disdainfully over some

flattened droppings left by one of the carriage horses. "Anyway, we're always here, you idiots just don't notice anything that doesn't shove itself in your faces. You've never spotted the elves, either, and they're taking up half the tables at Per Se every night."

"Hey, Belcazar," a cat said, walking by.

The unicorn very slightly flicked his tail. "Social climbers, cats," the unicorn said with a sniff after they had passed farther on.

"Belcazar?" Alison said, eyeing his tail, long and white-furred with a tuft at the end, like a lion's. "So, if I help you get the baby unicorns back, this is all going to stop, right? I don't need to be hearing cats talking."

"Who does?" the unicorn said evasively. "This way," he added, and trotted across Columbus Circle to take Broadway downtown.

Otto Penzler lived on Gramercy Park in a neat three-story brownstone with an honest-to-God front yard and fresh flowers in the window boxes.

"I guess he can just magic up money or whatever," Alison said, staring in through the fence bars. She'd been spending a lot of time in libraries reading the *New York Times* to find classified ads for jobs she wouldn't get, so she had picked up what this place had to cost.

"Not unless he wants the Treasury Department to decide he's a counterfeiter," Belcazar said. "He probably has a day job. Come on."

He jumped the ironwork fence in a single spectacularly graceful leap and trotted to a side window. Alison rolled her eyes and just went through the unlocked front gate. "What's the plan, here, exactly?"

Belcazar touched the window with his horn. The latches on the inside slid by themselves, and the window rose smoothly open. "You climb through, let me in the front door, and then we find the baby unicorns and get out, hopefully before the wizard even wakes up," he said.

"Uh," Alison said. "I hate to break it to you, but he's not keeping them in there."

"How would you know?" Belcazar demanded.

Alison pointed inside the window. "If he blew that much money on hardwood floors, I do not think he is letting a bunch of horses walk on them. He's got to have them somewhere else."

Around back there was a padlocked cellar door. Belcazar backed away from the lock with a snort. "Cold iron," he said unhappily.

"Would it help if it was *warm* iron?" Alison said. "I have a lighter."

"Very funny, not," Belcazar said. "That must be where he's got them." He looked at Alison expectantly.

It was New York, so there was a twenty-four-hour hardware store a couple of blocks away. The guy at the cash register had a vague expression on his face as he handed Alison the crowbar and put one of Alison's last five-dollar bills into the register.

Belcazar was standing just inside the door; he had somehow managed to cram himself in between the folding ladders and the mops.

"If I get locked up for this, you are so busting me out," Alison said shortly after working the crowbar into the lock and leaning on it. The padlock popped open like a gunshot, and she looked up and around to make sure no one had gotten curious and stuck their head out a window to see her breaking into some nice upstanding wizard's cellar in the dead of night.

"I'll hire you a goblin lawyer," Belcazar said. "Hurry up before it gets light."

She was still careful opening the doors, keeping them as quiet as she could, lifting them slowly. She wasn't sure what she was expecting; this all still seemed unreal, the streetlamp casting Belcazar's shadow with the tapering horn on the ground next to her. But you could get used to pretty much anything, if you gave it enough time—eating in soup kitchens, sleeping on the street. Unicorns were not that hard, and breaking into an evil wizard's basement was turning out to be easier than getting into the high school weight room after hours.

The doors opened on a broad staircase going down into black, with the annoying kind of fancy steps that were so long you had to take an extra step before you got to the edge, but not long enough to take *two* extra steps, so you were always going down on the same foot. She couldn't see the bottom, even after they had ducked all the way in.

Belcazar's horn glowed white as they descended, a sort of cool, unforgiving pearly light. The walls were weird and smooth and curved, like they were auditioning for an Escher painting. It seemed like they were trying to bend away from the light.

"Ew," Alison said, twenty steps down, with the dark cornflower blue rectangle of open sky above getting farther away than she wanted it, and a rotten stink getting closer. "Is this going to end up in the sewers or something?"

"Ugh, no; it's a troll," Belcazar said, stopping.

They hadn't quite stepped off the stairs, but they'd bottomed out in a small antechamber, pretty much just a landing with a door at the other end. Alison didn't see what Belcazar meant until the big lumpy pile of rock by the door sat up and unfolded concrete gray arms and legs and blinked little black pebble eyes at them. "Yum," the troll said, and came lumbering toward them.

"Uh," Alison said, backing away rapidly. Belcazar just stood there, though, and the troll got yanked up a foot short of the stairs by a chain around its neck.

"Yum," it said unhappily, stretching its thick stumpy arms out at them futilely.

"They won't stay put unless you chain them," the unicorn said to Alison a little loftily.

"Thanks for letting me know!" she said. "So now what? Can you kill this thing?"

"No," the unicorn said.

"I thought you guys could take out dragons?"

Belcazar pawed the ground. "Okay, *theoretically* I could kill it, but if it grabbed on to me, it's stronger, and it's not like there's a lot of room to maneuver in here."

"Well, I don't think it's going to let us by if we just ask nicely," Alison said.

"Yep," the troll said immediately. "Let you by. Go 'head." It backed up against the wall and waved a hand at the passageway. It even tried a hopeful smile, full of teeth like broken rocks.

"Nice try," Alison said.

"Aw," the troll said.

"You're a soldier!" Belcazar said. "Haven't you got any better ideas?"

"Oh, yeah, absolutely. I'll go upstairs, call around, and find someone in Manhattan with a grenade launcher, and we'll come right back," Alison said sarcastically. She wondered what a real marine would do. Probably shoot it with the gun a real marine would be carrying and know how to use, which wasn't a lot of help.

"Riddle game?" the troll said. "I get wrong, you go by."

"Will he stick to that?" Alison asked Belcazar.

"Of course not," Belcazar said. His sides heaved out in a deep breath. "I knew I should have let Talmazan do this," he muttered, and lowered his horn, his hindquarters bunching awkwardly on the steps.

"Wait, wait, hang on," Alison said, because the troll's hands were the size of basketballs and looked like they'd been carved out of solid rock. She didn't really want to see what they'd do to Belcazar if he got close enough to touch.

"I thought you didn't have any better ideas," Belcazar said, lifting his head.

And Alison didn't, at first, but then she said to the troll, "Are you only up for dinner if it talks, or would you be okay with chicken?"

The troll brightened right up. "Big Mac!" it said.

"Fabulous," Alison said, sighing.

"That isn't going to be more than an appetizer for that thing," Belcazar said when they'd come out of the McDonald's with the burger in a sack.

"That's why we're going to stuff it full of crushed Benadryl," Alison said, crossing the street toward the twenty-four-hour Duane Reade on the other side.

That wiped out the rest of her cash, but the troll bounced right up when Alison tossed it the burger. Then it spent about half an hour eating it slowly and lingeringly, one tiny bite at a time, and licking its lips after each one. Then it ate the fries, the wrapper, and the bag, said, "Yum!" and fell over snoring.

Alison and Belcazar stood warily, but the troll really did seem to be asleep. "Wait here," Belcazar said, and edged across the floor toward it.

"You aren't going to kill it while it's sleeping!" Alison hissed.

"Shh!" Belcazar said, and then bent his head and tapped the troll with his horn three times. Light went rippling down from the horn, washing over the troll's body, and its skin went pale like concrete drying out on fast-forward. It almost seemed to settle down into itself. The arms and legs and head curled in closer, until the separations turned into nothing but faint cracks in a lumpy rock.

"I can't believe you're worrying about the troll that was

going to *eat* us," Belcazar said irritably, raising his head again. "Anyway, it was just a pile of rock to begin with." He snorted. "Only wizards would go around trying to turn rocks into living things and think that was a good idea. Now come on. Let's find the baby unicorns and get out of here."

Alison crossed the antechamber and opened the door at the other end. She had a second to realize she was staring at a blank rock wall—the door didn't go anywhere. Then the floor dropped out from under her feet, and she heard Belcazar whinny in startled fright before she was going down with him in a flailing heap and a flying hoof caught her on the head.

Alison woke up with her head ice-cold-clear and a horrible taste in her mouth. A smiling white-bearded man was standing beside her, with a small brown glass bottle in his hand. "There. All better," he said, and she eyed him sidelong. He didn't really look like the evil wizard type, but then she noticed her wrists were chained to the wall, which, okay, was more supporting evidence than she really needed, thanks.

Belcazar was chained next to her, and the light had gone out of his horn. He bent his head and nosed at her anxiously as the wizard went to put the bottle back on one of the crammed-full shelves, and then to putter over a smoking cauldron in the middle of the room. "Are you all right?" Belcazar whispered.

"Totally not," Alison said. Whatever Otto the Wizard had given her, it wasn't anywhere near as nice as getting sobered up by a unicorn. Her head wasn't hurting exactly, but it didn't feel like everything on the inside was lined up right either. She dragged herself to sit upright against the wall, chains rattling. They had a lot of slack, but they didn't seem to have anything at all in the way of openings in the shackles.

Otto straightened up from the cauldron and waved a wand at the back wall of the room, muttering. The wall slid aside. "Belcazar, Belcazar," a few small voices said, calling. The baby unicorns were penned up in a iron cage, five of them crowded in together, looking sad and matted and scared.

"Okay, okay, stop bleating, that's not going to help anyone," Belcazar said, pawing the ground with a hoof, sending up sparks. "All right, wizard, stop being an ass. You can't make yourself immortal by sacrificing baby unicorns."

Otto laughed without looking up from the new stuff he was throwing into the cauldron. "I know the baby unicorns aren't enough," he said. "Fortunately, I now have a *grown* unicorn— and its chosen virgin."

"Oh my God!" Alison said. "I'm not a—ow!" Belcazar had just kicked her in the thigh.

"Would you believe it's harder to find a virgin than a unicorn in New York?" Otto added, throwing some more bunches of herby stuff into the cauldron. "People get very suspicious if you start hanging around teenage girls. I even tried Craigslist, but I'm reasonably sure all of the responders were lying."

"Well, I'm shocked," Alison said, and then she started scrambling up, braced against the wall, because Otto was coming over with a bowl and a very sharp knife.

"Don't worry," Otto said cheerily. "I only need a little bit at this stage. The actual sacrifice will be painful, of course," he

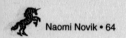

added apologetically. "But that won't be for a few hours yet."

The chains were pulling tight, dragging her wrists up over her head. "That had better be a clean knife," Alison managed, her throat dry, as Otto reached up to cut a thin shallow slice across her upper arm and held the bowl underneath.

"Oh, completely sterile," Otto assured her, seriously, and carried the bowl of blood over to the cauldron. The chains relaxed and came loose again.

"You really aren't?" Belcazar whispered to her anxiously. "Because this would be a bad time to find out you—"

"I'm really not!" Alison spat back.

"Good, then you should probably—," Belcazar began, and then Otto tipped the blood into the cauldron and the whole thing went up into a giant mushrooming cloud of black smoke that billowed out and filled the entire room.

Otto yowled as whatever had been boiling in the cauldron went pouring over his alligator-skin shoes and steaming over the floor. He whirled and came at them with the wand. "What did you do? How did you do that? I'm going to flay the skin off your bones—" Then he got close enough that Alison could pull the Princess Leia maneuver and throw the chains around his neck.

She jerked them tight and dragged him in close as his face went purple and red, and she snatched the wand out of his hand.

"What do I do with this?" she yelled at Belcazar.

"Touch my chains!" Belcazar yelled back, while Otto made choked strangling noises. The wand popped open Belcazar's shackles, white light blooming through the whole room as he began to glow again.

In the light the wand seemed to writhe and squirm like a snake, shining greasily. Alison ughed and flipped it out of her hand onto the floor, and Belcazar pounced on it, touching the twisting, gnarled stick with his horn. It glowed red and smelled like rotten eggs for a moment, and then it went up in a whole bunch of colorful flames.

"No-o-o," Otto said, the *O* dragging out of him like the whine of a deflating balloon. It wasn't just the sound, either; he was sinking in on himself, skin going greenish-white, and bones toppling slowly inward as a horrible rotting smell exploded outward. Alison covered her mouth with one hand and then the other as she did a little frantic dance trying to shake the chains loose of disgusting bits of Otto as he started falling apart.

"Hold still, do you want me to poke an eye out?" Belcazar demanded irritably, and then he tapped the shackles on her wrists with his horn. They popped open and clattered to the floor, along with the gaping remains of Otto's skull, his teeth scattering away loose over the ground.

"That was so unbelievably gross," Alison said, trying not to heave, or for that matter to look too close, "and I am saying that after I slept in a bus shelter yesterday."

"You can throw up after we get out of here," Belcazar said, whacking the lock off the baby unicorns' cage. "Yes, yes, you're all very grateful and happy to be rescued, I know," he added to them.

"I'm hungry," one of the baby unicorns said, popping out of

the cage and shaking itself head to toe. The mats all fluffed out, leaving it looking a bit tufty, and then smoothed back down into place, neat and glowing.

"I want to roll in the grass," another one said.

"I want some chocolate milk," another one said.

"Chocolate milk, chocolate milk!" all the baby unicorns said, clamoring.

"Do not even look at me, I am cleaned out," Alison said when Belcazar looked over at her in desperation.

"Okay, nobody back at the herd hears about this, you understand?" Belcazar said to the baby unicorns as they nudged and shoved against each other to get to the bowls Alison had set out, their hooves sliding and leaving streaks on the hardwood floor. "They really shouldn't be drinking that," he added fussily.

"Mm," Alison said, tipping back a glass herself.

Belcazar eyed her darkly, and then he nudged her shoulder. "Give me a bowl too."

Otto had kept a giant bag full of cash and diamonds upstairs in a wall safe that fortunately had been made out of steel, to keep out burglars instead of unicorns.

"I bet if I keep this, I'm going to get in trouble or something," Alison said, looking at the money while the unicorns finished drinking. She hadn't counted it yet, but the bag was crazy huge, and it was almost all in thousand-dollar bills. "Also, oh my God, we just killed that guy."

"He was fairly close to dead to begin with," Belcazar said, lifting his head and shaking chocolate milk off his nose, "so I don't think anyone is going to miss him. Give that here." He tapped the bag with his horn, and the money all riffled quietly like a deck of cards before settling back down, looking somehow cleaner and more crisp. The diamonds glowed briefly. "I hope you don't plan on spending any of it soon."

"What?" Alison said.

"I'm certainly not herding five baby unicorns home *alone*," Belcazar said. "They'll end up in New Jersey."

"So, where is home, then, the Bronx?" she asked.

Belcazar straightened his neck and tossed his head back a little, somehow managing to avoid putting a giant dent in the ceiling with his horn while he shook his mane out. "The entrance is in Fort Tryon Park," he said.

"To what?" Alison said suspiciously.

"Er," Belcazar said. "Home."

"Fairyland!" one of the baby unicorns said, lifting its head up. "I want to go home!"

"Fairyland, Fairyland!" the others chimed in.

Alison looked at Belcazar.

"The *correct* name is actually the Land of Faerie," Belcazar said stiffly, somehow managing to squash in a whole bunch of extra vowels. "Only infants and idiots call it—okay, you know what, just shut up and give me some more chocolate milk."

"Bougainvillea"

Justine: Carrie Ryan's zombies are solidly in the Romero mold: the death that haunts us all. Her undead are also a reminder that this debate is not about which creature is cooler or nicer, but about which creature makes for better fiction. Zombies are clearly far more versatile than unicorns. In Alaya's story, zombies were more or less the heroes; in Carrie's world, they are neither villain nor hero, but a force of nature the protagonist must rise above. If she can.

(And in doing so, our heroine reveals yet another of the important advantages of zombies—they're way more fun to kill.)

Holly: If you think that zombies are more fun to kill, you obviously don't know the truly messed-up folks that I do. Actually, "Bougainvillea" is a great example of one of the things about zombies that unnerves me the most—they never stop, never slow, and inevitably they will win. I hate that!

Justine: Death takes us all, Holly. Denial ain't going to stop the ole Grim Reaper.

Bougainvillea
By Carrie Ryan

1. BEFORE

Last year, Iza turned fifteen and her father threw a massive *quinceañera*. It was the largest party anyone on the island had seen since the Return, lasting an entire week. Every captain who wanted to curry favor with Iza's father and gain access to Curaçao and its port or dry dock paid a visit at some point. They pushed beribboned boxes into Iza's hands, their eyes always on her father to see if he approved of their offerings.

They brought Iza jewelry that she shuddered to look at, wondering which bracelets had once adorned reanimated arms. They brought scraps of useless money from various countries for her to collect. Many brought books that Iza couldn't wait to devour, all covered with raven-haired men and redheaded heroines.

But one of the men, a dark old Venezuelan with impossibly green eyes, brought Iza a game that belonged to his son. She knew it was the son's because the old man made *him* be the one to hand it to her. The boy did so with a rage in his eyes that seemed too violent an emotion to be contained in his skinny teenage boy body.

The game came in a box with edges worn white, the cardboard slightly warped, and the name "Risk" in faded red.

There were no instructions, and the old man spent a sweltering afternoon teaching Iza how to play before he had to get back to his leaky boat. His son refused to join them, and instead spent the afternoon standing at the edge of the cliffs, staring out at the ocean.

Iza spent weeks begging anyone to play with her. Some of the men and women who worked the *landhuizen* tried to play the game, torn between the fear of angering her father by not doing their jobs and the fear of his anger if they ignored his daughter. But they always let her win, and finally Iza would send them on their way.

Still, every afternoon Iza set the board up on the table in the shade of a divi-divi tree, the little red, yellow, blue, green, black, and gray men arranged in tight rows according to rank. She once asked her father if he could make the old Venezuelan come back and play with her, but he told her it was impossible.

"Why?" she asked, brushing away the yellow-breasted bird picking at the crumbs of her lunch.

"I had his ship banished from Curaçao," her father said.

Iza's eyebrows tilted into a frown. "Why?" she asked. The bird swooped in, nabbing a crust of bread, but she didn't care.

"Because you told me the son refused to play with you," her father said. He didn't even look at her as he rose from the table and walked away before Iza could respond. She felt slightly unsettled, her stomach twisted and queasy.

Hadn't she known that her father would take action if she told him about the boy refusing to play with her? Isn't that why she'd done it? The bird hopped over to the abandoned plate to scoop up the remains left by her father, and she didn't bother waving it away.

Alone, Iza was left to trace her fingers from continent to continent on the game board, memorizing the shape of countries that no longer existed. Before he'd left, the Venezuelan had taken out an old marker and drawn an *X* in the blue expanse of the Caribbean sea where Curaçao was supposed to be. Iza would press her thumb over it, wondering if it really was that easy to wipe out an entire world.

2. NOW

"You should be more careful when you leave the *landhuizen*, Iza," Beihito says to her one afternoon. Even after so many years on the island, she's not used to the way he says her name, like the word "pizza" without the *p*. Sometimes it reminds her of when she was a little girl before the Return, when she'd pull hot thin slices of greasy cheese out of a cardboard box. She closes her eyes, unable to remember the taste and burn of it.

She's lying on her stomach on the large dock at the base of the cliff and staring into the water. She used to have a snorkel and mask and loved to swim around and explore the reef, but her father took them away when he felt she'd grown too comfortable.

Iza grits her teeth, thinking about the way he stood in his office, long finger crooked through the chapped old rubber of the mask strap, telling her she was old enough to know better than to take such risks. She imagines herself stalking across that wide wooden floor and snatching it from his hands.

But of course she didn't, couldn't, and never would do such a thing.

Iza lets her fingers trail off the dock and brush the tips of the waves that glide under the warped old wood. "I'm technically still on my father's property," she tells Beihito. But the day is hot, the sun at a harsh angle, and she doesn't put much force behind her words. She watches as three flying fish leap out of the water, and she holds her breath, counting until the last splashes down again. *Bulladóe,* she thinks, and closes her eyes, trying to remember what it felt like to fly.

"Your father worries about the pirates," Beihito tells Iza. "They've been coming closer, making threats. He wants you to be safe."

Iza smiles just a little. Her father has barely spoken to her in a month; she hears his words only through others. Iza wonders if she should make it a game: How long can she go without speaking to him?

Beihito's knees crack a little as he bends over, setting a machete on the dock next to Iza. She opens her eyes and stares at the way the sun sparks off the edge of the blade. "At least until your father's men kill the pirates," Beihito says. *"Permití."*

Iza makes him stand here, a sigh building in him as he waits for her to promise. Beihito has many other things to do, and while he loves Iza like *un yiu muhé*, having no children of his own that survived the Return, she's old enough now that his day no longer includes watching her like a tired old babysitter.

Iza nods her head, deciding that it's not lying if she doesn't say the words.

3. BEFORE

She always heard when the pirate ships passed by the island at night. She could feel them in her bones, a shiver soft and sweet along her skin. The moans of the *mudo* slithered into her dreams, a tinge at the edge of her memory.

She woke up one night and stared into the darkness, the spin of the ceiling fan cutting the air. *"Here,"* the whispers called. She slipped out of bed and shuffled through the dew-damp grass to the edge of the cliffs.

It used to be that she could never see the pirate ships, only hear them as they slid through the darkness, the *mudo* lashed to their hulls. But ever since her father closed the port, they'd been inching closer, circling like *tribons*, teasing and toying, ready to bump the island in a warning, with their masts cutting the air like fins.

Iza wrapped her arms around her body as if she were holding who she was safe inside. Below her the waves crashed and crashed and crashed against the limestone, cutting away at her island.

In the distance, under the haze of the moon, the hulk of the pirate ship drifted by like a ghost in a skirt, tarps and sheets draped over the edge of the railings and covering the hull. Shapes huddled and strained beneath the tarps, sharp edges raking against the graceful arc of fabric that rippled in the breeze.

The corner of the tarp at the bow lifted, and Iza saw the bend of a bare knee, the curve of a shoulder. But it was the gaping mouths and desperate faces that she couldn't bear, the sound of the moans cutting over the waves and bounding against the cliffs. The *mudo* strained against the boat, reaching—always reaching and needing.

The tarp fluttered back into place, hiding the bodies lashed to the hull, concealing them until the pirates bore down on their prey. Iza saw dark shapes gathered on the deck of the ship, crowding at the railing. They watched her as they glided by in the night, and Iza wondered what was worse—the *mudo*, or the moon gleaming off the teeth of the pirates.

4. NOW

Iza is lying on her back on the dock, letting the sun burn her body, when the hand wraps around her ankle. She is at the edge of sleep and she's slow to react. Her fingers fumble as she grabs for the handle of the machete Beihito left, and by the time she pulls her foot away and scrambles to her knees, the man's already halfway out of the water.

Iza knows that a *mudo* could never be coordinated enough to climb onto the dock. Still her first thought is to strike at his head, to slice the blade through his spinal column.

"Wait," the man gasps as her muscles tense.

5. BEFORE

"Why don't we call them zombies?" Iza asked Beihito one day. It wasn't long after her father had taken over the island and hired Beihito to run the plantation and keep an eye on his only child.

"It's not respectful," Beihito said. They were standing near the edge of Curaçao's limestone cliffs, watching a giant iguana try unsuccessfully to hide itself in a kadushi cactus.

Iza kept tugging against the straps of her sundress where they left grooves in the baby fat on her shoulders. She'd outgrown almost everything shortly after arriving on the island and was tired of the way the tight clothes made her feel big and ungainly.

"But it's what they are," Iza whined. She was just getting used to the idea of her father's power. Just starting to understand that something about her father made her different. She tossed a strawberry at the iguana, seeing if she could temp him down.

Beihito pointed to the animal and said, *"Yuana."* Iza waved her hand in the air, brushing the word away.

"What does '*mudo*' mean, anyway?" She pronounced it like "mud," thinking of the way the ground looked after the snow thawed at her old home. She wanted to see how far she could push Beihito. She threw another strawberry.

"Mudo," Beihito corrected her, saying it "mood-o," no tinge of anger in his voice. "It means 'mute.'"

Iza rolled her eyes. "I know that," she said, her hand on her hip. She hated being talked down to. She hadn't been a child since the months-ago day when she'd turned seven and seen her first dead man rise and walk. "But they're not mute, duh. They still moan."

Beihito stared at her, perhaps with pity or maybe with impatience. "It also means 'speechless'—those who have lost their voice. They have nothing to say. They've lost who they are."

"They're dead," Iza grumbled. "They're nothing." She picked up a stick and walked closer to the iguana. She reached out to poke at it but Beihito closed his hot dry hand over her arm, stopping her.

She stared at the spot where he touched her—his dark wrinkled skin against her own. Rage seared inside her that he would stop her from what she wanted to do. A rage that she knew her father would act upon if she told him.

"There are things in this world greater than you or me," Beihito said then, and she wondered if there was something in the *mudo* that she couldn't see. Something about them that he understood and she didn't.

There was a crack then, and a loud hiss. The old man twisted Iza behind his back, standing between her and the kadushi. The branch holding the massive iguana cracked, and the iguana leapt into the air, thick tail swinging. It scrabbled on the edge of the cliff, its claws raking against the limestone until it finally found purchase. The cactus branch bounded down into the waves below.

Beihito had protected her. Iza wondered then if he would always protect her. Her cheeks blazed, her entire body a feverish red burn welling with shame. She turned and stalked back to the plantation house without thanking him. She vowed then that she would learn to be more like her father. He never thanked anyone.

6. NOW

Iza lunges forward and holds the sharp edge of the machete to the young man's throat just as he throws a knee over the edge of the dock. He freezes. They both pant and stare at each other.

Time still hasn't caught up to Iza, and she feels sleep-drugged and slow. She notices things about the man she shouldn't— how water streaks down his face like tears, breaking over high cheekbones. How his eyes are a bright green that doesn't seem to match the darkness of his skin.

His nostrils flare with each breath, puffs of air skimming over Iza's knuckles. His arms tremble with the effort of holding himself on the edge of the dock, half out of the water. He looks young, not still in his teens like Iza, but near to her in age.

"Please," he says. "Please, I promise I won't do anything. Please." He turns his head slightly as if glancing back to the open waves behind him. Iza doesn't let her gaze on him waver.

"Who are you?" she asks. Her voice shakes a little too much as the adrenaline from being startled works its way through her system. She clenches her teeth, knowing that her father's voice would never shake like hers. "Are you one of my father's men?" She's fairly certain she doesn't recognize him, and she's also quite sure that if he worked on the *landhuizen*, she'd have seen him. She knows for sure that if she'd seen him before, she'd remember.

Water drips from his chin onto her wrist and twines down her arm. "I was on a ship," he says. "I saw the lights on the island as we sailed by last night. I ran away. I jumped." He swallows, his throat pushing against the blade. Iza can hear the desperation in his voice, but that's nothing new. The entire world is desperate.

"They were pirates," he says. "You can't let them find me.

They were going to infect me and lash me to the boat with the others." He pauses, licks his tongue over his lips. Iza can almost taste the salt.

"Please," he whispers.

7. BEFORE

When Iza was young she had nightmares that the *mudo* were coming for her. She'd see the teeth of the woman who'd once been her babysitter and the hunger of the used-to-be gardeners. But more than anything she'd *hear* them, their pleading need for her. Iza always felt a deep ache at the moans and a desire to do anything to quench it.

Her father's men, the *homber mata*, were good at their tasks and always killed any *mudo* that washed ashore. There'd been small outbreaks on the island over the years, tales of *lihémorto* sprinting across the sticky dry desert inland, but they were always contained eventually.

Except for once. Except for the one who somehow got into the *landhuizen*. No one ever explained to Iza what happened— not even Beihito—and eventually she stopped begging for information when she saw the shadows in his eyes every time she brought it up.

All Iza knew was that the *homber mata* killed the *mudo*, but it was her father himself who killed her mother. She never saw her mother Return, and once, a few days after her death, she overheard one of the maids whisper to another that her mother had never actually been infected.

Sometimes Iza believes the rumor that her mother was never

bitten. Sometimes she wants to slit their throats for saying such a thing.

Her father added three more layers of fences to the land sides of the *landhuizen* and replaced the wide staircase to the floating dock at the base of the cliffs with a narrow ladder the *mudo* could never climb. For months after the uprising Iza was terrified of the water and imagined them coming for her, their fingers curling from the surface, their flesh prickled and gray.

She missed the taste of salt on her skin, the way it made her feel tight and itchy when she dried in the burning sun. She even missed the sting of fire coral. Her father ordered his men to dig a pool for her, but it wasn't the same.

8. NOW

"Please," the man whispers again. The muscles cording around his arms flex and shake. Dozens of tiny white lines fleck across his chest like cracks in glass.

Iza's father has instilled in her the need for discipline and order; every day of her life has been about rules and restrictions. "It's how we'll survive this," her father always says. "It's the only way."

She can sometimes remember the man he used to be before the Return, but only barely. He used to mow the lawn on summer Saturday afternoons, and on Sundays in the fall he would crack open a can of beer and eat chips and salsa as he watched football games. He used to always let her drink the first sip if she'd fetch it for him from the refrigerator, and she can still remember the sharp sting of metallic carbonation, the crisp clack of the can snapping open.

All Iza has to do is push the blade against the man's throat just a little more and it will either cut him or he'll be forced to let go of the dock and fall back into the water.

Her father would never have hesitated. She can hear his voice in her head screaming at her to kill this man, that he's dangerous and she's stupid to even consider letting him live.

But Iza thinks of the romance novels she loves and the pirates splashed across their covers. She thinks of all the times she stood at the edge of the cliffs and wanted someone to whisk out of the sea and rescue her.

Swallowing, Iza pulls the knife away from his throat and scoots down the dock a little, giving him room to climb the rest of the way up. He crouches on his hands and knees, his back arching as he draws in long deep breaths.

"Thank you," he says softly.

Iza shakes her head and stands. "Don't," she says, still holding the machete out in front of her. "The *homber mata* will kill you if they find you."

He looks up at her, deep green eyes in a sea of darkness. Something pulls inside Iza, making her want to help him. To know him and believe that things can be different from how they are. The flutter of desire and hope inside her aches so hard that she presses a hand to her chest to quench it.

"But there are caves," she says, waving the machete toward the limestone walls. "Hidden tunnels that will take you up beyond the *landhuizen*. You might have a chance that way."

She says it quickly, rushing to get the words out.

His eyebrows twitch, just barely. "Thank you," he says again.

Her father's training scrapes through her mind. She should kill this man. She squeezes her hand around the handle of the machete, imagining the blood dripping from his neck and seeping through the cracks of the dock into the waves—perfect petals of dissipating scarlet.

The image reminds Iza of when her mother used to toss bougainvillea blossoms from the cliffs, and she releases her grip on the wide-bladed knife. Before she can change her mind, as her father's rules dig through her skull, she turns and walks down the dock to climb up the narrow ladder. Behind her she hears the man's breathing, the small shudders of water dropping to the old beaten wood as he watches her fade away.

9. BEFORE

Iza stopped going to the little Curaçao school two years ago when her father declared it useless. There were too many tasks to be done to keep the island running for the children to spend wasted days in a classroom learning about the history of Holland or the life cycle of the barrier reef.

Instead he put them to work—everyone on the island worked for the right to remain a citizen and to enjoy the relative peace and safety. Even the people who'd lived there much longer than Iza and her family.

Of course, everyone worked except for Iza. As the governor's only daughter, she was left alone to do what she wanted. Most often she was nothing more than her mother's ghost, weaving from room to room, trying to stay out of the way of the gardeners, the housekeepers, the *homber mata*, the guards, and the rest of her father's men.

Iza chose instead to read, and discovered a love for books. To indulge her, or to keep her from complaining, Iza's father let it be known he was looking for books and that captains hoping to curry his favor and find access to Curaçao's ports could start by stocking his library.

The captain of an old gleaming cruise ship was the first to bring Iza boxes of romance novels with faded covers and pages soft with age. Iza devoured every one.

It was the pirate stories that gave her the biggest thrill. She'd spend countless afternoons sitting at the edge of the limestone cliff bordering her father's *landhuizen*, staring out toward the horizon and hoping for a dashing captain to come rescue her. He'd take her away from her father's rules, her mother's insanity, and the constant threat of death. He'd rescue her and they'd sail away to a place forgotten in time, a place that the Return never touched.

But that was before she learned that real pirates lashed *mudo* to their hulls. Or that they infected prisoners and forced them into cages that they dropped into the water so that the infected would die and come back to life as *lihémorto*—the fast-moving *mudo*.

10. NOW

Every evening Iza stands on the edge of the cliff and stares down into the water, heat lightning exploding in the clouds on the horizon.

"Are we safe?" she asks Beihito. It's the question she asked her mother every night before she died.

Iza's mother always told her yes and promised the world would recover. They'd kill off the hordes of undead, and soon enough everyone would be going home. One day she'd taste snow on her lips again.

The first time Iza asked Beihito this question he'd asked, "Do you want the truth?"

She'd said no, and he'd told her that yes, they were safe.

Tonight she says, "I want the truth."

Beihito pauses. "I don't know," he finally admits. The wrinkles at the edges of his eyes are heavier than usual, tugging his face down in a slow slide. Gravity pulls harder on troubles than on anything else.

Iza wants to ask him if it will end, if the *mudo* will ever go away. But she doesn't. Instead she watches the waves drive against the cliffs like the hands that pushed against the fences around the *landhuizen* during the previous wave of infection— never stopping, always needing. Fingers of lightning claw through the clouds. The water is so clear that she wonders if the *mudo* in their depths can see her and Beihito. If they can look through the surface and beg for their lives.

Beihito places his hand on Iza's shoulder. *"Spera,"* he says.

But she's not sure she wants to hope.

11. NOW

Tonight in the darkness before sleep, when the stars shine the brightest, Iza remembers the snow. She recalls standing in the front yard of their old house in the states before the Return, staring up at the sky and seeing nothing but puffs of white floating over and around her.

She remembers taking her mother's hand. Remembers everything being so white and pure and soft and quiet.

It's one of her only memories that doesn't have the moans of the *mudo* as a constant background hum. One of the few not tinged with the relentless heat of Curaçao.

She lets it pull her into sleep, falling deeper and deeper into the folds of the blinding cold whiteness.

Iza wakes up knowing something's wrong. She's been dreaming about the pirate ship. This time, though, rather than being the spirited damsel in distress getting rescued by the pirate, she'd been lashed to the ship with the *mudo*. She could feel the spray of the water as the ship cut through the seas, the salt stinging the gouges in her arms where the ropes and chains held her tight to the barnacled hull. All around her writhed the dead, sharp edges of bones cracking through skin and raking the waves. But she was not one of them; she was still somehow alive. In her dream Iza opened her mouth to scream and beg for mercy, but all that dripped from her mouth were moans.

In the heartbeat when she bolts upright in her bed, everything is muddled and Iza can't tell what's her dream and what's reality. It takes her too long to realize that the moans from her dream are still reverberating through the house. That's when she hears the pounding of feet running on the wooden floor outside in the hallway. That's when she hears the first scream streak through the darkness.

Iza's father has trained them for this, and she jumps out of bed. Her fingers shake as she tries to remember what to do first. She runs to the door. Panic begins to chew through her body and she swallows again and again. She flicks the light, but nothing happens. She snaps the switch up and down, up and down, and still nothing happens.

Even if the island's electricity is out, the *landhuizen* can be run by generators. Iza doesn't understand why they haven't turned over, why she can't hear their humming outside her window. The night becomes too dark and close and claustrophobic. She feels like she's underwater and can't breathe. She's about to throw open the door, needing the air, when something slams against it.

Fingernails crack as something, or someone, on the other side scratches to get in. Moans bore through the wood. Iza stumbles back into the room, tripping over the brass corner of the trunk at the end of her bed, and feeling a slice of pain shoot up from her shin. She looks down at the blood seeping into her white nightgown, knowing it will attract the *mudo*.

The banging and clawing grates against her as she fumbles with her dresser. She finally opens the drawer and pulls out the gun inside. She grabs a belt from the floor and loops it around her waist, sliding the machete Beihito gave her that afternoon into it.

And then she stands there. In the darkness. In the middle of her room. Listening to the screams and moans, and feeling the panic crushing her lungs.

The window, she thinks as the door begins to buckle under

the force of someone trying desperately to get inside. She pushes aside the fluttering curtains and crawls out onto the roof, scuttling to the side and hiding in the shadow of the dormer.

Overhead, heat lightning shoots the clouds with green and blue and orange, flashing open the world around her. With shaking fingers Iza switches the safety off her gun and tries to steady herself. She can't tell if the rumbling around her is thunder or gunshots.

Inside, the door bangs open. Feet pound against the floor. Iza's breath becomes a roar in her ears. They're *lihémorto*, the fast moving dead, not the slow, plodding *mudo*. This is the problem with living on an island cleared of the undead: If infection breaks out, the first to turn are always *lihémorto* until they reach that critical mass that renders the new ones *mudo*. It will be almost impossible for her father's men to kill the *lihémorto* before they infect half the plantation.

Iza feels rather than hears when the first one hits the window from inside. It's one of the groundskeepers, and most of his left arm is missing. He'd probably tried to cut it off after being bitten, which of course only served to hasten the Return.

He swings at Iza, reaching into the darkness with his teeth bared, eyes wild and moans rampaging. He smells like orange rinds and sweat and tobacco, and it reminds Iza of Beihito.

She holds out the gun as close to the man as she can while still outside his reach, and pulls the trigger.

It's not a clean shot. It wouldn't impress her father. But it still hits the man's head, tearing through his face. Iza can't take the time to let reality set in. She can't pause while the realization that she's just shot a man ripples through her. He slumps over the windowsill just as another *lihémorto*, a maid, lunges through the opening. This one tries to climb after Iza and slips from the roof, falling to the ground two stories below. Shards of bone jut through her leg, their tips glistening white in the echoes of heat lightning.

The maid hauls herself to her feet, the bad leg crunching under her, and limps to the wall, reaching for Iza still. Her fingers scrape and scratch against the stucco as she tries to climb, but she just keeps sinking back to the ground, the bones grinding farther out of her leg.

Iza digs her toes into the warm tiles of the roof already slick with her sweat. She wipes a trembling hand over her mouth, the smell of gunpowder hot and sweet. She tries to think of what to do next.

12. BEFORE

Iza's father was a businessman before the Return, an executive with access to the company jet and a yacht anchored in Miami. When news of the Return began to filter through the news channels, he didn't hesitate like everyone else.

He called the pilots, told them to ignore the flight ban, and took off for San Salvador Cay, a small Bahamian island with airport workers willing to take a bribe in the form of weaponry. From there he shuffled his wife and young daughter to the already waiting yacht, and they set sail for Curaçao, her mother's home.

While everyone else panicked in disbelief and denial as the Return unfolded, Iza's father had done research. He'd figured that an island would offer the best chance of survival during the onslaught of the undead. Curaçao was small enough that it was easily containable. It had a nice port, an oil refinery and plenty of oil, and a water purifying station large enough for the entire population. And it had the largest dry dock in the Caribbean—a necessity for the ships that planned to spend any length of time in the water in order to avoid the dangers of landfall. Most important, Curaçao was an island made up mostly of limestone cliffs, impossible for the living dead to climb. It also helped that Iza's mother had been born and raised on the island and still had family there with deep connections.

By the time Iza's father's yacht docked, Curaçao, like most of the world, was edging toward chaos.

Holland had abandoned it, and the local government wasn't equipped for the situation. Iza's father stepped in at the precise moment to take control, as he'd done with so many failing businesses in the past.

Once Curaçao was cleared of the *mudo*, Iza's father moved his family to the largest and most opulent *landhuizen* on the coast, erecting massive fences and gates around the plantation in case another wave of infection broke out. He used his wife's connections to broker deals with the locals and created an army of men—the *homber mata*—to keep the family safe.

That was when he began calling himself the governor and implementing his rules.

13. NOW

Of course Iza's father has prepared for a breach. Ever since the Return, he learned to be hypervigilant about every eventuality.

He had his men dig tunnels from the *landhuis* to caves in the cliffs that are stashed with supplies and close to ships moored and waiting.

Iza knows that she just has to reach one of those tunnels and find her father and everything will be okay. She flips the safety back on the gun and tucks it into the belt with her machete. While on the ground *lihémorto* moan and men run, she edges her way with sweaty fingers along the slick tiled roof. She crawls until she's perched against the dormer to her father's room, but she's afraid to look inside.

Even though she knows they've breached the *landhuis*, she can't imagine them getting to her father. She can't think of him being one of them. Even the idea of it causes her stomach to cramp and bright spots to explode in front of her eyes. Iza isn't sure she can survive without her father. She doesn't know if she's strong enough.

A lizard slides over her toes, and she jumps, her fingernails raking against the tiles as she scrabbles to stay put. She feels like someone has planted a tree in her chest and then pressed fast-forward on the world, branches growing and twisting and pushing her apart from the inside. It's hard to breathe in the thick night air, and she tastes the dampness of impending rain in the back of her throat.

Iza holds her breath and pushes her head around the corner of the dormer until she's looking through the window and into her father's room. He's standing by his wide bed, a pistol in one hand and the other reaching behind him toward the wall that hides an entrance to the tunnels. One foot is still raised as he walks backward, the pasty pale skin of his ankle jutting out of black pants.

He must sense Iza's movement, because he glances over at her. He swings toward her, his eyes widening at the same time as his finger twitches on the trigger. The window explodes. Iza recoils as tiny slivers of glass slice across her arms and face, the sound of the gunshot screaming in her head.

Her balance is off. She clambers to jam her toes against the sharp gutter as she's thrown backward. Blood seeps into her eyes, making everything blurry. But Iza can still see when the *lihémorto* rages into the room. She can tell the exact moment when it scents her blood and freshly flayed flesh.

Iza's father shouts her name, but nothing will stop the *lihémorto*. It bounds through the room toward her. Iza wants nothing more than to curl her hands around the windowsill, but she knows that her only chance is to let go. And so she does.

For years after they came to the island, Iza used to watch movies using an old DVD player. She remembers being able to click a button and have everything turn into slow motion— the show unfolding in front of her frame by frame. This is what she thinks about as she falls, everything happening frame by frame.

For just this moment Iza wishes she could stop everything, just pause the world and ask her father something—anything— to make her understand him. She feels like she can see every possible answer to her possible question on his face: regret, love, fear, shame, guilt, resignation, hope. And those emotions explode between them.

Iza watches as her father pulls the gun around straight. As the *lihémorto* lunges through the window for her. As she gives in to gravity.

14. BEFORE

"Un momentu," the men kept telling Iza, waving their hands in the air for her to get out of the way. Her father's men were unloading supplies at the dock, and she knew there were treats hidden in all the boxes. They'd been bringing provisions to the *landhuizen* for weeks, and every day something different arrived. Today she was hoping for some new books—everything she'd found exploring the dusty library was written in Dutch.

"What's for me?" she kept asking. She'd just lost her other front tooth the day before, and every *s* she pronounced came out with a soft lisp.

The men called her *Muskita*—little fly—because she buzzed around them, zipping between the boats. They brushed her away, passing the boxes over her head. She hadn't been on the island long enough by then to understand anything they said as their chatter filled the air.

Finally an older woman who smelled like baby powder and sweat dug around in one of the boxes until she found a stick of rock candy. She pulled Iza away from the boats where the men were working and handed her the treat. Iza was just touching her tongue to the dusky sweetness when a hand rose out of the water and grabbed the old woman's ankle.

She tried to pull away, tried to stay standing, her huge chest waving and the fat under her arms flapping as she clawed at the air. But the only thing she could have held on to was Iza, and she didn't want to risk pulling the little girl into the water with her. The old woman had worked for Iza's father for only a few weeks, but even so, she was like everyone else on the island: terrified of his wrath, and knowing she had a better chance against the *mudo* than she did against Iza's father.

The old woman didn't even shout or scream or cry as she toppled back into the waves, into the arms and teeth of the *mudo* waiting for her. She just closed her eyes and sighed as the water crested over her face, as if she'd always been waiting for that moment and was relieved it had finally come.

It was Beihito who grabbed Iza and carried her away from the dock, away from the men watching the frothing water where the old woman had fallen. He told her not to look, and so she stared into the sky and saw her father watching it all from the top of the cliffs. He didn't blink or wave or say anything.

Iza learned many things that day: that there was no such thing as being truly safe, that the ocean can change everything, that her father may have wanted her to live a normal life but it was Beihito who made it so.

15. NOW

Iza is drowning. She can't breathe. She's lying on her back on the ground and looks up to see her father in the shattered window of his room shouting down at her. She can't hear anything he's saying. Nothing penetrates the water around her. There is only silence and darkness, cut through by the lightning tearing apart the sky.

Iza feels the ground shudder as something falls next to her. She sees her father point the gun at her. She wants to tell him she's sorry, but she can't find the air. She wonders then if the rumors are true. If her father really did use the previous outbreak to kill her mother. If Iza has let him down as well.

Fingers wrap around her wrist, and she turns her head. His face isn't far from hers. It's Beihito, and his mouth opens and closes desperately. He tries to drag Iza's hand to his lips, but his arm is too broken. He tries to roll toward her, but half of his body refuses to move. She stares at his hand on her arm.

"Danki," she tries to tell him, because she'd refused to say it all those years before. Iza's staring into Beihito's eyes when her father's bullet rips into his head. The wisps of his moans still twine through her ears.

16. BEFORE

A few weeks after Iza lost her mother, Beihito brought her a stray kitten.

"Pushi," he said, handing it to her, always trying to urge her to learn the local language. She'd shrugged, and Pushi became the cat's name. Pushi was black and white, his legs too long for his body and his tail crooked. He was mean and spiteful, and Iza spent weeks coaxing him to like her, to be loyal to her.

Iza trained Pushi to follow her like a dog and to eat from her hand. Iza loved that cat more fiercely than she'd ever loved anything else in the world.

And then one night, Pushi didn't come to sleep with her. She found him in her father's bed, curled against his snores. She clicked her tongue against the roof of her mouth, trying to call the cat to her, but he refused to move.

Iza's father was the lodestone everyone else was drawn to; everything in this world was his. Iza wanted to slam the door, shut off the sight of him and Pushi. She wanted to run to the cliffs and fling herself into the water and dive so deep that sound and light and everything about her disappeared.

But instead she stood in the doorway while in the flashes of green gray dawn her father woke up and stroked his hand down Pushi's back.

17. NOW

Sensation returns to Iza's body like the sting of fire coral. She can't tell what's hot, what's cold, what burns, and what's torn. She only knows pain. She pushes herself to her feet, and the world spins and blinks. All around her is nothing but sound: moans, screams, gunshots, wails, thunder. The lightning is almost constant now, flashing scenes of men running, *lihémorto* chasing.

The rain comes at once, dousing everything in the thick taste of water. Iza looks back up at her father's window, but he's not there anymore. She thinks she can see shadows careening against the wall. Before she can figure out what's going on, someone is grabbing her.

She rears back, the blood and sweat and rain on her skin making her slick enough that she's able to pull away. She slips on the ground and throws up a hand as she's about to fall. Someone seizes it and steadies her. She recognizes him, the young man from the water that afternoon. The man she didn't kill. Iza winces, waiting to feel the tinge of teeth.

But it doesn't come. Instead he pulls her to him, wrapping her arm over his shoulder, sliding his other arm around her waist, helping her stand. Behind them is an explosion of wood and glass. They both look over their shoulders, their cheeks grazing. A *lihémorto* bursts from the house but is caught in the curtain, twisting and clawing at the fabric like the *mudo* under the tarps on the pirate ship.

They start to run, the man half-carrying Iza as they slip through the mud, the rain a blanket of water covering the world. Iza has so much blood on her from the broken window and the fall that even in the rain the *lihémorto* scents her and begins to chase, ripping free of the curtain, its moan grating through the darkness.

When they hit the edge of the cliff, Iza doesn't even hesitate. She just jumps, using everything left in her body to propel her as far away from the limestone wall as she can. The man's hand still grips hers, but as they fall, his hold falters and his fingers slip through her own.

In that moment, while Iza hangs suspended in the air, nothing hurts. Nothing shatters the stillness of the night, the cradling gentleness of the rain-soaked air.

And then she hits the waves, bubbles careening around her as the salt invades every scrape and cut. Iza claws at the water, scrabbling for the surface. The man finds her arm and yanks, pulling her up until she can breathe again. She kicks her feet to stay afloat and watches the water froth and churn closer to the cliff, where the *lihémorto* hit.

"My father," Iza says, still trying to catch her breath. "He has ships. Just around in the next cove." She points to the south, but the man shakes his head.

"We can make it," she tells him. "We'll be safe." She coughs as a wave slaps water into her face. "My father was prepared for this."

The man grabs Iza's arm, pulling it back into the water. "Your father's boats are gone," he says. She can barely hear anything beyond the sound of the rain slapping the ocean's surface like a hundred million children clapping at once.

Iza doesn't even know how to form the question, but she doesn't have to. "The breach wasn't an accident, Iza. All of this was planned from the beginning. Even saving you."

"I don't understand," Iza says. The world around them hushes in that moment, a gap in the rain. And that's when Iza hears the moans, but not from the direction of the cliffs. She looks back into the darkness beyond the breaking waves and in a flash of lightning sees the pirate ship. Its tarps have been pulled back, and the writhing mass of *mudo* strapped to the hull surge at the night.

18. BEFORE

Iza's mother wasn't built for the heat, even though she'd been born and raised in Curaçao, and she certainly wasn't raised to serve as a dictator's wife. She missed the snow, the university where she worked, and Starbucks coffee. She missed turning on the boiler in the winter and building a wood-fueled fire. She missed traffic and NPR and the buzz of Internet gossip.

In the beginning she told Iza to be grateful they were alive. Iza knew her mother tried not to think about all the friends she'd left behind, or wonder if they'd survived the Return. She tried especially hard not to think about them being undead. But at night, when her mother lay in bed and her father met with captains and the *homber mata*, Iza knew her mother thought about her ex-boyfriends and wondered if they'd died and come back.

Iza's mother joked with her husband that if only the Internet were working reliably, she'd be able to log onto Facebook or Twitter, and she was sure they'd have added a "Check here if zombie" box so she could catch up on the status of her friends.

Iza noticed her father never laughed when she wanted him to.

But both Iza and her mother knew that they were alive because of Iza's father. And everyone on the island also knew this. They knew that it was because of him they were surviving, and they treated him with deference, respect, and awe, until he came to expect it, even from his family, who'd known him from the before time. Who could remember what he looked like sheepishly rumpled and unshaven on a long weekend morning.

After a while, after the fences were set up around the beaches and port, and the *homber mata* secured the coastline, it became rare for people to die and Return.

Iza's father began to think that maybe he'd established one of the few pockets of sustainability in the world and that they could outlast the Return. He began to think that maybe Iza could be raised with a normal life. But her mother despaired even more. Because she couldn't stand a life that was close to normal. It only reminded her of what she'd lost.

That's when the ships began to arrive. Desperate, limping, starving, and often rife with infection, these huge floating cities would throw themselves upon Curaçao's shores. Men, women, and children would jump from the rails and swim for the cliffs, climbing old ladders, and huddling on tattered docks.

Everyone on the island, including Iza, could hear their screams for mercy. For help and water and food and shelter and life—everything that Iza had without a second thought.

Iza's father was ruthless. He knew that in order to survive, they had to keep the population of the island in check, and they had to be militant about keeping the infection from breaching the border. He set up patrols. He sent shiny white speedboats loaded with armed men to buzz around the island. Iza always thought of them as albino bees guarding an angry nest. Her afternoons were filled with the lazy drone of motorboats in the distance, puckered with snaps and pops as the *homber mata* killed the infected or anyone else not willing to follow her father's rules.

Before long Iza's mother would stand at the edge of the cliffs and watch the *homber mata*. In her hands she'd hold branches of bougainvillea, and one by one she'd pluck their petals and drop them to the water. Some days the waves at the base of the cliff would blaze red with their bright blossoms, and other days with the blood of people who'd been seeking any chance to survive.

Iza's father would remind them that this is what it took to

survive, but Iza could tell, looking into her mother's eyes, that this was no way to live.

Iza sometimes wondered if her father's need for order and utmost loyalty had killed her mother. If somehow her mother had fallen outside her father's tightly ordered rules and that was what had led to her infection. If she'd actually been infected.

19. NOW

Tacked to the limestone cliff is a small battered sign that reads THE BLUE ROOM in a black scrawl with a jagged red arrow pointing down into the water, the sole reminder of the old tourist site, now abandoned. Only in the lowest of tides does the mouth of the cave breach the surface of the water. Tonight the tide is high, and Iza and her savior have to heave in a deep breath and search against the cliff for the opening.

Iza's fingers brush the jagged edges of the limestone as she swims into the darkness. She kicks as hard as she can, her lungs beginning to buck. She purses her lips tight, her chest burning as her body chants, *Breathe! Breathe! Breathe!*

Her shoulder scrapes against the top of the tunnel leading into the cave, and she pushes at the wall until finally she feels her ears pop and her fingers touch air. The young man helps pull her onto a large flat rock in the middle of the cave.

On a bright day the sun dances through the water, throwing the entire room the most brilliant shade of blue Iza's ever seen, brighter than the bluest parrot fish in the reef. Now, as the storm begins to clear off, every now and then moonlight bubbles through.

Iza pushes herself to her feet and reaches out a hand until she can touch the wall to steady herself. The light bouncing through the water seems to make the entire cave dance and twirl and spin, and it makes her feel off balance.

She stares at the man, who just stands there. He glances at Iza's body, and then sharply away into the darkness. Iza looks down and realizes what he must have seen—her thin white nightgown almost transparent, the richness of her skin shining through it. With each breath it pulls tight against her.

For a heartbeat she wonders what it would have been like for them before the Return. If this had been some other night so many years ago and they'd both ended up in a hidden cave of blue light. Iza wonders how many lovers have rendezvoused here in the reflection of waves.

She tries to pluck the fabric away from her body, but it gets tangled in her belt, and so she unbuckles it, holding the machete in her hand. She has no idea what happened to her gun.

Iza crosses her arms over her chest. "The pirates," she finally says. Her voice sounds dull in the cave, and she shakes her head to dislodge the water from her ears. "You told me you escaped from them."

"I told you I jumped from their boat in the night and swam to the island. That was true," he says.

She curls her hands into fists, clenching the machete tighter. "You're one of them."

"No," he says. "I *am* them. The ship is my ship. The men are my men. I have made all this happen."

"Why?" Iza can barely even whisper the word.

"Your father is a ruthless man," the pirate says. "And this *isla* is too valuable."

"My father is fair—," Iza tells him, always his greatest defender.

"He uses his power to control people!" The pirate cuts Iza off, shouting so that his words echo around her.

"You have to be ruthless to survive," Iza says, her voice low. It's her father's mantra.

"If that's true, then why do you blame me for attacking? For being just as ruthless?"

Iza opens her mouth, and then closes it. "There were innocent people," she finally says. "You're going to end up killing the entire island."

"No, I'm not," the pirate says. "My men won't let the infection spread past the *landhuizen*. In a few days they'll kill the *lihémorto*, and Curaçao will return to normal."

"My father will never allow it."

"Your father will be dead!" the pirate yells, his breath hot against Iza's face like a slap. She stumbles under the weight of it. He seems to regret the words as soon as they leave his mouth, and he reaches for her hand, wrapping his fingers around her.

"I am not like your father," he says, stepping closer to her. "You have to understand," he continues. "I don't like this. I don't want this. I want the world to go back to the way it was before. I want it to be fair. That's all I'm trying to do is make it fair again."

Iza thinks about her mother tossing bougainvillea petals into the waves. All she wanted was for life to go back to the way it was before the Return, and Iza realizes that's what she's been waiting for as well.

And it's never going to happen.

"My father's men are loyal to him. The *hombrе mata* won't follow you. They'll avenge his death," Iza growls, ripping her hand free and pushing back against the cave wall.

"The *hombre mata* will follow your father's heir," the pirate says, stepping forward. "They will follow you. And you will follow me. And in return I will keep you safe."

The pirate takes another step forward. He brushes his fingers against her chin. Iza feels his chest against hers. *"Mi bunita,"* he whispers.

Iza's toes curl against the ragged edges of the rock. The water in the cave pulses like a dull heartbeat—in and out, in and out. She thinks about all the old romance novels she's read. All the times the pirate rescued the damsel in distress and she learned to love him for it.

"You don't know how long I've waited to make you my own," he says, twining his hand in her hair and pulling her head back. Prickles of pain itch against her scalp. Her throat feels awkward and bare.

Iza tries her best to pull away from his kiss. "How long?" she asks. "How do you know me?"

The pirate grins. He leans toward her, the heat of his mouth barely brushing Iza's forehead, her temple, her ear. "You don't remember me, do you?"

20. BEFORE

"Look," her father said. He took Iza's smaller hand in his and gently pushed her fingertips into the warm salty water. They were at an aquarium, standing with the other tourists around a low shallow tank filled with starfish and anemone and sea urchins.

He'd taken the day off just to spend it with her, to point out all the different types of fish weaving through the large exhibits. Together they'd sat in a huge amphitheater and watched a whale shark lumber around the graceful eagle rays.

Iza spent hours with her eyes wide open, leaning into the pipe-tobacco warmth of her father and listening to him explain how to tell a nurse shark from a hammerhead and a grouper from a jack.

But now that she was close enough to touch the creatures, she wanted to pull her hand back. She was too afraid of the spines and prickles of the sea urchins that looked as sharp as needles.

"It's okay," her father said, a laughing rumble to his voice she could feel in her chest. "Trust me."

Iza tasted the salt in the back of her throat, but whether it was from her tears or the open tanks she didn't know. She sniffed and pressed her lips together, holding her breath as she let her father brush her hand over the different creatures.

She jumped when she felt the sea urchin, expecting the sharp pinch of pain and not the soft bristle instead. Iza turned her head up to him then. He was smiling at her, and she knew he was proud of her bravery and strength.

She understood then that she wanted to be that little girl in his eyes forever. She would do anything for that feeling again, and she'd spent years chasing after it since.

21. NOW

"The game," Iza whispers. "Risk. It was yours."

The pirate smiles even larger. "Strategy," he says. "That's how I learned it. Your father should've paid attention."

Iza should have remembered his eyes, but the pirate was so skinny then. So young and full of rage that he hides so well now.

It becomes so clear to Iza how everything is her fault. Her knees go weak, so that the pirate has to loosen his grip on her hair in order to hold her body up. She pushes her fingers to her lips, tasting the dusky saltiness she'd tasted when the old woman had fallen off the dock because of her.

Her father always said Iza needed to be ruthless, but she hadn't believed him. She'd thought that the world could be something more. And she'd been the one to give the pirate access to the *landhuizen*. She'd had a knife at his throat and let him live. All because Iza wanted to believe that her father was wrong.

The pirate wraps his hand around Iza's wrist, and she glances down at where his dark fingers splay over her pulse. In her head all she can see is Beihito. At the way he looked at her when they fell, as if she were nothing to him. As if he'd never loved her as *djé yiu muhé*—his daughter.

She looks up at the pirate. He's wiped out the only man who'd ever found something inside Iza worthy of love.

Iza reaches one hand up and places it behind the pirate's head. His skin feels like the summer sun, damp with sweat and rough like a *tribon*'s body. "And my father's men will follow you because of me?" she asks. Her mouth hovers just against his. "And you'll protect me?"

He mumbles a yes as she presses her lips to his. Just this once Iza wants to know what it tastes like, this idea that the world can be beautiful and different.

She thinks about the old Risk board, about how the Venezuelan marked an *X* where Curaçao would have been. She remembers how she would put her thumb over it, wiping out her world. She wonders at how easy it is to erase everything you've ever known. Everything you've ever thought you were or wanted to be or should be.

As the pirate lets himself go against Iza, as he breathes her in, she pulls Beihito's machete up and presses it against his neck. Iza digs the blade in deep like she should have done before.

"Then they'll follow me," she says as the pirate clutches a hand to his throat, falling backward into the moon-drenched water. "And I'll protect myself."

Iza watches his body sink through the waves, his blood like bougainvillea blossoms blooming on the surface. She could do what it takes to survive. She could do what's necessary to rule her father's island.

Iza could be ruthless. Just like her father.

MARGO LANAGAN

"A Thousand Flowers"

Holly: Unicorns are a study in contradictions. They are portrayed as both gentle and fierce, spiritual and animal, healers and death-bringers. In addition to having healing properties, the horn that sits on a unicorn's brow is thought to be a deadly weapon and the unicorn itself is depicted as so fierce that it would rather die than be taken alive. Although often shown to be gentle, a unicorn will attack its natural enemy, the lion, without provocation. And the unicorn itself is found in medieval manuscripts associated both with celibacy and with desire.

Margo Lanagan's "A Thousand Flowers" is a masterful story exploring the contradictory nature of the unicorn.

Justine: Much as it saddens me to say so of work by a fellow Australian, this is by far the grossest story in the anthology. Eating brains, you say? So much less gross than Margo Lanagan's story. Here's why you should skip this one: B***iality as a defense for unicorns? I think I'm going to be ill.

Holly: Now, Justine, don't tell me a unicorn story made you feel squeamish? I thought we were supposed to look into the face of darkness? Face our fears?

A Thousand Flowers
By Margo Lanagan

I walked away from the fire, in among the trees. I was looking for somewhere to relieve myself of all the ale I'd drunk, and I had told myself—goodness knows why—in my drunkenness that I must piss where there were no flowers.

And this, in the late-spring forest, was proving impossible, for whatever did not froth or bow with its weight of blossoms was patterned or punctuated so by their fresh little faces, clustered or sweetly solitary, that a man could not find any place where one of them—some daisy closed against the darkness, some spray of maiden-breath testing the evening air—did not insist, or respectfully request, or only lean in the gloaming and hope, that he not stain and spoil it with his leavings.

"Damn you all," I muttered, and stumbled on, and lurched on. The fire and the carousing were now quite a distance behind me among the treetrunks, no more than a bar or two of golden light, crossed with cavorting dancers, lengthened and shortened by the swaying of storytellers. The laughter itself and the music were becoming part of the night forest noise, a kind of wind, several kinds of bird cry. My bladder was *paining* me, it was so full. Look, I could trample flower after flower underfoot in my lurching—I could *kill* plant after plant that way! Why could I not stop and piss on one, from which my liquids would surely drip and even be washed clean again, almost directly, by a rain shower, or even a drop of dew plashing from the bush, the tree, above?

It became a nightmare of flowers, and I was alone in it, my filth dammed up inside me and a pure world outside offering only innocents' faces—pale, fresh, unknowing of drunkenness and body dirt—for a man to piss on. Which, had he any manners in him at all, he could not do.

But don't these flowers grow from dirt themselves? I thought desperately. *Aren't they rooted in all kinds of rot and excrements, of worm and bird and deer, hedgehog and who knows what else?* I scrabbled to unbutton my trousers, my mind holding to this scrap of sense, but fear also clutched in me, and flowers crowded my eyes, and breathed sweetness up my nose. I could have wept.

It is all the drink, I told myself, *that makes me bother this way, makes me mind.* "Have another swig, Manny!" Roste shouted in my memory, thumping me in the back, thrusting the pot at me with such vigor, two drops of ale flew out, catching my cheek and my lip two cool tiny blows. I gasped and flailed among the thickening trees. They wanted to fight me, to wrestle me down, I was sure.

I made myself stop; I made myself laugh at myself. "Who do you think you are, Manny Foyer," I said, "to take on the whole forest? There, that oak. That's clear enough, the base of it. Stop this foolishness, now. Do you want to piss yourself? Do you want to go back to the fire piss-panted? And spend tomorrow's hunt in the smell of yourself?"

I propped myself against the oak trunk with one hand. I relieved myself most carefully against the wood. And a good long wash and lacquering I gave it—aah, is there any better feeling? I stood and stood, and the piss poured and poured. Where had I been keeping it all? Had it pressed all my organs out to the sides of me while it was in there? I had not been much more than a piss flask—no wonder I could scarce think straight! Without all this in me I would be so light, so shrunken, so comfortable, it might only require a breath of the evening breeze to blow me like a leaf back to my fellows.

As I shook the very last droplets into the night, I saw that the moon was rising beyond the oak, low, in quite the wrong place. Had I wandered farther than I thought, as far as Artor's Outlook? I looked over my shoulder. No, there still was firelight back there, as if a house door stood open a crack, showing the hearth within.

The moon was not the moon, I saw. It gave a nicker; it moved. I sidled round the tree very quietly, and there in the clearing beyond, the creature glowed in the starlight.

Imagine a pure white stallion, the finest conformed you have ever seen, so balanced, so smooth, so long-necked, you could picture how he would gallop, easy-curved and rippling as water, with the mane and tail foaming on him. He was muscled for swiftness, he was *big* around the heart, and his legs were straight and sound, firm and fine. He'd a grand head, a king's among horses, such as is stitched upon banners or painted on shields in a baron's banquet hall. The finest pale velvet upholstered it, with the veins tracing their paths beneath, running his good blood about, warming and enlivening every neat-made corner of him.

Now imagine that to that fine forehead is affixed a battle spike—of narwhal horn, say, spiraling like that. Then take away the spike's straps and buckles, so that the tusk grows straight from the horse's brow—*grows*, yes, from the skull, sprouts from the velvet brow as if naturally, like a stag antler, like the horn of a rhinockerous.

Then . . .

Then add magic. I don't know how you will do this if you have not seen it; I myself only saw it the once, and bugger me if I can describe it, the quality that tells you a thing is bespelled, or sorcerous itself. It is luminosity of a kind, cool but strong. All-encompassing and yet very delicate, it trickles in your bones; slowly it lifts the hairs on your legs, your arms, your chest, in waves like fields of high-grown grass under a gentle wind. And it thins and hollows the sounds of the world, owl hoots and rabbit scutters, and beyond them it rumors of vast rustlings and seethings, the tangling and untangling of the workings of the universe, this giant nest of interminable snakes.

When something like this appears before you, let me tell you, you must look at it; you must look at nothing else; your eyes are pulled to it like a falcon to the lure. Twinned to that compulsion is a terror, swimming with the magic up and down your bones, of being seen yourself, of having the creature turn and lock you to its slavery forever, or freeze you with its gaze; whatever it wishes, it might do. It has the power, and you yourself have nothing, and *are* nothing.

It did not look at me. It turned its fine white head just a touch my way, then tossed its mane, as if to say, *How foolish of me, even to notice such a drab being!* And then it moved off, into the trees at the far side of the clearing.

The rhythm of its walking beat in my muscles, and I followed; the sight of it drew me like pennants and tent tops on a tourney field, and I could not but go after. Its tail, at times, braided flowers into itself, then plaited silver threads down its strands, then lost those also and streamed out like weed in brook water. Its haunches were pearly and moony and muscular. I wanted to catch up to its head and ask it, ask it . . . What impossible thing could I ask? And what if it should turn and answer— how terrible would that be? So, all confusion, I stumbled after, between the flowers of the forest, across their carpet and among their curtains and beneath their ribbons and festoons.

We came to a streamside; the creature led me into the water, stirring the stars on the surface. And while I watched a trail of them spin around a dimple left by its passing, it vanished— whether by walking away, or by leaping up and becoming stars itself, or by melting into the air, I could not say, but I was standing alone, in only starlight, my feet numb and my ankles aching with the water's snowmelt cold.

I stepped out onto the muddy bank; it was churned with many hoofprints, all unshod that I could distinguish. There was no magic anywhere, only the smell of the mud and of wet rock, and behind that, like a tapestry behind a table, of the forest and its flowers.

Something lay higher up the bank, which the horse had fetched me to see. It was a person's body; I thought it must be dead, so still did it lie.

Another smell warned me as I walked closer on my un-numbing feet, on the warm-seeming mud, where the trampled grass lay bruised and tangled. It was not the smell of death, though. It was a wild smell, exciting, something like the sea and something like . . . I don't know, the first breath of spring, perhaps, of new-grown greenness somewhere, beckoning you across snow.

It was a woman—no more than a girl—and indecent. Lace, she wore, a lace-edged under-dress only, and the lace was torn so badly about her throat that it draggled, muddily, aside and showed me her breast, that gleamed white as that horse's flank, with the bud upon it a soft round stain, a dim round eye.

Where do I begin with the rest of her? I stood there stupidly and stared and stared. Her storm-tossed petticoats were the finest weavings, broiderings, laces I had seen so close. Her muddied feet were the finest formed, softest, whitest, pitifullest feet I had laid eyes on in my life. The skirts of the underclothes were wrenched aside from her legs, but not from her thatch and privates, only as far as the thigh, and there was blood up there, at the highest place I could see, some dried and some shining fresher.

Her hair, my God! A great pillow of it, a great swag like cloth, torn at the edges, ran its shreds and frayings out into the mud. It was dark, but not black; I thought in proper light it might show reddish lights. Her face, white as milk, the features delicate as a faery's, was cheek-pillowed on this hair, the open lips resting against the knuckle and nail of one thumb; in her other hand, as if she were in the act of flinging it away, a coronet shone gold, and with it were snarled a few strands of the hair, that had come away when she tore the crown from her head.

I crouched a little way from this princess, hissing to myself in awe and fright. I could not see whether she breathed; I could not feel any warmth off her.

I stood and tiptoed around her, and crouched again, next to the crown. What a creation! I had never seen such smithing or such gems. You could not have paid me enough to touch the thing, it gave off such an atmosphere of power.

I was agitated to make the girl decent. I have sisters; I have a mother. They would not want such fellows as those back at the fire to happen on them in such a state. I reached across the body and lifted the lace, and the breast's small weight fell obedient into the pocket and hid itself. Then, being crouched, I waddled most carefully down and tried to make sense of the lace and linen there, not wanting to expose the poor girl further with any mistaken movement of the wrong hem or tatter. I decided which petticoat piece would restore her modesty. I reached out to take it up with the very tips of my fingers.

A faint step sounded on the mudded grass behind me. I had not time to turn. Four hands, strong hands, the strongest I had ever felt, caught me by my upper arms and lifted me as you lift a kitten, so that its paws stiffen out into the air, searching for something to grasp.

"We have you." They were soldiers, with helmets, with those sinister clipped beards. They threw me hard to the ground away from the princess, and the fence they formed around me bristled with blades. Horror and hatred of me bent every back, deformed every face.

"You will die, and slowly," said one in deepest disgust, "for what you done to our lady."

They took me to the queen's castle and put me in a dungeon there. Several days they kept me, on water-soup and rock-bread, and I was near despair, for they would not tell me my fate nor allow me to send word to any family, and I could well imagine I was to spend the rest of my days pacing the rough cell, my brief time in the colorful out-world replaying itself to madness in my head.

Guards came for me, though, the third day. "Where are you taking me?" I said.

"To the block, man," said one.

My knees went to lily stalks. The other guard hauled me up and swore. "Don't make trouble, Kettle," he told his fellow. "We don't want to bring him before them having shitted himself."

The other chuckled high, and slapped my face in what he doubtless thought a friendly way. "Oh no, lad, 'tis only a little conference with Her Majesty for you. A little confabulation regarding your misadventures." Which was scarcely less frightening than the block.

From the stony under-rooms of the castle, up we went. The floor flattened and the walls dried out and we passed the occasional terrifying thing: a suit of armor from the Elder Days; a portrait of a royal personage in silks bright as sunlit water, in lace collars like insect wings; a servant with a tray with goblets and decanter so knobbed and bejeweled you could scarce tell what they were.

"Here's the place," said the humorous guard as we arrived at a doorway where people were waiting, gentlemen hosed and ruffed and cloaked, with shining-dressed hair, and two abject men about to collapse off that bench, they leaned so spineless and humiliated.

The guards at the door let us straight in, to a room so splendid, I came very close to filling my pants. It was all hushed with the richest tapis, and ablaze with candles, and God help me, there was a throne, and the queen sat upon it, and at the pinnacle of all her clothing, all her posture, above her bright, severe eyes and her high forehead filled with brains, a fearsome crown nestled so close in her silvering reddish hair, it might have grown into place there. Under her gaze my very bones froze within me.

"Give your name and origins," said the guard, nudging me.

"My name is Manny Foyer, of Piggott's Leap, Your Majesty."

"Now bow," the guard muttered.

I bowed. Oh, my filthy boots were sad on that bright carpet! But I would rather have looked on them than on that royal face.

"Daughter?" The queen did not take her attention from my face.

I gaped. Was she asking me if I *had* a daughter? Why would she care? Had she confused me with some other offender?

But a voice came from the shadows, beside, behind the throne. "I have never seen him in my life. I don't know why he has been brought here."

The queen spoke very slowly and bitterly. "Take a *close* look, daughter."

Out of the shadows walked the princess, tall and splendidly attired, her magnificent hair taken up into braids and knots and paddings so elaborate, they almost overwhelmed her little crown. Her every movement, and her white fine-modeled face, spoke disdain—for me, for her mother, for the dignitaries and notables grouped about in their bright or sober costumes, in their medals and accoutrements or the plainer cloaks of their own authority.

She circled me. Her gown's heavy fabrics rustled and swung and shushed across the carpet. Then she looked to her mother and shrugged. "He is entirely a stranger to me, Madam."

"Is it possible he rendered you insensible with a blow to your head, so that you did not see his face?"

The princess regarded me over her shoulder. She was the taller of us, but I was built stockier than her, though almost transparent with hunger at this moment.

"Where is my constable? Where is Constable Barry?" said the queen impatiently, and when he was rattled forth behind me, "Tell me the circumstances of this man's arrest."

Which he did. I had my chance to protest, when he traduced me, that I had not touched the lady, that I had only been adjusting her clothing so that my fellows would not see her so exposed. I thought I sounded most breathless and feeble, but while the constable continued with his story, I caught a glance from the princess that was very considering of me, and contained some amusement, I thought.

There was a silence when he finished. The queen dandled my life in her hands. I was near to fainting; a thickness filled my ears, and spots of light danced at the edges of my sight.

"He does not alter your story, daughter?" said the queen.

"I maintain," said the magnificent girl, "that I am pure. That no man has ever touched me, and certainly not this man."

The two of them glared at each other, the coldest, most rigid-faced, civilized glare that ever passed between two people.

"Free him," said the queen, with a tiny movement of her finger.

Constable Barry clicked his tongue, and there was a general movement and clank of arms and breastplates. They removed me from that room—I dare say I walked, but truly it was more that they wafted me, like a cloud of smoke that you fan and persuade toward a chimney.

They put me out the front of the castle, with half a pound-loaf of hard bread to see me home. It was raining, and cold, and I did not know my way, so I had quite a time of it, but eventually I did find my road home to Piggott's, and into the village I tottered late next day.

My mam welcomed me with relief. My dad wanted my word I had done no wrong before he would let me in the house. My fellows, farm men and hunters both, greeted me with such ribaldry I scarce knew where to look. "I never touched her!" I protested, but however hard I did, still they drank to me and clapped my back and winked at me and made unwholesome reference. "White as princess skin, eh, Manny?" they would say, or, "Oh, he's not up for cherry-picking with us, this one as has wooed royalty!"

"Take no notice, son," Mam advised. "The more you fuss, the longer they will plague you."

And so I tried only to endure it, though I would not smile and join in their jesting. They had not seen her, that fine girl in her a-mussment; they had not been led to her through the flowering forest by a magical horse with a horn in its head; they had not quailed under her disdain, or plumped up again with hope when she had looked more kindly on them. They had not been in that dungeon facing their deaths, nor higher in the palace watching the queen's finger restore them to life. They did not know what they spoke of so lightly.

I thought it all had ended. I had begun to relax and think life might return to being more comfortable, the night Johnny Blackbird took it into his head to goad me. He was a man of the lowest type; I knew even as I swung at him that Mam would be disgusted—Dad also—by my having let such an earwig annoy me with his crawlings. But he had gone on and on, pursuing me and insisting, full of rude questions and implications, and I was worn out with being so fecking noble about the whole business, when I had never asked to be led away and put beside a princess. I had never wanted picking up by queen people and bringing into royal presences. Most of all, I had not wanted, not for a moment, to touch even as much of her clothing as I touched, of that young lady, let alone her flesh. I had never thought a smutty thought about her, for though she were a beauty she were much too imposing for a man like me to do more than bow down before, to slink away from.

Anyway, once I had landed my first thump, to the side of

Blackbird's head, the relief of it was so great, I began to deliver on him all the blows and curses I had stored up till that moment. And hard blows they were, and well calculated, and curses that surged like vomit from my depths, so sincere I hardly recognized my own voice. He called pax almost straightaway, the little dung piece, but I kept into him until the Pershron twins pulled me off, by which time his face was well colored and pushed out of shape, the punishment I'd given him.

After that night people left me alone, and rather more than I wanted. They respected me, though there was the smell of fear, or maybe embarrassment—bad feeling, anyhow—in their respect. And I could not jolly them out of it, having never been that specimen of a jolly fellow. So I tended then to gloom off by myself, to work when asked and well, but less often to join the lads at the spring for a swim, or at the Brindle for a pot or two.

We were stooking early hay when the soldiers came again. One moment I was easy in the sunshine, watching how each forkful propped and fell; the next I came aware of a crowding down on the road, like ants at jam, and someone running up the field— Cal Devonish it was, his shirt frantic around him. As soon as he was within the distance of me, he cried, "They are come for you, Manny!" And I saw my death in his face, and I ran too.

The chase was messy and short. I achieved the forest, but I was not long running there before my foot slipped on a root, then between two roots, and the rest of my body fled over it and the bone snapped, above my ankle. I sat up and extricated myself, and I was sitting there holding my own foot like a broken baby in both my hands, knowing I would never run again, when the soldiers—how had they crossed the hay field so fast?—came thundering at me out of the trees.

"What have I done?" I cried piteously. They wrenched me up. The leg pain shouted up me, and flared off the top of my head as screams. "'Tis no less true now, what I said, than it was in the spring!"

"Why did you run, then," said one of them, "if you are so innocent?" And he kicked my broken leg, then slapped me awake when I swooned from the pain.

Up came Constable Barry, his face a creased mess of disgust and delight. "You *filth*." He spat in my face; he struck me to the ground. "You animal." He kicked me in my side, and I was sure he broke something there. "Getting your spawn upon our princess, spoiling and soiling the purest creature that ever was."

"But I never!"

But he kicked me in the mouth then, and thank God the pain of that shatterment washed straight back into my head, and wiped his ugly spittle-face from my sight, and the trees and the white sky behind it.

✫

Straight up to the foot of the tower he rode, the guard. He dismounted jingling and untied a sacking bag from his saddle. It was stained at the bottom, dark and plentifully.

"You have someone in that tower, I think, miss," he says to me. "A lady?"

"We do." I could not tear my gaze from the sack.

"I'm charged to show her something, and take her response to the Majesty."

"Very well," I said.

He followed me in; I conveyed his purpose to Joan Vinegar.

"Oh, yes? And what is the thing you're to show?" And she stared at the bag just as I had, knowing it were some horror.

"I'm to show the leddy. I've no instructions to let anyone else see."

"I'll take you up." Joan was hoping for a look anyway. So was I. He was mad if he thought we would consent to not see. Nothing ever happened here; we were hungry for events, however grim.

Up they went, and I walked back outside, glanced to my gardening and considered it, then followed my musings around to the far side of the tower, under the arrow slit that let out of the lady's room.

It was a windless day, and thus I heard clearly her first cry. If you had cared about her at all, it would have broke your heart, and now I discovered that despite the girl's general lifelessness, and her clear stupidity in getting herself childered when some lord needed her purity to bargain with, I did care. She was miserable enough already. What had he brought to make her miserabler?

Well, I knew, I knew. But there are some things you know but will not admit until you have seen them yourself. The bag swung, black-stained, before my mind's eye, a certain shape, a certain weight, and the lady cried on up there, not in words but in wild, unconnected noises, and there were thuds, too, of furniture, a crash of pottery. I drew in a sharp breath; we did not have pots to spare here, and the lady knew it.

I hurried back to the under-room. Her shrieks sounded down the stairs, and then the door slammed on them, and the man's boots hurried down, and there he was in the doorway, a blank, determined look on his face, the bag still in his hand, but looser, only held closed, not tied.

He thrust it at Joan as she arrived white-faced behind him. "Bury this," he said.

She held it away from her skirts.

"I'll be off," he said.

"You'll not sleep, sir, or take a bite?" said I.

"Not with that over me." He looked at the ceiling. We could hear the lady, but not down the stairs; her noise poured out the arrow slit of her room, and bounced off the rocks outside, and in at the tower door. "I would sooner eat on a battlefield, with cavalry coming on both sides."

And he was gone. Joan and I could not move, transfixed by the repellent bag.

"She has gone mad," I said.

"For the moment, yes," said Joan, as if she could keep things ordinary with her matter-of-fact tone.

We exchanged a long look. She read my question and my fear; she was not stupid. "Outside," she said. "We don't want to sully our living place wi' this. Fetch the spade."

We stepped out in time for a last sight of the horseman a-galloping off into the trees. The gray light flared and fluttered unevenly, like my heartbeats. Joan bore the bag across the yellow grass, and I followed her into the edge of the forest, where we had raised the stone for old Cowlin. Joan sat on Cowlin's stone. She leaned out and laid the bag on the grass. "Dig," she said, pointing. "Right there."

She did not often order me about, only when she was very tired or annoyed, but I did not think to question her. I dug most efficiently, against the resistance of that bastard mountain soil, quite different from what we had managed to rot and soften into the vegetable garden. The last time I had dug this was for Cowlin's grave, and the same sense of death was closed in around us, and of the smallness of our activity among the endless pines, among the endless mountains.

While I dug, Joan sat recovering, her fingers over her mouth as if she would not let words out until she had ordered them better in her head. Every time I glanced at her, she looked a different age, glistening like a wide-eyed baby the once, then crumpled to a crone, then a fierce matron in her full strength. And she would not meet my eye.

"There," I said eventually. "'Tis done." The mistress's wails in the tower were weakening now; you might imagine them whistles of wind among the rocks, had your very spine not attuned itself to them like a dowser's hazel rod bowing toward groundwater.

Joan sprang up. She brought the bag. She plunked it in my digging. Then she cast me a look. "You'll not be content till you see, will you."

"No."

"It will haunt your dreams, girl."

"I don't care," I said. "I will *die* if you don't show me."

"I will show you, then." And with her gaze fixed brutal on my face, she flicked back the corner of the sacking.

I looked a long time; I truly looked my fill. Joan had thought I would squirm and weep, maybe be sick, but I did not. I'd seen dead things before, and beaten things.

"It is her lover," I said. "The father of her bab," I added after some more looking.

Joan did not answer. Who else would he be?

I touched him, his hair, his cold skin; I closed the eyelid that was making him look out so frightening. I pressed one of the bruises at his jaw. I could not hurt him; I could push as hard as I liked. But I was gentle. I felt gentle; there is nothing like the spectacle of savagery to bring on a girl's gentleness.

"I am astounded she recognized him," I said.

"Oh, she did," said Joan. "In an instant."

I looked a little longer, turned the head to both sides and made sure I saw all there was to see. "Well, for certain he don't look very lovable now."

"Well, he was once. Listen to her noise, would you?"

I glanced behind me, as if I might be able to see the thin skein of it winding from the window. One last glance at the beaten head, at the mouth—that had been done with a boot toe, that had—to fix the two of them together in my mind, and then I laid him in the sacking in the ground, and I put the cloth over his face and then some of the poor soil on top of that, and proceeded to hide him away.

✧

Joan Vinegar woke me, deep that night. "Come, girl, it is time for midwifery."

"What?" Muzzily I swam up from my dream. "There are *months* to go yet."

"Oh, no, there ain't," she said. "Today has brought it on, the sight of her man. She is in the throes now."

"What should I do?" I said, frightened. "You have not had time to show me."

"Assist, is all. Just do as I tell. I must get back to her. Bring all the cloths you can find, and a bowl and jug of water." And she was gone.

I rose and dressed and ran barefoot across the grass and rocks to the tower. The silence in the night, the smaller silence in the tower; the parcels of herbs opened on the table; the bowl and jug there, ready for me to fill; the stove a crack open, with the fire just woken inside—all of a sudden I was awake, with the eeriness of it, with the unusualness, with the imminence of a bab's arriving.

Up I went with my bringings, into the prison room. It was all cloth and candlelight up there, the lady curled around herself on the creased bed. She looked asleep, or dead, as far as I could see from my fearful glances. The fire was built up big, and it was hotter in here than I had ever known it, hotter than it ought to be, for the lady was supposed to enjoy no comforts, but find every aspect of her life here a punishment.

Joan took the cloths from me, took the jug and bowl. "Make up a tea," she said, "of just the chamomile, for now. Lots of blooms, lots of leaves, about a fifth what is in my parcel there, in the middling pot."

"No," murmured the lady, steeling herself for a pain, and Joan almost pushed me outside. I hurried away. I had only heard screams and dire stories of childbed, and the many babs brought healthy from its trials had done nothing to counter my terror of it.

Down in the lower room I went to work, with Joan's transmitted voice murmuring in the stairway door, wordless, like a low wind in a chimney. I tidied the fire and put the pot on, then sat with the stove open and my face almost in the flames, drinking of their orange-ness and stinging heat, listening for a sound from the lady above, which did not come; she must noise loudly for her dead man, but stay stalwart for babbing, it seemed. They are a weird folk, the nobility; they do nothing commonsensically.

I took up the tea, and Joan told me the next thing to prepare, and so began the strange time that seemed to belong neither to night nor to day, but to happen as an extremely slow and vivid dream. Each time I glanced in at the door, the lady would be somewhere else, but motionless—on the bed, crouched beside it, bracing herself against the chimney-breast, her hair fallen around her like a cloak, full of snarls and tangles. Joan would hurry at me, as if I should not be seeing even as much as I saw. She would take what I had brought and instruct me what next she needed. Downstairs was all smells and preparations—barley mush with honey and medicine seeds crushed into it, this tea and that, from Joan's store of evil-smelling weeds, warmed-over soup for all of us, to sustain us in our various labors.

The fear came and went. Had I a task to do, I was better off, for it took my whole mind to ensure in my tiredness that I performed it right. When I was idle by the stove with Joan murmuring in the stairs, that was worse, when I could not envisage what awfulness might be happening up there, when only the lady's occasional gasp or word, pushed out of her on the force of a birth pain, stoked up my horrors. "Girl?" Joan would come to the door and say down the stairs, not needing to raise her voice. And then my fear would flare worst, at what I might glimpse when I went up, at what I might hear.

Then a new time began, and I could avoid the room no longer. Joan made me bring up the chair from the kitchen, and sit on it, and become a chair of sorts myself, with the lady's arms hooked over my thighs, my lap full of her hair. "Give her a sip," Joan would say, or, "Lift the hair off her neck and fan her there; she is hot as Hades." And in between she would be talking up into the lady's face, crouched before us, and though she was tired and old and aproned, I could see how she once must have been, and how her man might still desire her even now, her kind, fierce face, her living, watching eyes, her knowing what to do, after child after child after child of her own. She knew how to look after all of us, the laboring lady and the terrified girl assisting; she knew how to damp those two great forest fires, grief and fear, contain them and stop them taking over the world; she was in her element, doing what she was meant to do.

In the middle of one of the pains, the lady reared, and there was a rush and a gush, and Joan exchanged sodden cloth for dry, out of sight there, under the lady's nightgown. She looked up exultant, over the bump of the baby. "That's your waters popped," she said. "Not long now, love-a-do."

I was almost in a faint, such a strong scent billowed out from the soaked cloth beside us, from the lady herself. Jessamine, I thought. No, elderflower. No—But as fast as I could name the flowers, the scent grew past them and encompassed others, sweet and sharp, so different and so strong my mind was painted now with scattered pinks, now with blood-black roses and with white daphne.

"Oh," I whispered, and drank another deep breath of it, "I can almost *taste* the sweetness!"

The lady's head lolled to the side; released from the pain, she faded into momentary sleep, her face almost rapturous with the relief. Beyond her, Joan held the nightgown out, and watched below, shaking her head. "What is coming?" she said softly. "What is coming out of you, lovely girl?"

"A little horse," said the lady in her sleep. "A little white horse."

"Well, that will be a sight." Joan laughed gently, and arranged her cloths beneath.

What came, four pains and pushes later, was of course not a horse but a child—but a child so strange, a horse might almost have been less so. For the child was white—not white in contrast to Moorish or Mongol or African prince, but white like a lily, white like the snow, like the moon, entirely without color, except . . . He was a boy-child, and the boy spout on him was tipped with wrinkled green, like a bud, and the boy sacks on him—a good size for one so small—were also green, and darker, like some kind of fruiting, or vegetable.

He was small, he was unfinished, he did not live long. Joan gave him into the lady's arms, and I sat behind her on the floor and supported her, and over her shoulder I watched as he took a few pained breaths of the sweet, heated air, and then took no more, but lay serene. He was barely human, barely arrived; he was an idea of a person that had not got quite properly uttered, not properly formed out of slippery white clay; and yet a significance hovered all round him quite disproportionate to his size. He smelled divine, and he looked it, a tiny godlet, precise in all his features, delicate, pale, powerful like nothing I had seen before, like nothing I have seen since.

"What is that on his forehead?" I said. Perhaps all newborns had it and I was ignorant.

Joan shrugged, touched the crown of his tiny head. "Some kind of carbuncle?"

The lady held him better to the light.

"It looks like a great pearl there," I said. "Set in his skin. It has a gleam."

"Yes, a pearl," said the lady distantly, as if she had expected no less, and she kissed the bump of it.

Joan gave her a cloth, and she wrapped him, her hands steady, though I had begun to cry behind her, and were dripping onto her shoulder.

There was business to deal with—a body that has birthed needs to rid itself of all sorts of muck, and be washed, and dressed cleanly, and laid in a clean bed to rest, and it can only move slowly through these things. We proceeded calmly, Joan saying what I should do, task after simple task, and always I was aware of the little master, in his wrappings there by the fire, as if to keep his small deadness warm, and the dance we were doing around him, in his sweet air, in the atmosphere of him.

When she was abed, the lady asked for him, and the three of us sat there in a row very quiet, and she held him, unwrapped, lying along her up-propped thighs. Quite lifeless, he was, quite bloodless, with the scrap of green cord hanging from his narrow belly; he ought to have looked pitiful, but I could feel through the lady's arm against mine, through the room's air, through the *world*, that none of us pitied him.

"He looks so wise," I whispered. "Like a wise little old man."

"Wise and wizened," said the lady. *I have never known anyone so tranquil and strong as this lady,* I thought. Whoever she was, all I wanted that night was to serve her forever, me and Joan together in that tower, bonded till death by this night's adventure, by the bringing of this tiny lad to the world, and the losing of him from it.

In the morning the flower scent was gone; the fire had died, the tower was cold, and the air felt rotten with grief. *He will haunt your dreams*, Joan had told me, of that lover's head, but in fact he filled my waking mind, so well remembered in all his details that it was as if a picture of him—his ragged neck flesh, the turned-up eye—went before me, painted on a cloth, wherever I went, to the well or the woods or wherever. And when he was not there, his son, pale as a corpse candle, floated before me instead.

The lady gave the bab into Joan's hands, a tight-wrapped, tiny parcel, banded and knotted with lengths of her own hair. "Oh, of course!" I said when Joan brought it down the stair. "So that he always has his mam around him! And such a color, so warm!"

She laid him on the table. "So we've more digging to do, for him and the other birth leavings. It is best to bury those, with proper wordage and herbery."

"How is she?" I said timidly. I was unnerved that our bond was gone, that we were three separate people again.

"Resting," said Joan. "Peaceful."

Then I must have looked very lost and useless, because she came to where I sat on the bench, and stood behind me with her hands on my shoulders, and she held me together while I cried into my apron, and "There, there," she said, and "There, there," but calmly, and patiently, as if she did not expect me ever to stop, but would stand quiet and radiant behind me, however long I took to weep myself dry.

✧

I sent the girl home. She was in too much distress to be much use to me, and I could not let her near the lady. I thought it odd—she had hardly been squeamish at all when that head was brought in. I had had hopes for her. But the bab undid her, whether its birth or its death or its strangeness, or the fact that its mam shed no tears over it but sank straight back away into the stupor we were used to, as if she had never been childered, as if she had never raved and suffered over her man's death.

With the rider who brought supplies and took the girl away,

I sent a message to Lord Hawley that the mistress was delivered of a dead child, and what were we to do now? For my contract with him had only specified up to the birth, but now that the bab was gone, could not some other woman, without midwifing skills, be brought to the task of guarding my lady? For though I could use the good money he was paying, I felt a fraud here now, when there were plenty of childered women in my own village to whom I could be truly useful, rather than playing nursemaid here.

For answer he sent money, money extra upon what he had promised, as if the death of the bab had been my doing and he wanted to show me favor for it. And he bid me stay on while they sorted themselves out at court about this state of affairs. I could see them there in their ruffs and robes, around their glasses of foreign wine, discussing: Ought they to humiliate the lady with further exile, or ought they to allow her back, instead to be constantly reminded of her sullied state by the faces and gestures of others?

And so I stayed nursemaid. Although there were only the two of us now, I kept to my contracted behavior and did not keep company with my prisoner, but only attended her health as long as that was necessary, and made and brought her meals, emptied her chamber pot, and tended her small fire. I was under orders to speak to her only when spoken to, and to resist any attempt she might make to engage me in conversation, but had I obeyed them we would have passed our days entirely in silence, so to save my own sanity I kept to my practice after the birth of greeting the lady when I entered, and she would always greet me back, so that we began each day with my asserting that she was a lady, and her acknowledging that I was Joan Vinegar, which otherwise we might well have forgot, there being nothing much else to remind us.

A month and a half we lived together, the lady and me in our silences, the mountain wastes around us. The lord's man came with his foodstuffs and more money, with no accompanying message. He told me all the gossip of court, sitting there eating bread and some of the cheese and wine that he himself had supplied, and truly it was as if he spoke of animals in a menagerie, so strange were their behaviors, so high-colored and passionate. He filled the tower room with his noise and his uniform. I was so glad when he went and left us in peace again that I worried for myself, that I was turning like that one upstairs, entirely satisfied with nothing, with watching the endless parade of my own thoughts through my head.

I stood, with the man's meal crumbs at the far end of the table, and a cabbage like a great pale green head at the near end, and the gold scattered beside it that I could not spend, for how much longer yet he had not said. She was silent upstairs. She had maintained her silence so thoroughly while the man was here, he might have thought me a hermit, hired only to do my prayers and observances for sake of the queen's health, not to attend any other human business. And none of this made sense, not the gold, or the cabbage, or the smell of the wine dregs from the cup, or the disturbance his cheerful voice had wrought on the air of the usually silent room, but all flew apart in my senses like sparrows shooed from a seeded

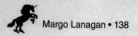

field, in all directions, to all quite different refuges.

My lady's womb ceased its emissions from the birth, and paused awhile dry. Then came a day when she requested cloths for her monthly blood. I wondered, as I brought them, then later as I washed them, whether this was good or bad, this return to normal health. Would Hawley have preferred—would he have showered me with yet more gold?—if she had died in expelling her child, or thereafter from some fever of childbed? Had I been supposed to understand that she was not to return alive from this exile? Had I failed in an unstated duty?

"Well, she is as *good* as dead," I said to myself, rinsing the scrubbed cloth and watching the pink cloud dissipate down the stream. "If you ask me."

Dreams began to trouble me. Often I dreamed of the dead child. Sometimes he lived, and made wise dreamish utterance that carried no sense when I repeated it to myself in the morning. Sometimes he died, or fell to pieces as he came out of his mother, or changed to a plant or a fleeing animal on emerging, but always these dreams were filled with the scent of him, maddening, unplaceable, all flowers and fruits combining, so strong it seemed still to linger in the room even after I woke, and slept again, and woke again in the morning, so tantalizing that several times I hunted on my hands and knees in the meadow around the cottage for the blossom that might be the source, that I might carry it about with me and tantalize myself further with the scent.

I woke very suddenly from one of these dreams, and lay frightened in the night, washes of color flowering forth onto the darkness, with the surprise of the wakening to my heart and blood. My hearing had gone so sensitive, if one of my grandchildren had turned over in his sleep back home, I think I would have heard it. Outside a thud sounded, and another, earthen, and then another; a horse was about, not ridden by anyone, but perhaps it had pulled itself loose when tied to browse, and now wandered this unfruitful forest and had come upon our meadow in its hunger.

When I had tamed my heart and breath, I left my bed and quietly opened the cottage door, to see whether the animal was wild or of some worth. I dare say I had it in mind how useful a horse would be, if it were broken and not too grand, how I might add interest to my dreary life here with excursions, with discoveries of towns within a day's ride of the tower. I might spend a little of my gold there; I might converse with sellers and wives. Figures and goods and landscapes flowed across my imaginings, as I stepped out into the cold night, into the glare of the stars, the staring of the moon.

The air was thick with the flower-scent of the dead boy-child—such a warm, summery smell, here in autumn's chills and dyings! The horse stood white—a stallion, he was—against the dark forest. He was down the slope from the tower. He had raised his head and seemed to gaze at the upper window.

"Perhaps you are too splendid," I whispered, but I fetched the rope anyway, and tied a slip-loop. Then across the meadow I crept, stepping not much faster than a tree steps, so as not to frighten the horse away.

At a certain point my breathing quieted and the night breeze eased to where the low noise issuing from my lady's window reached me. That rooted me to the meadow ground more firmly, her near-inhuman singing, her crooning, broken now and then with grunts and gutturals, something like triumphant laughter.

I have often been thought a witch myself, with my ugly looks and my childbedding, but I tell you, I have never evoked any such magic as shivered under that fine horse's moonlit hide, as streamed off it in the night, fainting me with its scent and eluding my eye with its blown blooms and shining threads. And I have never cast such a spell as trailed out that window on my mistress's, my charge's, song, if song it were. It turned my bones to sugar ice, I tell you, my mind to sweet syrup and my breath to perfume.

And then among her singing another sound intruded, with no voice to it, no magic, no song. It was an earthly sound and an earthy: stone scraped on stone, heavily, and surreptitious somehow.

Then I knew what she was about, with her mad singing, with her green-tipped baby, with her caring so little for the shame of the queen's name and family. And I ran—more, I *flew*—across the meadow grasses and around to the tower door. I must be quiet, or she would hurry and be gone before I reached her; I must be quick!

I took the prison room key from under its stone and managed to open the tower door silently. I sped up the stairs, put the key in the lock and turned it, with its usual squeaks and resistance. From inside, loud now, undisguised, came the grinding, the push of stone on stone.

"My lady!" I forced the stiff key around.

More grinding. Then, and as I flung myself into the room, the stone the girl had loosened from the arrow slot—months of labor in the night, it would have taken her!—thudded down into the meadow at the foot of the tower.

"My lady, no!"

She darkened the hole with her body, for the moments it took me to cross the room. My fingertip brushed the hem of her nightgown. Then moonlight and starlight whitened my reaching hand.

"Madam!" I screamed to the waiting horse, but through my scream I heard the impact of the lady below, the crack of breaking bone.

"Madam, no! What have you done?"

I pressed myself to the arrow slot, peering down. The horse stepped up the grass, and I gasped. He bore a fine long spiraling horn on his brow, like some animals of Africa, anteloupes and such. I could smell him, the sweet ferocious flower-and-fruitishness of him, so powerfully that I was not surprised—I did not gasp again—when my lady appeared, walking across the meadow, not limping as she ought, or nursing any injury that I could see. And when she embraced him, he bowing his head to hold her slight body against his breast, and crooking his knee to further enclose her, the rightness and the joy of it caught me in belly and groin, like a birth pain and a love pang together, and I drank of the sight as they each seemed to be drinking of the other, through their skins, through his coat and her clothing, from the warmth they pressed into being between them.

She held and held him, around his great neck, her fingers in his mane; she murmured into him, and rubbed her cheek on the nape of him and kissed him; she reached along his shoulder and the muscles there, holding him to her, and no further proof was needed than that embrace, and the sight of her lifted face, and the scent in my nostrils of all that lived and burgeoned, that the two of them were lovers and had loved, that the little green-tipped boy had been issue of this animal and this maiden, that the carbuncle on the boy's brow had been the first formings toward his own horn, that I had been witness to magic and marvels. The world, indeed, was a vaster and much mysteriouser place than queens and god-men would have us believe.

My mistress led the horse to the tree stump I used for chopping kindling on. She mounted him from there, and rode him away. I shook my head and clutched my breast to see them, so nobly did he move, and so balanced was her seat to his movement—they were almost the one creature, it was clear to me.

And then they were gone. There was nothing below but night-lit meadow, giving onto black forest. Above, stars sang out blindly in the square of air where my lady had removed the stone. The prison room was empty; the door yawned; the window gaped. Everything felt loose, or broken. The sweetness slipped out of the air, leaving only the smell of the dead fire, and of cold stone.

I left the door ajar, from some strange notion that my lady might return, and require to imprison herself again. I walked down the stairs I had so lately flown up. Slowly I crossed the lower room to the other gaping door, and stepped out into the meadow. Brightly colorless, it was, under the moonlight, the grass like gray straw, the few late flowers leaning or drooping asleep.

I rounded the tower. There she was, her head broken on the fallen stone. I scarce could believe my eyes. I scarce could propel myself forward, surprise had frozen so thickly around the base of my spine, where all the impulses to walk begin, all the volitions.

"My lady, my lady!" I *fell* to my knees rather than knelt to them. How little she was, and fine, and pale! How much more delicate-crafted are noble ladies, aren't they?, than us countrywomen, all muscled for fieldwork and family life! But even my thick skull could not have prevailed against that stone, and from that height. Blood had trickled from her eye corner, and her nose and mouth, and poured through her hair; now she seemed glued blackly to the stone, staring to the forest, watching herself ride away.

This is the end of my story. I told a different one to Lord Hawley when I walked out of the mountains and bought myself a strong little bay mare to ride to the palace and give my information. My lord—I had not seen him in person before—was small, and his furs and silks and chains and puffed-out sleeves made him seem as wide as he was tall. He listened to my tale most interestedly, and then he released me from my contract, paying it out in full though I had four months to serve yet, and adding to that amount the sum I had paid for the mare, and double the sum I had outlaid for bed and food to visit him,

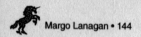

so that I should not arrive home at all out of pocket. He gave me a guard to protect me and my moneys all the way to Steeping Dingle; that guard, in time, was to marry my youngest, little Ruth, and sire me four grandsons and three granddaughters.

I had no reason to complain of my treatment by the queen's house; every royal man gave me full courtesy and respect. And though I was sworn to secrecy over the whole affair, the fact that I had had royal dealings, as evidenced by my return with the guard, did much for my standing, and from that time on I made a tidier living bringing out babies than all the other good-women combined, in my village and throughout the surrounding country.

MAUREEN JOHNSON

"The Children of the Revolution"

Justine: Maureen Johnson's brain does not work like that of most people. Possibly because it's already infected. Consider this story a report from the inside and a warning to begin your search for a zombie-proof abode NOW. Stock it well!

Holly: One of the things I find particularly upsetting about zombies is the idea of being trapped in your own head, unable to think clearly, but still conscious. Forever. It's pretty much the worst thing I can think of—ugh. Just writing about it makes me shudder.

Justine: Once again, I thank you, Holly, for pointing out further awesome aspects to writing about zombies. While, yes, I do, indeed, love zombies qua zombies, it's also true that they are the most resonantly powerful metaphor of all time.

The Children of the Revolution
By Maureen Johnson

Maybe I really should have guessed the moment I saw the children and the room they were kept in. Sure, there's no way I could have known what was *specifically* going on . . . only a lunatic could have guessed what was *specifically* going on . . . but something was clearly wrong with the picture.

The room was a child's wonderland. What had once been formal dining rooms and sitting rooms and reception rooms had been turned into one massive, long room, separated only by bits of load-bearing walls or massive fireplaces that could not be removed. The walls and ceiling had been painted to look like a blue sky, full of cartoonish clouds. The wood floors had been covered by colorful squares of heavy foam rubber and carpet. At the far end there was a full-size jungle gym, complete with a purple and red tube slide and a small ball pen. There was a fake tree that rose all the way to the ceiling, with a tree house and a swing. There was a book nook, and a play kitchen with plastic pots and pans. There was a section for throwing balls. Televisions were mounted high on the walls. In one corner there were five little beds—a little race car, one that looked like a plastic castle, one that looked like a rocket, one that was covered in sparkles, and one designed to look like a half-moon in a puddle of starry sky. There was everything needed to keep small children very happy. The enormous windows had clearly been treated with something to keep out prying eyes, and were barred for safety.

The whole thing was sealed off by an extraordinary baby gate—about five feet of a clear fine mesh of very strong plastic, clamped from wall to wall. The mesh was as tall as the average adult and was soft and strong enough to take any assault a child could inflict upon it. A wayward ball had gotten loose, and their mother tossed it softly over the top of the gate.

"I can't really take them outside," the woman explained, "so I tried to bring the outside in."

They certainly looked like they needed a little outside time. Their lips were all very dry, their eyes all very milky. Their skin had no luster. I was prepared to blame almost anything on England at that point, but these kids . . . It wasn't just the bad weather. They moved like toddlers, even though they were older than that and should have had more of the easy grace of kindergartners. They needed the vitamin D of the sun. They needed to run and play and get a healthy glow and some coordination.

"They come from all different countries," their mother went on. "None of them are native English speakers. They know a few words. They're learning. Watch. Everyone! Look at mommy! Listen to mommy."

Five little heads turned. The one closest, a girl started to drool. A long strand of saliva loosened from her mouth.

"Mommy has to go on a trip. A very short trip. Mommy has to go to London, just for a day. Just for a day."

This brought a collective noise of interest from the children.

"It's all right, it's all right. Look at the nice friend mommy has brought to stay with you! Isn't she nice? Isn't she pretty? You like her, don't you?"

The children all examined me with baffled stares.

"Ugggnnhhhhhh?" asked the oldest boy, pointing at me. It seemed a little judgmental to my ears.

"Yes," said their mother, who apparently understood this. "This is Sofie. You like her!"

One of the girls stumbled and fell over for no reason at all. She hit the ground with a solid thump, but the thick rubber easily cushioned the fall. She pushed herself back up, and promptly fell again.

So, yeah. I should have known that these were not normal children. But I thought, Celebrity children. Well, they're just different. You can't apply the same standards you apply to regular children. And though they were clearly not doing well, I guess the voices in my brain were telling me that these kids had dietitians and had spent a lot of their short lifetimes on private aircraft (that has to mess with your inner ear balance), and maybe that's just what being really rich looks like.

But there was another voice in my head—a quieter one, way in the back, telling me to leave, to get out of the house and away from them, to go back into the rain, to hitchhike to London or starve or even just call home.

While I can still assign blame, I want to make sure you know this was *all Franklin's fault.* . . .

Come to England, he said. We will have a romantic summer together picking berries on an organic farm, he said. Wild ponies roam free around the farm, he said. Imagine us with our organic berries surrounded by the beautiful wild ponies, he said. We will read to each other, he said. We will write long letters in real handwriting, he said. We will enjoy the quiet and fresh air and be together all the time, he said. Learn to live, he said. Look at this website I found, he said.

The website talked about the free room and board on the farm. Three square organic meals a day in the fecund countryside. It presented images of an ecologically friendly, healthy, progressive wonderland with a house full of people from many countries. It showed pictures of carrots and berries and ponies and little English towns and a big English fireplace with a roaring fire. *This* is where Franklin wanted us to go to be together.

Of course, he showed me this one afternoon when he was skipping class. When trolls cut classes, you think they are losers. When the beautiful and/or reasonably erudite do the same thing to sit on the library steps and read poetry, you think they are on to something deep. You see only deep brown wavy hair and strong legs, well honed by years of Ultimate Frisbee. You see that book of T. S. Eliot poems held by the hand with the long, graceful fingers, and you never stop to think that it shouldn't take half a semester to read one book of poems . . . that maybe he is not so much reading as getting really high every morning and sleeping it off on the library steps, forcing the people who actually go to class to step or trip over him.

At least if you are me. Looking back, I made a number of bad decisions that now seem glaringly obvious. But that's hindsight for you.

I mean, I was a freshman at college, overwhelmed, with too little sleep and an experimental haircut and a bipolar roommate and little to no idea what I was doing with my life. I was out of my depth with Franklin—a beautiful junior, so very dreamy eyed. (Again, I know what that means now.) We met when I basically fell over him on my way out of the library, which led to three weeks of I-fell-for-you jokes that he laughed at every time. (This is because he was very, very high and had no memory of my telling them before, and also he laughed at everything, including sneezes and radiators and doorknobs and long silences.)

I guess I was just a little too easily impressed with people that seem beyond me socially. I mean, Franklin had been *an actual catalog model* for J.Crew when he was thirteen. I think you can maybe understand why it took me a few weeks to catch on to the fact that he was completely and totally full of shit, and that all of his ideas were bad. Specifically, I caught on when I was up to my ankles by the side of an English road weeks later, yanking reluctant blackberries out of a bush full of thorns that tore at my skin while cars whizzed by my back. Alone. In the misting rain.

See, what Franklin did not mention—or, more likely, did not know—was that "Come live and work on our organic farm in remote England this summer!" actually meant "Be our slaves, stupid students!" No one mentioned that the farmhouse was uninsulated and not really weatherproof, and that the huge fireplace was in the owner's house. Our accommodation had no such fireplace. The roof leaked on the third floor, and the floors leaned and creaked, and the beds were World War II surplus cots. The website didn't convey the all-pervading damp and boredom, that it was the land of daily rain and sweaters in mid-June. That the owners were mean and cheap, that hot water was unknown, that there was no washing machine (except in their house, and they certainly weren't sharing). That the nearest town was a mile and a quarter away down a road with no shoulder. That it was the land of godforsaken wild ponies that charged at you through the bushes when you were least expecting it, looking for apples in your pockets and hating you for not having them, butting you with their massive heads in retaliation.

And it was a land of absolutely no weed, which is probably why Franklin took off after two weeks—two utterly miserable weeks. Because a non-stoned Franklin was actually a grouchy, extremely lazy Franklin who made other people pick his berries while he sought out other ways of getting high. Then, one very wet day in the middle of the second week, he just dropped his plastic berry basket and said "I'm going to London. You can come if you want, but I'm not paying for you."

Franklin had cash. I, however, did not. I had blown everything I had on the stupid ticket to England. I tried to explain this to Franklin, and he just said "Sorry" without sounding sorry at all. He put on his backpack and walked to town.

I was alone. My days were filled with watery organic vegetable soup and tasteless organic curry and mysterious organic mash. (What I would have given for solid food.) And then, of course, there was the death match for the berries themselves—the berries that came out of the hedgerows along the road. I'm not even sure that the farmers *owned* these bushes. I suspect the bushes were wild and on public land, and the farmers were having us steal berries from the English government to fuel their fascist jam-making empire. Those who brought the most berries got the best rooms, the warmest blankets, the occasional cup of extra tea or ride to town to do laundry.

Every night, I thought about giving up and going home. I could fall on my parents' mercy and beg them to pay the difference to get my ticket changed. But that would mean that every single thing I tried to do for the rest of my life would only bring trouble. "Remember that time you thought it was a good idea to run off to that stupid organic farm with that guy . . . What was his name?" they would ask. "And then he left and you were stuck there and we had to bail you out?" Oh, my parents had guessed that something like this would happen. They *always* thought my ideas would turn out badly. They had seen Franklin, and they knew.

No. It was unthinkable to run home. Sometimes it is worth any amount of suffering just to prevent giving your parents the opportunity to be right.

What I needed was some money, that was all. Then I could go to London too, and get a room with some people and a job somewhere. I could survive on just a little for a few weeks. Fuck Franklin. I could do this myself.

This is all I thought about, day and night, for a week after Franklin's vanishing act. I walked to town every day, risking life and limb on the non-road, as English people in nice, warm cars, went to their homes. "Town" was about as depressing a place as you could ever hope for—a booze shop, a betting shop, a pub full of old dudes, a knockoff "American Fried Chicken!" place, and a place to make copies.

Of all the places in town, the Laundromat was actually the best. Even though it was just cracked linoleum and a bunch of industrial washers and driers, it was warm and snug. The owner was an older man named George with a flushed red face who wore the same navy blue fleece every day. He kept a bowl of hard candies on the counter and was kind to all of the students on the farm. He knew the farm scam well, and he knew what the owners were up to. So he would let me come in every evening and use the rickety old computer in the corner, the one that was supposed to be for customers only. I used this to research my escape.

The one thing that was immediately clear was that it was going to be very hard to get a job in London. I wasn't very qualified for anything that required a résumé, and for all the other jobs, you had to turn up in person to apply. Which was all part of the problem. Every night, I played this game with myself before walking home down the road with no shoulder, praying that I wouldn't be hit. Or sometimes, that I *would* be.

One miserable, murky afternoon, as I worked my little blackberry patch, George's rusty little car pulled up behind me.

"Hello!" he called cheerfully. "You making out all right there?"

"Not really," I said.

"I've got something for you," he said. "You know the big house up on the hill?"

I didn't.

"Well, there's a big house on the hill. There's an American up there who needs someone to take care of her children. Pays very decent. Generous lady. She don't want a local, because locals around here talk too much. Everything gets around the village. American college student, that's just what she wants. My wife does some of the cleaning for her, and they got to talking. I'd imagine it's a lot nicer up there than where you are. If you're interested, you just let me know. I can drive you up there tomorrow, or whenever . . ."

"Give me fifteen minutes to get my bag," I said.

It took ten. Never in my life had I packed so quickly, shoving my mud-soaked clothes into my bag. I didn't even tell the farm owners that I was leaving. I walked away from the farm without looking back once, and got into George's car, where he was listening to a football match on the radio.

"So fast?" he asked with a chuckle. "Funny, they always leave that way. Come on, then. Let me take you somewhere nicer."

Even riding around in a run-down car with an old man on a bleak afternoon was a massive improvement. My summer had tanked so terribly. We drove past some grim collections of houses that looked all the same, and a Little Chef restaurant, and a mile or two of nothing. Finally we turned down an unpaved road of dirt and small stone, cut between a solid bank of trees. It wound up and up, through more and more dense nothing. I was just thinking that this was the least-promising vista I'd ever seen, and then . . . it came into view, the wide expanse of gray stone with the ivy-covered facade. A massive building, with long, high windows, and little turrety bits.

"That's . . . a house?" I asked.

"Well, I suppose you'd call it a manor," George said pleasantly as the car popped and bumped its way up the long stone-filled drive. "Sometimes they go vacant, and people buy them up. She's done quite a nice job with this one."

We had pulled up to the front door now. Just like that—a big black door with a black lion's head knocker.

"She's expecting you," George said. "I've had a word. Just knock. You'll be quite all right here. She's lovely."

I was reluctant to get out of the car and shut the door. If there were no one home, if it didn't work out, I was stuck. Stuck in the middle of nowhere, up on this hill, in the rain, in the middle of England. But this was clearly where he was leaving me. I grabbed my bag, thanked him, and got out. The knocker was heavy and slick, and it squeaked terribly when I lifted it and brought it down on the door with a heavy clank.

Then I stepped back and waited. It took a few moments, but the door opened. A woman stood there—maybe in her early thirties, long brown hair tied back, glowing cheeks, friendly face.

"Hi!" she said. "I was just feeding the kids! Are you from the farm? Sofie, right?"

It was the tattoos that I picked up on first—the signature eight-pointed star on the inside of her wrist. The Sanskrit running down her arm. My eyes followed the muscled arm in the form-fitting black T-shirt up to the face. The face had been ingrained in my mind, through hundreds of posters and articles and websites. My brain struggled for a moment, trying to connect the physical reality in front of me with the confluence of images surging through my memory. I didn't even realize how much I knew about this woman. I had never consciously *studied* her. She was simply so famous that everyone knew all about her. She was a concept, not a person.

"Yeah," the famous actress said, with a smile and a shrug. "Sorry. I'm who you think I am. I didn't mean to startle you. Come on in. Want a cup of tea?"

I nodded dumbly. I found myself staring at one of the world's most frequently photographed asses, now wearing a pair of yoga pants, as it lead the way into the house. The actress was really tiny—maybe two inches taller than me, but absurdly small in frame, like a child who'd had an awkward growth spurt.

According to all the papers, the actress had just jetted around the world on an adoption spree, and was now the mother of five. The papers also claimed that the children lived in a huge house on Malta, in the middle of the Mediterranean. Or maybe in Aruba. Possibly in Spain. Perhaps a ranch in Colorado. A compound in California. The actress and her partner, the equally famous actor, were vigilant about their children's privacy—aside from long-distance shots taken at the time of the adoptions, no one ever scored a picture of them.

"Your children are here?" I asked.

"My publicist plants stories so no one ever knows where

they really are," she said with a smile. "Come on. Let's go to the kitchen and talk."

We passed through an airy entrance hall with a fireplace, yellow walls, several portrait paintings, and a fine carved wood fainting couch covered in black damask woven through with images of Chinese dragons. There were many doors, many nooks. A tiny reading space under the stairs. A long hallway that wound back, deep into the house. And then, a kitchen.

Aside from the fact that it could have housed a small airplane, it was sort of a normal kitchen. The long marble counter was loaded down with bottles of vitamins and glass jars stuffed with herbs. There were piles of reusable grocery bags, and a stainless steel compost pot sitting in the corner. The huge silver two-door refrigerator was covered in schedules and children's drawings. A set of shelves was filled with vegetarian cookbooks, books on nutrition, and at least a dozen books with titles such as *The Lazarus Kitchen, Cooking for Life, The Eternal Diet, Eating Toward Forever, Lazarus Healing, The Never-Ending Meal,* and *Lazarus Kids.*

A lot had been made of the actress's strange religion— Lazarology, which had something to do with living forever by taking vitamins and doing a lot of exercise. Some people said it was a cult, that she and her boyfriend collected blood, that they went through all kinds of weird rituals and treatments based on the teachings of their crackpot guru, some insane scientist guy who had died about twenty years before. All the Lazarines were waiting for him to wake up. Some claimed he already had. They were all nuts, every last one of them. Lazarology had been banned in at least a dozen different countries.

Mostly, though, it seemed to be about eating a lot of uncooked vegetables, doing yoga, and purifying yourself in New Agey ways. Harmless, friendly stuff. No one ever claimed the actress wasn't *nice*. A little dumb, maybe. But nice. Here she was pouring filtered water into some kind of clay kettle and making me a cup of tea.

"George says he likes you," the actress said, getting out a mug. "He said the farm isn't so nice."

"He's right," I said.

"Well, George says you're okay, and that works for me. I need a little help around here."

"You don't have anyone?" I asked. The actress was supposed to have a whole harem of nannies.

"Nope," she said. "I have to keep it small. People talk. Sometimes my life can be really complicated. What I really need is just one normal babysitter."

There was a goofy earth mother quality to the actress, and I got the distinct impression that she didn't think things all the way through. She got so busy talking that she forgot that she was boiling water until it started hissing and spitting in the kettle.

"I just need a hand, that's all. I have to be away tonight, so I just need you to keep an eye on them. The most important part of the job—the only thing you really have to do is feed them. But it's really easy. All their meals have been prepared."

She opened one door of the fridge. There were stacks of colorful plastic containers, perfectly organized by color and design. There was a pile of pink ones, a pile of ones with dinosaurs, another with Elmo, a Disney princess stack, and one with Harry Potter. Under each stack was a name card: Melissa, Lily, Ben, Maxine, and Alex.

"Meal times," she said, tapping a piece of paper held to the side of the refrigerator with a magnet. "Breakfast, lunch, snack time, and dinner. Everything is prepared and measured out. You just give them the containers."

"I don't have to cook the food?"

"Nope," she said. "We follow a raw diet."

Somehow, I already knew this. I must have read it somewhere.

"So, I just take the lids off . . ."

"You don't even have to do that," the actress said. "The lids keep it all fresh, and the kids love ripping the tops off things. Just give them the containers. Actually, it's kind of fun. I'll show you. It's snack time, anyway. Come meet everyone."

We headed back to the main entrance hall and she opened one of the doors. This is when I saw the room for the first time, and the five blank, stumbling children that lived in it.

"They have everything they need in there," the actress went on. "Beds, toys . . . and this is how they get their snacks."

There was a small glass hatch in the wall, just under the window. She opened this, placed the containers inside, shut it, and hit a switch. Tinkling music started to play "The Farmer in the Dell." The children got very excited and drifted over to the wall. A small conveyer belt, also encased in plastic, started to move, carrying the containers along it. As the containers moved along, little colored lights came on along their path, marking their progress. Then the song stopped, there was a *ding*, and another small hatch opened. The children crushed into each other to each get a container.

It was both one of the most adorable and one of the most disturbing things I had ever seen. Truly, the rich and famous were not like normal people. They didn't just take their kids into the kitchen and feed them chicken nuggets. They fed them raw food through a musical conveyer belt.

The actress pointed them out. Alex was a little boy from Kenya. Melissa was a brown-haired girl with a slightly pushed-in face from Turkey. Ben was from Vietnam. Lily was a tiny blonde from Ukraine, and Maxine was from Burundi. For such a diverse group of kids, there was a sameness about them, something in their expressions and the way they moved. They had to be between five and seven, but they acted much younger, like toddlers.

"They'll be busy for a few minutes," the actress said. "Let me show you your room. It's just across the hall."

My room—the guest room—was such a welcome sight that I almost cried. There was a four-poster bed covered in filmy white gauze. The rest of the furniture consisted of heavy perfectly refinished antiques. More important, there was a large television mounted on the fireplace mantle, and an en suite marble bathroom with a cavernous tub, and a towel warmer, and a little gold chair to sit on while you got ready for a hot bath.

"Do I give them their baths here?"

"Oh, don't worry about that. They can go a day without a bath. Bath times around here are kind of chaotic. Let them play for a day. It's incredibly clean in there, anyway."

"And when they have to . . . go to the potty?"

"Oh, they have one in there. You really don't have to do anything. Just give them their meals at the right times. That's it. Just don't go into the play area, okay? And don't take them out. They're fine in there. I have to get going."

It was that fast. She strode out of the room, with her bouncy little-kid walk, thigh bones jangling in the hip sockets. She took a tiny purse from the fainting couch and slapped on a pair of sunglasses, despite the grayness of the day. The actress needed no bag. Famous people didn't lift or carry things. I could imagine it—everything waiting at the hotel. The dress. The makeup artist. The hairstylist. The famous actor would be there, and her every need would be provided for.

"You'll be fine," she said cheerfully. "I'll see you around noon tomorrow. Oh, and here."

She reached into her purse and pressed a folded stack of pound notes into my hand. A moment later she was out the door, and I heard the purr of a motor and the sound of crunching on the drive. When she was gone, the house creaked a bit, and then an unsteady quiet descended. I looked at the money in my hand. She had given me eight hundred pounds for a night's work.

Again, you might be thinking that the flags should have gone up, that they must have been waving wildly. But what would *you* have done? A famous person comes along, asks you to do the easiest job in the world for one night, and hands you enough cash to fix all your problems. So, okay, the whole situation was a bit freaky. Fine. But it wasn't unpleasant or illegal or deeply, morally wrong. I was just an overpaid babysitter working for a famous, friendly nutcase.

When I went back to the playroom, the children couldn't be bothered with me. SpongeBob had somehow appeared on one of the televisions, and they clustered close underneath it to watch. There was plenty of room for everyone to see, but they were knotted together, and they had no concept of viewing distance. They planted themselves right under it and stared up, craning their necks.

I felt the heavy plastic of the gate. It was just taller than I was, made of something strong and flexible. I pushed on it, then leaned on it, then dropped all of my weight onto it. The gate could handle it easily.

It had always been said that the Lazarines did some weird things with their kids, that they kept them pure. They didn't believe in medication of any kind, some sources said, not even vaccines. I hadn't believed a lot of that stuff, but here were five kids in a pen, unable to be touched. I pressed my hand against the plastic mesh again. It was so fine that not even a little hand could get through. Clear enough to see through perfectly— dense enough to prevent real contact.

How could this even be happening? How could someone that rich and famous just leave their children with a stranger?

The second SpongeBob was over, the television shut itself off. This caught me by surprise, and I jumped. The kids didn't flinch. They also didn't move from their spot. They watched the screen even though it was off, at least for a good five minutes.

The house settled again. And aside from a very slight, confused mumbling from the kids, there was no noise.

"All right," I said. "You guys? I'm Sofie. Sofie."

This got some interest, but just for a moment. The children turned and came toward me as a group.

"Sponnn . . ." Little Ben was pointing at the television. "Sponnnnn . . . Baaaaaa . . ."

"Yes," I said. "SpongeBob. You like SpongeBob."

"Spooonnnn . . ."

"SpongeBob is done now."

Ben turned to the television hopefully. "Spoonnnnn?"

"No more SpongeBob right now."

Lily came over and reached up her arms, wordlessly requesting to be picked up, drooping against the plastic fencing. I put my hand against hers. Lily smiled and drooled a little.

They definitely looked happy. Not *smart*, but happy. Ben was aloof, sitting in the corner for most of the day, scowling and occasionally knocking over a pile of blocks. Melissa talked a lot, a low, endless, incomprehensible noise. She was also the bossiest, pushing the others around, making endless circuits with the toy shopping cart. Alex just stared into the depths of the toy oven. Melissa was somewhat sly. Lily was the most obviously dim-witted. She opened books and banged them on her own head.

At six o'clock the television turned itself on again. This time the show was the BBC news, which I assumed had to be a programming error—but the children raced over to watch. They seemed to like the news even more than they liked SpongeBob. They got particularly excited when war coverage was on. They were lulled by a long interview with an economist. At seven, the television switched itself off, and once again they stood there, watching the gray screen for five or so minutes before meandering off in different directions.

Seven o'clock was a mealtime. I retrieved five of the plastic containers.

"Who's hungry?" I called.

This got a reaction. A chorus of excitement. Something to do. This felt so weird, just sticking the food into the hatch for these strange children, sending it on its colorful, musical way into their playland. But those were the instructions. Once again there was a cluster around the hatch, a struggle to reach for the containers. They ate so quickly that I couldn't even see what they had. Then they dropped the containers and went right back to playing.

At nine o'clock they watched a police drama.

Summer days in England were long, and it was around ten o'clock before the day passed into anything I could be certain was called night. The kids were still glued to the television, taking in the sight of an autopsy with quiet fascination. A surprising amount of light streamed in through the windows . . . maybe more than during the day. The moon was nearly full and provided an almost fluorescent glow over the flat landscape, bringing into sharp relief the black outlines of trees.

Click.

All the lights went out. I lurched, but in a moment realized that, like everything else, the lights were on a timer. The darkness didn't bother the kids. I saw their little shadows moving from toy kitchen to jungle gym to television set. Someone threw a ball, hard, but no one caught it. It dribble, dribble, dribble, dribbled its way to rest next to what I thought was little Lily, who was still "reading."

There was nothing to do now. Not even stare at them. I could go to my room in good conscience, turn on the TV, and eat. I took a quick trip down to the kitchen and got some of the food that the actress set aside for visitors. There was plenty of it too—good ham and bacon and sausages, all in fancy packaging. All the delicious meatiness that I had been denied for weeks. I decided to make the most disgusting decadent thing I could think of—a big grilled cheese and bacon sandwich, chips on the side. As the bacon was sputtering away in a pan, I took *Lazarus Healing* from the row of books and let it fall open. It looked like an official publication—boring and hard-core crazy in a looping print, with lots of pictures.

We understand that our sleep need only be temporary, that the time is coming when True Health can come through re-an. As such, it is crucial to keep the original body in optimal health. Western medicine and household chemicals disturb the body's balance, making re-an more difficult; therefore, it is critical to eliminate all of these from the system. . . . Though the mech for True Health exists, it is not fully available yet. But the time is coming very soon when the re-an period will start, and it's important to prepare your mind for the transition, for your first eternal morning . . .

Which was bad enough. But then I got to the picture section in the middle and saw a picture of a dead girl on a surgical table, her abdomen sliced open. It looked like a normal autopsy, much like the one they had just seen in the show, except her smiling family members stood nearby.

Madeline, the caption read, *seen here with her mother and sisters after she went to sleep in June. Her internal organs are being lovingly removed and stored for reuse before the embalming process. As mech goes forward, this step will be skipped, and the body will go right from sleep to True Health . . .*

"Wow," I said, flipping through some more pages. "The tabloids don't even know how crazy you are."

I took my two (I figured if I was going to the trouble of making all that bacon, I might as well use it) sandwiches, and some chips, and a roll of cookies, and two sodas back to my room. Up here on the hill, in this warm house, everything finally seemed good. It made all the difference to have a decent (a relative term) dinner, and a television, and a soft bed with a weighty duvet. I switched on the television and lost myself instantly. I'd been so starved for some mindless entertainment.

At two o'clock I found that I was still awake, still eating, still watching television, and hungry for another round of snacks. Since I was up, it made sense to go and check on the kids again. They were still up. In fact, they were all pressed against the plastic gate now, straining against it, their little faces urgent and sad.

"What's the matter?" I asked, coming over.

But they couldn't say. They spoke only in wide, sad eyes and outstretched arms. All the loneliness and misery that I had felt the last few weeks came to the surface. A motherly instinct stirred in me. These were just little children awake in the middle of the night, their mother gone, trapped in a strange playpen.

No one had put them in pajamas and tucked them in. They didn't know what to do. They were tired and confused. They pressed their hands deep into the mesh, reaching for me. . . .

Funny how this all fell apart, how all the shit came down simply because I was following one of my nobler instincts. All the times in my life when I'd done things for all the wrong reasons and walked away unpunished? I guess it was just time to pay.

So, yeah. *Screw it,* I thought. *These kids need a hug, a tuck into bed, some kind of reassuring presence.*

I strode over to the corner, where the gate was attached to the wall. It was like riot fencing, this huge webbing. All of this to keep in five tiny children. Seeing what I was doing, they gathered close in the corner, urgently waiting for me to open the gate.

"It's okay, you guys," I said. "It's okay. Just . . . back up. Okay?"

But the children didn't understand "back up." They shook the gate, making it impossible for me to get it open. They pulled on the heavy plastic, shaking the catch. I looked around for a remote control for the television, but there was none. But there was the conveyer belt. I hit the switch. "The Farmer in the Dell" started up, and the colorful lights glowed brightly. Surprised, the children trundled over. Left alone for a moment, I was able to work at the catch again. It was designed to hold tight, and it took all of my strength to release it. But it finally gave way, and the gate slid easily back on its track. I pushed it open wide enough to make a doorway-size opening for myself.

The kids were still clustered by the conveyer belt, which had stopped playing and glowing, their hands still inside the hatch, reaching around for containers that obviously weren't there.

"Hey!" I called.

Turning. Shuffling. Pushing each other out of the way.

They were just a few feet away from me when some instinct deep in my brain told me that I had made a mistake. I wasn't sure what the mistake *was*, but the fact that one had been made was obvious. They were so eager, so needy, with their little arms and adorable little faces, and their skin . . . so ashen in the moonlight. They all looked gray.

Melissa reached me first, pushing aside little Ben and Lily and knocking them down. She got to me, grabbed me around the thigh in a strangely urgent hug, and pressed her face into my pajama bottoms. By this point Alex had gotten to me as well, and had me by the arm.

"It's okay, guys," I said.

And then Alex opened his mouth and clamped down just above my left wrist, digging his little teeth right in, tearing at my flesh and immediately drawing blood.

"No! No! No!" The universal word had no effect. I tried to shake loose, tried to push Alex's head back, but nothing would detach him. In the next moment I felt Melissa make a similar attempt on my leg. I jerked my knee up hard, knocking Melissa off. She fell onto a pile of plastic toy pans.

Alex was sinking his teeth in harder. No amount of prying, pushing, or shaking would get rid of him. So the next reaction was just as automatic. I swung out with my right fist and punched little Alex in the face. I hit him with enough force to dislodge him and send him flying backward. He landed against the mesh and slid down, then put his little hands over his face and started to cry, loud screaming sobs.

The other three were just a foot or two away.

"What the fuck . . . ," I cried, scrambling backward. I stepped outside of the gate and tried to pull it closed, but the kids grabbed at it, preventing this. Ben was already out and making his strange, unsteady way toward me. I ran for the door and slammed it behind me. There was no lock on it. Instinctively I grabbed one of the chairs and propped it under the knob. That's what people did in movies. It was supposed to do something.

I ran for the kitchen and switched on the light with a shaking hand, fumbling around on the wall until I got it. Then I saw my wound for the first time. The pain truly came with the visual. There was a full bite profile. The blood was dripping down my arm, down to the floor. There was something cold running through my veins, starting from the bite and running up the arm. And the area around the bite was starting to go black. I grabbed a kitchen towel hanging from a hook on the wall and wound it tight around the wound. I was woozy, suddenly exhausted. I needed to get in bed for a little while. All the horrible weeks I'd been here, and now this. . . . Rest. I needed to rest.

I shuffled back down the hall, pausing just for a second by the door to the playroom. I could hear gentle shuffling inside. The children were still in there, moving around, playing. There was a faint, light moaning. Alex was still crying. The door rattled lightly.

For a moment I was flooded with guilt. These were just children . . . small, very confused children who had led weird lives. They couldn't communicate with anyone. They ate raw food that came off a conveyor belt, like they lived in a sushi place. No wonder they bit me when they had the chance. They had no sense of normal. Maybe the bite hadn't even been intentional, just an overenthusiastic attempt to make and keep contact. *Stay with me.* That's what it had probably meant.

I still wasn't opening that door.

I kept right on going, falling headfirst into the bed. I didn't even have the energy to get under the covers. I just folded the duvet over myself and closed my eyes. Just a minute of rest . . .

When I woke up, there was light. Soft, diffused light. Birds were cooing.

I felt heavy, truly heavy, like my body had been cast in concrete and the supremely soft bed shouldn't have been able to support my weight. But there was no pain anywhere. In fact, aside from feeling heavy, I had pretty much no sensation at all.

It took some effort, but I managed to turn my head on the pillow. I was under the blankets now. It appeared that I was wearing pajamas. I didn't recognize them, but they were very nice. When I turned my head the other direction, I saw the actress standing in the doorway. She came and sat on the edge of the bed.

"How are you feeling?" she asked, reaching over and kindly stroking a stray hair back from my forehead.

"Kind of weird," I said. "Tired."

"You had a bad bite. But you'll be okay now. I did say not to go in—but I understand. You were drawn to them. I know the feeling."

She stroked my hair for a moment. It felt so nice. Ever have anyone stroke your hair? It's amazing.

"I need to talk to you about your friend," she said.

"My . . . friend?"

"Franklin. He was at the farm with you? I think he's your boyfriend."

"Was," I said.

"Don't think of it that way. There's no ending, okay?"

I had no idea what to say to that, so I just let her continue to pet me. God, I was tired.

"It wasn't his fault," she said quietly. "It was just so dark."

"Dark?"

The actress sighed deeply.

"He was just . . . in the road. Walking. It was dark. There aren't any lights out here. I didn't see him until he bounced off my hood."

That woke me up—a little, anyway.

"Bounced off . . . You hit him?"

"He's doing *fine*," the actress said quickly. "That's why I wanted to help you. I knew he must have come from the farm. I asked around, and George told me about you. He said you came together. You must have been worried sick when he went out and didn't come back. . . ."

"I managed," I said.

"He really wants to see you. I told him you were here, and he's just been asking for you over and over."

"Really?" I said. "He's asking for me? Where is he?"

"He's here. And he asks about you all the time! I'll go and get him and bring him."

I shouldn't have cared about this, but a part of me was glad that Franklin was sucking it a bit, getting bounced off car hoods. That he was sorry that he'd left me. But how was he here? I'd been here all night and hadn't seen him.

A few minutes later she helped him in. It was Franklin, all right. He looked like hell—his skin ashen, his eyes glassy, his lips dry. He was wearing some yoga outfit that I'd never seen before—probably one that belonged to the famous actor. And bizarrely, he was wearing a surgical mask tied snugly around his mouth.

"Sooofie . . . ," he mumbled. There was a drag in his voice, a slurring distortion that wasn't caused by the mask.

"Franklin?"

"Soooofie . . ."

He moved toward me, almost falling over. The actress was practically holding him up. She was strong.

"He's still recovering," the actress said, straightening him up. "I had to give him a little something to calm him down because at first he was a little . . . disoriented. Sometimes he seems agitated. But he's okay now."

I'd seen Franklin very righteously stoned, but never quite like this.

"Soooooofie . . . ," he said, almost in a moan. There was real longing behind it, like he wanted nothing more in the world than to be near me.

"I think he needs to go back and rest," the actress said. "I just wanted you to see him."

"Sooooooooofie . . ."

Franklin strained to keep looking at me, even as he was negotiated out of the room, banging against the doorway in the process.

I decided it was time to have a look at my own injury.

It took all the effort I had to pull my arm from beneath the thick duvet, and as soon as I did, I wished I hadn't. While it didn't hurt, my arm was clearly *not well*. It was whitish-gray from the tips of my fingers to just above my elbow. The wound itself had become engorged and pus-filled, green and purple and blue-black and angry red and every color of the rainbow that my hand could be except its usual one. You didn't need a degree in medicine to know that that kind of a wound was *seriously fucking bad*, and that whatever herbal teas I had been given, or whatever magical rocks had been placed on my sleeping body to aid my recovery, hadn't worked and were never going to work.

This woman had hit Franklin with a car and brought him back here to recover, and to cover up what she had done, and now he looked deranged. He was probably infected, delirious. She had weird children penned in the living room. And now I was going to get some hideous old-school infection if I didn't get the hell out of here.

Just outside the window I could see the actress's car. I had to go outside, and take it and drive to town, somewhere with a hospital. I wasn't worried about driving on the other side of the road, or that I was stealing. How could she report me when she'd mowed Franklin down with a car and not told anyone?

Get the car. Drive. Before I got any sicker.

The act of pushing back the duvet felt like pushing a piano up the stairs with one hand, but somehow I did it. I got out of bed. All my movements were unsteady. My feet couldn't be relied upon to move as I wanted them to, not with a normal gait, but I could get forward and out of the room, to the hall, to the door. Slowly. So slowly. I was walking like I was tangled up in nets.

The actress caught me as I was just a few shambling steps away from the door.

"There's something I need to explain to you," she said, her voice pleading, urgent. "And it's *really good news*. See, death doesn't really exist. That's why we don't call it death. We call it sleep."

She smiled and nodded and took it as read that I had any idea what the hell she was talking about.

"My kids," she went on. "They're very special. They were all asleep. I woke them up using the mech. I'm not supposed to have the mech. But . . . one of the lab heads . . . I met him at Star Center. . . . That's the special center for, you know, famous people. . . . He gave me a little bit. But it works! It's true re-an . . ."

This was all a jumble in my mind, but I can honestly say

I wouldn't have understood it any better even under ideal conditions. It was a bunch of Lazarus crap.

"Re-an?" I repeated.

"Reanimation. True Health. My kids were asleep. I woke them."

Piece by piece I clicked this all together. The picture I was assembling was very odd.

"You're telling me that your kids were . . . dead? And you brought them back?"

"There is no death," she said. "Remember? Just sleep."

I wanted to point out that there are in fact a number of differences between death and sleep, like breathing and generally being alive. But then she added something that made me drop the nit-picking.

"Just like your boyfriend."

There was a faint ringing noise in my ears.

"Franklin's *dead*?"

"Not dead! You just saw him. Did he seem dead?"

I had no answer to that question. Thinking in general . . . It was getting harder by the moment. I just had to keep going. Get to the door. Get to the door.

"The mech is the answer," she said, following me. "The end of death. He's better now! Everyone will be better! It's a revolution, Sofie. Against death itself. And my children are the start, and Franklin . . . and you. You'll be with your boyfriend. You two will be together! You'll *always* be together!"

With Franklin. Forever. Forever with that idiot. The idea was so horrible that I lunged forward, smacking myself against the door as I reached it. Moving was so difficult.

"I think it's in you," she said, coming toward me. "The mech. It transferred to you in the bite. Don't you understand? Don't you understand how wonderful this is?"

The famous actress got between me and the door and wrapped those famously tattooed and toned arms of hers around me in the warmest, most motherly hug imaginable.

God, she was warm. People are so warm. And her *pulse*. It's so weird, that pulsing. It was like a drumbeat, a drumbeat that made me outrageously angry. I opened my mouth to scream but lost my balance and found myself pulled into the actress's neck, bare and exposed.

It was like I hadn't eaten in days and then someone had shoved a perfect, juicy burger under my nose, fresh from the grill, still running with those delicious juices that you get right as the meat comes off the flames . . . and I knew it was a neck and not a burger, but it had become one and the same, and there was only one thing to do . . . one thing . . . so I bit. I bit so hard! I was so strong! I clamped down, and then . . . delight, blind delight . . . a happiness I had never known! I didn't even mind the screaming. And my face was all wet. I guess blood, but that was *right*. It was all right. It was right, it was right, it was right, it was . . .

Excited. Don't know why just happy now. Machine on wall with pictures comes on. Is television. Right, is *television*. Why so hard remember? *To* remember. Ugh, so hard thinking. Would think is sick but feel so good so must not be sick.

"Sponnnn?" Franklin say.

Franklin happy too. And so pretty lady. She say "Spooonnnn" too. Little ones happy too. Everyone like sponge.

Not always here. Remember other place. Hard remember but try. Like room and machine with sponge . . . *television* . . . and tree. Nice room. But know other place. Car outside. Car *is* outside. Can go places! Like drive. Maybe when no more sponge we drive. Remember big place wanted to go to. Big city. Yes. Nice there. Can take car to big city. London is called!

But when sponge done. Sponge first. Then car to big city. *To London*.

Franklin touch hand, smile.

"Spoonnnnn," he say again. Franklin so pretty.

We happy.

Diana Peterfreund

"The Care and Feeding
of Your Baby Killer Unicorn"

Holly: Although few people believe in unicorns today, there was a time they were referred to by naturalists as casually as you might refer to cats. Researchers looking back on those writings often try to identify what might have been "misrepresented" as a unicorn. A rhinoceros is one possibility, an antelope seen from the side, so that both its long horns were perceived as one single horn is another, and of course, narwhal horns are thought to be the material with which kings inlaid their thrones and their cups.

But the possibility remains, as Diana postulates in her marvelous "The Care and Feeding of Your Baby Killer Unicorn," that unicorns have been here all along, hunted into near extinction, but now ready to come back and make themselves known.

Justine: I suspect that some of the Team Unicorn partisans are currently muttering under their breath about my unfairness to their team. Utter rubbish, of course, but in case you think I am entirely one-eyed on this subject, I will confess that I like Diana Peterfreund's killer unicorns. Frankly, they're the only interesting unicorns in the entire book. I can trust an animal that's out to kill us. It's the rainbow defecators I don't hold with.

Of course, the unicorn obsession with virginity remains a concern. Some of us nonvirgins are quite lovely, you know. Why do they shun us? Of course, it should be pointed out that the Peterfreund's killer unicorns are even fussier: You also have to be a descendant of Alexander the Great. Yeah, I'll get right on that.

Holly: I see even you are weakening, Justine. The lure of the adorable killer unicorn must be great indeed.

The Care and Feeding of Your Baby Killer Unicorn
By Diana Peterfreund

"Cool. It's a freak show," says Aidan. "I didn't know they had those anymore."

I don't think we're supposed to call them freak shows. Though I know my parents would freak if they knew I was anywhere near one. Too much nudity, too many pathways into the occult.

The tent is near the back of the carnival, decorated with garishly painted plywood signs and lit by a string of lights at the entrance flap that does little more than cast long shadows, obscuring most of the ads.

So far, the carnival has been pretty lame. There's a Ferris wheel, but it costs four dollars to go around a single time—Yves says they must have to pay a fortune for insurance. The hot dogs look ancient and shriveled, and taste more like jerky. The cotton candy is deflated, the funnel cake soggy, and they aren't selling anything cool like deep-fried Twinkies. I had to beg my parents to let me come too. You see, the fairgrounds back up to the woods, and I'm not allowed anywhere near the woods anymore.

Maybe if we played some games on the midway it would have been fun, but Aidan pronounced them childlike and insipid, suitable only for jocks and their sheeplike followers, and we all agreed. Except for Yves, in a move clearly designed to recall my collection of bobble-headed monkeys that we'd amassed over several summers spent being childish and insipid at the Skee-Ball range down the shore.

Yves loves telling cringe-worthy stories about the dumb stuff we used to do, especially since last fall. Most especially whenever he catches me flirting with Aidan.

"Ewww," says Marissa, insinuating herself and her bare-midriff top between Aidan and me. "A two-headed cow? Is it, like, alive?"

"Probably not," says Yves from behind us. "I bet it's pickled."

I look over my shoulder and wrinkle up my nose at him. Yves's eyes are dark, framed by even darker lashes that were always too long and full for a boy. His hands are balled up in his jacket pockets and he's giving me one of those long piercing looks that have been another one of his specialties since last fall.

Summer refuses to go inside the freak show, citing how inhumane it is to put people with deformities up on display. But a quick glance at the signs out front reveals only one sideshow performer whose "qualities" don't seem self-inflicted: the wolf-boy. The others are a tattooed man, a sword swallower, and some guy called the human hanger who looks like his claim to carnival fame is dangling stuff from his body piercings. Gross. Maybe my parents have a point. I move down to examine the next sign, and freeze.

VENOM

THE WORLD'S ONLY LIVE CAPTIVE UNICORN
They said it couldn't be done, but we have one!
Be one of the few to see this monster . . .
and SURVIVE!

There's a bad drawing beneath the words, nothing
blurry photos on the news, or the pictures you've seen of
corpses. The unicorn on the sign looks like one from the old
fairy books, white, rearing, its mane flying out behind it in
artful spirals. Just like a fairy tale, except for the fangs and the
blood red eyes.

I stumble back and almost trip over Marissa. "A unicorn?"
she says. "But it can't be a real one."

"Of course it's not," says Aidan. "They'd never be allowed
to put it on display. Way too dangerous. It's probably pickled
too."

Marissa points at the sign. "But it says it's alive."

"Maybe a fake one," says Katey, clinging to her boyfriend,
Noah. "They have this patented process where they graft the
horns of a baby goat together, and it grows up with one horn.
Like a bonsai tree. We learned about it in bio class."

I shudder and move away from the tent. Before unicorns
came back, people used to do that and pretend it was this
gentle, magical creature. No one realized the old stories were
lies.

"Well, that's totally worth five bucks," says Aidan. "I want
to check it out. A killer unicorn! You know they never caught
the one that killed those kids in the woods last fall."

"They can't," says Noah. "They say no one can catch one,
and no one can tame one either. This one has got to be a
fake."

My arms tangle up, hugging myself to keep out the cold.
But it's a warm spring evening. Nothing like last fall, with its
cold gray skies, crisp leaves, bloodcurdling screams.

vehemently. "Yeah, I'm definitely

"It isn't a real one. If it were, it
some sideshow tent."

mer. "Be lame." He cocks his head
at me, g

If my folks disapproved of body piercings and the occult, then a unicorn was definitely off-limits. Especially for me.

"Wen?" Yves's voice comes from way too close. He's the only one outside my family who knows. "You don't have to."

I turn to him. He's offering me his hand like we're still six years old. Like holding his hand will be as simple as it was when we were kids. Like holding *him* can be as natural as it was last fall. But like I told him then, it was an accident. A mistake.

I stare at him. He's holding out his hand like things can ever be the same between us again.

"Hey!" I call to Aidan and the others. "Wait up."

It isn't a fake.

I can tell the instant I'm inside the tent, though I can't even see it yet. But it smells like last fall in here, the weird scent that at the time I thought was someone burning leaves, or plant matter rotting after the October rains.

The interior of the tent looks like a museum gallery, with a dark, winding path snaking past individual exhibits that stand out like islands of amber red light in the gloom. Noah has already pulled Katey into a dark corner behind the sea serpent bones to make out. I can see them even better inside the blackened tent than I could in the glare of the midway.

It's the unicorn that does this to me. Its evil tingles along my nerve endings, waking them, tuning them like a drug so that everything is clearer, stronger, slower.

The two-headed calf is, in fact, pickled; a fetal calf mutation preserved in a giant tank that glows green to heighten the creep factor. Aidan and Marissa gape at it, then skip over to watch the sword swallower do his thing. I close my eyes and try to push the unicorn out. I'm hot all over, like that time my cousins Rebecca and John and I got into the brandy at Christmas.

The sword swallower licks the sword from end to end, grinning at us, then leans his head back and lifts the rapier into the air, poising it carefully over his mouth. I watch each inch of it descend into the man's gullet, see every movement of his neck muscles, every twitch as he fights to suppress his gag reflex.

The suppressed magic breaks free, loosing within me a painful clarity, every moment of time stretched out to encompass unbearable detail. I can hear Marissa's heartbeat, quickened because of the sight before her, quickening more when she shivers in disgust and leans against Aidan. Blood pounds in my ears, like that time my cousins Rebecca and John and I bet to see who could hold their breath longest at the bottom of their pool.

I can even feel the soil beneath my soles, and I let myself be pulled along in my steps like I'm a train car on a track, tugged inexorably toward something that lies in the darkness beyond.

Like the time my cousins Rebecca and John and I went out to the woods near their house last fall and I watched them die.

I never should have come in here. It was wrong; I knew that, but I'd wanted to show off for Aidan.

There's a woman seated on a metal folding chair in front of a curtain partitioning off the back of the tent. Over the flap is another drawing of a unicorn, rampant red against a black field. She stamps out her cigarette. "You here to see Venom?" she asks. She's dressed in flowing skirts and a corset, but looks more like a biker babe than a fairy-tale princess.

"Yes," says Aidan, behind me.

"I have to go with you," says the woman, pulling herself to her feet. "For safety."

Marissa stands back. "So it is real?"

Aidan rolls his eyes. "Part of the show. Like the sword swallower popping those balloons to show it was sharp."

I take a deep breath. And like the sword swallower, this is real. They have a real unicorn back there. Poisonous. Man-eating. We should run. Now.

The woman holds open the flap and ushers us inside, and the others jostle around me, but I can't take another step. In my head I hear my cousins screaming. No one here knows, and Yves is still outside. They were two years older than me, seniors at another school. No one knows those kids who were killed by a unicorn were my cousins. No one knows I was there.

My parents said not to tell. Fewer questions, then, about how I'd survived. Less temptation, then, to explore the evil that dwells in my blood.

"Coming, Wen?" Aidan asks, and grabs my hand. Something like an electric shock breaks through my thoughts, and I follow him beyond the curtain. There's a small observation space in front of a sturdy-looking metal grate. Beyond the grate: darkness and a tiny pool of yellow light.

The woman lifts a whistle on a chain hanging around her neck and blows a low, warbling note. Beyond the bars the unicorn steps into the light. Or actually, it hobbles. It's a small one, not like the kind that killed Rebecca and John. Each of its cloven hooves is encircled with heavy metal clamps, and they are chained, left to right, front to back, so the unicorn can take only tiny steps. The front leg irons connect to a Y-shaped metal pole ending in another metal clamp securing the beast's neck. Thus chained, it can only hold its head out straight, the better for us to admire its goatlike face and long corkscrew horn.

The unicorn is enormously fat. Underneath a coat of sparse, wiry white hair, its belly distends almost to its knobby knees. Patches of its coat are bare, and in the bald spots I can see scabs and even open sores, like it's been chewing itself.

The unicorn's watery blue eyes glare at each of my friends in turn. Its mouth opens in a snarl, revealing pointed yellow fangs and unhealthy-looking gums. It growls a low, bleating growl at Noah and Katey, at Marissa and Aidan. And then it turns to me.

Its pupils dilate, its mouth closes, and then it moves toward the bars.

We all jump back.

"Venom!" yells the woman. The unicorn's horn scrapes the bars. It bends its knees now, struggling to lower its head in the confines of the irons, bleating as the edges of the neck brace scrape against its skin.

"Venom!" the woman screams. "Get back. Now!" The unicorn does not obey.

My friends take another big step back toward the curtains. "Lady . . . ," Aidan says. I can hear their heartbeats pounding away. But I can't take my eyes off the unicorn.

The monster limps and stumbles, trying to put one knee on the ground and then the other, constrained by its bonds, never breaking eye contact with me, never letting go of the pleading look in its eyes.

The woman snaps to and turns to me. "You."

I blink as she grabs my arm. The unicorn stops what it's doing and begins growling again.

"You're one of us," she hisses at me.

Oh, no.

"Lady, get your monster under control," Aidan says. The unicorn bangs against the grate, and the bars *bend* under its weight.

Under her weight, I realize at once. It's a female.

"Who are you?" the unicorn wrangler asks, and her grip tightens. She's so strong. Insanely strong.

But so am I. I yank my arm loose, then fly back through the curtains, mindless of her shouts or my friends' shock or the soundless pleas of the unicorn. I run with speed I haven't felt since last fall. Speed that meant I was the only one who got away when that unicorn attacked my cousins and me on the trail. Speed that those people from the Italian nunnery mentioned when they came to my parents' house to explain to us that I'm something special when it comes to unicorns. I draw them in like unicorn catnip. I'm immune to their deadly venom. I'm capable of hearing their thoughts. When I'm around them, I'm blindingly fast and scarily strong. And I, unlike most of the people on the planet, have the ability to capture and kill them, if properly trained.

They said they had a place to train girls with powers like mine. They called us unicorn hunters. My parents kicked them out. My father said they were papists at best and exploiters and magicians at worst, and there was no way he was letting me get anywhere near a unicorn. After all, we'd already seen what those monsters had done to Rebecca and John.

I flee with this inhuman speed through the twisting paths of the sideshow tent and break through the flaps into the benign neon night. And the first thing I see, when the moon stops spinning in the sky and the sense of unicorn fades, is that Yves and Summer are sitting on a bench in the shadows, and they're kissing.

Yves gives Summer a ride home, which means I'm sitting in the back. He turned sixteen last summer, which makes him almost a year older than the rest of our crowd. I choose the seat behind the driver's side, so I can't see Yves in the mirror, even if I wanted to. Summer chatters the whole way, splitting her monologue between the two of us, and I wonder what she thinks of me, and of the rumors about me and Yves. When we arrive at Summer's house, Yves gets out of the car and walks her to her front door, and I stare as hard as I can at the moon. It seems to take a really long time for him to get back. He doesn't move to put the car in gear.

"You staying back there? Am I your chauffeur?"

I kick the back of his seat.

"What was the unicorn like?"

"Real." I say, and then, to keep him from asking anything else, "What was Summer's tongue like?"

Yves peels out.

As soon as Yves pulls into his driveway, I open my door and tumble out, unsteady because the car is still moving. I sprint across his lawn, jump over Biscuit, old Mrs. Schaffer's annoying yellow cat, and am halfway up my front walk before I hear the engine die, before he shouts at me.

"Wen! Wait, Wen, we should talk about this!"

And then I'm inside my house, and I can't hear him yelling anymore, and I can't see the moon, and most of all, I can't feel that unicorn calling out to me from all the way across town.

That's the part I still don't get, after I've knocked on my folks' door to say good night and changed into my pajamas and said my prayers and gotten into bed. Because if I'd done like those Italian nuns had asked, if I'd gone off with them, I'd have trained to be a unicorn hunter. A unicorn killer.

But there was no mistaking that unicorn. She wanted my help. Did she want me to kill her? I could easily believe that living in captivity, confined day and night by all those chains, might be unbearable. Was that what she wanted? A mercy killing?

I punch my pillow down and pull the covers over my head

to protect my eyes from the moonlight, which seems so much brighter now than it did at the carnival. *Just stop thinking about the unicorn. Just stop.*

For six months I lived in fear of waking up one morning and finding a whole herd of monsters in my backyard, such was my power to draw their evil down on me. But now that I've met another unicorn, now that I know what it is to have one near, I understand. I recognize what it feels like now. I just have to overcome it. The trick is to think of something else. Something pleasant.

So I imagine I'm kissing Aidan, that he is touching my back the way he touched my hand in the tent tonight. It's probably not the right image, though, because the only experience I have kissing anyone is with Yves, last fall. And instead of feeling Aidan's long blond hair between my fingers, I am feeling Yves's dark, wiry curls; I'm feeling Yves's full lips against mine; I'm hearing Yves whisper my name, just like he did last fall, like instead of grabbing him by the shoulders and kissing him I'd waved my arms and conjured lightning out of a blue sky.

I'm glad for Summer. I really am. I want Yves to find a girlfriend and forget about trying to go out with me. I want him to forget about kissing me, even if it was his first kiss as well. And I want to forget too.

I want to forget it all.

Yves isn't waiting for me at my locker on Monday morning. He and Summer spend lunch canoodling at the far end of the table. Which is fine by me. Less fine is that Marissa hangs off Aidan all through the food line and arranges the seating so he's nearest her and farthest from me at lunch. Plus, they only want to talk about their current events class. Apparently the government napalmed some unicorn-infested prairie out West somewhere to try to control the spread of the monsters. It didn't work.

"The pictures on the news didn't look anything like that thing we saw at the sideshow," says Aidan. "Maybe it was a fake."

I keep my mouth filled with coleslaw. Least fine of all is that the unicorn has been calling to me all weekend. Even in church on Sunday. I almost told my parents, but I was too scared by what they'd say. Like maybe if I still feel it, it's because I haven't been trying hard enough to banish this evil from my heart.

I can feel it tugging on me now.

"Of course it was a fake," says Marissa. "Everyone knows that unicorns can't be captured."

"*Everyone* knows a lot of things," Noah points out. "Like how you can't kill them with napalm. But then they also show unicorn corpses on the news. Who killed them, and how?"

I dare to look up then, and I notice that Yves is focusing on me. Only we know who is really killing unicorns, and I swore Yves to secrecy last fall.

Right before I kissed him.

Katey shudders and pulls the crusts off her sandwich. "Fake or not, it was scary. Unicorns are awful—the ones on the news, the little fat one at the fair—doesn't matter. I hope whoever is killing them gets that one in the woods. The one that killed those kids last fall."

"Don't you think there are better things to do than just wipe them out?" Summer asks. "They're an endangered species."

"They're *dangerous*," Noah corrects, slipping his arm around Katey. "I bet you'd drop your whole animal rights act if you had seen that thing try to break through the bars and eat Wen last weekend."

"It tried to eat you?" Yves asks abruptly.

You'd know that if you weren't so busy macking with Summer, I almost snap at him. But the truth is, I don't think it was trying to eat me. Get to me, certainly. But eat me?

I wonder what else they say about unicorns that isn't true. I wonder, if I'd gone with those guys from Italy last fall, would I know now?

After school I head straight to the library, because if not, Yves might think I want a ride home, which would probably complicate whatever after-school plans he has with Summer. In the library I do a little bit of homework and a lot of thinking, and eventually I go over to the computers and look up the city bus routes online.

It takes me three different buses to get out to the fairgrounds, and I almost turn around and go home at each change. I probably shouldn't be doing this, but at the same time, I have to know. Maybe I'm imagining it, letting the fear of last fall put all sort of ideas in my head.

The sun's already low in the sky by the time I reach the

entrance gate, and once inside the fairgrounds, I lose my nerve. I buy and drink a soda. Then I play ten straight rounds of Skee-Ball and win so many tickets that the carnie manning the machines starts giving me the stink eye, so I finish up and trade my tickets for the first thing my eyes land on: a unicorn doll.

"Not a common choice," the carnie says, digging it out of the pile of teddy bears and puppy dogs. "Not these days, anyway. Kids are too scared by the news stories."

He hands me the doll, and its gilt horn sags over one eye. I focus on it and say nothing, worried for a second that he's calling me a sicko for picking up such a macabre doll.

"You know we have one here, in the sideshow?" says the carnie, who apparently never learned when to leave well enough alone. "At least, that's the pitch. They keep it locked up real tight, though, so maybe it is real."

I nod.

"But they weren't showing it today." He shrugs. "Said it's sick."

And then, over the din of bells and alarms on the midway, over the screams of the people on the rides and the raucous music emanating from every speaker on the fairgrounds, I hear her. The unicorn. She is sick. And she needs help.

And before I know it I've taken off, backpack flouncing hard against my spine, unicorn doll grasped firmly in my fist. The same speed that carried me far away from the unicorn last Saturday now takes me back to the sideshow tent, but I know—somehow I know—she's not inside. It never occurs to me to stop, to push this unicorn sense away, to pray for God's protection from this evil. Instead, I just go.

I wave at the guy manning the entrance, and as soon as his attention's elsewhere, I sidle toward the side, pretending to read the garish posters advertising the acts within, then skitter around the corner. The side wall of the tent comes flush with the fences surrounding the fairgrounds, but I can see that the tent actually extends a ways beyond that. I press against the canvas walls, but they're pulled snug, with little room to maneuver around, and massive bungee cords secure the sides to the fence so no one can sneak inside the fairgrounds—or, apparently, sneak out.

I'm ready to go back to the entrance of the fairgrounds and walk all the way around the outside, when I hear the unicorn cry out again. And this time it's not in my head but a shrieking roar of anguish so loud that I can see the people on the midway pause in surprise.

And then my foot is on the lowest bungee cord and I'm pulling myself over the top of the fence with one hand. I drop to the ground on the other side, soft as a cat. The sun has dipped below the horizon, and twilight blurs the edges of the trailers, caravans, and Porta Potties that fan out haphazardly over the dirt. Still, I know exactly where she is, and I beeline toward her.

What I'm going to do once I get there, I don't know. Even if the unicorn wants to die, I have no clue how to kill her.

The unicorn wrangler's trailer is dented and in need of a new paint job. I plaster myself to its rusted sides as I hear a voice coming from a tentlike patio spilling out the back. I recognize the voice as the woman who grabbed my arm last weekend, and she's saying words my father would wash my mouth out for.

The unicorn is alternating pitiful little bleats with full-on growls, and I edge closer, trying to peek between the trailer and the canvas flaps and see what's going on. The canvas lean-to is secured to the top of the trailer with ropes and staked into the bare ground like a picnic cover on a camper. Is the woman beating the poor thing? Or maybe punishing it for eating a fellow carnie?

"Don't you dare—," the woman puffs, out of breath. "Not until I come back, do you hear?"

The unicorn moans again, and I hear a screen door smack against the aluminum siding. I drop to my stomach and peek through the gap between the ground and the canvas tent flap. The unicorn is staring at me. It's shifting from foot to foot, lowing, and as it struggles to turn, I can see that there's something weird sticking out of its butt. It looks like two sticks or something, but then I peer closer and realize they are legs. Two tiny legs ending in cloven hooves.

The unicorn's not fat. She's in labor.

She struggles to lie down on the hay coating the ground, pulling against her chains so she can lick her backside. I hear the screen door open again, and my view is blocked by the women's feet and the dirty hem of her skirt.

"I said wait," the woman snaps at the monster, who merely growls in response. "I don't have it ready yet." She sets down a large bucket, and cold water sloshes over the top and splashes me.

That's weird. I've heard of people boiling hot water before

births—though I'm not sure why—but a bucket of cold water?

The unicorn pauses in her labor pains and lays her head against the ground. One big blue eye bores right into mine.

"You better pray this one is stillborn, Venom," the woman says, and her foot taps the earth near my face. "I hate doing this."

The unicorn stares at me, her bloodshot eye wide with terror. And with a shudder that goes from the top of my head into the tip of my toes, I get it.

The unicorn bleats and moans and licks and pushes, and slowly I can see the baby's head pushing out to meet those spindly legs. The head is mottled white and red, and its eyes bulge out from either side of its oblong cranium. Between the baby's eyes is nothing—no horn. Maybe it grows in later, like antlers on a deer. Some sort of glossy membrane encases the baby's body, and it's turning translucent in the air, or maybe because it's being stretched. I can't tell.

I'm scared someone will come round the corner and catch me peeping underneath the tent. I'm terrified the wrangler will lean down and see me. I can't believe I'm watching the birth of a unicorn. How many people alive have ever seen anything so extraordinary?

The unicorn wrangler is clearly one of them, as I can hear her hissing with impatience, and her foot hasn't stopped its restive tapping. The unicorn turns to lick at the baby, and the membrane splits wide. For the first time I see the baby unicorn move. It blinks and wiggles and slides even farther out of its mother.

The wrangler hurries over to the unicorn, grabs the baby

by its slimy two front legs, and yanks it the rest of the way out. Venom screams in pain, and then the ground is covered with some sort of foul-smelling liquid.

"Jesus, Venom!" cries the woman, dangling the baby just out of my sight range. "You reek." She takes a single step back toward the bucket, and the unicorn pauses in its anguish to lock gazes with me.

My hand shoots out beneath the flap and tips the bucket over.

Cold water floods the hay inside the tent and spills outside to soak the front of my shirt and pants. I bite back a gasp, but I needn't bother, since the wrangler is screaming bloody murder. She drops the baby unicorn, who tumbles into the wet hay in a heap. Then the woman snatches up the bucket and vanishes into the trailer.

The baby shifts feebly on the ground, bits of membrane and hay sticking to its wet hide as it tries to slither back toward its mother's warmth. But there's something wrong with Venom. She keeps trying to raise herself and move toward her child, but can't. She looks at me again, pain and pleading shooting at me like an arrow.

"No," I say. "I can't."

From inside the trailer I hear water running. She's refilling the bucket. She's going to come out here any minute, and then she's going to drown that baby. That poor, innocent little unicorn baby who never killed anyone's cousins. Who never did anything but get dropped moments after it was born. How can it be evil?

Venom pulls herself over to the foal, licks the rest of the membrane away, and rubs it all over with her snout. The baby's crying high-pitched, pitiful little bleats and trying to crawl under its mother's fur. The unicorn glares at me and growls.

I say that word the wrangler used, stuff the doll into my backpack, and pull myself beneath the tent flaps, smearing mud, wet hay, and much nastier stuff all over my clothes. As soon as I'm inside, Venom nudges the baby at me with her nose.

"I can't," I repeat, but then why am I here?

The pitch of water hitting bucket grows higher. Soon the bucket will be filled. Venom bleats again and, with much effort, shoves herself to her feet to face me.

I stumble backward as Venom bends her knees and bows, touching her long corkscrew horn to the ground. She looks up at me from her supine position, and her desperate supplication hits me with the force of a blow.

The sound of running water dies.

I snatch up the baby and run, not looking back when I hear the screen door slam, not stopping when the wrangler screams, not noticing until I'm miles away how fast I'm going. Or how I don't even feel out of breath.

When I finally do arrive home, it's black out. I sneak around the side of the house into the garage and unwrap the foal from my gym uniform, which is now every bit as streaked with afterbirth and mud as my clothes. I don't know how I'm going to explain the mess to my mother.

I don't know how I'm going to explain the unicorn, either.

The baby unicorn hasn't shivered since I wrapped it up in my clothes, and its skin is dry and crusty now. I'm pretty sure its mother would have licked it clean, but I'm not about to do that. Still, I know I need to keep the baby warm. And find it something to eat.

Our garage is too stuffed with junk to fit the car anymore, but that makes it a perfect hiding place for the foal. I shove aside boxes of picture albums and Christmas ornaments and pull down a ratty old quilt we sometimes use for picnics. If I can make a nest of the blanket, maybe I can put it behind the storage freezer. The heat from the motor will probably be enough to keep the baby warm overnight. I look back to where I left the unicorn on the pile of my dirty gym clothes. The foal is pushing itself up on wobbly feet and taking a few tentative steps.

Uh-oh.

Near the door there's an old plastic laundry basket filled with gardening tools that I dump out onto the concrete. I arrange the blanket inside, hoping the tall sides of the basket will be enough to keep the unicorn from getting out. And the sides and lid have enough holes in them that I won't worry about the baby suffocating. I wedge the basket in the space I've made behind the freezer and put the unicorn inside. As an afterthought I pull out the unicorn doll I won on the midway and put it in there with the baby.

It's bleating again, but you can't hear it above the sound of the freezer. Bet it's hungry. I wonder what I can feed it, since unicorn milk isn't an option. I grab my book bag and head inside, making a beeline for the stairs.

"Wen!" my mother calls from the kitchen, but I don't stop. "Wendy Elizabeth, you get down here!"

I grimace at the use of my full name. "Can't," I call from the top of the darkened stairwell. "My, um . . ."

Mom starts up the stairs, so I duck into my bedroom and pull off my clothes, stuffing the dirty stuff into the back of my closet. I'm in my underwear when she tries the door and I push against it.

"Mom!" I cry. "I'm not dressed!"

"You're late for dinner! Why didn't you call?"

I lower my voice, and then I tell my mother a lie. "My, uh, my period started at Katey's house and it made a mess and I was too embarrassed so I walked home."

"Oh, honey." My mom's voice is softer now. "Well, wash up and come downstairs. Make sure you get your pants in the laundry tonight, though, so it doesn't stick. There's stain remover by the washer downstairs."

"Thanks," I say. If the blood does stain, how will I explain getting my period all over my *shirt*? But that's the least of my problems. After washing the blood off my arms and face—which grosses me out more than I can say—I pull on fresh clothes and log on to the Internet. I look up both how to care for orphaned deer fawns and how to care for orphaned lions, figuring that if anything, a unicorn is a mix of the two.

This is going to be harder than I thought. Apparently it's not as simple as just giving them milk. Fawns drink something called "deer colostrum," and lions take special high-protein baby formulas. Neither of which I have any ability to get my hands on.

What am I doing? I can't take care of a baby unicorn. Even if I could figure out how to feed it, it can't be legal! And it can't be right.

Back downstairs Mom and Dad are waiting at the table. I slide into my seat, and Dad says grace. Dinner takes forever, and I can barely eat a bite. Dad doesn't eat much either, because Mom is trying out a Moroccan recipe she got from Yves's mother, and Dad thinks anything more exotic than spaghetti is too weird to count as food.

But it does give me an idea. Yves's mom sometimes cooks with goat's milk. Maybe that's closer to unicorn than cow. After the endless dinner and the even more endless washing up, I turn to Mom. "Can I run over to Yves's house really quickly? I need to get his notes from history class." Lie number two.

"Be quick," my mother warns.

Yves answers at the kitchen door. "Hey," he says, leaning against the frame. "What's up?"

"I need to borrow some goat's milk."

"Borrow?" He raises his eyebrows. "Like you're going to bring it back?"

"No. I mean I would like you to give me some goat's milk. Please."

Yves shrugs and heads toward the fridge. "Just so you know," he says, retrieving the slim carton from a shelf on the door, "it's pretty nasty all by itself. What do you need it for?"

So I lie again. "My mom has this new recipe she's trying out and she, uh, remembered you'd have some . . ."

"At nine o'clock at night?" Yves's big, dark eyes are staring right through me. It's not fair. It's hard enough lying to my parents, but Yves?

"Yeah. It needs to . . . marinate overnight or something. I don't know. She just sent me over here." I look away. "So, in case we ever need to get more, where does your mom buy this stuff?"

"There's a Caribbean grocer downtown," Yves says, handing me the carton. "Hey, Wen, you okay?"

I step off the stoop into the darkness so he can't see my eyes. Biscuit the cat is off on another of his nocturnal strolls. He's shredding Yves's mom's flower bed. Mrs. Schaffer really needs to get that beast under control. "I'm fine."

I'm not fine. I haven't been this not-fine in months. And we both know what happened then.

Part of me expects him to come forward and touch my arm the way he's been doing since last fall, but he doesn't. He stays on the stoop, and there's a space the size of Summer between us.

"Well, see you at school," he says.

I return to my own yard and approach the garage with trepidation. I hope this works. I hope I'm not too late. How soon after birth should a baby unicorn eat?

What if it's already dead? I catch my breath, freezing with my hand on the door. What if I went through all this and the unicorn died while I was eating dinner? All that effort, all that terror, and it might just croak in my garage, alone, without its mother nearby.

And maybe that would be all right. Maybe the wrangler knew what she was doing when she tried to drown it. After all, these things are deadly. Dangerous. Evil. Maybe she had the right idea, to never let it grow up. But then I remember the look in Venom's eyes, and I rush inside.

Behind the storage freezer the laundry basket is still and silent. I open the lid, and the unicorn is curled up inside, nestled up against the plush unicorn doll on the blanket. I reach inside and touch its flank. A heartbeat flutters through its velvety skin. It starts from its sleep and turns its head toward my hand, noses my palm and wraps its lips around my finger. Something inside me lets go. Yes, it's a tiny little man-eating monster. But it needs me.

I grab an empty water bottle, a rubber band, and a pair of my mother's rubber-tipped gardening gloves. I cut a finger off the gloves and poke a hole in the tip. Then I fill the bottle with the goat's milk and secure the glove finger onto the opening with the rubber band. A few moments against the back of the freezer, and the milk loses its refrigerator chill. That's going to have to be enough.

"Come here, baby," I say to the unicorn, lifting it out of the nest and cradling it against me. I try to get the bottle into its mouth, but the unicorn is having none of that, and struggles while goat's milk streams out of the hole in the glove and smears over us both.

Gross. The unicorn begins to cry, soft little bleats, and tries to burrow into my torso. I bite my lip, knowing just how it feels. What do I think I'm doing? Goat milk. What a dumb idea.

I pull off the rubber and stick my finger into the bottle.

"Here," I say again, pushing my milk-coated finger past its lips. This time the baby unicorn suckles, its tongue surprisingly firm. I plunge my finger into the bottle again and again, and slowly, painstakingly, we make it through about a sixth of the bottle. This is going to take a while. There has to be a better way.

I put the glove finger back on the bottle, then squeeze my finger over it, covering both the bottle opening and the pinprick hole in the glove tip. Milk dribbles out and down my finger, but slowly, controlled by the pressure of my finger on the rubber. I place my finger back into the baby's mouth and let it eat.

Its eyes are closed as it suckles, its spindly legs drawn up against its body for warmth. Its skin is mostly white, covered with a soft, velvety down. It doesn't look dangerous at all. I guess this early, without its venomous horn, it's not. Just soft and fragile and dainty. I run a finger down its delicate snout. Between its eyes is a reddish mark, like a starburst or a flower.

"Flower," I say, and it opens its eyes for a moment and looks at me.

Oh, no. Now I've named it.

I can't sleep. Down the hall, my parents' room has been dark for hours, but I'm tossing and turning, trying to imagine what it's like for the little unicorn, alone in the garage. Is it awake? Hungry? Suffocating? Dying of carbon monoxide poisoning from the fumes off the freezer?

Finally I toss a jacket on, slip into my flats, and tiptoe down the hall. Outside, the moon is bright on the lawn, and I realize

I should have brought a flashlight. If my parents wake up and see the light on in the garage, they'll freak out.

But once I'm inside the garage, I find I can see just fine. Maybe it's the moonlight. Maybe it's the unicorn. I peek into the laundry basket. Flower is curled up next to the doll again, and I can see its chest move as it breathes. I hope it's a girl. Flower would be a pretty funny name for a boy.

Except, wasn't the skunk in *Bambi* a boy? His name was Flower, and that turned out okay. Bambi, also, was a boy with a girl's name.

I lay my head against the side of the freezer. I can't name this thing Flower. I can't keep it either. It's so dangerous, not only to my parents, who might have to come into the garage for the lawn mower and end up eaten—but also for me. It's magic, and it's all around me, and that's just not right.

Did God place this unicorn in my path as a temptation meant to be overcome? I stare down at the tiny creature curled up in the basket. It's so fragile, like a lamb. How is it to blame for its lot in life? I rest my hand on the unicorn's back, just to feel it breathe. I watch its eyelids flutter, its tiny tail swish slightly against the blanket.

When I wake the next morning, my neck is killing me from sleeping hunched over, and I can't feel anything below my elbow, since the rim of the laundry basket has cut off my circulation. The sun is peeking into the windows of the garage, and the air is stained with the scent of sour milk. The unicorn stirs, yawns adorably, then proceeds to have diarrhea all over the picnic blanket.

No goat milk. Check.

As I'm cleaning up—Flower is now cuddled on a red and white Christmas tree apron—I realize that I'm going to be gone at school all day. I'll have no chance to feed the baby before I go, and what if my mom comes in here and wonders where her gardening stuff has gone and why the freezer is pulled away from the wall?

Flower starts bleating again as I leave the garage and make my way into the house. In the kitchen my dad is eating oatmeal and grousing about how Biscuit peed on the newspaper again. The funny pages survived; the business section did not. He takes in my pajama pants and jacket.

"Where were you?"

"You weren't in the woods, were you?" Mom's eyes are wide with fright.

"No!" I'm so tired of lying. "I was looking for something in the garage."

This, of course, sets off another round of lying, as I try to make up a non-unicorn-based object that I was looking for, and my mother offers to scour the garage for it later, and I tell yet more lies in order to convince her to keep out of there.

Here's a question for Sunday School: Can one lie to one's parents in order to save a life?

I hop in the shower, throw on clean clothes, say a quick prayer that Flower survives and goes undetected until this afternoon, and head to school. School consists of the following: English, math, and history classes, where I fail to pay attention while I fret about Flower; lunchtime, where I brainstorm ideas about what to feed the unicorn and try to avoid glancing at the end of the table, where Summer is sitting on Yves's lap; study hall, where I think about how if I were the kind of girl who knew how to skip and sneak out of school, this would have been an excellent time to slip home and check up on the unicorn; gym, where we play kick ball; and then bio class, where the teacher says our new unit is going to be on endangered species and extinction, and how there are all kinds of animals that we once thought were extinct (like these tree frogs in South America) or imaginary (like giant squids and unicorns), and it turns out that they were just really endangered, and how changes in the environment can either bring the population back or else put the animal in danger.

"So we might have all these unicorns around this past year because we destroyed their natural habitat?" asks Summer, sitting in the front row with Yves.

"They've got the woods all to themselves now," grumbles Noah. After what happened to Rebecca and John, the government closed all the local parks and the state forest that backs up to so many of our housing developments until they could determine the risk to the public. The deer hunters and the Boy Scouts are still pretty livid about it. As for me, even if they ever do open the woods again, I won't be allowed to go back. Not until the unicorns are gone.

"Not anymore," says Aidan. "Didn't you hear? They caught that unicorn, the one that killed the kids. It's dead."

My head whips around. "What?"

Aidan is sprawled out behind his desk, and as usual, he's

gotten half the class's attention. "Was on the news last night. They showed the corpse and everything."

My knuckles grow white, my breath grows shallow, and it's funny but I can feel Yves's gaze on the back of my head as easily as I could feel Venom calling to me from across the fairgrounds. Class devolves into a discussion of what they are not showing us on TV, until the teacher manages to regain control.

They caught it. A chorus of angels are singing somewhere in the vicinity of my sternum. They caught it. I don't care what my folks said about the special unicorn hunters. Maybe they use magic, but they answered my prayers. Someone avenged my cousins' deaths. We're all safe.

And then I remember Flower.

When school lets out, Aidan invites me to go with him and the others to the mall, but I need to tend to the unicorn in my parents' garage. I head to the grocery store, where I buy a real baby bottle, some formula, and some hamburger meat. I'm terrified of what the lady at the checkout counter will think of my purchases, but she says nothing, just takes my money and watches me stuff everything into my backpack.

Yves honks at me as I hit the street. "Need a ride?"

"Stalker," I say, and climb in. "Aren't you going to the mall?"

"Nah." He shrugs. "Summer has yearbook, and I don't need an Orange Julius." He pulls out onto the road and casts me a sidelong glance. "So, they caught that unicorn."

"Yeah." I look out the window.

"How do you feel?"

"Better." And as soon as I say it, I realize it's the truth. Who knew I had such viciousness inside me? I wonder if that's what comes of spending the night communing with a killer unicorn. Even a newborn one. I'm sure my parents would agree.

Then again, they are probably also thrilled to hear that my cousins' killer is dead.

We ride the rest of the way home in silence, and my heart plummets as I see my mom on our front yard wielding hedge clippers.

"Hey, Mrs. G," Yves says as we get out of his car.

I clutch my backpack to my chest and try very hard not to look at the garage. Does she know? Even from here I can tell Flower is scared, starving, alone. Is it possible my mom didn't see it? Or doesn't know what it is she saw? After all, Flower has no horn.

My mom brushes her hair out of her eyes and waves, and I can breathe again.

"How did that marinade work out for you?" Yves asks Mom.

She cocks her head to the side. "I'm sorry, dear?"

Yves fixes me with a look. "Never mind. I must have been confused."

I beeline for the house, hoping Mom will stay outside long enough for me to snag the blender without notice.

"*Thanks for the ride, Yves!*" Yves calls after me. "*You're my knight in shining armor!*"

My knight has another damsel. Not that I care.

I dump my textbooks on the kitchen table, grab the blender off the counter, and shove it into my backpack.

Back outside, Yves is nowhere to be seen and my mom looks like she's packing it in. She stretches and rolls out her neck muscles.

"I can take those clippers back to the garage for you," I say quickly.

"Thank you, sweetie." My mom brushes dirt off her knees. "I need to get better at keeping my gardening stuff in one place. You know I had these clippers under the porch all winter?"

Well, that was a close call. I go to take the clippers from her, but she doesn't let go.

"I'm . . . glad to see you going out with your friends again, sweetie."

I tug on the clippers and keep my eyes down.

"I know the past few months have been hard on you, with all our restrictions." She places her other hand over mine. "But it's for your own safety—your life *and* your eternal soul. Those monsters—they're demons."

"They're animals," I reply, and pull the clippers away. "We learned in bio class that they're back because of environmental degradation of their habitat."

Mom smiles at me and nods. I half-expect her to pat me on the head. "That's the science, my dear. But what happened to Rebecca and John—that was the work of the Devil. And what happens to you when you are near the creatures? It's sorcery. The snake in the Garden of Eden was an animal as well. Remember that. Don't let that evil into your heart."

She leaves me on the porch, blinking back tears. I want to run inside and climb into her lap and have her sing me lullabies or hymns or whatever it takes to drown out Flower's cries of fear and hunger. The unicorn has been calling to me since the second I got out of Yves's car.

What if I just left it there? It won't be able to survive alone much longer. If Flower dies, I won't be able to hear it cry, won't feel its pain. I won't be caring for a demon, like Mom says. No matter how innocent the baby unicorn looks, I know what lurks within. It was foolish of me to obey Venom yesterday, foolish of me to defy my parents and everything I knew was right.

Maybe after it's dead I can go and bury it. Or drag it into the woods. Or . . .

Except how could I save it from drowning, from the quick death the wrangler offered—only to subject it to a day and night of terror and hunger and loneliness? What right do I have to torture it so?

Ignoring the garage and my backpack filled with groceries, I head to my bedroom. I do my homework, I surf the Internet, and I pray to God to deafen me to the baby unicorn that screams inside my head.

I resist it for two hours, and then I find myself on my way to the garage, backpack in hand. All my life I have learned that my God is a God of love, and that above all He wishes me to be compassionate. And then He places in my path a monster. If this is a test, then surely I am failing.

Inside the garage the unicorn is standing and pushing its face against the lid of the laundry basket. It has made a mess inside again. I sigh and empty out the basket. While I get its formula ready, the unicorn takes a few tottering steps on the concrete floor, unsteady on its matchstick legs, then wipes out and starts crying. I do my best to ignore it while I blend the formula according to directions, then add a few handfuls of raw hamburger and set the blender to puree. The resulting mixture looks and smells like something you'd see on a reality television show, and I wonder if this will be any more palatable to the unicorn. Baby birds eat regurgitated bits of bugs or other meat from their mothers, though. Maybe unicorns work the same way.

Flower seems to like it, sucking from the bottle like a pro and pawing at me for more. After eating, it settles down pretty quickly into the cardboard box nest I've made for it. It drifts off to sleep as I'm rinsing out the blender, but when I cross the garage to return Mom's gardening tools to the laundry basket, the unicorn wakes up and starts crying at me.

I swallow until I can speak. "Stop."

Bleat, bleat. Bleeeeeaaaaaaaaaat.

"Stop, please!" Why couldn't I kill it? Why couldn't I let it die? I clap my hands over my ears and squeeze my eyes shut.

Bleeeeaaaaaat. I hear Flower throwing itself against the sides of the box.

"No!" I say sharply. "Stop it. Settle down."

And, amazingly, the unicorn listens.

By the end of the following week, I've fallen into a routine. My life circles around Flower—when to feed the unicorn, when to clean out his box, when to sneak out of the house, how quickly I need to run home from school to take care of the little monster. In the middle of the night, I can tell when he stirs from his sleep, when he needs me. Oh, yes, it's a boy. I made that little discovery the other day when I got a good look at his backside.

Flower thrives on the burger-formula solution and begins growing by leaps and bounds. Wooly white hair sprouts all over his body, and I worry less about whether or not he will be too cold at night. I've taken to sneaking out of the house to walk the unicorn around the backyard, hoping to tire him out enough that he won't go wandering around the garage the next day. Luckily, he seems to be a nocturnal creature, happy to snooze the day away. I'm not so lucky, and I walk around school half in a daze, doze off in class, and suffer long, concerned looks from Yves at his place at the other end of the lunch table. He hasn't spoken to me since the goat milk incident.

If I weren't so tired, I'd wonder about that, and also about the damage this behavior is doing to my eternal soul. Every night I pray to God to send me strength, but it's never been enough to kill Flower, nor even to leave him alone long enough to let him die. Apparently my parents had nothing to worry about. Even if they had let me go with those people, I'd never have been able to bring myself to hunt unicorns.

Saturday afternoon our crowd has a picnic at the newly reopened park. All around, families are walking the trails, playing Frisbee in the fields, or barbecuing in the pavilions.

"I think it's premature," says Katey, unpacking sandwiches

and bags of potato chips from a cooler. "They caught one unicorn. Doesn't mean there aren't more."

"If you're so scared, why did you come?" asks Marissa, pulling out a six-pack of sodas. Today she's in a pair of shorts cut almost to the crotch.

Katey gives Marissa a smile that is more like a growl. "Noah will protect me. Won't you, sweetie?"

Noah is standing next to Marissa, but moves really quickly. Yves is sitting on the picnic table, and Summer is on the bench, propped up against his knee. Aidan is stealing carrots from the plate where I'm setting out vegetables. He grins at me, his mouth a row of baby carrots laid end to end.

"Hey," he says through the veggies, "did you see the corpse they put on the news yet?"

I have not. My parents deemed it unnecessarily macabre, and not only forbade me from watching the news, but also hid the metro section of the newspaper the following day. Aidan has brought the video, downloaded from YouTube, on his cell phone. We cluster around to watch. The audio is terrible, and the first minute is all the mayor shaking hands with the wildlife control people, none of whom, I note with interest, look like they could be unicorn hunters. To start with, there's not a single girl in the bunch.

There's a ticker running across the bottom of the screen that explains what neighborhood watch group found the corpse. Apparently the wildlife control folks aren't the ones who killed the unicorn after all. Then the video cuts to another scene, where photographers and people with cameras cluster around

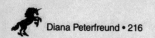

a small table in the police station. The camera zooms in on the corpse.

It's Venom.

I reel back from the group, a gasp lodged in my throat. How I recognize the remains of Flower's mother on a two-inch screen, I don't know. But it's her. The unicorn from the carnival. The one that bowed before me and begged me to save her child. *Dead.*

When? How? Did the wrangler kill her when I escaped with the baby? Venom wasn't looking too good that night, was having trouble standing after the wrangler ripped Flower out of her. Did she somehow injure herself then?

But what I know for certain is it's not the unicorn that killed Rebecca and John. It's not even the same kind. That one was big, and dark, with a horn that curved instead of twisted.

And then I realize something else. If the unicorn they "caught" was Venom, it means the one terrorizing these woods is still out there. Which means that all my friends, all these people in the park—they're in terrible danger.

Even more because they are here with me.

I turn and sprint away as my friends start calling my name. I run into the parking lot, breathing hard and wondering how I can get the city to close the parks down again. I hear feet pounding behind me, then feel a hand on my arm.

"Wen!" It's Yves, and Summer and Aidan are right behind him. They each stop a few feet away, giving me space, but not enough. I back up again.

"Get away," I tell Yves. "Don't come near me." I breathe the air, tasting it for any trace of unicorn. We're safe, so far.

"It's okay, Wen," he says.

"What's wrong?" asks Aidan.

"It's the unicorn," Summer explains. "Those kids it killed—they were her cousins."

I rip my arm out of Yves's grip and glare at him so hard he stumbles backward. *You told her?*

"Wen," says Aidan, coming forward. "I'm so sorry. I didn't know. Man, I'm such a moron. I—"

"That's not it. That unicorn, in the video. That's the one from the fair. They have the wrong one. The one that killed Rebec—it's still out there." I'm crying now, words choking me, breath stinging my throat.

"What do you mean?" Yves says.

Oh, no. This burning, this clarity, this smell of rot and forest fire. I know it. It's coming.

"Get away!" I scream at him. "Get away from me right now!"

And then I start to run.

They say on the news that no one died in the attack. Yves calls from the hospital, reporting that the unicorn knocked Aidan down and broke his arm, then ran right by them.

Of course. It was trying to get to me.

I huddle under an old afghan on the couch while Mom makes me hot chocolate and smoothes my hair. I can hear the helicopters overhead, watch as their searchlights scour the woods behind our house. The parks and forests have been closed again, and the whole town is on lockdown. I wonder if the unicorn is waiting out there for me, or if it has enough sense to go back into hiding.

"You did the right thing," Mom says. "Running away from a populated area. It was stupid to reopen the parks, to think there was only one of them out there. . . ."

I sip my hot chocolate and don't correct her. After all, it's true that there *was* more than one unicorn in our town. And even if they do kill this one, there's still Flower, tucked away safe and sound in the garage.

Sometime late that night they report that the unicorn has been eliminated, but that the wilderness shutdown remains in full effect, for public safety. Yeah, right. They couldn't have gotten hunters over here from Italy so fast. My parents, now seated on either side of me, praise God for his protection and mercy, but I just sob into their hugs and reassurances and promises that they can keep me safe. My parents are so much older and wiser than I am. How can they be so wrong about this? How can any of us be safe when I'm raising the instrument of our destruction in our own garage? How can we guard ourselves against unicorns when I'm spending half my nights feeding one from a bottle?

I excuse myself, claiming I need some alone time. This is, miraculously, not a lie. Then I head to the garage.

In my father's toolbox is a small hand axe. I'm doing this for the right reasons. The wrangler was correct all along. Maybe she was in the same situation I'm in. Tricked into caring for a unicorn that became increasingly dangerous, that created little monsters of its own. Maybe she was right to try to drown

Venom's offspring, to let Venom die—or even kill the unicorn herself at last. Maybe the wrangler possessed the grace that I could not muster on my own.

I approach Flower's box. I can tell he's happy I've come, but something's wrong. There's a hole chewed in the side of the box. The box is empty.

"Flower?" I say, spinning. He's still in the garage, hiding. He thinks this is a game. Flower's joy is palpable. He's so proud of himself. Clever beast, escaping. Freedom. Showing off for me when I come home. Each emotion is clearer than the last, and I realize that every moment I spend with the unicorn is giving it more access to my mind, to my soul.

I tighten my grip on the handle of the axe. I *must* cast it out. "Come here, Flower."

The unicorn usually obeys my every command, but he's hesitant now. Perhaps he's even smarter than I thought. Perhaps since I can read his thoughts, he can read mine and knows I mean him harm. I try to project my usual tenderness.

"Flower," I coax, following my senses through the garage, behind the saw table, under the disused weight bench, over to the old camping equipment. There are holes in the bag where we keep our cooking supplies, and utensils are strewn all over the floor. "Come here, baby."

I hear rustling from the darkness. Flower is unsure of my motives, confused by my tone.

"Flower," I try again, my voice wavering over more sobs. How do soldiers do it? How do the real unicorn hunters? The trained ones? "Don't you get it? I have to! I *have* to . . ."

The unicorn steps out of the shadows, his blue eyes trained on me. His mouth is open, panting slightly, so that he almost looks like he's smiling. I can see brand-new white teeth breaking through the gums. Teeth that helped him chew through the cardboard. Teeth he might use on my parents, or my friends.

I have to, I cry to the unicorn inside my head. Flower's matchstick legs wobble a few steps closer, and he watches me, eyes full of trust. This is the creature I've held and fed every night and every morning.

The flower in the center of his forehead is red now, glistening, enflamed and engorged like a massive, starburst-shaped boil. The horn is coming. The horn, and the poison, and all of the danger that marks this monster's—this demon's—entire species. I can't let him survive. I can't.

This is the animal I caressed until he fell asleep, who I crooned to while he cried, who I dreamed of every night, who I've run through the yard by moonlight, who I rushed home to day after day. I watched him be born; I held him in my arms, still wet from his mother; and I crushed him to my chest so he wouldn't freeze. I've hidden him and protected him and given up everything to keep him safe.

Flower bends his forelegs and lowers his head to the floor. He bows before me, just like his mother, and stretches out his neck as if for sacrifice. I could do it now; it would be so easy.

I drop the axe and fall to my knees.

Under cover of twilight I take Flower out to the woods. The deadly woods. The forbidden woods. With an old rubber-coated bicycle chain for a collar and a leash made from steel cable that Dad uses to tie his boat to his truck, I secure the unicorn to a tree, then create a makeshift shelter in the brush right next to it. From a few feet away you can hardly tell there's anything unnatural there. And at least he's out of our yard. No one will go into the woods—not after this new attack.

Flower is quiet while I work, and still, as if he knows how close he came to death. He trots obediently into the shelter and settles down on a pile of leaves. I leave the unicorn a package of ground turkey for dinner. Now that his teeth are in, I don't even need to bother with the blender anymore, but I figure that the food should still be soft. Baby food, for a predator.

The woods are still now. No helicopters, no searchlights. No sounds of birds or insects, either, as if they also recognize the presence of my monster. Beyond Flower, I can sense no unicorn. I stretch out my awareness to its limit, searching for the other one I know must still be alive, and I find nothing. It feels incredible, but then I recoil from the magic.

After all, haven't I sinned enough for one day?

In Sunday School the next morning, we talk about the Book of Daniel. When we get to the part about the one-horned goat, everyone goes quiet. It's bad timing on the teacher's part.

"Ms. Guzman?" A boy raises his hand. "Do you think that's a unicorn? That one they put on the news the other day—it kind of looked like a goat."

"It's possible," Ms. Guzman says. "In fact, there are older translations of the Bible that call it a unicorn. When this translation was made, however, we didn't know there were unicorns, so they called it a goat instead. If Daniel did see a unicorn in his prophetic vision, what do you think it meant?"

"That whatever was coming would be much more vicious and dangerous than if it was a goat," says one of the girls. "If it really was a unicorn in his vision, that makes it a much scarier one."

"And it makes more sense if it is a unicorn," says another girl, "because it goes on to say that neither the ram nor anyone else was strong enough to withstand the goat's power. And that's what they say about unicorns, that no one can cure the poison, that no one can catch or kill them."

"Someone can catch them," I find myself saying. "And maybe the goat kind of unicorn—Well, maybe they aren't vicious. So maybe the vision meant that Daniel should—"

"What?" asks the boy. "Hang out with the man-eating monster?"

"He hung out with man-eating lions," I snap.

"I think we're getting a little off topic," says Ms. Guzman. "The point is, no matter how powerful this unicorn might be— and the angel Gabriel explains to Daniel that the unicorn in the vision represents the pagan king Alexander the Great—all these kingdoms, the ram, the unicorn, all of it, are destined to fall because they are man's kingdoms, human kingdoms, and not the kingdom of God."

Ms. Guzman talks about God a little more, but I can't pay attention. I've been praying to God about Flower for weeks, hoping He'll forgive me for lying to my parents, hoping He'll forgive me for betraying Rebecca's and John's memories by taking care of a unicorn. I've been waiting for a single sign of violence from Flower, a clear sign that he is as dangerous as all the others so I can kill him with a clear conscience—but I've not seen anything. Is it because Flower isn't a killer? Or is it because I'm like Daniel in the lion's den? Is God protecting me?

And if so, why didn't He protect Rebecca and John?

Weeks pass, and Flower remains my secret. The unicorn is eating real food now—chicken thighs and kidneys and pork shoulders and anything else I can find on sale at the supermarket. I'm burning through my savings at an alarming rate, but I know my mom would notice if I started stealing meat from our fridge. Flower must be deadly bored, hanging out in the makeshift shelter all day, but he's out of sight of my parents and out of reach of any danger, so that's all that matters. With the woods off-limits to everyone in the neighborhood, the only thing that could hurt him is one of his elders, and I haven't sensed any during our nightly runs through the forest. The unicorn likes when I run alongside him, I've learned, and I admit, I love how fast we can go together. Branches and roots are never in my way when I'm flying through the forest with the unicorn at my side. If only he weren't illegal, I'd keep Flower around and slay on the track team.

But if I tried that, the unicorn might try to eat the spectators. Plus, Aidan would totally call me out on being a jock. Not that it matters. Even if Aidan did decide he liked me, I could never go out with him. Every time I see his cast, I'm reminded that it's only through God's grace that I avoided being the cause of his death. I could have killed them all, and yet I persist in this defiant path through my own weakness.

School is torture now. Since finding out about my cousins, Summer writes my odd behavior off as post-traumatic stress when it comes to unicorns. Yves doesn't correct her, and I don't enlighten any of them. They know unicorns are deadly, my parents tell me that they are evil, and I know everyone is right.

But I still love mine.

Flower is already half as tall as his mother, and his silver-white coat turns long and wavy. I draw the line at brushing it, but I'm pretty sure that if I bothered to, Flower would look as pretty as any unicorn in a fairy story. Even his dangerous horn is pretty—a smooth, creamy gray that twists like a corkscrew and seems to grow longer by the day. You can hardly see the remnants of the flower-shaped marking that gave my Flower his name.

One night, as I sneak into the woods for our usual evening romp, I catch a strange scent in the air. The reek of unicorn is as strong as ever, but there's something else carried aloft on the summer breeze. Something horrible. Flower rustles in the shelter as I approach, and the unicorn's elation stings like a cramp. What kind of life have I consigned this animal to? Alone all day, chained to a tree, never allowed to run except for a short half hour each night when I should be in bed?

From my pocket I retrieve the bits of ham I secreted away from dinner and hurry toward the clearing. The smell grows stronger, and as I round the last tree, I put my foot down in something slick and sprawl onto the forest floor.

At eye level is a rabbit. Or what used to be a rabbit. The remains—mostly skin—are almost unrecognizable, except for a pair of floppy ears.

A few feet farther on is the half-digested skin of a chipmunk. Then a squirrel, and a scattering of sparrows.

I raise myself on my elbows and try not to gag.

In the center of the carnage sits Flower, with what looks like leftover raccoon all over his snout, and his chain lying in crumpled chewed-up chunks at his hooves. Flower looks at me, proud as punch, and thumps his tail against the earth.

Flower? Try *Flayer*.

My killer unicorn is finally living up to the name.

I fix the restraints, but the unicorn gnaws through them again. I spend the last of my savings on the heaviest chain the local hardware store supplies. Flayer, as I've taken to calling him, takes four days to chew up this one and then, in retaliation, procures a feast. I find the unicorn on his back in the shelter, four hooves in the air, drunk with the blood of small woodland creatures.

Oddly enough, this new evidence of the unicorn's deadly abilities only confuses me further. I wonder if killer unicorns are really the work of the Devil. I've seen Flayer in his natural element, covered in gore, tearing apart flesh and bone, and loving every minute—and though he's not exactly a candidate for a petting farm, neither does he seem like an evil demon. Dogs and cats and great white sharks do that too. Biscuit likes leaving mice and frogs and crickets as gifts on old Mrs. Schaffer's porch.

I eat cows and chickens and pigs and fish. Flayer is a predator. That's not against God's plan.

But then I remember what that other unicorn did to my cousins, and I'm not so sure. Perhaps my ability to accept these acts of violence in my unicorn is nothing more than a sign of my own corrupted soul. I defied my parents, indulged the magic, raised a killer unicorn by hand. Maybe I'm past all redemption.

As if to prove the point, on our run this evening Flayer decides to snatch bats out of thin air for an evening snack. I hear him crunch their little bones, listen to them squeak their last, and shut my eyes to the sight of him tearing through their leathery wings. An animal that eats bats must be a creature of darkness, right?

We return to the shelter and I get Flayer settled down for the night, encouraging him to lie quietly and remain here, and above all, not to destroy the final length of chain. Thankfully, even when he has escaped his bonds, the unicorn hasn't wandered too far on his own yet. With the woods being off-limits, I can only hope that whatever slim precautions I can take will be enough to protect him from people, and enough to protect people from *him*. I've read stuff online about how baby fawns will wait in the brush for their mother to forage, but Flayer's obviously not going to be a baby much longer. He'll graduate from bats to people. Then what will I do?

I think about this on my much slower walk back to my yard and as I edge around the moonlight on my lawn, sticking to shadows in case my parents are randomly looking out the window.

They aren't. But someone else is. As I am rounding the back porch, I catch movement out of the corner of my eye. Yves is standing at his bedroom window, and he's staring down at me.

I successfully avoid him the entire next day at school, and volunteer to accompany Mom on a shopping trip on Saturday, so I miss both of his phone calls and the time he drops by the house for a chat. My parents raised me to return calls, but I find that disobeying them concerning the unicorn is indeed a slippery slope, and I avoid calling him all evening. He's waiting for me on the porch after church on Sunday, though, and since my parents are there, I can hardly run past him and into the house—or worse, up to the woods.

"Hey there, Wen," he says. "Long time, no see."

If I were any good at lying, I'd have explained to my folks that I was mad at Yves. If I were any good at lying, I'd tell Yves he was imagining things in his bedroom that night.

But I'm not, and Yves knows it. And as soon as the screen door closes after my parents, the smile fades from his face.

"What's going on with you?" The spring sun suddenly feels more like the glow of an interrogation lamp. I can feel my church skirt sticking to the back of my knees.

"Nothing."

"Don't give me that. You're hiding from everyone in school, and you're sneaking into the woods."

I look away. Old Mrs. Schaffer is shuffling down the street, pausing at telephone poles and mailboxes and peering into open garage doors.

At church today I prayed that God would show me a way out of this mess. I can't let Flayer go, but I can't keep him either. I can't tell my parents what I've been up to. I can't figure out what to do. I know now why the lady at the carnival was so upset. Like me, she was trapped.

And Venom ended up dead. My throat closes up if I try to picture a future like that for my unicorn.

"Do you have a death wish?" Yves's voice cuts through my reverie.

"What?" I turn back to him.

"Are you out there looking for—for unicorns? You think you can kill them or something, because of what those people said to you?"

I laugh. "Trust me, Yves. If there's one thing I'm positive I can't do, it's kill a unicorn." Spoil it rotten with hamburger meat? Teach it to come when called? Treat it like a jogging partner? Sure. But kill one? Forget it.

Yves's collar is open, and there's a dab of moisture in the hollow at his throat. I wonder how long he's been waiting out here for me. And if it's this hot for him, Flayer must really be sweltering in his shelter—if the unicorn is even there, and not out on a rampage.

I shut my eyes for a moment. If I don't stop dwelling on Flayer, Yves will be able to read the truth on my face. If I don't stop staring at him, things will get even weirder.

"Wen, I *saw* you." He takes two steps, and suddenly he's on top of me, speaking in a voice that's so low I almost need my unicorn senses to hear him. He puts his hand over mine on the porch railing, and it practically sears my skin. "Tell me. You know you can tell me anything."

"Hello, children." Mrs. Schaffer's standing on the walk. "You haven't seen my Biscuit around anywhere, have you?"

"No, ma'am," Yves mumbles. Beside him, I stiffen. He glances at our joined hands, and when I try to pull away, he clamps down. He knows me so well.

"I haven't seen the poor thing since Friday morning."

I can't swallow. I certainly can't speak. Yves squeezes my hand in his, and it's not hard enough to bring tears, but somehow they're welling up in my eyes.

"I'm just so worried about him," Mrs. Schaffer goes on.

I hate that mangy old cat. It pees on our newspaper. It rips up our flower beds. It tears down the wind catchers Mom hangs on our porch.

And it's totally toast.

"I'm sorry, Mrs. Schaffer," I choke out. "I—"

"—hope you find him soon," Yves finishes, and tugs my hand. "We have to go."

I stumble, blind with tears, into the backyard. I've hated Biscuit for years, but that doesn't make him food. Random, nameless rabbits and raccoons are one thing. But Biscuit? Mrs. Schaffer loved him like I love Flayer. What have I done?

Yves pulls me into the shade behind the kitchen door and makes me look at him. We used to make mud pies back here. We used to make dandelion crowns and willow swords.

"It's a unicorn, isn't it?" he asks. "A unicorn ate Biscuit."

I nod, miserably.

"Oh, no. Wen, I'm so sorry." He pulls me into a hug. "I know it was just a stupid cat, but it must remind you of—"

"No." I shove the word out as I push him away. "You don't understand. It's my fault."

"Stop saying that," he cries. "This is exactly what I'm talking about. You have to stop blaming yourself for this. Stop punishing yourself. Stop going into the woods and endangering yourself. I don't care if you think you're irresistible to unicorns or whatever stupid stuff those people told you."

"Invincible," I say with a sniff. "*And* irresistible, I guess."

"Listen to me," he says, and tilts his head close to mine. "Look at me."

I do. I see a hundred Sunday afternoons and a thousand after-school playdates and one very black night last fall. Yves's eyes are dark and clear. "Rebecca and John weren't your fault, and Biscuit isn't either."

"It is. This one is." I take a deep breath, but I don't look away. "Yves."

"Wen." It's a whisper.

"I have to show you something. You're the only one who'll understand."

He doesn't hesitate, not even for a moment. I'm the girl who beats him at Skee-Ball; he's the first boy I ever kissed. Yves takes my hand, and I lead him into the forbidden woods.

I can feel the unicorn, sleeping through the afternoon heat. We'll just have to keep our distance, like with Venom at the sideshow. Flayer is chained, so Yves will be safe.

As we reach the shelter, Flayer rouses and bounds out, tail wagging, silver hair shining in the sunlight, horn still streaked with the blood of his latest kill. The beast pauses as he sees Yves, then bares his teeth in a growl.

And in the slowness and clarity that comes with my powers, I can see my fatal mistake. It took Flayer four days to chew through this chain the last time, and that was Thursday night. It's Sunday afternoon. I've cut it too close. The chain dangles at the unicorn's throat, mangled beyond hope of repair.

I hold fast to Yves's hand as the monster lunges.

"No!"

My sharp tone stops the unicorn short. Yves gasps.

"Sit."

Flayer parks his behind on the earth and looks at me in frustration.

"Wen?" Yves's voice trembles.

"Down," I order. The unicorn grumbles, and lowers himself to the ground, tilting his deadly horn up and away. I grab the broken end of the chain, hold on tight, and turn back to my friend. "This is Flayer."

Yves looks as though he might faint.

"Remember that night at the carnival?" I crouch next the unicorn and rub his stomach. "The unicorn there—Venom— she was pregnant."

"Pregnant," Yves repeats flatly.

"And I went back a few days later and found her giving

birth. And . . . I can't explain it, but it was like she asked me to take care of the baby. So I took it."

Flayer lifts his hind leg in the air and bleats. I intensify my massage.

"I've been caring for him ever since." The unicorn's mouth opens, and his bloodstained tongue lolls between fanged jaws. "And, aside from Biscuit—well, and I guess some squirrels and stuff—"

I babble on. I don't know for how long. It feels so good, to confess all this to Yves. I tell him about the goat's milk, and the laundry basket. I tell him about the hamburger and the bicycle chains. I tell him about the moonlight runs through the forest. I tell him about the time with the axe, and the way Flayer can call to me from half a mile away.

Yves listens to everything, and then he says, "Do you have any idea what you've done?"

I nod, staring down at my pet. "Yeah. Broke the law. Endangered our entire neighborhood. Lied to everyone."

He shakes his head. "Wen, you *trained* a killer unicorn. No one can do that. No one can catch one, no one can kill one, no one can tame one! But you did!"

"I—"

"Even the one at the carnival was covered in chains. They're wild, vicious, but this one . . ." Yves gestures to Flayer, who wags his tail like Yves is about to throw him a ham hock. "He listens to you! He stays where you want him to. It's a miracle."

I stare down at the unicorn. *A miracle.*

I've been praying to God to deliver me from my unwelcome

powers, the curse of my dangerous and unholy magic. I've been praying for Him to direct my hand, to give me strength to destroy the demon unicorn He placed in my path. And all this time, I thought He'd refused because of my own sins— my defiance of the law, my disobedience toward my parents. I thought I'd failed Him.

But what if . . . God *wanted* me to care for this unicorn? What if He sent it to me to discover a way to prevent what happened to my cousins from ever occurring again?

What if my powers aren't a curse at all? What if they're . . . a gift?

"We have to tell the world," Yves finishes.

I snuggle the unicorn close to my chest. "No way. If I come out of the woods with Flayer by my side, he'll be taken from me, experimented on, destroyed. What chance does this little guy have against helicopters and searchlights? Against napalm?"

Yves says, "There has to be something. Maybe your parents—"

"My parents think unicorns are demons and my powers are witchcraft."

It'll never work. Too many lives have been destroyed by unicorns. Even Yves looks uncertain as I continue to cuddle the killer unicorn in my lap.

If only they could feel what it's like to run through the woods by Flayer's side. If only they knew how much Flayer loves me, and I him. I never feel so free, so right as I do when I'm alone in the forest with the unicorn. If only God would reveal His plan to them as well.

"Okay," says Yves. "What about those people in Italy? The unicorn hunters? They understand your powers, right?"

Yeah, but even they wanted to use my powers to help them *kill* unicorns. Maybe I could show them how to use our gifts for this instead, but first I'd have to persuade them to spare my unicorn. I scratch the base of Flayer's horn, where the tiny flower marking is barely visible. Protecting Flayer is what matters most. The world can wait.

"Stay," I say to the unicorn as I join Yves again. "What if I left?"

"You mean, like, run away?" Yves looks stricken. "Wen, you can't—"

"Flayer and me, we're safe in the forest. And I can keep an eye on him, make sure he eats only wild animals. And me . . . I used to be a really good camper."

"But what about school? What about food? What about the other unicorns?" Yves shakes his head. "No, there's got to be another way."

"A way where I can save Flayer?" I ask. "What way is that? Everyone in the world wants him dead but me!"

"We could—" Yves casts about desperately for an alternative. "We could ask Summer. She's involved in the Sierra Club, she knows people at the World Wildlife Fund . . ."

Right. Her.

"Yves." I bite my lip, but it's too late and the words pour out. "I know you and Summer—"

He kisses me then. Full on, noses smashing. Our arms go around each other, and Flayer bleats in surprise, but I don't care.

Last fall may have been a mistake, but this isn't. I just wish I had figured it out before. Before Summer. Before Flayer. Before I feared I'd never see him again.

We're still kissing when Mom and Dad come up over the hill. I feel Flayer's alarm, hear him start to growl, and I pull away from Yves. My parents' faces are dark with fury, dim with shock. Their daughter, their little Wen. Lying. Woods. Magic. *Kissing.*

I move to stand beside my killer unicorn.

"Inoculata"

Justine: I'm probably disqualified from expressing my opinion of this story on account of knowing Mr. Westerfeld rather well.[1] So let me confine myself to just the facts: This story is about love, lust, evolution, and zombies.

The job of every generation is to discover the flaws of the one that came before it. That's part of growing up, figuring out all the ways your parents and their friends are broken. So pity the first people to reach puberty after a zombie apocalypse, who would have some truly heavy lifting in this department. How do you fry up the sacred cows of a previous generation who are all traumatized survivors?

You become whatever they fear the most. Now *that's* evolution.

Holly: Wait, you mean they become unicorns?

Justine: Holly, you're delusional. So. Very. Delusional.

---

[1] Justine Larbalestier and Scott Westerfeld are married. To each other.

Inoculata
By Scott Westerfeld

1.

"Flat tire drill!" Dr. Bill shouts through the busted front window.

Sammy's next to me in the driver's seat, pretending to drive. He makes a noise, "Rrrrrrr . . . kupuch!" and spins the wheel, bouncing around the front seat spraying spittle and explosion sounds. He winds up with his head in my lap, his eyes rolled back and tongue sticking out.

"Um, dork?" I say. "This is a flat tire. Not a car wreck."

His answer: "I call shotgun!"

"Fine." I shove him off me. "Then *I'm* doing the jump and roll."

He scrambles into the backseat of the rusted-out Ford, pulling the shotgun from the floorboard. I unstick my sweaty T-shirt from the seat back, check my empty pistol one more time, then open the door.

"Call out the steps, Allison!" yells Dr. Bill. Back in the before, he was a medic in the U.S. Marine Corps. He thinks that lots of shouting equals lots of learning.

So I shout, "Step one: three-sixty check!"

Sammy and I make a show of looking in all directions. Kalyn and Jun are waiting in the insect-buzzing trees with their arms folded, which means we aren't supposed to see them. Kalyn winks at me as I pretend she isn't there.

"Step two: jump and roll!" I throw myself hard—farther than arm's length—and roll sideways in the soft dirt with my pistol pointed back beneath the car.

For a moment I imagine cold eyes staring at me, something waiting in the darkness, hungry for an unwary ankle to grab. A tingle awakens on my skin, and my eyes start twitching. I can almost remember how it felt outside the wire. It's like this in my running dreams, the whole world shiny like metal.

But there's nothing underneath the car. Just dirt and fern leaves. The nearest zee is two hundred yards away on the other side of the main gate.

"Clear!" I shout, and Sammy bounces out, whirling around the old Ford, waltzing with the shotgun, also unloaded.

"Dial it back, Sammy," Dr. Bill says, and Sammy mostly does. He's still bouncing from foot to foot, as dialed back as he ever gets with a shotgun in his hands, even the crappy, rusted Remington we use for drills.

I stand up. "Step three: post a guard."

"That's me, Ally!" Sammy says, like I've forgotten. He climbs up onto the car roof, the tired metal sagging under his weight. He turns in place, maintaining our three-sixty, but I can tell he's cheating, keeping a close eye on Kalyn and Jun.

"Step four," I say, slapping a mosquito on my arm. "Change the tire."

Also known as "the pretending part." The Ford barely made it through the gates four years ago, and it squats like a dead thing in the middle of the clearing, all four tires reduced to rubber puddles.

I can barely remember when the Ford still ran and we were still outside the wire and going places. These days the paint is peeling, the windows are broken, the upholstery is fried to crackling by the Mississippi sun.

As I holster my pistol, the world gets less shiny. It's pathetic that the only car I've sat in for the last four years is this hunk of rust, except for a couple of driving lessons in the Benz with Alma. Back in the before I'd have a driver's license by now, but inside the wire there's nowhere to drive, and outside, the roads are falling to pieces.

But still we drill.

"Which tire is flat again?"

"Right rear," Dr. Bill says with great assurance. Behold the power of running the drill.

The Ford's trunk doesn't really open anymore, so the jack's just sitting on the ground. I kneel and set it under the rear bumper.

"For real?" I ask.

"Why not, Allison?" Dr. Bill smiles. "Nothing wrong with working up a good sweat."

Yes, he actually said "a good sweat." Because I wasn't planting potatoes all day yesterday in hundred-degree heat.

Oh, wait. I was.

But I start pumping, or jacking, or whatever it is you do with jacks. The car lifts in slow increments, the ancient tires drooping from their rims like rolled down socks.

This is the boring part—when nothing happens. It's supposed to teach you that *mostly* nothing happens, even outside the wire. There are plenty of spots in the world where you can change a tire without any of the six billion shambling along. So sometimes Dr. Bill just leaves everyone waiting in the wings, watching while you fix a flat or clean your gun or count your precious bullets. . . .

And the zees don't come. Just mosquitoes.

But you can't let your guard down. That way lies death, zombification, and lost dessert points.

"Hey, Ally!" shouts Sammy. "Um, I mean—zee alert!"

I stand up and draw my pistol, smiling. Despite the very important lesson they teach, those nothing-happens drills are *really* annoying.

Kalyn and Jun have unfolded their arms. They're coming toward me, feet shuffling through the broken safety glass and ferns. Jun looks like he's about to bust out laughing, but Kalyn's zee shamble is eerily perfect. Her long black skirt drags in the dirt, the hint of a zee limp rippling down its length.

She hangs out by the wire in her free time, watching the six billion. I hang out there too, watching her.

But right now I'm all business. "Okay. Get a count!"

Sammy keeps his shotgun trained on the zees while I take a quick circuit of the car. There's only four of us kids, but Dr. Bill can be tricky. Sometimes he makes the grown-ups join in, just to keep things interesting.

But there's nobody else in sight.

"I got two."

"Me too," Sammy says. "I mean, also."

"Okay, so no guns." When Sammy makes a whining noise,

I holster my pistol and add, "Silence is golden, and bullets are precious."

This show of restraint will surely win Dr. Bill's favor.

I pull the tire iron from the base of the jack, spinning it in my hands, and take a step toward Jun. I'm still on my backswing when he falls to the ground, like a damsel fainting. He used to be a pretty good zee, for a ten-year-old. But he's been a wimp since last summer, when I accidentally whacked him with a shovel in a camping drill. I don't know what his problem is. He was barely bruised, and *I* was the one who lost five dessert points.

"One down!" Sammy calls, bouncing on the car roof.

I wait for Kalyn to come to me, enjoying her shamble. She's been wearing makeup lately, going for a zee look. Not enough to freak the grown-ups out, just little smudges of ash beneath her eyes. It makes her look wiser, somehow, like she knows what a joke this all is—the drills, Dr. Bill, our whole broken little tribe.

I don't rush. For the next few seconds I don't have to hide that I'm looking at Kalyn. I can gaze straight into her dark brown eyes, and the world gets shiny again.

She gazes back at me with a cool zee stare, but there's a smile playing on her lips. I want to ask her what she's thinking, even if we're in front of everyone. I want to stand here and let her bite me.

But Dr. Bill is watching, and a few shambled steps later she must die.

I heft the tire iron, getting a solid grip with both hands, sharp end pointed at her. With a giant step I thrust it forward like a spear. The point stops two inches from her left eyeball, but Kalyn doesn't blink. She gives me a little drama as she drops, sputtering like a zee with a tire iron jammed through its brain.

So there we are: Kalyn lying in a crumpled dead-looking heap, Jun with his hands behind his head, like it's movie night and I'm the star.

I pretend to wipe the tire iron off. "How's my back?"

"Two down!" Sammy yells, bouncing up and down on the car roof. "Stains for brains!"

I glance at Dr. Bill, whose expression is all about Sammy's dessert points draining away.

"Yeah, but how's my *back*!"

"Oh, right." Sammy spins around, still bouncing as he checks our three-sixty. And suddenly the rusty metal under his feet is bouncing with him. His zee-killing dance has stumbled on the Ford's natural frequency . . .

The next few seconds unroll in slow motion. The jack folds, popping like a match snapped between two fingers. The car's rear end thumps down in the dirt, and Sammy's arms are wheeling. The dropped shotgun smacks barrel-first off the hood, the metal *boom* so loud I flinch, thinking for a second the gun's gone off.

Sammy spins in place once, then tumbles off the far side. . . .

The thud of him landing sounds like a punch in the stomach. Everyone runs over, Kalyn and Jun reanimating to scramble across the dirt behind me.

Sammy's on the ground, his eyes shut, his neck at a weird angle.

Kalyn bends over him—much too close. "Are you okay?"

He doesn't say anything. He looks twisted and broken and very wrong.

Dr. Bill pulls Kalyn away, practically throwing her across the dirt. I taste panic and vomit in the back of my throat, but my hands do the right thing and draw my pistol. And I'm thinking, *Fuck, fuck, fuck—it isn't even loaded.*

But I aim at his head anyway.

Sammy opens his eyes and makes a gurgling noise.

"Rrrrrrr . . . kupuch!" he says, then busts up laughing.

We're all staring down at him, Dr. Bill and me with pistols drawn, and Sammy's laughing like an idiot. Like a moron, like a pathetic fourteen-year-old waste of gravity.

But not like a zee.

"Got you, dorks," he finally says.

Dr. Bill holsters his gun. "Yeah, you got us. And you, my friend, have lost *all* your dessert points!"

The words come out quietly, but are as serious as teeth marks. This shuts Sammy up for a moment, but then he's laughing again.

Why shouldn't he? Sammy hasn't been outside the wire since he was ten. He's never pointed a gun at a real zee. He's never seen anyone turn in front of his eyes. So this clearing in the swamp, this rusted-out Ford, these drills—what are they supposed to mean to him? What are they supposed to mean to any of us?

It's not worth pretending, even for the promise of canned chocolate pudding or pears in syrup. Maybe Sammy has finally realized what Jun and Kalyn and I have known for ages, except he's brave enough to say it out loud.

Or maybe he's just totally high.

2.

The thing is, we live on a pot farm.

Not that we're drug addicts or anything; we plowed under most of the original crop when we got here. We weren't looking for pot, just safety and sustenance.

The safety part was easy. We'd traveled past plenty of places with thick zee-proof walls: prisons, army bases, airports, gated communities. But those all had people in them in the before, so they were swarming with zees. On top of that we needed to plant our own crops. Aircraft runways and prison yards make for pretty crappy farmland, and we had only one season's worth of precious cans to learn how to grow food.

So that was our problem: most high-security establishments don't have farms in them, and most farms don't have big-ass fences around them.

That's when the beautiful Alma Nazr, our most awesome zee slayer and my previous crush, had her brainstorm. Back in the before, she was a federal marshal, wasting bad guys instead of dead guys. She'd been assigned once to a secret farm in Mississippi where the government grew pot for research purposes. In the last few years of the before, the states were legalizing medical marijuana. So the feds were making the farm bigger and the fences around it taller, just in case one day they wanted to sell the stuff.

So the wise grown-ups of our tribe led us southward, saying unto themselves, "Primo farmland, primo barbed wire, and maybe even some primo weed!"

Dr. Bill claims that last part didn't come into it, of course. It was all about safety and sustenance. But he also says that the wire will last forever, that chocolate can grow in Mississippi, and that one day we'll learn to inoculate for zee bites, or maybe even cure the six billion.

Dr. Bill is generally full of shit. Just like the rest of them.

3.

That night I'm spying on Kalyn again.

She always goes to the same place along the wire, where two fences meet at an acute angle, a pie slice jutting out into the swampland around the farm. Alma says it's because the wire follows the old property lines exactly. It's weird how the whole planet was divided up into little pieces back in the before, every square inch owned by one of the six billion.

These days there's just two kinds of real estate: ours and theirs, human and zee.

Kalyn's standing almost where the fences meet, so close to the wire that Dr. Bill would crap his pants if he could see her. He makes us use the words "arm's length" in practice sentences a lot, and yells if we don't put the apostrophe in, like bad punctuation will get us bitten.

Kalyn is definitely within arm's length of the wire, maybe elbow's length. But the chain-link is woven pretty tight, so it's only fingers sticking through, along with a few tongues and broken jaws and loose bones. She's not even wearing a pistol.

Some of the grown-ups stood like that in early days—right by the wire or close to a limbless zee—to "desensitize" themselves. But then one day a very pregnant Mrs. Zimmer reached out by accident (or committed suicide by zee), and the grown-ups made the arm's length rule.

I crouch there watching Kalyn for a while, the darkness falling around us, the bugs in the swamp starting to buzz, and I tell myself a story. I imagine her long black skirt caught by some withered stick-thin hand. Kalyn looks down in horror, but it's too late to pull away. She stumbles and her arms wave around, and so her billowy sleeves are snagged by all those bony fingers. I run to her rescue, appearing out of nowhere to slash her clothes right off her.

And she falls into my arms.

"Allison?" she says back here in the real world.

I am busted.

I stand up, wondering how she spotted me. She hasn't even turned around.

"Oh, hey." I'm all casual. *Yeah, just passing by. Not spying on you in some non-world-repopulating girl-crush way.*

"Thought that was you," she says.

Thought *what* was me? I wasn't making a sound, and even if we don't bathe much anymore, it's not like she can smell me over the zees.

"Yeah, it's me. What are you . . . doing?"

She turns around, her smile catching moonlight. "Waiting for you."

Okay. The world is definitely getting shiny again.

As I walk into Kalyn's pie-slice corner of fence, the zees all shuffle to face me, like they've gotten bored with her. The metal flexes with their shifting weight, the chain-links grinding. Except for the insect buzz, the night is quiet.

I can still remember right after the before, when the zees made a gargling noise whenever they saw us. Now they're too dried out, Dr. Bill says.

It's nicer this way.

Kalyn's looking at me, her pupils huge in the dark.

"Anyone you know?" I ask. It's an old joke, but it gives me an excuse to glance away into the crowd, arm's length from the intensity of her stare.

"No, never," Kalyn says, and turns back to the faces pressed against the fence.

Her ash-smudge makeup is more careful tonight, like she's made an effort for the zees. I know how weird that is, but it's not like there's much else to get fancy for. No one celebrates birthdays since the shed with the calendar marks burned down, and the parties weren't much fun anyway. The liquor's been gone for ages (and I never got any of it), the precious Ping-Pong balls are all broken, and the dartboard's green with mold.

Movie nights are a big deal, I suppose, since we only run the generator once a month these days. But Kalyn dressed up for . . . this.

Is it to perfect her zee impersonation? To desensitize?

I don't care which, as long as I get to stand here, closer to her than the zees pressed in around us. She's so close that her hair moves when I breathe.

Breath's length, and my heart's beating like I'm on the other side of the wire.

"Do you think Alma's right?" she asks.

"That Sammy's a waste of gravity?"

"No," Kalyn says. "About the other thing."

"Oh . . . us all dying."

Last year when Dr. Bill had the squirts from a dented can of beans, Alma Nazr was in charge of us for a whole week, the epicenter of my crush on her. She showed us how to crack skulls with police batons, how to reload a shotgun with one hand, and explained why we were doomed.

More zees come to the wire every day. We don't know why. In the early days we thought sound drew them to the living. But there's no way they can hear us from the other side of the swamp, and yet they come. They just know we're here.

Alma says it's only a matter of time before there are too many. Enough to crush the fence. Or to stack themselves higher than its uppermost coil of barbed wire, like rain forest ants using their own bodies to cross a river.

So we should leave soon, before the crush gets too thick to drive through. Before the roads get any worse, especially here on the rainy kudzu-choked Gulf Coast. You can already see the asphalt breaking down outside the front gate. If we wait too much longer, we'll have to walk out shooting.

And bullets aren't forever.

Dr. Bill came back to teaching early, still sickly and squeezing crap-farts into his pants. Alma wasn't supposed to say that stuff to us kids, I guess. She probably wouldn't have, except that the other grown-ups had stopped listening to her. They can't imagine ever going outside again.

Even Dr. Bill, for all his drills and shouting, never talks about leaving.

And the thing is, the grown-ups are right. If we roll out of those gates now, the zees will eat us in five minutes.

Alma's right too, of course. The wire can't last forever.

Doomed if we do, doomed if we don't.

But I decide to sound strong. "Don't worry. The zees won't break through."

Kalyn sighs with disappointment. "So we're stuck in here forever?"

"Well . . . no. Not that either." Here at breath's length, I want to say whatever she wants to hear. "What I mean is, we'll have to leave *way* before the zees crush the fence."

She turns to me, her eyes bright. "Really?"

"Sure." My mind is scrambling. "Sooner or later, something random has to happen."

"Um, random how?"

"Like . . . a tornado."

Kalyn laughs, opening her hands to the triangle of sky above us. "You mean it'll scoop up a bunch of zees, then drop them inside? Like a rain of frogs, but zombies?"

"Okay, maybe not a tornado. But what about a major hurricane? They come around every ten years or so. That could pull this fence up. Then we'd *have* to leave."

She nods slowly. "Everything random is inevitable. You just need enough time."

I'm nodding stupidly, because our eyes are locked again. It's much better than the zee stare she gave me that afternoon, and this time no one's watching.

I wish there were a drill for this. Step one: take her shoulders?

But I look away again. "We should start having tornado drills. Dr. Bill would love that."

"Yeah, he would." Kalyn snorts a laugh. "But he won't like it when the zees come raining down."

"Step one . . . kiss your ass good-bye."

"Maybe, maybe not." She reaches for the fence.

My fingers circle her wrist. Her skin is cool in the night air. "Quit that."

"Does it make you nervous?"

"Um, yes. Because it's kind of *insane*." I squeeze her hand, remembering Mrs. Zimmer growing paler every hour until they finally put her in the isolation hut. "You could get bitten. Don't you want to be around for the inevitable rain of zees?"

"Mmmm," she says softly. "That's the weird thing. I already did."

4.

I stand there for a moment, her hand in mine, the insect buzz growing louder in my ears. I'm not sure what she just said.

"Um, you've already seen a rain of zombies?"

"No. I already got bitten."

"Very funny."

Kalyn drops my hand and stretches out her left arm, rolling up the puffy black sleeve of her shirt. Her forearm gleams with moonlight, darkened by a purple scar in the shape of a nine millimeter shell.

"Right there."

I shrug. "Looks like you cut yourself on a can of peaches. Dessert points of evil."

"That's not from metal. I was standing right where you are, looking straight up at the sky. Remember back in the before, how there were, like, . . . a few hundred stars? And now there's so many, like the souls of the six billion all flew up there?" She runs a finger across the scar. "I sort of got dizzy thinking about them. And I took a step sideways, with my hand out so I wouldn't fall."

Kalyn reaches out toward the fence, and I'm frozen, watching her. Her hand is too close to one of the ruined faces—finger's length—but the zee doesn't react at all.

It's looking at me instead.

"Scratched it pretty bad," she says. "On bone."

"When was this?" My hand is on my pistol.

"A month ago."

Relief runs through me in a shiver. "You cut yourself on the wire, then."

"It wasn't metal. It was bone."

Kalyn reaches out to grab my shoulders. I pop the button on my holster, but she's only steadying me. I'm inches from the fence, dizzy from all this. She pulls me closer to her.

"Be careful."

"Quit fucking with me, then!"

She shakes her head, hard. "I felt like shit at first, and puked up meals for two days. I was going to tell everyone, I swear. But then I felt better."

I take a deep breath, reminding myself that this all happened a month ago. Her scar is old and dry; the ones that turn you never have time to heal.

"Then it was psychosomatic. Or you got infected with something else. A bad can of beans, like Dr. Bill."

"But I feel better now, Allison. Not just well—*better*." She does a spin in the narrow space, her skirt flaring out to brush against the fences. "You have to try it."

"Try it?" My mouth feels as dry as a zee's. "You want me to stick my hand out there?"

"No, silly. You'd turn. Whatever got inside me must be pretty scarce, or we'd have seen it before."

"Seen *what* before?"

"Cowpox. Think about it, Allison. Out of all the mutations churning inside the six billion, there must be one that's cowpox."

"Cowpox?" I remember the word from Dr. Bill's vaccine fantasies, but I'm too shaky to put it together.

She explains slowly. "In the old days people who milked cows never got smallpox, because they'd already been infected with *cow*pox. It's close enough to make you immune, but it doesn't kill you. It's a natural vaccine."

"Bullshit," I say. "I mean, yeah, I remember all that. But why would it happen *now*? After everyone's already *dead*?"

"Anything random is inevitable," she says, as serene as a

prayer. "You just need enough time, and billions of zees carrying trillions of variations, until that lucky mutation pops up."

I shake my head. "But why would *you* get it?"

"By accident, Allison." She shrugs. "Accidents happen. I almost fell over, and something bit my hand. So I can leave here if I want. Want to come?"

I turn and walk away from the wire, from the zees straining to get us, from Kalyn's madness.

But five seconds later I drift to a halt, processing what I've been seeing while staring into her eyes—she's not wearing makeup. That's not ash; it's something underneath her skin.

And something else . . . She said it's been a month since she was bitten. And how long since I started noticing her? Suddenly started seeing her, like a switch flipped, and I forgot all about Alma and the girls in the dirty pictures on the rec room walls.

Like something lucky came along and made Kalyn *better*.

A cool hand settles on my shoulder.

"They'll kill me if they find out," she says simply. "But I know you won't freak out and tell them."

"Trust me, I'm freaking out."

Kalyn turns me around. "I *do* trust you, Allison, because you saw it in me. From that very first day, you noticed. That's why I chose you to join me."

"Join you?" I force out a dry laugh. "How's that supposed to work?"

"It's inside me now." Kalyn reaches down and pulls a precious sewing needle from the hem of her dress. She holds it between her thumb and middle finger, the pointy end resting against her fingertip, not breaking the skin yet. "One drop, to start."

I stare at my own fingers, then at her. I'm about to explain that noticing her was something completely different. But she leans in and kisses me, like it's not two different things. Like it's all wrapped up at tongue's length—my obsession and her mutation and a way to leave the wire behind.

Kissing her isn't wet and slippery, like I've always imagined it. Her mouth is fever-hot and dry. Her breath draws me in and spins me dizzy. I cling to her so I don't fall over.

When we pull apart, the needle has broken her skin.

Kalyn smiles and squeezes her finger so a drop wells up, black and shiny in the moonlight. She hands the needle to me.

I still don't believe any of this, I tell myself. Her illness was psychosomatic, so her *betterness* has to be too. She scratched herself a month ago and didn't die from it, and in this piece-of-shit postapocalyptic pot farm, that much luck is enough to make anyone ecstatic. It was enough to make her beautiful.

So why not play along? Maybe she'll kiss me again.

I take the needle, lick it, and stick it home. I watch the blood well up from my middle finger, as shiny as hers in the moonlight.

We press our wounds together for a while—blood's length.

And then we kiss some more.

That night I throw up my chocolate pudding.

5.

It feels like the flu at first, my whole body responding to an invasion. My joints ache and buzz, like the swamp bugs are eating the insides of my kneecaps. My skin is on fire. Nothing stays in my stomach, not even water. I puke up every trickle of saliva I swallow, becoming dry and silent, like the zees.

My brain is buzzing too, wondering if Kalyn has it wrong. Maybe it's not the virus inside her that's lucky. Maybe it's *her*. What if she's immune, a carrier like Typhoid Mary? I'm blood sisters with Zombie-fucking-Mary.

Which means I'll turn, and they'll put a precious bullet in my head like they did with Mrs. Zimmer.

I lie to the grown-ups and say I haven't been anywhere near the wire, and they decide it's food poisoning. With no airplanes to bring us new flus, it's all food poisoning these days. Or maybe an infection from a cut, but our last amoxicillin went bad two years ago, so all they can do is keep me hydrated. Someone's always with me, forcing me to drink water that I'll only puke up. They keep me in the isolation hut where Mrs. Zimmer died, even though food poisoning isn't contagious, and they try not to make a big deal about the pistol on the bedside table.

You can't be too careful, after all.

But why isn't Kalyn here? She could have volunteered to watch me. Is she as worried as I am that she got it all wrong?

On the second day I'm still puking, and Alma Nazr comes in and strips me in a no-nonsense way, looking for teeth marks. Dr. Bill watches with a shotgun pointed at the floor. Alma's hands feel hot on my skin, like she's the one with a fever. She turns me around and around, going over every inch of me, like in the dreams I used to have.

She doesn't notice the pinprick on my middle finger.

But I can see it, the little purple circle where Kalyn and I mingled at blood's length. The rest of me may be turning cold, but that one spot stays warm and tingling.

On the third day everyone relaxes a little, the pistol disappearing from the bedside table. No one's ever taken three days to turn, so it must be a dented can or some mundane infection.

They don't notice that mosquitoes have stopped biting me.

I'm seeing things. There are flickers in the corners of my vision when I puke, and at night I can see the tribe sleeping around me, even through my eyelids, even through the walls. Human bodies are hot sprays against the cool of night, like fireworks on a dark horizon. Every night they're more spectacular, the relentless little engines of their heartbeats astounding me. Five days after my infection I can see them in the daylight, even halfway across the farm.

Slowly I start feeling . . . better.

And one night when no one's watching, Kalyn comes for me.

6.

She takes me to the tree house, the watchtower overlooking the front gates. The grown-ups never use it anymore, but we do.

"I'm so sorry," Kalyn says for the fourteenth time. We're sitting cross-legged, and her fingernails are scratching at the wooden floor on either side of her. "But I was scared you'd turn."

"*You* were scared? How do you think I felt?"

"I didn't know it would be like that, Allison. I only puked

after meals." She leans forward, taking my hands. "No one even noticed I was sick."

"Well, that's just *more* annoying." But instead of pulling away I squeeze her hands tighter. "I thought I was going to die."

"I know. I heard you moaning." Kalyn sighs at my expression. "*Yes*, I came by. But I was afraid to go in. Like, if Dr. Bill saw you and me next to each other, he'd figure out what we were."

She reaches up and traces the smudges under my eyes. My infection is a deeper color than hers. A pair of black eyes, like I've been fighting demons in my dreams. Her fingers are cool against the heat beneath my skin.

"You're so pretty now," she says.

For a moment I wonder what she means by pretty "now." I can't complain, though. Kalyn only flipped my switch five weeks ago. Before she was infected, I only wanted Alma. But Alma seems like a different species now, just like the other grown-ups, broken and stuck in the before.

And she'd kill me in a second if she found out what I was. Any of them would. They didn't make it this far by being gun-shy.

"Did Dr. Bill notice your eyes?" Kalyn asks.

"Yeah, he noticed. He said that puking can burst blood vessels. Said it should go away in a few weeks."

"Don't worry. It'll never go away." Her hand falls from my face, takes the collar of my sweatshirt and draws me near. Our lips press together.

This time my mouth is as dry as hers. Water tastes foul now, but I'm thirsty for the fireworks inside her. She isn't showering sparks like the others, but something serene and endless flickers inside her. It's deep blue, like the hottest part of a flame.

The fireworks must be how the zees find us humans, why they stack up outside the wire, waiting for a stray finger poking out, or a hurricane to pull up the fence. And that's why Kalyn and I can leave anytime we want now—we aren't so dazzling anymore. We look more like the zees outside the wire, with their mean, unwavering little lights.

We're something halfway between, eternal but not rotten. On the way to the tree house, Kalyn made me stick a finger out, and none of the zees even glanced at it.

"I'm sorry I got scared," she repeats after we pull apart. "That always happens when I kiss someone the first time."

"Always happens? Hah. You were, like, *eleven* back in the before."

She gives me the smallest smile. "Maybe I've kissed someone since then."

I stare at Kalyn, making a mental list of everyone on the farm. Even including the people who've died since we got here, everyone's so old. Except . . .

"Not Sammy?"

She nods.

"When?"

"It was only one kiss, *ages* ago, and it only made me giggle." She smiles. "Jealous?"

"Of that waste of gravity? Hardly."

Her eyes close, and she moves closer. "Glad to hear that won't be a problem."

We're like that for a while longer, then we lean out to look at the six billion stars. Their twinkle is stronger than it used to be. Maybe my vision is sharper, or maybe aliens live on those faraway planets, and I can see their fireworks too.

I'd make a great astronaut now. No water, no food, ageless.

"Do you think we'll live forever?" I ask. "Like zees do?"

Kalyn turns from the stars and sighs. "Dr. Bill says they don't, because of that thermodynamics law. Just because they're dead doesn't mean they won't run down. Eventually."

"What's there to run down? Their hearts don't even beat."

She puts her cool palm against my neck. "But yours does."

"I guess so. Too bad." I can feel it pulsing where her hand rests—so much for being an immortal astronaut. I'm going to die, or run down, so I'm wasting time here on this stupid farm. "What should we take?"

"Well, we don't need food. We don't need guns. We can go into the cities for new clothes." Kalyn smoothes her homemade dress. "*Real* clothes, finally. So we don't have to take anything."

"Sure. But I want a car—the Benz. That's the only one that still runs."

"You want to drive?" Kalyn thinks that's funny, like she wanted to shamble out of here. "Do you even know how?"

"Alma showed me once. It's easy. You point the car and push the pedals down." I was paying more attention to Alma than the car, but it didn't look too hard. "There are no other cars on the road, not moving ones anyway."

It feels a little weird to be talking about stealing the Benz, because it's Alma's favorite. But it's not like she's ever leaving here, not without the rest of them. And they've got their pot plants and their movie nights, their stacks of cans going bad. All those dessert points carved into the dining room wall.

They'd never trade all that for freedom.

Even if we infected them, they'd probably just shoot themselves. Kalyn hasn't even mentioned the possibility, and I'm certainly not going to. I want her all to myself, forever.

And I want to learn to drive before the highways break down into asphalt puzzles.

"Okay, Allison, we'll steal the Benz. Four days from now."

I smile, thinking of a few favorite things I'll bring. Maybe one of Alma's raid caps, black with DEA in big silver letters on the front. Her raiding days are over, and mine are just beginning. Might as well bring a few guns, in case we run into living people who annoy us.

"Why not tomorrow? Why not *now*?"

"Four days."

My smile disappears. "Why?"

Kalyn sighs, pulling back a little. Her fingers drum on the wooden floor. The wind steals through the open windows of the watchtower, sending a cool finger down my spine.

Then she says it:

"Because I don't want Sammy puking in the car."

7.

It's four days later and we're stealing the car—all four of us.

Yes, that's what Kalyn was doing while I puked and moaned

and *almost died*. She was going after Sammy, bleeding her pox into him. Kissing him.

Ages ago, my ass.

And then, two days after our conversation in the tree house, we both decided we couldn't leave Jun behind. He's only ten; we can't leave him here alone with the broken grown-ups.

He changed the easiest of all of us, the little twerp. Didn't vomit once.

So here we are, stealing the Mercedes-Benz together, one big happy semi-zombie family . . . and we are total crap.

"Push the clutch down first," Sammy whispers, like anyone outside the barn can hear us. Can't he *see* that no one's awake? All those little fireworks are tucked safely in their beds, hearts slow and steady.

"Cars don't have clutches, dork." I shift into drive, keeping one foot down hard on the brake.

"The Ford does. Dr. Bill showed me how it worked."

"Yeah, but the Ford's, like, a hundred years old. This is a *real* car."

"Then why isn't it *moving*?" Kalyn moans.

"Um, maybe because I don't want it to? The barn doors are closed."

We both look at Sammy, who jumps and rolls, then scuttles across the dirt floor. He stares at the barn door lock, which isn't locked—no one locks doors here. An open padlock is just stuck in the hasp, holding it together. We wait while he figures it out.

Like I said, we are crap.

It's lucky we don't have to bring anything. We would've been crap at packing, too.

Sammy swings the doors open, and I consider plowing past him, just crashing through the front gates and leaving him behind. If the grown-ups wake up quickly enough, they can probably stop the zees from pouring through the hole.

But I couldn't do that to the Benz's paint job. Alma spent hours keeping it beautiful while the other cars slowly fell apart.

As my foot comes off the brake, we ease into motion. Kalyn grasps my knee, like everything's fine between us again. Like she didn't lie to me about kissing Sammy and everything else.

Well, everything except the pox itself. She was telling the truth about that, and how it feels amazing to be one of us. Every day is better.

I touch her hand. We're really leaving.

I remember this feeling now, from back in the before and the early days outside the wire—how you can just sit in a car and watch the world slide by.

Sammy jumps onto the hood as we ease from the barn, and soon we're rolling past the rec hall and the isolation hut, waving good-bye. Past the storage sheds and the barrels full of rusty-tasting rainwater. Past the crappy Ford in its muddle of deflated rubber and broken safety glass.

Toward the wire.

Jun giggles in the backseat, even though we've threatened to dump him if he makes a single noise. He was six the last time he sat in a moving car. This must be like Disney World for him.

A little spray of fireworks flares in a corner of my vision.

Someone's waking up. Even on a hot night with the insects buzzing, the sound of a car engine is alien enough to stir the brain.

I let the brake up a little more, pointing us at the front gates.

Fifty feet away Sammy jumps off the hood and runs ahead. Kalyn scrambles out the door to follow, the hem of her long, impractical dress bunched in one hand.

This is the part of our escape plan we've actually thought about—getting through the front gates without letting in a thousand zees. We owe the grown-ups that much. Even if they're broken and pathetic, they kept us after our parents were eaten.

Sammy's climbing up the chain-links, right at the split between the gates, while Kalyn slides the heavy bar across. The zees shuffle around a little, but they're not looking at her—they're watching the fireworks behind us. More people waking up.

I hear a shout, and roll forward again.

The bar falls to the ground just as I reach the gates. The Benz's bumper scrapes chain-link, pressing the mass of zees backward. Kalyn jumps onto the hood, and Sammy swings overhead as the gates slowly open.

Behind us, bright little showers of consciousness are erupting from every building. I hear them shouting, calling to us, trying to understand.

The zees push back against the gates, but the Benz is stronger, rumbling beneath me as I let the brake out more. I'm driving with two feet, which Alma said was bad. But I'm scared to take my feet off the pedals, like I'll never find them again down there in the dark.

A gunshot sounds. Probably an alarm, but I wonder if they'll think of shooting out our tires. They must think we've gone insane.

The Benz finally slides through the open gates, zees pressed against every window. On the hood Kalyn is reaching out to pat their heads, and a nervous sound comes from the backseat.

"It's okay, Jun," I say sweetly. "They can't hurt you anymore."

The zees are surging now, trying to get past the car and at the people waking up inside the wire. But the implacable Benz crowds the opening, and the zees at the sides will only push the gates shut once we're through. A few may slip past, but Alma will make short work of those. I can see her sparking back there, very awake now, an automatic in each hand.

The gates scrape down the flanks of the Benz, ruining her paint job. Then we're past, and I see the gates swinging closed. I shift into reverse and complete the work of shutting them, grinding zees beneath my tires.

This is where Sammy comes in. He rides the gates closed, then lashes them together with chain and padlock. It should hold until the grown-ups get the bar back on.

He lands on the car roof with a *thump*, and I wince a little. I hope he doesn't start bouncing.

I shift back into gear and push ahead again. Not too fast, with one passenger on the roof and another on the hood. Not with a hundred zees pressing against us, still trying to get at the gates.

The road is worse than it looked from inside, broken down

by rain and kudzu. We bump along at a shambling pace, and I notice that some of the zees are following.

They stare in through the windows at me, rotten hands sliding against the glass. What if we were wrong, and suddenly they want to eat us?

But they aren't trying to get Kalyn. They don't even look at her, just keep plodding alongside the car like mourners following a hearse.

Another shot rings out, and a zee head splatters across the right backseat window.

"Shit!" Sammy cries, rolling from the roof onto the hood. "They're trying to save us!"

"Morons," Kalyn says, ducking low.

More booms rumble behind us, and the back windshield splinters.

"Stay down, Jun!" I shout, wondering if they're shooting *at* us.

Maybe they've figured out somehow what we've become. Sammy and I got food poisoning at the same time, and Dr. Bill can't have missed that all four of us have dark circles under our eyes.

Then a hail of gunfire erupts, fully automatic, like the air ripping itself in half, and the back window shatters completely. They *are* shooting at us!

Because we've changed? Or because they'd rather have us dead than eaten alive, or turning into zees and shuffling back to haunt the wire.

But then it gets much stranger. Through the splinters of

back window glass, I see fireworks winking out behind me. Humans are dying back there. . . .

They're shooting at each other now.

It's Alma—I can feel her blazing, stopping the other grown-ups from stopping us. Or it's all just mayhem, caused by the gates opening for the first time in four years. A few zees slipping through has shattered everyone's fragile sanity, and they're spilling precious bullets like it was the old days. Back when every moving thing was a target.

We've made a mess, it seems.

But the sheltering crowd of zees presses closer around the Benz, taking our hits for us. If one falls, another takes its place.

We bump painfully along the broken highway, the gunfire fading behind us minute by endless minute.

And after a while the night is silent again.

8.

Kalyn is sitting up on the roof, her heels banging on the front window. Sammy sits beside her, his sneakers dangling across my view. I can hardly see the road, and I can't tell what they're doing up there.

They better not be kissing.

A piece of jumbled asphalt bangs against the underside of the floorboard, but the Benz keeps rolling. The zees, of course, keep shambling.

We drive for a while.

The road should get better, sooner or later. Maybe not in this swamp, or anywhere in rainy Mississippi. But we'll find deserts eventually, with roads lying flat and empty in the sun.

It occurs to me that a map might have been useful. Where did they sell maps back in the before? Gas stations? Bookstores? I can't remember.

Sammy's face appears, hanging upside down against the front windshield. He taps the glass.

I roll down my window.

"You guys should see this!" he yells.

"See what?" Jun asks.

"Just come up here. Both of you. I'll drive!"

I doubt he knows how, but I'm happy to switch places. I put the Benz into park, the zees shambling to a halt around us. They hardly notice when I open the door and step out. They're waiting patiently, still staring straight ahead.

Jun scrambles over the seat and comes out my door, sheltering himself from the zees behind me.

Sammy doesn't bother to touch the ground, just crawls in through the passenger-side window. So I lift Jun up, shut the door, and then climb on top of the car.

Kalyn is standing there in her long black dress, so we stand beside her.

The moonlit road behind us is full of zees.

Thousands of them choke the narrow road between the trees, the line stretching back to the gates, at least two miles. Most are still pressing ahead, like they haven't gotten the word yet that we've stopped. The floodlights at the farm gates have snapped on, showing the zees back there still flowing after us.

"What the fuck?" I ask.

"They're following us," Jun says.

"No kidding. But where did they all *come from*? There weren't this many at the gate!"

Kalyn nods. "There weren't. So they must be coming from along the wire. It's like they're all on one long piece of string, and we're pulling it."

I see what she means. The wire must be five miles around. So if all the zees that have showed up over the last four years follow us, there'll be tens of thousands in the line. A parade of zombies.

"But *why*?" Jun asks.

"Yeah, really," I say. "They don't want to eat us. So why?"

Kalyn doesn't answer, and we stand there silently until Sammy manages to get the car in gear. We stagger for a moment, then squat there on the roof, still facing backward.

The Benz makes its slow way along the broken road, bumping even worse now that Sammy's driving. The swamp trees grow denser, brushing our heads with cool fingers now and then. The shadows of moonlit leaves flicker across our zombie hosts.

Finally we lose sight of the farm, the last glimmer of floodlights disappearing around a bend. But the zees don't turn around.

"Why are they following us?" Jun asks again.

Kalyn says, "Maybe they were bored too."

"Bored?" I say. "They're *zees*, Kalyn. All they do is stand around."

"Yeah, but they were watching, too. All day. So they must

know that nothing was happening back there. Those drills, those fucking dessert points, all those people going bad like beans in a dented can." Behind Jun's back she takes my hand. "It's death back there, tornado or not. But the zees have *us* now."

She turns around and sits, dangling her feet against the front windshield again. Jun and I join her, facing the empty, broken road ahead.

I wonder if she's right.

It's their planet, after all. The six billion have all the real estate, except for a few little patches that are slowly dying. Maybe they want to do something with it but don't have any ideas.

They aren't strong on ideas, the zees.

Sitting there gets annoying fast, with Sammy smacking into every bump like the waste of gravity he is. So I stand up on the roof again, figuring my knees are better shock absorbers than my butt. I put my hands out for balance and spread my feet a little bit apart, like I'm surfing in extremely slow motion, the parade of zombies in my wake.

And then I realize that Kalyn's right, and everyone else was wrong—from the government scientists in the early days to the know-it-all radio stations who faded out one by one. The six billion didn't really die. Their lights are still burning around us, however dimly. I mean, just *look* at them.

Maybe they're not as mindless as we thought, or so dedicated to turning every last human into one of them. Like Kalyn says, they were just bored, waiting for something better to happen.

And that better thing is us.

"Princess Prettypants"

Holly: Unicorns exist in pop culture as bubble-gum colored, riding over rainbows, full of sparkles and stars. They have been made into stickers, posters, and adorable toys. Unicorns of this type are often used as symbols of pure happiness, hope, and awesomesauce.

You might see this kind of unicorn on the T-shirts of hipsters, in ironic animated videos, and as an antidote to unpleasantness on blogs.

Meg Cabot's "Princess Prettypants" is a fantastic and hilarious send-up of a unicorn of this type, dropped into the very real world. It also features one of my favorite explanations for why unicorns have recently come back from extinction.

Justine: Once again Team Unicorn cannot hide its shame. Little known fact: Meg Cabot is a zombie lover and would have much preferred to be on Team Zombie, but Holly was getting desperate for Team Unicorn members so Meg succumbed to pleading and bribery and joined Team Wrong, er, I mean, Team Unicorn.

The result is yet another anti-unicorn story. Which even the ringleader of Team Unicorn admits is a send-up of the dread rainbow-farting unicorn. It seems churlish to mention that Team

Zombie has won this contest hands down. So I'll just say that my pity for Team Unicorn continues to grow.

Holly: It is sad to me that Team Zombie is apparently without any love of irony.

Princess Prettypants
By Meg Cabot

It was Liz Freelander's seventeenth birthday, and so far it could not have been going worse. It had been her turn in debate, and the critique notes she got back afterward—which were supposed to be anonymous, but of course Liz recognized everyone's handwriting because she'd been going to school with almost every single person in the class since the first grade—ranged from the banal to the offensive:

Good job! And happy birthday, Kate Higgins, who had the same birthday as Liz, wrote, adding a winking smiley face.

Kate was the most well-liked girl in their grade, revoltingly perky even at eight in the morning when school started, and always screaming the loudest at the Venice High Gondolier pep rallies.

And yet Kate had never asked Liz to come to a single one of her birthday parties, even though she threw one every year in the huge media room in the basement of her parents' house in town. Everyone else in their entire grade was invited, to dance to Kate's parents' incredible sound system, play pinball and air hockey, and more recently to drink themselves to unconsciousness in Kate's parents' newly installed outdoor hot tub.

At least three girls had passed out in the hot tub at Kate's birthday party last year. Liz knew this only because her (now ex-) boyfriend Evan Connor had taken her to the party, *not* because she'd been personally invited.

Kate obviously just felt Liz would prefer to celebrate her birthday with her own family and friends.

The only problem with that was, with the exception of Alecia and Jeremy—and Evan, of course, but not anymore, because of what had happened in his dorm room last month— Liz had hardly any friends to speak of.

And when Liz opened the next critique note from her debate, she remembered why:

Debate on success of second-wave feminists? Sucked. But don't worry, you got your two biggest POINTS across: ^ ^ *!!! Love them titties!!!*

Liz felt her cheeks heat up. What the hell? She looked down at her chest. She was wearing an embroidered top her aunt Jody had bought for her on her last trip to the Adirondacks, where she'd gone last year with her friends from the Society for Creative Anachronisms. It was a very girlie top—like all the other things Aunt Jody gave her as presents, since Aunt Jody seemed to think Liz was still seven years old and fond of all things pink and princess-themed—and Liz wouldn't have considered wearing it to school if all the rest of her clothes hadn't been in the wash. It was pink, and not at all revealing, especially considering the fact that Liz was wearing a bra . . .

. . . except that, thanks to the brutally cold temperature at which the sadistic staff of Venice High School kept the building in order to lower their electricity bill, Liz could see both her nipples poking out under the soft cotton fabric . . .

. . . something Douglas "Spank" Waller apparently found objectionable, since he'd seen fit to mention it in his critique.

Liz recognized his handwriting immediately from the notes he'd frequently left on the windshield of Evan's truck after school last year. The two of them had been on the football team together, and—despite the fact that Evan was a year older and, in Liz's opinion, light-years more sophisticated and mature—they'd been as thick as thieves. Liz was sorry to say she'd spent more than a few nights cruising around downtown Venice in Evan's truck with Evan, Spank, and whichever cheerleader Spank had been dating that week, stealing lawn ornaments out of people's yards, then hiding them in Liz's barn.

(Although she'd often been bothered by the immorality of this, Evan, a soon-to-be poli-sci major, had argued that this was a socially conscious act. Most lawn ornaments—such as plaster geese wearing frilly aprons and bonnets or yellow raincoats—were hideously ugly, and by removing them from the public eye, Evan felt that he and Liz and Spank were beautifying the community . . .

. . . an argument that Liz had tried, unsuccessfully, on her friend Jeremy, when he'd found out about her nocturnal activities and expressed disapproval.

"No," Jeremy had said, shaking his head. "Nice try, Liz. But it's actually called petty theft."

After reading Spank Waller's note, Liz turned in her seat to throw him a look of disgust.

He caught her glance, winked . . .

. . . then ran his tongue lasciviously around his lips.

Liz had to look away, or risk feeling the tacos and Coke she'd had for lunch in the school cafeteria come back up. She

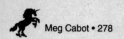

then turned her attention resolutely back to Mrs. Rice. Mrs. Rice was, as every student in the whole school knew, completely unqualified for the job of teaching eleventh-grade debate, since she'd actually been hired to be a PE teacher.

But that's what came from living in a town the size of Venice.

Venice, Indiana, that is.

Liz sighed. Should she really have been surprised that her birthday was going so horribly? The day had started off badly, with her father joking about the "big surprise" that would be waiting for her in the barn when she got home from school.

Had Liz's family been like any other, she'd have gotten her hopes up that the metallic blue Volkswagen convertible Beetle she'd always wanted would be parked in the barn when she got home, with a big white bow on the hood.

But because she knew her parents couldn't afford extravagant gifts on what they'd been pulling in lately from the family farm, she was certain what she'd find in the barn after school instead would be something more along the lines of a laptop—most likely purchased secondhand and refurbished by her dad, who was good with his hands.

Or possibly, if she were very, very lucky, her parents would give her back her old cell phone.

Which was extremely unlikely, considering the bill she'd run up earlier in the semester, texting Evan every night. She'd sworn she'd pay her parents back, and she was still trying to, working weekends at the Chocolate Moose downtown and babysitting whenever she could.

Mostly, though, she was just mad that Evan, after first

making her promise not to date other people while he was away at his freshman year of college, and then swearing that he himself wouldn't desert her for some gorgeous religious studies major with naturally straight hair, had immediately gone and done so . . .

. . . but only after stringing her along for seven weeks and twelve hundred dollars in texting fees (not to mention what Liz had paid for birth control pills the whole time they'd been going out . . . at least until she'd walked in on him and that religious studies major in bed together during a surprise visit to his dorm one weekend. She'd paid another two hundred and eleven dollars in round-trip bus fare for that pleasure).

She should have known her day wasn't going to go well when, that morning on the bus to school, Jeremy and Alecia had decided it would be funny to sing "Happy Birthday" to her.

But even that couldn't have prepared Liz for Spank's critique note during Mrs. Rice's fourth-period debate class.

"He's disgusting," Liz said to Alecia when school finally let out and they were heading toward their bus. Spank had just elbowed past them on the way to his Camaro in the student parking lot.

"Douglas?" Alecia pushed her glasses up her nose. "I thought you two got along. Besides, I think he's hot."

"That's because you were homeschooled for nine years," Liz reminded her.

Spank chose that moment to notice whom he'd just pushed out of his way. He turned around and yelled, "Is it a half hour before dusk? Because Freelander's got her headlights turned on!"

"Oh, hey," Alecia squealed excitedly, grabbing Liz's arm. "He's talking to you!"

"Yeah," Liz said. "He's making fun of my nipples, all right? Just keep walking."

"Oh." Alecia smiled. "My mom says if a boy teases you, it means he likes you. Isn't that right, Jeremy?"

Jeremy made a face. "Uh," he said. "No. In the case of Spank Waller, I suspect it just means he's an asshole."

Alecia's lower lip jutted out. "That's not what my mom says. She says that's why Douglas is always making fun of my glasses and the fact that I wear such long skirts every day. Because Douglas likes me. And, Jeremy, you shouldn't swear."

"Yeah," Liz said, shooting Jeremy an aggravated look. "That must be why, Alecia. Because he likes you." She grabbed her friend by her enormous backpack and steered her onto the bus. Jeremy, standing behind them both, gave Liz a perplexed look.

"Why'd you tell her that? You know Spank Waller doesn't give a shit about her."

"She's got a crush on a guy who in a million years will never like her back," Liz said. "She has so little. Let her have her fantasies."

"Whatever," Jeremy said with a shrug as he swung himself up onto the bus behind Alecia. "Spank thinks he can do whatever he wants, without consequence. Because he can, and as you know perfectly well, he has. His dad is the sheriff. Believe me, no good will come of encouraging Alecia's crush on him."

Liz rolled her eyes as she followed Jeremy to a seat toward the back of the bus.

"Guess where I'm going tonight?" Jeremy said as he sat down.

"Let me guess," Liz said. "Kate Higgins's house, for her birthday blowout."

"No. Your house. Your mom's having a surprise party for you."

Alecia, seated in a row ahead of theirs, squealed, "Jeremy! You weren't supposed to tell! Now you've ruined the surprise."

Liz blanched. "Tell me you're shitting me."

"Liz!" Alecia looked scandalized.

"*High School Musical* theme," Jeremy went on. "Your mom got matching hats and plates and everything half off from Party Kaboose. You know Debbie Freelander always knows what the cool kids are into."

"Seriously," Liz said. "This has been the worst day of my life. I think I'm going to slit my wrists."

"Liz!" Alecia cried. "Don't even say such a thing! You know you can't get into heaven if you kill yourself. And I want to be your best friend in heaven, too, the same as I am here on earth."

Liz looked at Alecia and wondered if she could somehow get a new best friend for her birthday, in addition to a whole new life.

"Seriously," she said to Alecia and Jeremy. "Don't come."

"Oh," Jeremy said, "I'm coming. I want to see your expression as you cut into your Troy 'n' Gabriella cake."

"Don't," Liz said as the bus engine roared to life. "Please. Not Troy 'n' Gabriella. You're making that part up."

"I'm going to come," Alecia assured her. "But if it's all right with you, I'm going to leave a little early, to go to Kate Higgins's party. My mom said she'd pick me up from your party to take me to Kate's. Because I've never been to a party with boys before. No offense, Jeremy. I mean, I don't really think of you as a boy."

"None taken," Jeremy said amiably.

Liz, however, frowned. It wasn't, she knew, that Alecia didn't think of Jeremy as a boy. It was just that she and Alecia had spent so much time over the years in Jeremy's company, either at his house or one of theirs, that it wasn't easy to think of him as someone in whom one might have a romantic interest, even though he was their age.

Lately, though, Jeremy had started to look quite . . . There was no other word for it: *manly*. He'd taken up tae kwon do, and breaking large piles of wood with his hands and feet had caused some undeniable muscle definition.

How could Alecia have failed to notice? Liz had been going out with someone else for almost a year, and even she hadn't been able to help noticing.

"So," he said when they got off the bus at their stop. "See you at your surprise party later?"

"Jeremy!" Alecia yelled from the bus window, where she was eavesdropping on their conversation. Her stop wasn't for another few miles. "You're ruining it!"

"See you then," Liz said unenthusiastically, and turned to start down the long gravel driveway to her house.

Though she looked for unfamiliar tire tracks, a clue that her family might be hiding a metallic blue Volkswagen convertible Beetle in the barn, all Liz found when she got home was her mother busily preparing for the surprise party that Liz knew no one but her friends Alecia and Jeremy would be attending (and Alecia was leaving early for Kate Higgins's party).

Her mother bustled around the kitchen with a happy air, forbidding Liz from having an after-school snack ("You'll spoil your appetite for dinner!"), while Mr. Freelander, done suspiciously early with work around the farm for the day, sat in the living room pretending to be engrossed in a spy novel, giving Liz the barest of glances as she breezed by on her way to her room. She didn't remark on the *High School Musical* party blower in the front pocket of his shirt.

Upstairs Liz discovered her younger brother, Ted, hanging around the open door to her room.

"You're really going to like your birthday surprise," he said.

"Is it a car?" Liz asked, knowing it wasn't.

"No," Ted said. "It's better."

"There's nothing better than a car," Liz said.

With a car of her own, she'd no longer have to get up at five forty-five in the morning in order to catch the bus at six thirty, often in the pitch black of predawn, in order to make it to school by eight.

With a car of her own, she could go into town whenever she wanted and not be dependent on her parents for rides.

With a car of her own, she could finally get the hell out of Venice.

It wouldn't have to be a nice car. It could be any old car. Jeremy had been working on the engine of his grandfather's old Cutlass Supreme, trying to get it running again, just so he could have something of his own to get around in, something other than his mother's minivan or his father's pickup (which both his parents were notoriously stingy about loaning).

It was horrible, living as far out of town as they did and not having cars of their own.

"It's way better than a car," Ted assured her.

Liz looked at him tiredly as she pulled her homework out of her backpack.

"Nothing's better than a car," she said.

"This is," Ted said.

"Would *you* want it?" Liz asked.

"Yes," Ted said.

Her parents were definitely, Liz thought, giving her old cell phone back to her.

When her mother called her down to dinner, Liz went into the bathroom and applied a quick layer of lip gloss, then fluffed out her hair. Not that she cared about how she looked in front of Jeremy. Why would she? It was only Jeremy.

But still.

She came down the stairs, through the living room, and into the dining room. Her mother had taped streamers that said *High School Musical 3!* on them all around the room. In the middle of the big round dining table was a sheet cake that, just as Jeremy had assured her, had a photo image in icing of Troy Bolton and Gabriella Montez from *High School Musical* on it. Liz's mother, father, and brother all stood on the far side of the table, wearing *High School Musical* party hats and blowing *High School Musical* party horns excitedly as Liz walked into the room. Not far from them stood Jeremy and Alecia. Each of them wore a party hat as well, though Jeremy was wearing his around his face, so it looked like an enormous beak.

Alecia was squealing anxiously, "Surprise! Surprise! Aren't you *surprised*, Liz? You didn't suspect a thing, did you?"

"Oh, my gosh," Liz said. "I'm so surprised."

"Are you really, honey?" Mrs. Freelander asked, beaming. "I was sure you knew. When you wanted something to eat and I wouldn't let you because I said it would spoil your appetite for dinner, I was sure you knew."

"Heck, no," Liz said. "I had no idea."

Liz could tell Jeremy was smirking behind his party hat by the way the skin around his eyes was crinkled up. He refused to take the hat off his face, even when Ted begged him to show him a *bandal chagi*, or crescent kick.

"No tae kwon do in the house, boys," Liz's mother reminded them as she came out of the kitchen with her homemade lasagna, Liz's favorite. This was rapidly consumed on *High School Musical* paper plates. "I know you're too old for *High School Musical*, honey," Mrs. Freelander explained. "But it was that or *Dora the Explorer* at Party Kaboose. And I wanted your party to be festive. A girl only turns seventeen once."

Then it was time for cake and presents. Liz took a big bite out of Zac Efron's head. Her gift from her parents was a brand-new cell phone. It was the kind that, unlike her old one, could download music, take pictures . . . everything.

"Oh," she said, genuinely surprised. "Oh my God, thank you."

"Happy birthday," Mr. Freelander said in his quiet way.

"You've been working so hard to pay us back what you owe, so your mother felt—"

"You're on the family plan," Mrs. Freelander interrupted him. "So don't be texting . . . well, everyone you know, all night long."

She knew what her mother meant by "everyone."

"No worries," she said. *Everyone* was long gone. She and Evan hadn't spoken since that day she'd paid that surprise visit to him, walked into Edmondson 212A, seen him in the arms of that girl, and walked out again without another word.

Liz stared down at the bright orange gadget. If this was in her hand, then what was in the barn?

In the distance a car horn honked.

"Oh, I'm sorry," Alecia said, apologetically gathering up her jacket. "That's my mom. She's picking me up to go to Kate's. Liz, here's your present. It's a gift certificate to buy music for your phone. Your mom told me what you were getting."

"Oh, great," Liz said. She gave her friend a hug good-bye. "Thanks so much. Have fun!"

"I will," Alecia said. She had an excited sparkle in her eye, and was wearing her best denim ankle-length party skirt and Mariah Carey party T-shirt. Her waist-length hair had been brushed to a sheen. "Bye!"

Alecia left, slamming the screen door behind her. Mr. Freelander looked disturbed.

"Where's she going?" he demanded.

"Kate Higgins's house," Liz explained. "You know she has the same birthday as me."

"Is that where everyone is?" Mr. Freelander asked, looking

around the empty dining room. He asked the same question every year on Liz's birthday.

"Yes, Dad," Liz said.

"Well, she's going to miss the main attraction," he said. "Her loss."

"I thought this was it," Liz said, waving the phone.

"That's not it," Mr. Freelander said. "It's in the barn."

"Oh, honey," Mrs. Freelander said to her husband. "Not yet. She's not done opening all her other gifts. She hasn't opened her gift from Jeremy."

"It can wait," Jeremy said, finally removing his party hat and setting it on the table. "I want to see what's in the barn."

"You won't believe it," Ted said. He grabbed Liz by the arm and started tugging on her. "Come on. You have to see it. Come on. *Now*."

"All right, all right," Liz said, laughing and putting the phone into her pocket. "I'm coming."

It was a long walk from the house to the barn. It had gotten dark out, though there was enough light from the moon and coldly glinting stars to see by. The frogs in the pond were calling to one another so loudly that it was almost a shock compared to the peaceful quiet of indoors. The air smelled sweetly of cut grass and of the wood Liz's father was burning in the fireplace in their living room. Jeremy strolled companionably beside her, his hands in his pockets, as the grass soaked their boots.

"So," he said as they watched Ted and Liz's parents hurry before them, eager to get to the barn and open the doors to show Liz her surprise. "Do you think it's a car?"

"Ted says it's not a car," Liz said.

"It's got to be a car," Jeremy said. "Why else would everyone be so excited?"

"I don't think they can afford another car," Liz said.

"You deserve a car," Jeremy said.

Inexplicably Liz felt herself blush in the cool night air.

But it was different from when she'd blushed in debate class after getting Spank Waller's note. Then she'd blushed with anger and shame.

Now she was blushing for a different reason entirely.

But before she had time to think about that, her parents were throwing open the barn doors, and Ted was yelling, "Look! Look! Aunt Jody sent it! She got it on her latest trip with SCA!"

As soon as Liz heard *that*, she lowered her expectations accordingly, and stepped into the barn.

At first Liz thought her aunt Jody—a widow who lived with her four cats and a Pomeranian named Tricki in a gated community outside of Boca Raton—had bought her a large white horse for her birthday.

Which would not have been the most unusual thing in the world, since Liz did, in fact, live on a farm and had once had a pony named Munchkin.

But although Liz had loved Munchkin very much, it had been some time since she'd expressed any enthusiasm whatsoever about owning another horse, Munchkin having passed on to that great pasture in the sky some ten years earlier.

It would not have been unlike Aunt Jody, however, to have

mixed up age seventeen with age seven and think there'd be nothing little Liz would want more than another horse to replace the dearly departed Munchkin.

But what stood in the barn in front of Liz, glowing softly with a kind of inner luminescence that seemed to have nothing to do with the electrical light from the bulbs hanging from the rafters some thirty feet overhead, was not a horse.

Or rather, it had a horse's body—a huge one, nineteen hands high at least—sleek, with a gorgeous white flowing mane and tail, soft blue muzzle, and purple fetlocks.

But jutting from the center of its forehead was a twisting, sparkling, three-foot-long lavender horn.

What her aunt Jody had sent Liz for her birthday was, in fact, a unicorn.

"You," Liz could not help blurting out, "are shitting me."

"Elizabeth!" her mother cried in horror. "Watch your language!"

"But that," Liz said, raising a finger to point at the monstrosity that even now was lowering her noble head to tear at some of the grass poking from Munchkin's old hayrack, "is a *unicorn*."

"Of course it's a unicorn." Her father walked over to the animal and gave her a hearty smack on her gleaming white flank. The unicorn tossed her head, her silky mane flying, and let out a musical whinny. Liz got a whiff of her breath, which smelled like honeysuckle. "Your aunt's always sent you the nicest gifts. Remember that Christmas she sent you that hand-stitched pink fairy costume with the tutu and the detachable wings made out of real swan feathers?"

"Jesus Christ, Dad," Liz said, flabbergasted. "I was five years old. This is *a live unicorn.*"

Both Mrs. Freelander and the unicorn eyed Liz reproachfully. Neither of them seemed to appreciate her colorful language. The unicorn in particular seemed disapproving as she delicately chewed the hay Liz's father had left out for her. Her irises were the same lavender color as her horn. There was no denying it. They were as sparkly as Troy Bolton's.

"What's wrong with it?" Mr. Freelander asked defensively. "I think it's great. Who else do you know who's ever gotten a unicorn for their birthday?"

"Uh, no one," Liz said. "Because they don't exist." Even Mrs. Rice, the worst teacher in the world, knew *that.*

"That's not true," Ted said defensively. "They've been extinct for a while, but they're making a comeback. It's all in Aunt Jody's card. Right, Dad? Give her the card, Dad."

Mr. Freelander fumbled in his back pocket for something, then drew out a folded card that he passed to Liz. She opened it, and saw that it was as lavender and glittery as the unicorn's eyes. On the front, next to a cloyingly sweet picture of an unnaturally thin blond girl in a white dress sliding down a rainbow, it said, *To my beautiful niece, on her seventeenth birthday.*

Opening the card, Liz read, *Happy birthday to a niece who brings sunshine wherever she goes! A niece like you is . . .*

> *Naturally nice*
> *In her own loving way.*
> *Each smile that she smiles*
> *Can brighten a day,*
> *Especially when she's so pretty and gay!*

What the hell, Liz thought. She read on.

Just want to tell you what a joy it is to have you for a niece, and how much beauty you bring into the world, Liz! her aunt Jody had written. *That's why when I saw Princess Prettypants at the renaissance fair I attended with my friends from the Society for Creative Anachronisms last month in the Great Smoky Mountains, I just knew I had to buy her for you. I know how much little girls adore their fairies, princesses, and unicorns!*

Holy shit, thought Liz.

And I know you'll make sure Princess P. gets a good home! Aunt Jody went on. *Unicorns have been extinct for years, of course, but a few Appalachian breeders have discovered how to clone them from a perfectly preserved specimen found in a peat bog and are hoping that they'll make a comeback. Soon they should be as popular as VCRs!*

There was some other writing at the bottom of the card, but after Liz got to the words "Princess Prettypants," she could barely stand to read any farther.

Princess Prettypants?

Liz glanced over at Jeremy. Seeming to sense that she was looking at him, he raised his gaze to meet hers.

Liz mouthed the word she was thinking: *eBay*.

Seriously. With any luck she'd be able to make enough selling Princess Prettypants to pay back all her debts and put a down payment on a decent car. Not a metallic blue Volkswagen convertible Beetle. She'd given up on that dream. Just any car. She'd take any amount of money to get rid of Princess Prettypants, who at that moment let out a delicate fart, filling the barn with rainbows and the scent of night-blooming jasmine.

"Oh, sweet Jesus," Liz said.

"Elizabeth Gretchen Freelander," her mother said sharply.

"Well, I'm sorry, Mom," Liz said. "But I'm seventeen years old, not nine."

Mr. Freelander sighed.

"I told you she wouldn't like it, Debbie," he said sadly to his wife. "I told you."

Liz bit her lower lip. What was wrong with her? Here her aunt had gone to all this trouble to ship what was probably a very expensive gift all the way from the Great Smoky Mountains.

The least she could do was be gracious about it.

"No," Liz said. She noticed that everyone, including the unicorn, was staring mournfully at the barn floor. "No, I like it. I do."

"No, you don't," Ted said. He too was still looking at the floor, kicking at some feed that had fallen from the hayrack. "You think you're too cool for unicorns. Well, you know what?" Ted lifted his gaze, and Liz was surprised to see that there were tears gleaming in his eyes. "Evan Connor's little brother, Derek, told me you guys are the ones who've been going around stealing plaster geese out of people's yards!"

Mrs. Freelander gasped. "No!"

Liz's father just shook his head, looking as ashamed of her as he had the first time he'd ever heard her use the F word upon accidentally stubbing her toe.

"That's right," Ted raged on. "I found them hidden in Munchkin's old stable! Eleven of them, all in different fancy outfits! I wasn't going to say anything because I thought you were cool, Liz. My cool big sister. But now that I know you don't like unicorns, I don't think you're cool at all. And . . . and one of those plaster geese you stole was from my best friend Paul's house. *And his mom wants it back!*"

With that, Ted ran from the barn, obviously hoping to escape before the tears gathering in his eyes started to stream down his face.

"Oh, for God's sake," Liz said in the ensuing silence, during which Princess Prettypants shifted her weight, causing one of her glittering silver hooves to strike against the barn floor and set off a musical chime that sounded not unlike the bells that rang out from the Venice Freedom Evangelical Church every Sunday morning.

"*You're* the one who's been stealing plaster geese from people's front yards?" Mrs. Freelander asked, giving Liz an incredulous look. "The one they reported about in the Police Beat in *The Venice Voice*? That was *you*?"

"Mom," Liz said, shame causing her own eyes to suddenly fill with tears. "I'm really sor—"

"Young lady," Mrs. Freelander interrupted furiously. "*You are grounded. Forever.*"

And, wrapping her sweater more tightly around herself, she stormed from the barn.

Mr. Freelander sighed and gave the unicorn one last pat on the rump.

"Now you've gone and upset your mother," was all he said as he turned to follow his wife. "And she worked so hard to give you that nice party."

When he was gone, Liz walked over to the stall door across from where Princess Prettypants was standing and sank down

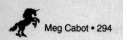

onto the floor, leaning her back against the rough wood. She wiped her eyes with the back of a wrist.

"Ted's right," she said, swallowing against the sudden lump in her throat. "I'm not cool."

Jeremy crossed over to Princess Prettypants and laid a hand on her shimmering neck. She rolled her purple-eyed gaze toward him appreciatively.

"Selling her on eBay is kind of extreme," he said. "Don't you think? She seems like a nice horse."

"Unicorn," Liz corrected him. She *really* wanted to cry now. Jeremy hadn't disagreed with Ted about her being uncool.

Well, Jeremy had always made it perfectly clear that he hadn't approved of her going out with Evan—and, okay, that *had* been a mistake . . . almost as big a mistake as stealing the plaster geese. She'd been dazzled by Evan's good looks and his fancy TAG Heuer watch and the fact that he'd wanted her. *Her*, out of all the girls in school.

She had failed to notice the small fact that Evan, like his friend Spank, was a douche bag.

She stretched her legs out in front of her, then crossed her ankles, keeping her gaze on her feet in order to concentrate on not crying.

"It's not a horse," she said, her voice tear-roughened. "It's a unicorn. And do you have any idea how much money I still owe my parents?"

"Well," Jeremy said. His voice didn't sound too steady either. "This should come in handy, then. Here."

He dropped something into her lap. When Liz looked

down, she saw through her tear-blurred gaze that it was a key. With a red ribbon wrapped around it.

"What's this?" she asked.

"Your birthday present," he said.

She glanced up at him questioningly. He appeared to have something more he wanted to say to her, but he was holding himself back for some reason. . . .

Which was unusual, because she'd always thought they could tell each other anything.

Well, *almost* anything.

"I gotta go," he said suddenly, removing his hand from the unicorn's neck. "I'll see you around."

"But . . ." She looked down once more at her present. "What's it a key to?"

But when she glanced up again, Jeremy had already left the barn.

She didn't get up to go after him. She didn't want him to see her cry, any more than he, apparently, wanted to stick around to talk.

She sat there in the barn, staring first at her present from Jeremy and then at her gift from Aunt Jody, wondering how she could have messed up so badly. The unicorn continued to munch on the hay, occasionally turning her head to eye Liz. Her horn sparkled in the overhead light. Her hooves glimmered like Cinderella's slippers. When she shifted her weight, they made a sound like the purest of bells ringing out on Easter Sunday. Every once in a while, she farted.

It sounded like a beautiful wind chime.

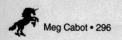

And smelled like a florist's shop.

Liz wondered what on earth she was going to do. Not just about the geese, and her parents, and Ted, and Jeremy.

But about the fact that her aunt had given her a unicorn—a *unicorn,* for God's sake!

Finally she heard footsteps outside the barn door, and thought, with relief, *It's Jeremy. He's come back!* She clutched the key he'd given her. *What could it be to? His heart? Oh, don't be such a dork, Freelander. What's* wrong *with you today?* She climbed to her feet. She was a little amazed at how her heart swooped in eager anticipation of seeing him again. What was up with *that*?

But it wasn't Jeremy who came in the barn doors. It was Ted.

"Your friend Alecia's on the phone," he said grouchily. "She sounds upset. That's the only reason I came out here and got you. So you owe me one."

Liz's heart came crashing down to earth the moment she recognized that it was her brother and not her next-door neighbor stepping out of the darkness.

But she said, "Listen, Ted. I'm sorry about the geese. And you're right. I'm not cool. I'm the opposite of cool. And I'm going to give Paul's mom's goose back."

"You don't even know," Ted said as the two of them walked back to the house, "which one is hers."

This was true. Which one had been Paul's mother's? The one in the polka-dot bonnet and apron? Or the one dressed as the Venice High School Gondolier? How would Liz ever figure it out?

"Hello?" she said, picking up the phone in the kitchen. Her parents had retired to the den to watch a television drama about sexual predators who preyed on young attractive women in New York City.

"Liz?" Alecia sounded as if she were in tears. There was a lot of screaming and loud music in the background.

Liz pressed the phone more tightly to her ear. "Alecia? Where are you? Are you at Kate's party? Are you okay?"

"No," Alecia said. She was crying. "I mean, yes, I'm at Kate's party. But, no . . . I'm not okay. S-something happened. C-could you come get me?"

Liz's grip on the phone tightened. "What?" she said. "What do you mean, something happened?"

"I'm sorry to interrupt your b-birthday." It was hard to hear Alecia with the sound of all the partying in the background. "And to call on the house line. I didn't have your new cell number. It's just that Sp-Spank—"

Fear clutched Liz's heart.

"Spank what?" she asked through panic-deadened lips. "Tell me, Alecia. What did he do to you?"

"He . . . he . . . Oh, *Liz.*" Alecia let out a sob. "Please just come get me. As soon as you can."

They were disconnected. Either Alecia had hung up or . . . Liz didn't even want to think what else could have happened. It was Spank they were talking about, after all. *Spank thinks he can do whatever he wants, without consequence,* Jeremy had warned her. *Because he can, and as you know perfectly well, he has.*

After staring at the phone in her hand for a second or two,

Liz hung up and went into the den where her parents sat, her hands and feet feeling strangely numb.

"Look," Liz said, "I know I've been a total bitch tonight. And I'm really sorry. But Alecia's in trouble and I need to borrow the car to go get her."

Mr. Freelander tore his gaze away from the screen to look at her. "What part of your mother telling you that you're grounded forever did you not understand?"

"But," Liz said, her voice rising, "it's Alecia! I think Spank Waller may have done something to her. Something bad."

"Why should we believe you?" Liz's mother demanded. Her eyes, Liz saw, were pink-rimmed from crying, and her cheeks were flushed. "You're a thief! A liar and a thief. All those nights you were out with that Evan Connor, saying you were going bowling or to the movies, you were really robbing people! Robbing our friends and neighbors! I don't know how I'm going to show my face in town anymore, knowing my daughter— my own daughter—is the one who has been stealing everyone's plaster geese. And they've been in Munchkin's stable this whole time."

Liz's stomach clenched. She felt awful. She realized that Jeremy had been right all along . . . that what she'd managed to convince herself had been a community beautification plan just might, to everyone else, have been theft of rightful property. Maybe she'd never have to go to juvie for it because Spank had been involved, and his dad would see to it that they'd never be prosecuted.

But that didn't make it any less wrong.

"I'm sorry," Liz said, her eyes filling with tears. "I'm going to return the geese. I really am. But please. Please. I think something bad might have happened to Alecia. You have to let me borrow the car."

Mrs. Freelander turned her head back toward the television screen. Liz's father looked Liz dead in the eye and said, enunciating carefully, "No. If Alecia's in trouble, call her mother. She can go pick up Alecia."

Liz thought about doing as her father said. She really did. It made sense to call Alecia's mother.

But if Alecia had wanted her mother to know what had happened, wouldn't she have called her?

Only she hadn't. She'd called Liz.

Alecia wouldn't, Liz knew, tell her mother what Spank had done to her. She'd be too embarrassed. Alecia's mother was a good woman, but she was deeply religious, which was why she'd insisted on homeschooling Alecia for nine years, only agreeing to let her daughter attend the public high school when the burden of homeschooling Alecia in addition to her seven younger siblings had become too much.

And there was no use calling the police. In Venice, Indiana, Spank Waller's father *was* the police. In Venice, Indiana, Spank Waller was king.

No. This was all Liz's fault. *Believe me, no good will come of encouraging her crush on him,* Jeremy had said when Liz had agreed with Alecia that Spank liked her. Why, oh why, had Liz ever opened her big mouth? Whatever had happened was all Liz's fault.

After stumbling back outside, and being greeted by the almost deafeningly loud ribbits and chirps of the frogs from the pond, Liz stood there, wondering what to do. Should she steal her parents' car? No. She was already in big enough trouble.

And then she heard it: the peal of Princess Prettypants's silver hooves ringing out as she shifted in place in the barn.

It was crazy. It was insane.

Except . . . Well, she was technically a *horse*, wasn't she?

And horses were made to be ridden.

Liz ran for the barn. Princess Prettypants looked up, flicking her velvety ears forward as Liz came in, and letting out a gentle, musical neigh. The fragrance of night-blooming jasmine, which Liz had only smelled before on a trip to Florida to visit her aunt, filled the air. Princess Prettypants had yawned.

Well, that's it then, Liz thought.

Liz had no choice but to ride bareback. Munchkin's saddle, of course, would have been far too small, and besides it had been sold in a yard sale years earlier. Liz had ridden bareback a few times before, because Alecia's family had horses and sometimes when it was hot they rode them saddleless for fun.

But this was different. This was a stately, elegant unicorn that stood nineteen hands high (extremely tall, for a horse), with a three-foot sparkling horn and lavender eyes.

Then again, she also farted rainbows. So.

Since there was no stirrup for her to step into, Liz found a crate and, after setting it next to the unicorn, climbed on top of it and said, knowing Munchkin had always liked it when she'd spoken to him in a soothing voice, "Hello, Princess, er, Prettypants. I'm just going to climb onto your back now, if that's okay. And we're going to go on a little trip. Okay? Great. Here I—"

But when Liz laid her hands on Princess Prettypants's impossibly silky back to boost herself up, the unicorn gave a start, reared back, and darted quickly away from her, giving Liz an extremely insulted look with her now wildly rolling violet eyes.

"Whoa," Liz said, holding up both her hands to show she hadn't meant any offense. "I'm sorry. I didn't know. Honestly. It's just . . . I really need to get to town."

And then, before Liz knew what was happening, she'd broken down into tears. She was standing there in the barn, sobbing to a unicorn. A freaking *horse*. With a stupid *horn* coming out of its head!

"I'm sorry, but I've had a really bad day. And now my friend is in trouble. She has this crush on this bad guy, and I sort of encouraged it, and so it's my fault, and he did something to her at this party, and I've got to go to her and make sure she's okay, but my parents won't let me use the car, so—"

A second later Princess Prettypants calmed down. She tossed her head, stopped rolling her eyes, and gave a musical nicker.

Then, to Liz's utter surprise, she folded one foreleg beneath her, stretched the other out before her, and bowed elegantly in front of Liz, like a prima ballerina, with her horn tipped toward the floor and her lavender-eyed gaze on Liz as if to say, *At your service, madam.*

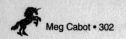

Liz stared at her, her mouth agape.

"Wh-what are you doing?" Liz asked, as if the unicorn could respond.

Of course Princess Prettypants said nothing, just stared at Liz patiently, clearly waiting for Liz to get on her back.

"Oh," Liz said, flustered. "Oh my God. Thank you so much . . ."

She climbed onto the unicorn. It was like sliding onto the back of the softest imaginable pillow . . . or like the fairy wings made from swan feathers her aunt had sent her for Christmas when she was five.

She was barely seated before the unicorn lurched to a standing position. Liz had to plunge her hands into the silky mane to hang on. Then, the strong back muscles beneath her moving powerfully, the unicorn turned and headed for the barn doors . . . so swiftly that Liz had to duck in order to keep from hitting her head on the top of the jamb.

"Hey!" Liz turned, and saw her little brother Ted coming toward the barn with an armful of apples, apparently for Princess Prettypants, stolen from the kitchen crisper. "Where are *you* going?"

"Um," Liz called down to him. "Just out for a ride. Tell Mom and Dad I'll be home soon."

"I thought you didn't even *like* Princess Prettypants," he said, looking suspicious.

"She's really growing on me," Liz called as the unicorn lurched into a gallop. "I gotta go. See ya!"

And suddenly, with Liz clinging to the unicorn's mane

for dear life, they were moving through the night-darkened countryside, Princess Prettypants cantering at an unbelievable speed—faster than any car Liz had ever traveled in—toward town. The unicorn apparently had no need of roads—or of Liz steering, or giving directions. She seemed to know exactly where Liz wanted to go, taking a direct route through fields, along the grassy medians of highways, through parking lots of shopping malls and cineplexes—her hooves making fiery sparks and a symphony of bell-like tones as they struck the pavement— and finally through other people's yards, simply hopping over anything that stood in her way, including walls, fences, and cars . . .

. . . causing a great many astonished looks, though traffic was generally light this time of night in downtown Venice.

Liz could only hang on and tell herself to remember to breathe as they flew past the people—and their hastily upraised cell phone cameras—they encountered along the way to Kate Higgins's house.

Liz completely understood their astonishment. She couldn't quite comprehend what was happening herself. She'd only had to picture the house where she needed to go, and Princess Prettypants—such a horrible name for such a noble creature!— was dropping her off there. True, they were coming up around the back . . . right up to the hot tub, into which no less than a dozen people seemed to be crammed.

But still, in no time at all Liz found herself behind the Higginses' downtown split-level colonial. Empty beer bottles were strewn all across the backyard. Loud music was pulsating from the house. People were milling around everywhere, some of them dancing, some of them laughing, some of them throwing up, but hardly any of them noticing the approach of a second birthday girl . . . this one on her new pet unicorn. Only one highly inebriated young man, who happened to be relieving himself upon a leafy oak tree near where Princess Prettypants slowed her pace upon her approach, cried, "Holy crap! A unicorn!"

He then promptly passed out in a heap behind some bushes.

Liz knew they had definitely come to the right place.

With a pealing neigh, Princess Prettypants bowed and allowed Liz to dismount. After she'd done so, Liz turned and extended both hands toward the unicorn and said, "Ummm . . . wait here, please?"

Princess Prettypants, giving the locale a skeptical glance, bowed her head and began to pull tufts of the Higginses' plentiful lawn into her powerful jaws and gnaw on it.

Satisfied that her ride was going to remain in one place for the time being, Liz crossed the yard, taking her cell phone from her pocket and dialing Alecia's number.

"H-hello?" Alecia asked when she picked up, not recognizing Liz's number.

"It's me," Liz said. "I'm here at the party. Where are you?"

"Oh," Alecia said, sounding grateful but still in tears. "Thank you. Thank you so much for driving over to get me!"

"No problem," Liz said. She didn't think it would be particularly useful at this point to mention that she hadn't exactly *driven* over. "Are you inside?"

"Yes." Alecia's voice sounded tiny and hurt. "I'm in the bathroom on the first floor."

"The bathroom?" Liz echoed.

"Yes," Alecia said again, in the same bruised voice. "And could you hurry, Liz? I think the people in line to use the toilet are getting kind of . . . angry at me. But I can't help it. I just can't come out alone. Not if *he's* around."

"I'll be right there," Liz said, and hung up, hurrying toward the house. As she went by the hot tub, she caught a glimpse of a number of naked chests. One of them belonged to Spank Waller.

Another, she saw, with a feeling that was akin to being run over—or how she supposed it must feel to be run over—belonged to her ex, Evan Connor.

Well, and why not? Why wouldn't Evan come back to town for the biggest party of the year? He was still one of Venice High's most popular graduates of all time, a golden boy who could do no wrong in most people's eyes. If a cache of stolen plaster geese were found in *his* parents' barn, everyone in town would just laugh it off.

Liz looked away, swallowing down a little bit of Troy Bolton icing–flavored vomit before she opened the back door and stepped into the house.

Inside, the music was pulsing even more loudly, and the house was so full of cup-holding, grinding bodies that Liz could hardly see where she was going. She managed to catch a glimpse of a line, however, and figured she'd find a door there leading to a bathroom. After what seemed like half an hour of elbowing people aside, she found the door, outside of which some extremely angry-looking girls, who obviously had to pee very badly, were yelling, "Open up! We gotta go!"

Liz went up to the bathroom door and tried the knob—it was locked, of course.

"Alecia?" Liz called, hoping Alecia would be able to hear her over the loud music and desperately shouting girls. "It's me, Liz."

Immediately the door opened a tiny crack. Liz saw Alecia, her eyes red behind her glasses, peering out at her.

"Hi," Alecia said, sniffling.

Several of the girls in line behind Liz, alert to the slightest motion of the door, pushed, trying to get inside to use the toilet.

But Liz pushed back, then snaked her way into the bathroom, and slammed the door, locking it.

When she turned to face Alecia, she saw that she'd sunk down onto the edge of the bathtub, and had her head in her hands.

Alecia, Liz saw with some relief, *looked* all right. All of her clothing was still on, and in no disrepair. Nothing was ripped or dirty or bloodstained.

True, her long hair was no longer brushed to a sheen. It was really messy, in fact. And her Mariah Carey T-shirt, of which Alecia was quite proud because she thought it was very stylish, was untucked, which wasn't really like Alecia.

But other than that, she looked perfectly presentable.

"Alecia," Liz said. "What's wrong? What happened?"

"I can't tell you," Alecia said, her long brown hair hiding her face. "It's too shameful! Oh, I've done the most terrible thing, Liz! You'll hate me!"

Liz knelt down on the bath mat beside her friend's feet.

"Alecia," she said, "you have to tell me. I went to a lot of trouble to get here tonight. You wouldn't even believe how much trouble if I told you. So you had better explain to me exactly what happened. I promise I won't hate you."

Alecia lifted her face from her hands and looked at Liz. Her tears had fogged the lenses of her glasses.

"It's just," Alecia said, her voice catching. "You know Douglas, right?"

Liz frowned. It took her a second to remember who Alecia was talking about. "You mean Spank?"

"Douglas," Alecia said. She'd always refused to call Douglas by his nickname, the origins of which were murky. "Well, when I got here, he acted really excited to see me. He said he wanted to dance. So we were dancing. Slow dancing! It was like a dream come true. I couldn't believe it. Douglas Waller had asked *me* to dance! I'm not anyone."

"That's not true," Liz said. She couldn't help remembering feeling similarly honored the first time Evan had singled her out . . . not at a dance but in their chemistry class, as his partner. It was only later that Liz realized this was because she was a chem whiz and he was anything but. "You *are* someone. But go on."

"It *is* true," Alecia said emphatically. "You're just saying that because you're my friend. But anyway, while we were dancing, Douglas whispered in my ear, 'Do you want to go somewhere to be alone?' I don't know what I was thinking, but . . . I figured it was because he wanted to kiss me. And even though I knew it was wrong, because he hasn't met my parents and we aren't engaged or anything—" Liz fought an impulse to roll her eyes. "I said . . . Oh, Liz, I said yes! And the next thing I knew, Douglas was taking me into a bedroom. I think it was Kate's. It had all these teddy bears everywhere—and we were kissing, and, oh, Liz, he started taking my shirt off! And I let him! I know it was wrong, but I did, it just felt so good."

Now Liz knew why Alecia's T-shirt was untucked. Feeling a little sick to her stomach and not wanting to hear any more—but knowing she had to—Liz said, "Go on, Alecia."

"This is where the shameful part comes in," Alecia said tearfully. "Although the whole thing is shameful, really." She took a deep, shuddering breath. "Once Douglas got my shirt off all the way, and I was standing there in my . . . my bra, he . . . he . . ."

"He what, Alecia?" Liz asked, prepared for the worst.

"He snapped a photo with his cell phone." Alecia buried her face back into her hands, sobbing. "Then he ran out, laughing!"

Liz knelt there on the bath mat, staring at her friend, perplexed.

"Wait," she said. "That's all he did? Kissed you and took a photo of you in your bra?"

"What do you mean, that's *all*?" Alecia lifted her face, looking furious. Two bright spots of red stood out on her cheeks, and her eyes, behind the lenses of her glasses, blazed. "He's going to send that photo to everyone! I'll be humiliated in front of the entire student population of Venice High! And what about my parents? When they find out—and they will—they'll yank me out and start homeschooling me again! I'm ruined! Don't you understand? Spank Waller has ruined me! And it's all my own fault for ever being stupid enough to think a guy like him could like a girl like me."

Alecia started to sob again . . . deep, heartrending sobs that Liz felt all the way to her core, like the bass of the music that was thumping outside the bathroom door.

Liz was relieved Alecia hadn't been physically hurt.

But remembering Spank's note from that morning—and what had happened in Edmondson 212A—she knew that that kind of hurt could be just as painful, in its own way.

She had to do something. What, she had no idea. But something.

Because, despite what Alecia thought, none of this was her own fault. If anything, everything that had happened to Alecia had been Liz's own doing. Jeremy's words still haunted her— *Believe me, no good will come of encouraging her crush on him.*

A sort of red haze descended over Liz's vision.

She put a hand on her friend's back.

"It's going to be all right, Alecia," she said.

"How?" Alecia moaned into her hands. "*How?* I can't go back to homeschooling, Liz. I love Venice High. I love it. The pep rallies. Even Mrs. Rice. All of it. But how is any of this going to be okay?"

Liz had no idea.

"I'm going to take care of it," she said, as if she did know what she was doing. Maybe some part of her did—some part that had been frozen, petrified in a bog since that day she'd walked into Edmondson 212A, a part that was finally waking up at the sight of Evan cavorting half naked in that hot tub like nothing had happened between them. "Come with me."

Liz got up and went to the bathroom door. She unlocked it, and a horde of girls dying to use the toilet came spilling in. Alecia, startled, had no choice but to get up and hurry out after her.

"Liz?" Alecia asked. "Where . . .where are we going?"

"You'll see," Liz said in a less calm voice as she made her way across what had once been Mr. and Mrs. Higgins's media room—which had now been torn apart and puked on by frenzied partygoers. "We're just going to have a little talk with Spank."

"Oh, no," Alecia said, her eyes widening. "I really don't think that's the best idea. . . ."

But Liz was already smashing open the screen door to the backyard with her fist. Outside, the moon was still high, and the stars still glinted coldly down from the dark sky.

But the air in downtown Venice didn't smell of cut grass or wood smoke the way it did on Liz's parents' farm. Instead it smelled of spilled beer from the keg in Kate Higgins's backyard and of chlorine from the hot tub toward which Liz was striding.

"Liz," Alecia said nervously. "Seriously. What are you doing?"

"It's okay," Liz said over her shoulder. "I'm fine."

"I don't think you're fine," Alecia said. "I just want to go home. . . ."

"Spank Waller," Liz said when she got to the side of the hot tub. Spank was crowded into it with five girls and six other guys, including Evan. The hot tub was made to fit only eight, so they were squeezed in there nice and snug. One of the girls, wearing a bright blue bikini and holding a cup of beer, was Kate Higgins.

"Oh, hey, Liz," Kate called cheerfully, giving her a wave. "I'm so glad you could make it!"

Liz ignored her. Why was Kate acting like she was glad Liz had come, when she hadn't even invited her? Kate was so fake. Liz would deal with her some other day.

She'd deal with Evan—who nearly choked on his beer and said, "L-Liz?" when he noticed her—later too.

"Spank Waller," she said instead. "You took an inappropriate intimate photo a little while ago of my friend Alecia without her permission. So I want you to hand over your cell phone. Now."

Spank, holding his cup of beer high in order to avoid it filling with foam from the jets, just laughed.

"No freaking way, Freelander," he said. "Nice nips, by the way."

Liz didn't have to turn around to see why all the people in the hot tub, including her ex, had suddenly started screaming and scrambling for cover. She knew without looking.

It was because a giant milk white unicorn had reared up behind her, angrily pawing at the air with its forelegs. Princess Prettypants had let out a neigh . . .

. . . only, this time, that neigh hadn't come out sounding like churchbells or a children's choir.

It had come out sounding like all the demons from hell, screaming in pain at the same time because someone had stoked the coals burning beneath their squirming pustular bodies.

Liz was pretty sure this was because someone had said

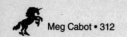

something to really piss off Princess Prettypants's mistress.

"Yeah," Liz said, feeling her hair flutter as one of those colossal silver hooves brushed just inches past her ear. "You might want to rethink your decision not to hand over your cell phone to me, Spank. Or my unicorn is going to smash in your face."

Spank sat frozen in the hot tub, the only person remaining in it. Everyone else had bailed, running for the shelter of the house or ducking behind nearby shrubbery. Evan was crouched next to the keg, gibbering like a monkey, his bare feet in two inches of muddy beer ooze.

Only Alecia had stayed where she was. Alecia's gaze was fixed not on the unicorn but on Spank.

"Not so high and mighty now, are you, Spank?" Alecia demanded, in a voice that was a little too high-pitched. "You said you were keeping that picture of me for your collection and that I'd better not step out of line, or everyone in school was going to get a peek!"

Spank said nothing. He was still staring up at the unicorn. Instead of the smell of night-blooming jasmine coming from her soft blue muzzle, the odor had turned to sulfur. And Princess Prettypants's lavender eyes had turned to stop sign red.

Liz just shook her head. This was all so sad and unnecessary.

Liz said, "Alecia. Go find whatever Spank was wearing when you two were dancing, and look in his pants pocket. The phone will be there."

Alecia pointed nervously at the unicorn, who was snorting and pawing at the ground, making a huge hole in the Higginses' lawn. The hole looked not unlike a grave.

"It's okay," Liz assured her. "That's not for you."

Alecia nodded and went to pick her way through the mud to the side of the hot tub. It took only a second or two for her to find what she was looking for. While she was gone, Liz found herself enveloped in another sulfur-scented cloud. She didn't take her gaze off Spank, who continued to stare at her in terror. She couldn't help feeling irritated. Clearly unicorns were not supposed to consume ordinary horse feed. She'd need to get in touch with her aunt Jody about Princess Prettypants's obviously unique dietary requirements.

"Here it is," Alecia said timidly, handing Liz Spank's cell phone.

"Don't give it to me," Liz said, stepping aside. "Put it there, where it belongs." And she pointed at the unicorn's massive front hooves.

Alecia darted another nervous glance toward Princess Prettypants.

But the unicorn only batted her long blue eyelashes demurely, as if to say, *Me? Hurt you? Never! I'm a lady!*

Alecia knelt and put the cell phone next to one of Princess Prettypants's gleaming silver feet.

Which the unicorn delicately lifted and, with a surgeon's precision, set down on the phone, obliterating it.

"Hey!" Spank yelled from the hot tub.

Liz shot him an annoyed look.

"Do you want to be next?" she asked.

"You can't go around doing that to people's personal property," Spank said, standing up. He was, she saw, wearing trunks, which were bright red and baggy.

Maybe it was because the trunks were red.

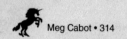

Or maybe it was just because he was Spank Waller.

In any case, Princess Prettypants, once the cell phone was crushed to her satisfaction, began moving in his direction.

"You can't just come in here, Freelander, and have your freak of a circus horse, or whatever it is, step on my phone." Spank was standing in the middle of the hot tub, pontificating to whoever would listen. "Do you know who my father is?"

It was at that moment that Princess Prettypants, coming around behind Spank, scooped him up by the bottom of his red swim trunks with her three-foot-long lavender horn and began to prance around, with Spank adorning her forehead like a live hood ornament.

"Oh," one of Kate Higgins's friends cried, wincing as they crouched with Kate behind her parents' barbecue grill. "Horned up the shorts!"

"That is twisted, Liz," Kate said, shaking her head. "You have one twisted unicorn."

"I know," Liz said, although of course she'd had no idea. She felt proud of her birthday gift.

The partygoers, beginning to emerge from their hiding places now that they sensed Liz's unicorn was otherwise occupied, produced their own cell phones and began to take photos of Spank's difficult situation.

"Hey!" Spank cried. "Stop taking pictures! Liz! Make your unicorn put me down! This isn't exactly the most comfortable position to be in. Look, I swear I won't do it again. I swear!"

Liz looked at Alecia. "Do you think he's learned his lesson?"

Alecia nodded. She looked considerably happier. She'd

stopped crying, and there was a tiny smile playing on her lips.

"I think so," she said.

Liz called to Princess Prettypants, "You can put him down now."

The unicorn lowered her head, and Spank fell to the ground, into the grave Princess Prettypants had dug for him beside the keg. A terrified-looking Evan got splashed with mud. He eyed Liz apprehensively, certain that he was next on her list.

"Liz," he said, holding his hands up, palms out, in front of his naked chest, which was flecked with spots of brown beer-soaked lawn. "I know how things might have looked that day in my dorm room. But you ran out before I could say a word in my defense. I was drunk. And she meant nothing to me. You've always been my everyth—"

"You," Liz interrupted him, "owe me fourteen hundred and eleven dollars."

Evan gaped at her. "What?"

"You heard me," she said. "That's how much you owe me. For texting fees, bus fare, and various sundries I don't care to discuss in public. Where's your wallet?"

Evan shook his head, his blue eyes wide. "Are you crazy? I don't . . ."

. . . *owe you anything* was what Liz was fairly certain he'd been about to say. But a snort from Princess Prettypants behind her caused him to modify that statement to a more benign, and slightly terrified, ". . . carry that kind of cash on me."

Liz realized he was telling the truth. He wasn't exactly going to lie when there was an angry unicorn behind her, glaring at him with glowing red eyes.

"Fine," she said, and pointed at his wrist. "That'll do."

Evan glanced down at his watch. "My *TAG*?" he asked. His voice broke with sorrow and disbelief.

Princess Prettypants took a threatening step forward. Evan quickly undid his watchband, saying, "N-no, it's okay. You can have it. You'll get at least that much for it."

Liz took the watch from him and dropped it into her pocket. She gave Evan a final, scathing look, wondering how she ever could have loved this person, who was not only a liar but had no honor either.

She must have stared at him a little too long, because Princess Prettypants stepped forward, nudging her horn toward his swim trunks.

"No, no," Liz had to say, grabbing the unicorn by the mane and steering her head away. Not that Evan didn't deserve it. "Whoa, girl."

Evan, looking pale, backed up, tripped on his own feet, and fell into the beer-soaked mud, much to the amusement of everyone present.

Spank, meanwhile, cried for someone to let him borrow their cell phone.

No one did. Instead everyone hurried to snap more pictures of Princess Prettypants. A few even took short films with their cell phones to upload later to their YouTube channels.

"Well," Liz said, conscious of there being many more things that she had to do in order make amends to everyone she'd wronged. "I have to go. Alecia, do you think you can get your mom to come pick you up?"

"Oh, sure," Alecia said. "This party is about to be over anyway." She pointed at Spank, who had managed to wrangle away someone's cell phone and was whining into it, "Dad, some girl sicced her pet unicorn on me. *No*, I haven't been drinking again. I *haven't*! No, don't come get me! Don't—"

Kate, overhearing this, whirled on Spank and, slapping him, cried, "Omigod, your *dad* is coming over here? Do you have any idea how many laws I'm violating here? And you just called your dad? Are you *crazy*?"

After the mad rush that followed to go before Sheriff Waller showed up, few partygoers remained, with the exception of Alecia and Liz.

Contented, Liz gave Alecia's arm a squeeze. "I'll see you tomorrow."

"Thanks," Alecia said, and hugged her. "I guess when boys tease you," she whispered into Liz's hair, "it doesn't *always* mean they like you."

"Actually," Liz said, "it does. It just doesn't mean they're necessarily nice guys."

Alecia pulled away and nodded. "I get it now." She gave a shy glance toward the unicorn, whose eyes had turned back to their normal sparkly lavender. "Thank you . . . um . . . What's her name?"

"Princess Prettypants, officially," Liz said. "But I'm really going to have to rethink that."

✿

The spray of small stones hit Jeremy's bedroom window a few hours later. Looking bleary-eyed, his hair sticking up in dark tufts, he opened it and looked down. "What time is it?" he asked, confused.

"After two," Liz replied cheerfully. "Come down."

Jeremy rubbed his eyes. "Is that Princess Prettypants?"

"Gloria," Liz corrected him. "I changed her name. Princess Prettypants didn't really suit her."

"Gloria," he said thoughtfully. "After Gloria Steinem, queen of the second-wave feminists, I assume?"

Liz nodded. "Exactly."

"Fitting," Jeremy said.

"Come down," Liz said again from where she sat astride Gloria in the side yard beneath Jeremy's bedroom window. "I want to show you something."

"I'll be there in a few," Jeremy said, and shut the window. A little while later he was opening the front door to his house and coming out onto the porch in jeans and boots while buttoning a clean white shirt. Liz tried not to feel distracted by his naked chest, which had quite a different effect on her than the sight of her ex-boyfriend's had earlier in the evening.

"Hey," Jeremy said, coming to stand beside her in the moonlight.

Liz patted Gloria on the neck, and the unicorn obligingly knelt down, allowing Liz to slide off her back and into the dew-moistened grass.

"Whoa," Jeremy said, impressed by Gloria's good manners.

"Right?" Liz said, glowing. "Isn't she great? She's fast, too. When we were putting the geese back—"

Jeremy looked surprised. "You put them *back*?"

"Yeah," Liz said. "Just now. Well, Gloria and I did. It was kind of hard, because I couldn't remember which one went where. So some people may have gotten geese wearing the wrong outfits. But at least they got their geese back. Maybe they can all get together and swap. But it didn't matter, because all I had to do was picture the houses in my head, and Gloria knew right where to—"

"Why'd you do that?" Jeremy wanted to know. "Put them back?"

"Well, I had to," Liz said, blinking up at the moonlight. "I can't really afford to do the wrong thing anymore. Or someone could end up being killed."

She looked meaningfully over at Gloria, who was contentedly pulling up large segments of Jeremy's parents' lawn and eating it.

"Oh, no," she said with a groan. "Gloria! No. We have apples and sweet hay at home. Stop it! Great, now she'll be making rainbow farts all night."

Jeremy shook his head. "I don't get it."

"Oh, right." Liz pulled her aunt Jody's birthday card out of her pocket and opened it. "See, I missed that part at the bottom of Aunt Jody's card. I have to make sure everything we feed her is organic and sweet. Also, there was a warning that unicorns take on the emotions of their owner. So, like, if I get mad, Princess Pretty—I mean Gloria—gets mad. There was already an incident earlier this evening over at Kate Higgins's house—"

"Wait," Jeremy interrupted, laughing. "*You* went to Kate Higgins's party?"

"Yeah," Liz said, putting the card back into her pocket. "I had to. It turned out you were right about me encouraging Alecia to like Spank Waller."

Jeremy's smile died on his lips. "Why? What happened?"

"Let's just say that thanks to some negative reinforcement on Gloria's part, Spank won't be messing with any girls for a while." Liz cleared her throat. "I don't think Evan Connor will either."

Jeremy raised his eyebrows. But his tone was carefully neutral when he asked, "Oh? Evan was there too?"

"Yeah," Liz said. "'Cause he's the kind of guy who goes off to college but still comes back to town for high school parties, apparently. Which shouldn't be a big surprise to anyone. What may have come as a surprise to some people is how scared he was of a harmless little unicorn."

"So," Jeremy said, smiling again, "I take it you're not selling Gloria on eBay after all, then?"

Liz's jaw dropped.

"What? No way!" Liz looked appalled. "Why would I do that? She's the best present I ever got! Which reminds me. I really love your gift—" She held up the key with the bow on it. "But I still don't get what it's for."

His smile broadened. "Don't you? It's to the Cutlass Supreme. I finally got it running."

"Oh my God, that's fantastic, Jeremy!" Liz was so excited she couldn't help throwing both her arms around him and giving him a big hug, which he returned.

As she held on to him, however, Liz became uncomfortably

aware that this wasn't her old friend Jeremy she was hugging.

Maybe it was the unfamiliar muscularity in the arms that were around her.

Or maybe it was something else. She wasn't sure. Whatever it was, it caused her to let go of him abruptly and take a quick step backward, her face suddenly feeling as if it were on fire.

"B-but I can't accept this. You've b-been working on that car forever," she stammered. "Why would you give it to me?"

"Well," Jeremy said, his gaze on hers steady. "I just got to thinking that I don't really have anywhere to drive to. Everything I've ever wanted is here in Venice. Even," he added, his tone carefully neutral again, "as close as right next door."

At first Liz was sure she'd heard him wrong. Or that maybe she hadn't understood him correctly. Surely he hadn't said . . . He couldn't mean that he . . . not like *that*.

Then Liz felt a soft—but firm—muzzle at her back, and she was enveloped in the scent of night-blooming jasmine.

Gloria, fed up with her owner's obtuseness—and knowing, as she did, Liz's true feelings—pushed Liz into Jeremy's waiting arms.

Which was when Liz, gazing up into his eyes, realized what she'd known all along, but had never admitted to herself until that very moment: Everything *she* had ever wanted had been right next door all along, as well

Except, perhaps, a unicorn.

Cassandra Clare

"Cold Hands"

Justine: Cassandra Clare's zombies are more influenced by the voudin tradition of the possessed dead. They do not shuffle or leak from too many body parts, and they have no interest in eating anyone's brains. It's true that they're not the world's greatest conversationalists, but they're loyal and they don't lie. In fact, they are emo zombies who will love you forever. Entirely, up to you to decide whether that's a good thing . . .

I think you should also note how many of the zombie stories are love stories and how few of the unicorn ones are. Very telling, that.

Holly: Another story where I can just pretend that we're talking about an undead type that I like. There's not even any brain eating! Excellent for me!

Justine: Yet another story where Holly's secret zombie adoration is revealed. You know, Holly, you could just cut to the chase and admit that Team Zombie has won.

Cold Hands
By Cassandra Clare

James was the boy I was going to marry. I loved him like I'd never loved anything else. We were seven when we met. He was seventeen when he died. You might think that was the end of our story, but it wasn't. Death is never the end of anything, not in Zombietown.

Zombietown is what other people call it, of course. Those who live here call it by its name, Lychgate. In Old English, "lych" means "corpse." James says that means we're a town that's always been touched by death, but it wasn't always like it is now. Lychgate used to be a nice place to live. Orderly houses set out in neat arrangements, pretty rows of streets decked in flowers, and the Duke's palace at the north end of town, with Corpse Hill rising up behind it. Then, one day, in the early morning, when people were just getting up and starting to get the morning paper, and putting the coffee on, and turning on the radio to hear the Duke's daily address, Corpse Hill came to life. The dirt sloughed off the graves like old skin. The earth peeled back and the dead came out, blinking in the sun like newborn kittens. They limped and shuffled and crawled. They turned their eye sockets toward the path that leads down to the town. And then they began to walk.

✿

It was Saint John's Eve—one of the town's four big festival nights. All the streets were strung with colored lights. James and I were down in the old part of the city, and James was buying flowers from a dead woman.

Her name was Annie. She ran the flower stall down the street from the main square, and she sold the best flowers in town. I know what you're thinking—it's weird that a dead person could own a flower stall. Well, of course she couldn't own it. The dead don't have property rights. But ever since the morning the Curse struck, ever since the dead started coming back to the town, the town council has been struggling to figure out what to do with all the zombies. They're pretty quiet—they don't say much—but if you can't get a zombie to go back to its grave in the first week or so after it comes back, it'll just stay forever. So they hang around the town, sitting and staring, cluttering up the streets. Much better to give them menial jobs like road sweeping, and trash collection. And flower selling.

James handed me a bunch of blue roses, which are my favorite—the same color as his eyes. I watched him as he took out a handful of coins, each stamped with his uncle's face, to pay Annie. The bones of her fingers clacked together as she took the money.

He turned back to me, his eyes searching. "You like the flowers?"

That was one of the things I loved about James. No matter how long we had been together, no matter how many times he'd given me gifts, or I'd given them to him—though I could never match what he could afford—he always worried about whether I would like something or not. He always wanted to please me.

I nodded, and he relaxed, starting to smile, starting to slide his wallet back into his pocket. That was when the car came screeching around the corner. James saw it; his eyes widened and he shoved me back, toward the sidewalk; I fell, and scrambled around just in time to see the car knock him down, then speed away with its tires screeching.

Annie, the zombie, was going crazy, making those weird noises they do, and shuffling around in a frenzy, knocking flowers off her cart by the handful until torn petals littered the street. People had started to come running, but I hardly noticed them. I was crawling toward James, who was lying partly in the road, partly out of it, his legs bent at strange angles. I still thought he might be all right—broken legs are survivable—until I got to him and pulled him into my lap. When he looked at me, blood bubbled up out of his mouth, so I never knew what his last words were.

Annie screamed and screamed when he died. It was like she'd never seen anyone die before.

It was James who told me the truth about the Curse. Everyone knows that it started about a hundred years ago, the dead coming back. We all know it had something to do with a sorcerer in Lychgate, someone who summoned up the dead and then couldn't put them back. What James told me was that the sorcerer was a member of the Duke's—of *James's*—family and that the dead man he summoned up cursed him and cursed his town, too, for good measure.

That's why the Curse sticks to the inhabitants of Lychgate like glue. Even if we move away from the town, our dead will follow us. They belong to us. They come after the ones they knew when they were alive—their living friends and family. They want to be with them. That's why no other town will have us. That's why we can't ever leave.

I don't really remember what happened after James died. I know there were the flashing lights of the police cars, and the EMTs who arrived in the ambulance and tried to pry him out of my arms. I wouldn't let him go. What was the point? He was dead anyway. There was nothing they could do for him. They were trying to convince me to let go of him when the Duke's limousine pulled up. I'd ridden in that limousine plenty of times, to events at the Duke's palace, sometimes just home with James after school, watching the town go by through the tinted windows.

The door opened and the Duke got out. James's uncle, who'd married his mother after James's father had died. He'd known me since I was nine. Been at my sixteenth birthday party. He'd given me a teddy bear—a weird thing to give a sixteen-year-old, like he thought I was still a little girl. He'd smiled at me. He had blue eyes like James, but they were weirdly lifeless, like doll eyes. James said it was because the responsibilities of being Duke tired him out, but I'd never liked him. I looked forward to the time when James turned eighteen and became Duke and we never had to see his uncle again.

Now Duke Grayson looked through me like I wasn't even there. "Take the boy from her," he said to the EMTs, who were standing around looking miserable.

"We've tried. She won't let him go," I heard them murmur.

"Take him," said the Duke. "Break her arms if you have to."

He walked back toward his limo without looking at me again.

It was my parents who finally came to get me, to put me in the back of their car and drive me home. My mother sat next to me, murmuring soothing words; my father sat up front, looking shattered. I could see all his dreams of his daughter marrying the next Duke leaking away like James's blood had leaked into the gutter at the side of the road.

"It was just an accident," my mother said, stroking my hair. Blue petals clung to her fingers. "Just an accident. At least it was fast, and he didn't suffer."

"It wasn't an accident," I said coldly. I could tell my mother was upset that I wasn't crying. "He was murdered. Duke Grayson had him murdered so he'd never turn eighteen."

My father jerked the wheel so hard that we ran off the road and bumped up over the curb, the wheels grinding. He whirled around in his seat, his face as white as paper. "Never say that again. Do you hear me, Adele? Never say that again, to anyone. If you do . . ."

He left the sentence hanging in the air, but we all knew what he meant.

Murders don't happen in Lychgate often. The punishment is always death, and they carry out the hanging or shooting in the town square. Everyone comes to watch. They bring picnic lunches—egg salad sandwiches in brown paper bags, warm bottles of soda pop, bars of chocolate. They cheer when the Duke gives the order for the execution to begin. After that the priests bring the bodies of the guilty up to Corpse Hill for burning, and the air turns black with smoke, and for a few days people walk around with surgical masks on to keep out the ash and grit. The other towns don't like it—they can see the smoke at a distance—but they know what happens in Lychgate if you don't burn the vengeful dead. They've heard the stories—doors ripped off their hinges, whole families slaughtered, judges and jury members dragged out into the street by walking corpses whose eyes burn like angry fire.

Murder isn't the only crime that can get you hung. Stealing from the Duke will do it. Vandalizing ducal property. Or slandering a member of the Duke's family. All are crimes punishable by death.

The Duke came to my parents' house the next day. The doctor had come that morning and given me a shot that made me feel as if my head had separated from my body and was floating away somewhere. I couldn't move from where I was lying on the bed. Everywhere around me were the big silver-framed photographs of me with James that I had been collecting since we had met in first grade. James and I at the playground as children, at the beach when we were older, holding our All Hallows' Day soul candles as we painted our faces to go out, hand in hand on Hanging Day. James with his sandy hair and his blue eyes and his big grin, looking down at me from everywhere and all

331 • Cold Hands

around as my parents sat downstairs with the Duke and his wife, James's mother, listening to their sad words.

I knew they were stunned by the honor. Even though I had been with James for so long that everyone knew it was inevitable that we would marry—even though the Duke, by law, *had* to marry a commoner—my mother and father were still struck speechless at the idea of actually welcoming Duke Grayson into their home. They just agreed when he told them that I couldn't come to the funeral. "It's just for family," he said, "unfortunately, and the ceremony is elaborate. We're concerned it will be too much for Adele to handle."

I heard my father make soothing noises, telling them it would be all right, while I lay on the bed and wished that I could die too.

Not everyone who dies comes back. Sometimes they come back to right a wrong. Sometimes to reveal a secret no one else knows, or to tell family members where a treasure was buried. Sometimes they just can't bear to be dead. Or, like the girl in the song whose bones were made into a harp, they return to sing a song of the one who killed them. It was always my favorite of the songs the Christmas carolers would sing door-to-door in the winter—especially the part where the bone-harp speaks and accuses the one who murdered her.

> *The very first song that the harp did play*
> *"Hang my sister," it did say.*
> *"For she drowned me in yonder sea,*
> *God, never let her rest till she shall die."*

There was more to the song too, about how the older sister was sentenced to death, but came crawling back out of her grave because her guilt would not let her rest. She spent her long unlife sitting on the cliffs near her old home, cradling her dead sister's singing bones. So you see, there are lots of reasons the dead come back. Sometimes they even come back for love.

If you love someone, you're not supposed to want them to come back. Better a peaceful sleep in the earth than the life of a zombie—not really dead but not really alive, either. You're supposed to pray for a quiet death for your loved ones, for dark oblivion in the earth. But I couldn't bring myself to pray for that for James. I wanted him back—no matter what.

The funeral was the next day, and true to the Duke's word, I wasn't allowed to attend. Instead I watched from my bedroom window. Even at a distance I could see the mourners like black ants wending their way up Corpse Hill. It was raining and the path was slick with mud. I saw some of them slip and fall as they went up, and I was glad. They deserved it, for being allowed to attend the funeral while I was shut out.

Though the Duke had refused to televise the event, they had set up loudspeakers on every street corner in town, and were blasting the funeral service for everyone to hear. I suppose it's not every day that the Prince of the town dies. I could see people gathering in damp huddles, their faces upturned as they listened to the voice of the priest booming down the streets.

"'For thou wilt not leave my soul in hell, nor suffer thy Holy One to see corruption. Behold, I show you a mystery; We shall not all sleep, but we shall all be changed: for the trumpet shall sound, and the dead shall be raised incorruptible, and we shall be changed. But your dead will live; their bodies will rise. You who dwell in the dust, wake up and shout for joy. Your dew is like the dew of the morning; the earth will give birth to her dead.'"

The loudspeaker crackled then, and I heard Duke Grayson telling the priest to lower the coffin. I shut the window, hard, before I could hear the sound of the dirt clods hitting the lid.

James didn't come back the next day. Or the next. I waited patiently for the shuffle of his feet on the paving stones outside my house. The cold knock of his dead hand on my front door. The graveyard whisper of his voice.

But he didn't come.

It can take the dead some time to return, I reminded myself. They wake up inside the coffin, disoriented and confused. They don't remember dying, most of them. They don't know where they are. In the old days they used to bury people with a rope inside the coffin that was connected to a bell aboveground. When the dead rose, they could ring the bell, and the graveyard keepers would come and dig them up and pour salt into the coffin and rebury them. That was before they started burying the dead in mausoleums, the way they do now, stacked one on top of the other with the most recently dead keeping the others down. I think of them sometimes, one on top of the other, whispering down to each other through the dirt and the bones.

✿

For a week after James died, my parents kept me home from school. They were afraid I wouldn't be able to handle the whispers and the stares. It had been one thing when I'd been the Prince's girlfriend, when they'd all known I'd be the Duchess of Lychgate someday. Then I'd had power, power enough to hold the stares back, to wave away prying questions. But now I was nothing. Just another commoner who'd known the Duke once. A commoner who was never going to be anyone special. I heard my father whispering to my mother in the kitchen, so quiet he thought I couldn't hear him. "We can't let her go back," he said. "They'll tear her apart."

Finally I convinced my parents to let me leave the house. I wore a hat and dark glasses to keep people from recognizing me, though it didn't really work. I could feel their eyes on me as I walked down the street. I saw a news van slow down next to me, the antenna on its roof spinning lazily, as if whoever was inside was trying to decide whether it was worth bothering to get out and start talking to me. Eventually it sped away.

Even the zombies seemed to be staring. Normally I barely noticed them as they shuffled silently along the sidewalks, or moaned to themselves as they sat hunched on benches or crouched with their begging bowls by the side of the road. But they seemed unusually alert today, turning their heads to watch me go by like weird, dead sunflowers following the passage of the sun.

But that wasn't what was making me cringe as I walked,

making me wish I'd never left the house. I kept seeing James everywhere, like a ghost, though I knew ghosts didn't exist. When I was buying CDs in the music store, I went to the listening stand and put on headphones and heard his voice. When I went to the supermarket, the Muzak on the speakers was James, saying my name. When I passed the window of the electronics store, the flickering images on the televisions inside were images of his face. I heard him in the crackle of the fire, the sputtering static of a dead telephone, the breath of the wind.

As I hurried home, the street corner speakers flared into crackling life, saying that the murderer of the Duke's nephew had been found, and would be put to the death on the next Hanging Day. I froze for a moment, staring up at Corpse Hill, still in the twilight.

I knew what I had to do.

I got up at midnight that night and put on black. Black pants and a shirt, my hair tied back, black shoes that wouldn't make a sound as I walked up the path to the cemetery. I stole my father's power drill, a shovel, and a pair of gardening gloves. The moon was the only light as I walked between the graves, which were clothed with winding sheets of mist. First I went past the graves of the poor, marked only by concrete slabs. Those lanes gave way to the wide, paved roads of the area where the richer families were buried. Here each family had a mausoleum, marked over the door with the family name and with stone cemetery angels kneeling at either side.

The Duke's mausoleum was by far the biggest. It towered

over the rest in white marble and wrought iron, with the names of all the members of the royal family carved down the sides. There were still visible remnants of the funeral that had been held that week—flower petals strewn all up and down the path leading to the mausoleum's front door, and glittering grains of salt from the burial ceremony, scattered like mica in the dirt.

I put my hand to the latch of the iron door, and it swung open. Inside, the crypt was silent but not dark: There was an electric light in the ceiling that gave enough light for me to see that there was a small chapel inside, with marble benches, and either wall was lined with vaults, like the inside of a bank's safe-deposit room. There were marble slabs on the floor too.

I stood by the slab that had James's name on it and wedged the narrow end of the shovel into the space between the slab and the next stone. I pushed down on it with all my strength, until the slab began to move, with a grating sound so harsh that my ears sang with pain. My shoulders were aching as the slab slowly inched up. I shoved, hard, and it slid to the side, revealing the dark square hole beneath.

In the hole was the coffin. I dropped the shovel and knelt. The coffin was bound in brass, heavy and elegant-looking. I took my father's power drill and turned it on.

The screws came out of the coffin hinges easily, as if they had never been tightened. Once I had them all out, and had pushed the lid back, I realized why.

I set the power drill down and stared. Tears burned my eyes.

The inside walls of the coffin were made of brass, etched all over with prayer words meant to seal the bonds of death. The coffin itself was full of salt; James lay amid the salt like a body washed up on a beach, surrounded by sand. There were huge brass circles sunk into the sides of the coffin at his hands and feet. They were connected by thick chains to manacles around James's wrists and ankles. I imagined him waking in his coffin, struggling against the manacles that held him, choking on the salt in his mouth. I had never seen anything so cruel.

"James," I whispered.

He opened his eyes. His skin was as pale as ashes, his blue eyes now the black color that the eyes of the newly dead often turn. He wore a white shirt and black pants and the big heavy emblem of the ducal house around his neck on a chain. He could have died an hour ago. His gaze fastened on me where I knelt over him with the drill in my hands.

He smiled.

"I knew you'd come for me, Adele," he said.

We sat on the steps of the mausoleum and looked out over the town. There were lights down in the streets, and bright illumination in the center of town where they were setting up the stage for tomorrow's Hanging Day.

"I woke up in the coffin," he said. "It must have been days ago. I yanked and pulled at the manacles, but all that happened was this." He showed me his ragged wrists. There were wounds braceleting them, torn but not bloody. The wounds of the dead never heal, but they never bleed, either. I had seared the metal of the manacles with the drill until they'd come apart and fallen away. I was wincing as I did it, terrified I would hurt him even as I knew I couldn't.

"Your uncle did this," I said. "He didn't want you coming back to accuse him."

"He must have planned this for a long time. Had the coffin made. The manacles put in. Paid the maker to be silent. Hired a man to run me down." James was looking toward the town. Toward the brightly illuminated gallows. "They're hanging him tomorrow, aren't they?"

I nodded. "They're calling him a drunk driver. Your death was an accident, but he still has to die for it."

"It wasn't his fault," said James distantly. "No one says no to the Duke." He turned to look at me. "If it weren't for you, I'd still be in that coffin."

I looked at him. He was still the same James, his beautiful face hardly changed at all. But something behind his eyes had gone away, something indefinable and strange. I said, "What's it like?"

"What's what like?"

"Being dead."

He reached up and put his palm against my cheek. His hand was cold, so cold, but I leaned into it anyway, fitting the curve of my cheekbone to his palm as I had so many times before. "When I woke up, I could hear everything." His black eyes reflected the lights of the town like mirrors. "I could hear you. I could hear your heart beating. But I couldn't sleep in my grave without you."

"James . . ." I swallowed. "In the morning they'll know what happened. That I dug you up. We have to get out of town—run away. Maybe we can go to the city—"

"No one runs away from Lychgate." He tilted his head to the side, slowly. "Where can we go? In any other town, when they look at me, they'll see a walking corpse. They'll chase us away with pitchforks and torches."

"Then what can we do?" I looked at him. I wondered when the black had eaten the blue in his eyes. Had it been gradual, or had it happened all at once?

"I want you to come with me," he said. "To Hanging Day, tomorrow."

"James—" I was horrified. "Your uncle will be there. If he sees you, he'll know what I did. That I got you out. I'll go to jail."

"No, you won't." He sounded completely confident.

"You can't be sure of that."

"Adele." He turned to me. "Do you trust me?"

I hesitated. He was James, still. I had always trusted him. Even if his skin was the papery color of an old book now, and his eyes were black instead of blue, and he smelled of cold stone and fresh dirt. "Yes."

"I won't let anything happen to you. Not while I—"

He hesitated. I knew he had been going to say *while I'm alive*. It was something he'd always said.

"Not while I'm here," he finished. He reached to take my hands. He wrapped his fingers around mine. His were like twigs carved out of ice.

"After that we can run away?" I said. "Hide somewhere, where they'll never find us?"

He leaned forward and touched his lips to mine. His were cold and tasted of salt.

"Whatever you want," he said.

Hanging Day began early, with crowds gathering in the square by nine in the morning. I had brought James some of his old clothes that he'd left at my house—a battered shirt and jeans would be much less likely to stir up notice than his somber funeral gear.

We stood at the outskirts of the crowd, in the shadow of one of the taller buildings. James kept his head down, his hair hiding his face. The return of the Duke's nephew from the dead would have been an event newsworthy enough to take the attention off Hanging Day, or even bring it to an end completely. He was totally silent, watching the stage, the scaffold, and the lectern where his uncle would stand. When he was alive, I could always read his face, but now I couldn't imagine what he was thinking.

Slowly the town square filled up with people. Teenagers in laughing groups, parents with their children on their shoulders, young couples carrying picnic baskets. And as I stood there with James, I saw something I had never really noticed before. I had always been close in to the festivities in the center of the square. But now that I stood outside everything, I saw that there were zombies here, clinging to the shadows, folding themselves into the darkness at the edges of the crowd. They stood with their black eyes fixed on the scaffold, their hands hanging empty at their sides.

It would never have crossed my mind that zombies would

enjoy a Hanging Day just like everyone else. But of course, we had been trained to ignore the undead. Not to see them when they were there. They were like trash lying in the gutter; you looked up and away, trying to concentrate on more pleasant things.

A shout went up from the crowd, and I looked to see what they were shouting about. The Duke's stretch limousine was sliding through the crowd like a shark through shallow water. The people in the crowd began shouting and waving. Behind the limo drove a police wagon with barred windows. I felt James, beside me, grow as stiff as a plank of wood.

The Duke's car drew up to the stage, and he was helped from the black limousine by his attendants. The crowd was surging; I could see only bits and pieces of what was going on—the policemen opening the back of the wagon, yanking out a terrified-looking man who was handcuffed and gagged. He struggled and kicked as they dragged him up the steps to the scaffold, where the executioner stood, all in black.

The Duke took his place at the lectern. He looked out over the crowd, smiling, as a few feet away the murderer was forced to stand over the square trapdoor cut in the stage's floor.

"Greetings, good folk of Lychgate," the Duke said, and a roar went up from the crowd.

James's hand tightened on mine. Suddenly he was moving, pulling me after him forward through the crowd. I tried to dig my heels in, but his grip was as hard as iron.

"Today we stand as one, united in our desire for justice," the Duke went on. "A terrible crime has taken place. The murder of my beloved nephew—"

His voice was drowned out by the crowd yelling. They were shouting James's name. None of them noticed that James was there among them, stepping on their toes and jostling their elbows as he dragged me closer to the stage. He was just some scruffy zombie pushing through the crowd.

"—The punishment for which, as I am sure you know, is death by hanging—"

We were nearly at the stage now. The Duke's amplified voice was deafening in my ears.

"—and burning, the ashes to be scattered on Corpse Hill—"

There was a police line around the stage, blocking the crowd from getting too close to the steps. As we neared it, an officer threw out his arm as if to stop us. James came to a halt, still holding my hand, and looked full in the officer's face.

The policeman lowered his arm slowly, looking astonished. "Your Grace?"

"—And if any among the crowd has an objection, or evidence of this man's innocence, bring them forth now!"

The Duke's voice rang out like a bell. He was required to say these words; the crowd could always come forth and speak up for the prisoner; no one ever did.

Except now. James raised his head and in his slow, dead voice, said loudly:

"I speak for the prisoner."

The Duke looked stunned. "Who was that? Who spoke?"

"It was me, Uncle." James took a step forward, but the

police officer blocked him. James gave him a stern look. "Don't you know who I am?"

"Y-yes," the man stuttered. "But—" *You're dead.* I could see he wanted to say it, but he didn't. Instead he stood aside and let James ascend the lectern. The crowd was screaming, watching James as he made his slow and steady way to the stage.

His uncle was staring at him. Duke Grayson was putty-colored, like a zombie himself. He looked as if he couldn't believe his eyes. "But—but—we bound you," he said, finally. "With salt, and bronze—"

"Bronze can be shattered," said James, "and locks broken. I stand before you today and demand to see my murderer punished."

Duke Grayson pointed toward the trembling man with the rope around his neck. "He's there, James."

James smiled a cold, unpleasant smile. "I meant you."

Now there was chaos. The crowd was screaming and milling. The police officer who had let James go by took me and set me on the steps to the stage, as if worried I would be crushed in the melee.

The Duke was blustering. "I don't know what you imagine happened, James, but I never harmed you—"

"Never harmed me?" James snarled. It was frightening to see the way he looked, his teeth bared and his black eyes glowing with the low light of the rageful undead. "You wanted to be the Duke. You never wanted me to live to eighteen. You hired someone to run me down, then found some poor vagrant you could pin the crime on and bribed the judge to make it stick. I *heard you*, Uncle. I heard you, paying off the murderer you hired. I heard you after I died."

The Duke spun toward the crowd. "He's gone mad," he said. "You know that death can shatter men's minds."

My heart was pounding. I had not known what James wanted to do here in the square, but I had not imagined a direct confrontation. *Trust me,* he had said. And I did. Even knowing there was no way out of this for him now. For us, now. Not unless James knew something I didn't.

"I am quite sane, nonetheless," said James, and I saw, from the way that the crowd was looking at him, that they believed him.

"The testimony of a dead man means nothing!" the Duke shouted. "Officers, take him away!"

But the police didn't move. James was the son of the old Duke, and both had been beloved in Lychgate. They would not move to hurt him, even in death.

"What can you possibly hope to gain by accusing me, boy?" the Duke demanded of James in a low voice that was half snarl and half wail. "You have lost the Dukedom. Accept it. If I die, there will be no one left with Grayson blood to hold the title of Duke of Lychgate. Do you want that?"

"No," said James.

"Then—"

"I will be the Duke of Lychgate," said James.

"But you're *dead*. A dead man can't hold a title—"

"Can't he?" The rage had faded from James's expression; there was a cool, calm smile on his pale lips instead. He turned to the crowd. "Who here would prefer a dead man to a murderer for their Duke? Who here wants the son of the *true* Duke Grayson as their ruler?"

The crowd stirred; I could sense their ambivalence. They had adored James when he was alive. I knew how much he had been loved; I had been there with him in the streets when they had stopped us both to wish him good health, or take photographs of him with their phones and cameras. But now he was dead, and the dead were not like us.

Duke Grayson smiled a thin smile. "Don't you see?" he said. "They don't *want* you. Officers, take my nephew—"

There was a rustle then, a sort of wave of sound that went through the crowd. I saw the Duke's expression change as he looked out over the people of Lychgate, and I stood up myself, to get a better view.

It was the zombies. They were coming forth from the shadows, moving in their slow deliberate way. Without making a sound they pushed through the crowd toward the stage and stood—at least a hundred of them—in a circle around it. The implication was clear. James was not to be touched.

Now it was James who was smiling. "You see," he said. "They do want me."

"They're dead," said the Duke. "They don't matter."

"Don't they?" said James. "I think it is time that we stopped pretending. Who among us cannot count a family member—a child, a parent, a wife or husband—or a friend who has returned from the dead? We know what they call this place—

Zombietown. We know that the Curse follows us. If it is even a curse. Maybe we should stop and ask ourselves if there is any real reason for us to be ashamed. In other towns death is the end. Here we see our dead. We speak to them. And they love us."

At that, he looked at me.

"Perhaps," he said, "it is time for Lychgate to have a Duke who represents what the town really is. A union of living and dead."

He held his hand out then. I stood. It was not as I had always imagined it would be. I had thought I would marry James before the entire town, with a carpet of white flowers spread out at my feet and James, handsome in a tuxedo, waiting for me in the gardens of the Duke's palace. Now he was asking me to stand up with him in front of everyone while there was grave dirt under my nails and clinging to the soles of my shoes. It flaked off in clumps as I made my way across the platform and took his hand.

It was as cold as ice.

We turned to face the crowd, together. I saw them. The faces of the town. They had never smiled when they'd looked at me, but now they smiled at *us*. We were young and in love. We were living and dead. The faces of the zombies shone as they gazed at us.

The crowd began to clap. Slowly at first, then fast, a sound like thunder. I heard the Duke cry out. He turned to run, but the zombies were there, blocking his way, encircling the stage. They looked to James for instruction.

He gave it.

"The Duke is yours," he said.

The dead swarmed up the steps like driver ants. They took hold of Duke Grayson and dragged him, struggling and screaming, to the trapdoor. The executioner released the innocent prisoner, who fled. The Duke was gagged and the rope placed about his neck. It was one of the zombies who pulled the lever that opened the trapdoor and dropped the Duke, twisting and kicking, into neck-snapping space.

So the town had its Hanging Day after all.

After the Duke's death, the officers led James and me to the limousine and helped us in. We drove slowly through the crowd, who watched us go—some cheering, some looking on with silent, stunned faces. I passed my parents, who were standing hand in hand, gawking like the rest. I rolled down the window to wave at them, but they looked at me as if they had never seen me before in their lives. I had become someone else to them.

I have not been home since. I live in the palace now, where there is a room made up for me. Because he is the Duke, my parents don't object to me living here. They know we have to stay together. The town accepts that their Duke is dead, because *I* am alive. I am the symbol. I am what proves that though James is dead, he is still human.

He has even found a priest to marry us. It used to be illegal, the marriage of the living and the dead. After this, I don't know. Everything is different now. Everything is changing. Because I am the betrothed of the Duke, I don't have to endure the curious stares of the townsfolk when I go out to the market, or to the square, or up to the cemetery to put salt on the graves of my ancestors. I ride in the town car, and I keep the tinted windows rolled all the way up so I don't have to see their faces when they look at me. I know they wonder what it is like, to love and be loved by the dead.

I would tell them it is much like it is to be loved by the living. James is not like he was when he was alive. He is quiet now; he talks very little, and does not share his thoughts with me. He does not sleep at night, and cannot dream. But many men are quiet, and most don't share their thoughts even with the ones they love. In many ways he is just like the James I always knew.

Except that when he touches me, even now, I can't help but shiver. If only the dead did not have such cold hands.

"The Third Virgin"

Holly: Unicorns are thought to possess healing powers. In particular, their horn is believed to remedy everything from bad breath to serious disease. Goblets inlaid with unicorn horn will purify poison poured into them, and candlesticks of the horn itself hold candles that burned especially brightly and very long.

But in addition to the much-coveted horn, other parts of the unicorn are also useful. Shoes made from unicorn skin will keep feet from having sores and bunions, a pelt of unicorn fur will cure fever, and ground-up unicorn innards will cure leprosy. Unicorns are useful creatures, hence all that creepy hunting of them.

Kathleen Duey's "The Third Virgin" explores what it means to have those healing powers—what the cost is, both to those who are healed and to the unicorn itself. I love this story; it still haunts me.

Justine: Wow. Obviously, I am anti-unicorn, but this story gives me ammunition I never even thought of. Who knew that unicorns are massive whingers? (For the Americans: A whinger is someone who complains constantly and lives in the land of half-empty glasses. It is not the same as being a whiner; it's much, much worse.) You don't see zombies standing around moaning about the awesome cost and responsibility of eating brains, do you?

This story also answers the question, "Unicorns? What are

they good for?" with an emphatic, "ABSOLUTELY NOTHING."

The anti-unicorn case rests covered in glory.

Holly: I'm not going to even touch what Team Zombie is covered in. Sores, maybe? Goo of some kind? Whatever that is, I wouldn't call it "glory."

The Third Virgin
By Kathleen Duey

I need a virgin.

I know, I know. But I do.

So I am hiding in the woods near a high school.

Pathetic, yes. But necessary. The virgin can't be an old man or a wee slip of a child or a man with a child's wits this time. I need strength and resolve. Am I the first to try this? More likely I am the ten thousandth. It hardly matters. I continue to starve myself. I don't know if I can keep it up—or if it will help. I can only hope that this is the last conundrum of my endless life.

I have no idea when or if I was born, nor what spawned me. I know when my memories began, because I still have every single one of them. It was a warm morning back in Cymru— the place they decided to call Wales, eventually—when I saw the sun rise for the first time. After that, I wandered.

Always alone.

Always hungry.

I was often frightened, and I envied the fawns and the fox kits their graceful mothers and watchful fathers. I coveted the way they all knew what they were meant to eat. I didn't. I tried everything. I spat out twigs and flesh, and vomited up berries, and had no idea what would still my hunger. And in spite of it, I grew.

When my body changed, my dapples faded into the silk white coat of adulthood. Then the horn split the skin of my forehead. It scared me, this long, sharp spike shoving its way outward. I had to walk differently, allow more breadth of passage in the forest. And I began to feel something beyond my constant hunger. It was a separate ache. A need. For what, I had no idea.

I was very young when I discovered I could not hurt myself beyond my ability to heal. There was no cut, no bruise, no broken bone that did not quickly repair itself. The first time, I watched the magic, both sides of the gash straining to touch, to cling, to erase the damage I had done. I thought all pain passed quickly, that all wounds healed in the course of a morning—until I followed a grounded bird flopping with a ruined wing. I began to watch. None of the other creatures healed like I did.

The first human I ever saw was nearly naked and filthy. She was running, screaming, bleeding. I understood her cries, but had no idea how to help. I hid as her pursuers passed me. I don't know if she died or lived, or what happened to her.

The First Virgin:

One drizzling gray morning a farm girl spotted me through the trees. She ran toward me, pleading with me to save her father, a coal miner nearly crushed when his bell pit collapsed. Her heart was a roiling mass of emotion that both excited and scared me. I bolted, but I could hear her behind me, shouting, begging, heartbroken. I stopped and looked back. Her desperation— even at that distance—felt sweet. As she came closer, I lowered my horn by instinct, even though I had no idea what I should do with it.

But she knew. She lay one trembling hand on my neck, and

guided me through the trees to a cottage. She coaxed me gently, waiting for me to puzzle my way through the open door, then to clop across the smooth wooden planks. Her father was dying. I could feel it. She stood close to me and showed me what to do, with gestures and words that made it clear she understood my fear and my inexperience.

I bent to touch her father's brow with my horn. The jolt I felt nearly buckled my forelegs. Something coursed through me, and I transmuted it into something I could give back to him, but not in full. I stole some of his life, without thinking, and my hunger was instantly stilled. For the first time in my life, I felt the strength that comes from eating. But was the man healed? Had I done it correctly?

He sat up. He flexed his legs. His weeping daughter was whispering, her hands light on my skin, thanking me, assuring me that I had done everything perfectly. And I only then realized that *she* could hear *me*; she was understanding my thoughts. I had lived all my life as silent as stone, hungry, aching, confused. All that was gone for a while. It was intoxicating.

There are legends about unicorns. I have heard—or overheard—most of them. I know there are paintings and tapestries that depict us looking love-daft, kneeling, staring up at a pretty girl. I am sure I looked as silly as any of them that first time.

But the virgins I have sought ever since cannot be defined in the narrow, idiotic way most people use the word. There are older, deeper meanings. Virginity means unmarred wonder, belief, new green grass, continuous rebirth. And even that is not enough for me to be able to talk, to be heard. There must also be a need so sharp that I feel loved, at least for a while.

I began searching all of Wales for people to heal and virgins to talk to. I found hundreds of the first and none of the second. I tried. Pure, hopeful, wondrous hearts are far less common than truly sharp need. And to find the two together? It is a very rare person who can hear a unicorn. So I pursued other intoxications.

Word spread, and those in need walked the woods, looking for me. I was stealing life, as well as giving it, every time. It felt entirely natural to me, in the way that a head shake violent enough to snap a rat's neck is natural for a terrier. I slowly came to understand that the ratio of gift to theft was mine to decide, that I could control it. And I quickly learned this: The balance between giving and taking impacted the exquisite physical thunder I felt when my horn touched human flesh. The more I stole, the better it felt.

At first I took more years of life from children. It seemed fair. I was saving most of them from very early death. Gray beards and prune-faced women kept more—because they had less to start with. And so it went. At first. Eventually I gave in to whimsy. There was a humble, kind man whose dog revered him. He kept most of his remaining years. The woman who wanted me to cure her small pox, but not her mother's, lost most of hers. At first this was amusing.

The day the game found its limits: A smelly, bestial old man slapped my muzzle when I bent to touch him with my horn. He had no idea what he was doing—disease had clabbered his brain. But still, it pissed me off. I jerked his last breath up and out of his mean, miserly chest and kept it for myself. It felt right. I did not heal him. I killed him. And killing him satisfied my hunger the way nothing else ever had. *Ever.*

I was afraid I would do it again. And I did. Over and over. Stealing a baby's entire life was the best. The jolt was violent, and the calm satiety that came after it lasted a long time. I loathed myself afterward, of course. And the loathing lasted much longer than the satisfaction. But it never stopped me. Here's an odd thing: The parents never blamed me. It was never my fault, always somehow theirs. Too late to find me, the wrong blanket the night before, something. They wanted to believe in the magic, I suppose. It made me feel filthy.

One sunny morning I stared at my reflection in a pond. My eyes were as dead as last night's coals. My coat was spattered with the blood of a child who had nearly killed herself falling from a barn beam. Because of me she was indeed dead now. And I realized that if I ever again found that special sort of virgin to talk to, I would have only horrific things to say.

That afternoon I waded into the sea and I pulled a long, slow underwater breath into my lungs, trying to die. I woke up on a rocky shore, a circle of human children around me, their faces lit with joy. I staggered away, gagging up salt water and coughing until I bled. Then I healed.

I was desperate to find others of my kind, to see if they felt what I felt, did what I did. I hoped they had found a way to stop killing. But I never saw another unicorn, not even from a distance. Maybe they had all found a place to hide. Maybe they were all dead. Maybe there is only one of us at a time. I don't know.

I kept searching for a pure heart with a terrible need so I could have the great relief of being listened to. I couldn't find one. I stumbled through fifty years of silence. Then a hundred. Sometimes I tried to hide. But I had healed so many people that everyone knew a story or two, and those stories were passed down. The parade of the injured and sick was endless—and an endless temptation.

I could sometimes be more or less fair for a while, but then I would slide backward again. Every time I thought about the feeling I got when I sucked the life out of a baby, I shivered and longed to feel it again.

I tried three more times to end my life.

It didn't work. I healed.

Obviously.

If I had managed it, I would not be watching the woods for a virgin this morning, would I? And these are not the woods I grew up in. I left Ceredigion County more than three hundred years ago because I overheard men talking about ships sailing to the New World.

Really? A new world?

It was huge, they said, and only the eastern coast was sparsely settled. I began to dream about a place with no people. No babies. Under a cold, yellow Welsh moon, I ran straight at a rock wall, over and over, until I finally snapped my horn off at the base. It bled, then scabbed. While it began to heal, I galloped all the way to Cardiff, to the sea. I found a dock and waited. When I saw livestock being boarded, I lowered my head, looked pitiful, and joined the party. I wasn't on the lading list, but the captain thought he could sell me in America, so he led me aboard.

I rubbed my forehead bloody on the rough stall planks to keep my horn from growing back, and I listened to the sailors. I listened to everyone in the Virginia colony where we went ashore too. They spoke several languages and it made no difference—I understood them all.

The man who bought me rode me only once. I arched my neck and posed so his friends would admire me, scabbed forehead and all. We trotted away from the manor house, and the men talked about their investments in a French settlement beside a magnificent river. Then one of them said this: "I've heard that western lands are so thinly populated that you could ride for years and never see another human being."

Full of hope, I pitched my rider into a ditch and galloped away, faster than any horse ever could. The bridle was easy. I ducked under a limb, hooked the leather strap behind my right ear on a stout twig, and backed up. Four days later I frayed the cinch with my emerging horn and left the saddle in a meadow.

I went west, not caring if I lived or died so long as I did it alone. It was rough travel across wild country, but every time I got hurt, I healed. One morning I saw mountains on the horizon. By evening I could tell they made the mountains in Wales seem timid and soft.

I stopped in the beautiful Roaring Fork Valley in what was later called Colorado. The people who lived there called themselves Nuutsiu. I could understand them when I overheard them, once every few years, and only by mischance. I avoided them. I lived alone. Entirely. I was constantly hungry, but I healed no one and stole no life. My appetite never slackened. And my other need, the ache to be heard, to not be alone, never dimmed either.

Thirty winters came and went. I bitterly envied every other creature I saw. Their appetites were natural, not magical. They killed honestly, not pretending to help or heal. Dragonflies knew they had to watch for birds. Birds knew they should stay away from foxes. And each creature had friends, a family. They lived, then they died. I envied that most of all.

One cold autumn day, after starving myself for a long time, I felt weakened from hunger. I began to wonder if I could die. The idea brought me joy. And so I tried.

There are two magnificent mountains at one end of that valley. Aspen forests give way to pines, then the slopes steepen into a bare crown of sliding knife-edged scree rock.

I climbed the northern peak. It took all day. I stood a long time on the top, looking down that almost cliff-angled slope. Then I took a run at permanent freedom, throwing myself into the air and over the edge. I hit so hard that I expected the sky to go dark once and forever. But it didn't. I bounced. My neck lashed to one side, then back. I felt my spine snap, then heard more bones break when one foreleg twisted beneath my weight. I slid sideways, writhing, tumbled over a ledge, hit hard again, and caromed downward across the jagged piles of scree.

I came to rest near the bottom, a white-coated bag of blood

and bone splinters. I lay pinned flat by more pain than I knew could exist. My right forehoof was altogether gone. I watched ribbons of my blood continue the downhill journey we had begun together, and I hoped that I might still die. I closed my eyes again and waited.

The next time I opened them, I noticed the tiny rim of a dark, clean new hoof already beginning to grow.

I lifted my head.

Then I heard a voice.

A voice speaking the language I knew best.

A Welshman had found me.

The Second Virgin:

His name was Michael. He had come from Wales with his uncle to work in coal mines near Glenwood Springs at the far end of the valley. He lay beside me on his bedroll blankets, keeping me warm. What he said broke my heart.

While I had been hiding from the Nuutsiu, the Irish had arrived in Denver City. There were hundreds of Galleghars, MacMahons, Gleasons, and Finleys there and in Leadville, to the south. Michael had always believed in unicorns, he said, and the miners and railroad men mostly did too. The Chinese railroad men called me Kilin, he said. The German miners prayed to a virgin named Maria Unicornis. "They all know in their hearts that you are real," he whispered. "Like I always have."

I closed my eyes and tried to concentrate on the warmth of his body and the gentleness of his hands while I waited for the pain to subside. I fell asleep, and while I rested, my new forehoof grew and the stringy stump above it healed, perfect

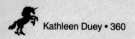

and new. Other parts of my body would take longer, I knew.

Michael had a garden of curly hair the color of ripe barley. His heart shone in his eyes. He was gentle and good, and he believed that I was too. "You are so beautiful," he said to me, quietly, his hand strong and steady on my twisted shoulder. "Please don't die. Please."

But I want to die, I said, and I could tell that he heard me, because his hand, stroking my shoulder, stopped, then went on again. I was lifted by the joy of that until I realized that if he could hear me, he had a need, a terrible one, and I would soon find out what it was.

The next night was colder. He built a little fire to warm us, and sat beside me humming and rocking himself like a child. I began to talk to him and ended up pouring my heart into his, in my own way—I told him everything except the truth. It was wonderful to not be alone. He sat with me all that day, listening, as my splintered bones sorted themselves out and my bloody bruises faded.

That evening Michael explained how he had chanced to see me falling. He had been on his way to the settlement for help when he'd seen me fall. His uncle was hurt. "Do you know what a bell pit is?" he asked me suddenly.

Yes, I told him and listened to the familiar tale. His uncle had made the pit looking for silver. It had collapsed, breaking most of his ribs and both of his legs. So, when I could walk, we started off.

Michael reached up more than once and placed his palm on my shoulder. He was a distinct and utter beauty, careful and kind in all he did, astonished by the sight of the rising moon. The silk of my white coat fascinated him. He loved textures and touching like an infant does. I had never felt less alone.

Sadly, Michael's dying uncle was a hard-faced bastard. Michael had been right. The uncle's ribs were all broken and his poor, black lungs were half full of Welsh coal dust, from his early years in the mines of Wales. He could barely take a breath. Still, he reached out and grabbed Michael's hair and wrenched him around, jabbing at the boy's face in anger because he had been gone too long. "I'll leave you here when I head northwest," he said, shoving the boy, then wincing and coughing. Michael ran to get tea. His uncle slapped it out of his hand when he brought it.

I lowered my horn and went through the motions for Michael. But I made no effort at all to heal. Instead I took the last little bit of life the uncle had and then watched Michael weep and shudder and mourn. All through that long night, I told him over and over that he had done all he could, all anyone could. He was so grateful to know it was not somehow his fault. But once that was eased, I felt his other fear: He had never made his way alone.

I still stayed until morning, sleeping close to the rough-made hearth, soaking up the warmth of Michael's heart and hands and gratitude. He was what people back then called a half-wit, of course. The first claim robber or the first bad winter would kill him. He knew it. I was certain he would beg me to stay when he woke. I almost wanted to. I also knew he would tell anyone he met about me, like a child with a pony.

I lay awake, thinking of all the Chinese men, the Welshmen,

the Irishmen who would eventually try to find me, especially once their womenfolk had followed them here and were having babies. I would fall back into terrible things. I was sure of it. So just before dawn I touched Michael's lips with my horn. He gasped awake, his eyes open wide in surprise. Then they closed, halfway and forever.

I lay beside him for a little while longer, feeling full. Sated. Angry. And sad. When I pushed open the wooden door and clip-clopped across the narrow porch, alone again, I thought, Northwest? Why not? It wouldn't matter which direction I took. I was determined never to feed myself again. *Never.*

My resolve lasted two days. My first lapse was a man-boy of about eighteen, shot in the back, squirming with pain. He thanked me a thousand times, saying it over and over in a soft Irish brogue. Had he known that I had taken all but a few of his years, and that he would have healed without me over a month or so, he might have been much less grateful.

Two days later I found a feeble old woman, left behind by a wagon full of her relatives because she was near death with cholera. I took away her pain and, I hope, her fear, and I left her just enough life to enjoy the sunset. The third, fourth, and fifth healings were children dying of various causes. Their gratitude was sweet and tentative. They were afraid of me, as well they should have been. I stole many years from each of them, but they lived. Maybe, I lied to myself, I could control my appetite.

I ended up in Portland, Oregon, ashamed, full of stolen vim and vigor, and determined to find a way to end my life. Or so I told myself. I have been here a very long time now and haven't even tried to suicide. I have so far contained my appetites.

Portland has been a good place for a unicorn to hide. Two big rivers meet here. The weather includes some snow, many rainy days, and warm summers, all of which encourage the dense pine woods that surround the city. Washington Park is my forest, now. It is four hundred acres of trails and arboretums and gardens. It runs into Pittock Park, which adjoins Adams Park, then comes Macleay, and that borders on Forest Park, which extends all the way out to Linnton Park and St. Johns Bridge. Thousands of acres, and I have been very careful not to be seen for more than a hundred years. I do not want people seeking me out, ruining my resolve.

I have gotten very good at eavesdropping. About five years ago I listened as a boy called a friend to say he was going to kill himself, and he got his friend to promise to scatter his bones. A fine sense of drama, and it set me wondering. What kind of friend could consider honoring a request like that? What kind of love would form that kind of bond? A few days later I found myself watching a mother with her baby and staring at couples holding hands.

The day after that I began this search for a third virgin.

Since the odds of finding a pure heart in exquisite need within a strong body are better among young people, I began spending most of my time here, in Washington Park, where it touches the city. There is a high school about half a mile away. The students come here to walk, jog, to do their drugs, kiss, touch, talk, and whatever else they can't do in their own homes. I am not impatient. In all the endless days of my life,

I have never done anything like this before. The uncertainty is wonderful.

I have been hiding in the pines in Washington Park during the hours before and just after dawn, then again in the evening, when I am harder to see. The rest of my days are spent in the deep woods with the creatures I have always envied. While they eat and play and make homes for their families, I daydream. I have been hoping for a woodsy boy—the son of an avid deer hunter. But early yesterday morning I saw a girl.

The Third Virgin:

She is tall and athletic, certainly strong enough, and she radiates both purity and pain. She was running alone, and I felt her careful, sweet heart—and her need—even before she was close enough for me to see her face.

She is covered with scars. Her nose is half gone. The discolored too-thick skin covers her right cheek, veers across her mouth and throat, and then disappears beneath her tank top. One hand is scarred too.

I saw her through the pine branches and was thinking how perfect she was, when she suddenly stopped, then lifted her head to scan the trees alongside the path like she had heard a voice. She had. Mine. I shivered with joy.

I was peeking through an apple-size gap in the pine boughs. I stared at her and tried not to think, but I couldn't silence my happiness at seeing her, so ugly, so hurt, and so lonely. I saw her blink when I had that thought. Then she pivoted, breaking into a long-striding run, glancing over her shoulder only once. When she was long gone, I galloped away, headed for the deep woods.

But late that evening I went back, hoping she had been as drawn to me as I was to her, that she would return, curious. She didn't.

After that I spent my daydreaming time deciding what to say—what I wanted her to hear first. I rehearsed it a hundred times, changing the words slightly, then changing them back again. Thinking about how to make her listen, how to win her pity, her gratitude, her love, and, eventually, her obedience, made me tremble. It took seven long days for her to come back. The anticipation was wonderful.

Before sunrise on the seventh morning, standing in the same tangle of pine boughs, I was telling myself that if she came back, if I could talk her into it, I would make it an even trade. I wanted it to be fair, in case the impossible happened. And if it did, I would welcome it.

I recognized the rhythm of her steps before I saw her. Her stride, her breathing, everything was already familiar to me. Familiar and precious. All my clever, practiced opening lines dissolved as she came closer. When she was finally near enough, I thought—loudly and clearly—*Please? Please. I need your help.* She kept going, but her stride was uneven, then she slowed. When she stopped and turned back, I took a deep breath. *I need help. Please.*

She stared in my general direction, her eyes wide. I knew she couldn't spot me. She turned to glance up the trail, and it was then that I saw the knife in her right hand. Not a kitchen knife. Longer and heavier.

Oh, no. Oh, no, I thought. *Not yet. Please. Let me explain.*

"Where are you?" she whispered.

I was afraid she'd run if she saw me, but more terrified she would end her own misery before I could talk her into loving me. I could feel her anger, her desperate pain, her beautiful need.

"Come out of the trees," she whispered. "Stand where I can see you."

Unicorns are fanciful creatures—pretty, even. But she might think she was going mad if I just stepped onto the path. I hesitated. There was another jogger coming. We heard him at the same time. She put the knife behind her back and stepped aside and waited until he had passed, was out of hearing distance. Then she turned to the dense scaffolds of pine boughs that hid me. "Why are you hiding?"

Such a good question. One I couldn't answer. She did not have a gentle whisper. More like a snake hissing a warning. She was not afraid. My heart rose. She was perfect. *Perfect*. This would be a very difficult conquest.

"Show yourself or I will . . . ," she began, then stopped when I heard a burst of music. She reached into her pocket for her phone.

Please don't answer that . . . and please don't leave. I really need help.

She looked at her phone, then put it back in her pocket and stared into the branches again. I did what I had done a thousand times with people who feared me. I took one step forward with my head lowered—just enough so that she could see the branches move, would know that I was too big to be a person, and the wrong shape. I heard her take in a long breath.

There is no reason to be afraid. I don't mean to startle you.

I took one more step and lifted my head slowly, arching my neck like a parade horse. It's a ridiculous pose, but I discovered a long time ago that humans love it. I heard her gasp.

Looking into her eyes, I pushed through the last of the pine boughs, slowly, slowly, until she could have reached out and touched my horn. *Will you take just a few steps this way? So I can stay hidden. If anyone else sees me, I will end up in the zoo.*

"And if I try to tell anyone, we might end up roommates?"

She smiled for an instant. Then she slid the knife into her back pocket and pulled her shirt over it. I pretended not to notice that she was watching me to see if I noticed. She took a single step toward me. I backed up one step, and waited for her. Then we did it again, like a beginner's dance class, until we were both swallowed by the tangle of boughs.

I looked at her steadily, holding the pose, trying to look noble and interesting and amazing and magical. She came closer, one thumb hooked in her jacket pocket. Her scars were truly awful. She was fortunate to be alive. I saw her stiffen, and I took control of my thoughts. *What do you know about unicorns?* I asked her.

She shrugged. "Only that they aren't real?" She smiled again, another quick one, and she was close enough that this time I understood why. The scar tissue was taut, thick—it probably hurt to smile. One eyelid was higher than the other. Both were crinkled, mismatched, odd shades of beige and pink. She had no eyelashes.

"A fire," she said, before I could frame another thought.

"The whole house burned down. My cousin lived in our basement and he was cooking meth. I knew, but I just didn't say anything. So my parents and my sister were killed along with him. I hate myself for that. I live in a group home, and I hate it, too." She paused, her chin high, staring at me. "Did I leave anything out?"

Her voice was brittle. How long had it taken her to work up that short, angry résumé, ready to throw at anyone who stared. I was framing a thought about being sorry for her misfortune, when she added this: "It was five years ago. Dr. Shrinkydink said I would begin to come to grips with things in about three years, but it turns out she was full of shit."

She sounded so weary, so defeated, that I knew I had been right about the knife. She hadn't brought it to cut mushrooms or to protect herself. Why had she stopped to talk to me? Had she been hoping someone would come out of the trees and kill her? I was thinking very quietly, but she heard the last part.

"It crossed my mind," she said. "It's nice to meet you, though, instead of Jack the Ripper. Or even just a white deer. But this must mean I am crazy now. On top of everything else."

You aren't insane, I told her. *I am real. I want what you want. If you will help me, I will help you.*

"You want . . ."

. . . to die. Yes. More than anything else.

"Why?"

She said it with such a gush of breath, her voice going girlishly high, that for an instant I could see the child she had been, pretty, happy, full of faith in herself and her life. And I knew, because she could hear me, that the childish purity was still within her.

Tomorrow morning, I began, *before it's light out, I want you to come with me into the woods, farther from the city. I will explain everything and—*

"Said the spider to the fly," she cut me off.

I had never heard the expression, but the meaning was clear. *I just want to help you and for you to help me—*

"No," she interrupted again. "You don't need help. Not if you're serious. Not if you really want to die. The ones who *try* to commit suicide make sure it doesn't work, make sure that someone finds them. With luck, the finder feels like a hero and sticks around for a while. I started there. I've been found twice—but this time I'm serious. I just want to be . . . finished. And I won't need help, thank you."

She was about to walk away, and I knew she would not come back. I said this: *If your scars were gone, would you want to live?* And then I held my breath.

She was quiet. Then she shrugged, looking at her feet. "Maybe. Because I wouldn't have to tell anyone I didn't want to tell. I could hide it sometimes." She lifted her head. "Maybe I could make real friends instead of just collecting a revolving cast of junior social workers."

I can erase the scars.

She stared. "Don't fuck with me."

Cut me.

She looked startled. I lifted one foreleg. *Not deep. I just want to show you something.*

She took the knife out of her pocket and held it loosely across her palm, like someone who has used knives and is comfortable with them. "It's razor sharp," she said, and I knew she had heard my thoughts. "It was my father's."

Did he ever take you hunting with him? I asked, hoping.

"Usually." She looked puzzled at the question. "Why do you want me to cut you?"

To prove something.

I set my hoof on a fallen log to make it easier. *Just deep enough to bleed.* She stared at me, then drew the thin, sharp blade over my skin. The cut was straight, finger length, and it began to seep blood.

She looked up. "What am I supposed to—"

Just watch. I touched my horn to the bloody place, for theatrics and to mislead her. Within a moment the bleeding had stopped. Both ends of the cut rejoined first, the little wound shrinking, my skin zipping itself back together. I can't begin to explain what I was feeling. I had watched my body mend itself thousands of times. I had never watched it *with* anyone. She glanced at me over and over, her eyes wide, then looked back at the cut.

I can heal you, just like that. And I will. And then you can help me die. I could tell she wanted to believe me. I turned aside and lowered my head a little. *Please. Meet me here tomorrow? Before sunrise?*

She looked down at my leg. There was no trace of the cut. She nodded slowly. "Maybe."

Bring that knife, a new pruning saw, and a heavy rope—and

put everything in a sturdy bag. You won't need a shovel. The river will take care of the memorial service.

She took one step back. "Oooo. Creepy. A serial-killer-unicorn-comedian?" Her chin was high, but her voice wasn't quite steady.

I am not a killer, I lied. *I will erase your scars. Then you will help me die. What you do after that is up to you.*

She hesitated, her tongue sliding across her lower lip. She was trying to decide. Or so I thought. But what she asked me was this: "What's your name?"

I blinked. No one had ever asked me that. *I don't have a name. What's yours?*

"It's Reeym. *Ree-um,*" she added, pronouncing it slowly and precisely in a joking hillbilly accent. It was another one of her practiced responses. "It means 'unicorn.' Weird, huh? People call me Ree."

I was stunned.

"It might mean 'a big bullock,'" she said a little louder. "Depends on which biblical scholar you trust. My parents . . ." She stopped to look at the sky, then back at me. "My mother loved unicorns. She would have fainted from fan-joy if she had ever seen you."

The last three words were squeezed into a whisper. I kept my thoughts still, excited that she was trusting me like this, with her sorrow, with her heart. She squared her shoulders. "Mom thought it was a lucky name, magical, that it would guarantee me a smooth ride. At least she didn't live to see this." She gestured at her own face. Then her voice changed, all the pain hidden again. "Knife, rope, saw, in a sturdy bag. Do you need me to bring anything else?"

Courage.

She stepped forward and slapped me. I was so startled that I reared, like a horse. It embarrassed me. She was backing away, talking fast. "Tomorrow, as soon as the sky is gray," she said. "If you change your mind and don't come, I'll just do what I meant to do today."

I will be here.

She didn't respond. She whirled and ran away without looking back.

I went deeper into the forest, my heart beating hard. I had never expected things to progress so quickly, for her to trust me so readily. I galloped all the way to the hidden meadow with its swift little creek, about twenty paces from the Willamette River.

I had found it years before.

It was still perfect.

I stood close to the water and waited. I could not stop imagining Ree's face when I explained what I needed her to do. She would agonize over it. But she would be very grateful to me for healing her scars. So maybe she would. Maybe I would know what it felt like to be loved.

In the morning I started off in the dark. Halfway there I smelled a campfire. I would take a different way back so we wouldn't stumble into a group of illegal overnighters. We? The word swung back and forth in my thoughts as I veered off to follow the least-used trails, sometimes just going through the woods.

I got there when the sky was just beginning to gray. I settled in to wait, savoring my fear that she wouldn't come. But she did, within minutes.

She appeared, her shoulders squared, walking, fast and sure.

My heart swelled. I loved her steadiness and I loved her scars—without them she would never have spoken to me. She had the knife, in a sheath this time, and she showed me what she called "loppers," along with the rest. I looked at her closely. No. She hadn't figured it out. She thought we were going to cut interfering branches, were going to make a hanging tree.

She looked at me. "Are you sure you—"

Yes.

"Really sure?"

I heard doubt in her voice. I had planned to talk to her as we walked through the woods, to convince her slowly, to give her time to get used to the idea. But maybe that would give her too much time to think about it—to back out. I shook my mane and pawed the ground, which made her laugh. *Have you ever ridden a horse?*

She nodded. "My father had three Appaloosas and a pack mule."

In a trice she was on my back, clutching the canvas bag. *You can hold on to my mane if you need—*

"I won't need to," she interrupted me.

I started off slowly, in case she was bluffing. Then I cantered—and we ended up galloping. She kept her weight centered and I barely felt her on my back. But it was still very strange. When I finally stopped, she slid off instantly, as uneasy with it as I was.

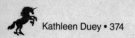

My skin was sweaty and warm where her legs had been.

The sun was coming up, and the dawn-dusk was lifting. She looked around the clearing and went to the creek, kneeling after a moment to wash her hands and splash her face. When she came back she was shivering a little.

"Have you picked out your tree?" she whispered. "I found instructions last night and practiced the noose knot."

I turned away, to hide my gratitude for her trying to make it easier for us both—and my fear that the truth would set her running. Staring at the trees, I explained, quickly, what I needed her to do like it was a detail, not something that might make her change her mind. Then I was quiet for a moment before I asked her if she would do it for me. And then I held my breath.

"This isn't what I thought," she said, very quietly. My breath caught. She exhaled, long, and came close enough to lean on me. I could feel her heartbeat and I was sure she could feel mine.

I know, I told her.

She slapped my shoulder. "Can't you heal yourself? Can't you make yourself happier somehow?"

No.

"Why?" She was angry. "I get that you're lonely, but you could make friends. You're beautiful, you're strong, and you're magical. You could do a lot of good if you—"

No, I said, to stop her, and then I spoke the truth. *I can't. I never have. I deserve this. I deserve much worse.*

She shook her head, and I could feel her pulling away emotionally. She didn't believe me. She thought I just wanted her to talk me out of it, and that pissed her off. She was two words and twenty heartbeats away from changing her mind. I couldn't let that happen. I wanted to feel loved more than I had every wanted anything. And if I died proving to myself that her love was real, it would be a perfect ending to my painful life.

I have stolen people lives, I said. *Lots of them.*

Her mouth opened. Nothing came out.

I described—as well as I could—how the jolt felt, that strange mixture of fear and need and hope that came pouring into me. I told her how I had used the people who'd come to me for help. I didn't tell her anything about the babies. I wanted her to love me, pity me, not hate me.

"You were an addict," she said when I had finished. "That's the way my cousin used to talk about meth. He hated himself for being that strung out, but every time he saw the needle, he'd just plunge it in and then tell himself it was the last time. He said he'd had hundreds of 'last times.'"

I sighed, as though the comparison were fair, even though I knew it wasn't. How many babies had the meth head killed on purpose?

"Maybe other unicorns have figured this out," she said.

I have never seen one.

"But if you're here, there have to be—"

Ree?

She met my eyes, and I lied again.

I can't find any other unicorns. I have spent more than five hundred years looking.

She took a breath like she was about to say something, then let it out. Then she took another breath. "Most people would love to live as long as you have. If you want to change your mind, I will under—"

No. Stand still. Trust me.

I walked closer, arching my neck for show, prancing a little. She smiled, one of her quick, painful smiles, as I lifted my horn high. Then she tipped her head back and closed her eyes, like she was waiting to be kissed by someone much taller than she was. I bowed my head so that the tip of my horn touched her lips. The jolt was the best, sweetest one I had ever felt, even though I took not one single second of her life. When I stepped back, I staggered a little.

She opened her eyes.

Smile, Ree.

She looked puzzled.

Smile. It won't hurt.

She worked her cheeks, and a glorious smile lifted her lips. Tears filled her eyes as she touched her face.

I did a trick-horse bow, and she laughed, giddy and high. She was beautiful. She ran to the creek and used it as a dull mirror, then ran back to me, jerking her shirt up. Her belly was soft and smooth. She turned away from me and pulled her shirt off, her chin ducked as she looked at her breasts. She got her shirt back on, then dropped to the ground and rolled up her jeans, running her hands over the calves of her legs. It was wonderful to watch her—limber, strong, and lovely. And happy.

When she turned to me, her face was contorted with emotion, her cheeks wet with tears. "Thank you. Oh, thank you."

I just wish I could have been there that night and— I stopped abruptly. It was a stupid thing to say. I might have helped. Or I might have decided not to singe my coat. And if I had saved them, who knows how much longer any of them would have lived?

She came close and put her arms around my neck. Her hair smelled like the woods, like pine gum and damp earth. When she stood back, she was wiping her eyes. "You could still think about this for a while and—"

It's all I have ever thought about, I said after a dramatic little pause. This was it. The test. If she didn't love me, she would never go through with it.

I need you to help me.

She took a breath that lifted her shoulders. Then she crossed the clearing and brought the bag to where we were standing. "Why the rope? Just to fool me?"

Yes. And because I thought that once you have a lot of the weight off, maybe you could hoist what's left of me up. It might make things easier.

She shuddered. "How many pieces to make sure?"

I loved her even more in that instant. *As many as you can stand,* I told her. *Some in the river. Some in the creek. Take what you can carry back with you and scatter it along the way.*

She nodded and clenched her teeth together. "Now?"

Yes.

She pointed. Her voice was a whisper. "Could you stand by that tree? In case I decide to use the rope?"

I led the way, and she followed, carrying the bag. She set it to one side, and when she turned toward me, she had the knife in her hand and tears were running down her cheeks. "If I cut your throat, you shouldn't feel anything after that."

I knew she was wrong, but I was sure I could lay still enough that she would think so—and I wanted her to, at least at first. Later, I would test the limits of her love, her gratitude. And I would let her live. Maybe.

"Okay," she said. "Are you ready?"

The fear and the determination in her voice were so equal, so raw, so honest, that I didn't respond except to lift my head high and close my eyes. The knife, when it came, was cold and sure. I felt the blood rushing out of my body. The wound hurt, but my thoughts were calm and clear. I lay down to make things easier for her, and to watch her face.

She was shaking as she picked up the saw. I was amazed at what I saw in her eyes. Her caring, the depth of her gratitude and love for me, that she would do something so horrifying because I had asked her to—all these things touched me deeply.

She began with my right forehoof.

The determination in her eyes made me very happy.

I was floating on an ocean of pain when I heard a metallic click and saw the loppers. I closed my eyes, listening to the sound of sharp steel meeting bone, then a thud. I could hear her crying. Grief. She was grieving *me*. It was delicious. I sighed, a long easy breath.

She suddenly stood up and walked away, carrying the bag down the slope to the river. Good. One hoof was a start. Later, I would suggest a bigger piece. She was gone a long time, then walked past me without speaking when she came back. Was she on her way to the creek to wash, then begin again? I didn't want to move, to scare her. So I waited hoping she would hurry. Through one barely open eye I could see her pacing, then sitting by the creek. I kept my thoughts as still as I could.

Time was passing. Too much time.

She finally came back, knelt and peered at my right foreleg. I felt her touch the cut she had made. She exhaled and rocked back on her heels and walked away again. I knew what she had seen. The bloody wound was nearly closed. I was healing. When she came back, carrying the bag, I felt my joy dissipating. And then I felt her hands—not the saw, not the loppers—her bare hands, soft, warm and gentle, pressing tattered skin and the ends of my bones back together. She hadn't thrown anything into the river.

Please don't do this, I begged her. *I need your help.*

She was making small sounds I couldn't categorize. Love? Anguish?

I lay flat on my side and closed my eyes, tired from the pain, feeling my body making itself whole again, disappointed that she hadn't tried harder. When I opened my eyes again, it was evening. I was sure she would be gone. But she wasn't. I could feel her warmth.

Ree was asleep, one arm over my back, her head resting on my neck. She was snoring quietly. I just lay there.

So.

It was over.

It hadn't lasted nearly as long as I'd wanted, but her emotions had been remarkable, even better than I'd hoped. I turned my head to watch her as she slept. She looked so different now. I wanted to leave, but it seemed unkind to desert her here. She might get lost in the woods. And I couldn't get up without awakening her. Would she tell anyone about this? About *me*? She would, eventually. Some handsome boy? I would be just one more story to tell as they exchanged secrets. Would anyone believe her? I lay still. I knew what I should do.

She stirred.

I love you, I told her when I felt her sit up. And it felt almost true, in a five-hundred-year-old lonely, selfish, parasitic way.

"Where should we go?" she whispered. "British Columbia is northeast of here. People say it's beautiful."

We? I could still feel the warm shape of her body against my skin. *You should stay here.*

"And explain my sudden lack of scars? First to the doctors and then the reporters?"

I let myself imagine it, keeping my thoughts very quiet. Maybe she could find deserving people and I would just steal a little of their lives, barely enough to feel the jolt. It might be easier with her helping me. But even as I thought it, I knew I would want to be alone when I started killing again—and I would eventually. Finding worthy people, virgins, making up ways to feel loved—it was all very hard. Killing strangers was very easy.

She stood up and took two steps, then faced me. "Don't worry. I don't mean it. I know you don't give a shit about me."

I lifted my head. *Yes, I do.*

She touched her face. "You don't want to die. You just

wanted to pretend someone loves you. You *enjoyed* all this shit."

Being cut? It hurt. I knew it was a stupid response, but I couldn't think of a better one. She was pacing, stiff-legged, almost rigid with anger. I could see her father's knife, back in its case, sticking out of her pocket.

"The first time I cut my wrists," she said, without looking at me, "I timed it perfectly—about three minutes before my roommate came in. She called 911, rode in the ambulance, started keeping track of me. And when she got a boyfriend, I bought more razor blades. But she was late coming home that night, so I staggered into the hall. The guy who found me thought he loved me for quite a while."

She exhaled and gestured at the bloody ground. "You're not magical. You're addicted to . . . terrible things." I saw pity in her eyes. "Maybe the other unicorns could tell," she said. "Maybe they hid."

Then, before I could react, she ran.

I wanted to chase her.

But while I had been asleep, she'd used the rope and all the clever knots she had learned. They tightened when I struggled, and I had time to think.

So she lived. I won't try to find her. I never want to see her again.

Because she was right.

About everything.

I think I'll head northeast. Why not?

LIBBA BRAY

"Prom Night"

Justine: A fitting end to the anthology is one of the book's most haunting stories. I could say a whole lot more but I don't want to ruin it for you. Read, enjoy, and appreciate how much richer and more poetic a tale of zombies is than a tale of—well, I think I've said enough on *that* subject.

Holly: "Prom Night" creeped me right out. You know what I need? A nice unicorn story to get the taste of zombies out of my mouth!

Justine: I'm going to ignore Holly's inability to appreciate one of the best stories in the anthology. It's never polite to dwell on someone else's complete lack of good taste. Instead, I would like to thank those of you who tortured yourself by reading the dread unicorn stories in addition to the brilliant zombie stories.

I know you could have easily skipped the stories with that horrifying little unicorn icon. But you didn't. Proving that you're made of sterner stuff than most of us. (Including me. I'll admit now that I only skimmed those stories.) You've gone above and beyond any reader's responsibilities. I'm proud of you. As a reward may I suggest a George A. Romero zombie movie festival? Go on, you know you deserve it.

Prom Night
By Libba Bray

The horizon was one long abrasion, the setting sun turning everything an angry red as it slipped below the dusk-bruised mountain range. Tahmina stood on the security platform and raised the binoculars to her eyes. A human skull appeared, the eyeholes absurdly large until she adjusted the magnification, shrinking the skull and bringing the stretch of desert into wider focus.

"Hey, got a new one for you," her partner, Jeff, said. "What's the difference between an undead and my last boyfriend?"

"I don't know. What?"

"One is a soul-sucking beast from hell and the other is an undead."

"Good one." Tahmina swept the binoculars over the stark landscape till they found the figure lurching quickly toward the electrified fence. "See him?"

"Yeah. About fifty yards out?" Jeff answered.

"Forty, I'd say."

"Damn. Is that . . . Holy shit. It is! Connor Jakes. Guess he didn't make it to Phoenix after all."

"Guess not."

The figure in the desert wasn't too far gone yet. His skin was gray, but it was mostly intact, just a few sores on his face.

His eyes were milky, though. And from the looks of his bloody mouth, he'd feasted recently.

Jeff put his binoculars down and shouldered his rifle. "Man, he used to be so hot. I had some serious jerk-off fantasies about him."

"Not so much now, though, I'm hoping."

"Nope. Can pretty much say this puts a bullet in *that* happy place."

"Ready?"

"I was born ready." Jeff's rifle fractured the stillness of twilight, and the flesh eater's head exploded. The body dropped, shook for a minute, and lay still. "And *that* puts a bullet in Connor Jakes. Boo-yah! High-five me, beyotch."

Tahmina kept her eyes and her rifle trained on the body lying ten feet from the electrified fence. "No popping corks until we see if he's reanimating."

"Dude, that was a direct hit. He's gone," Jeff said, a little hurt. They waited a minute, two. The body of Connor Jakes did not move. "Told you."

Satisfied, Tahmina shouldered her rifle, and they trudged down the wooden steps to the ground. She took the key from around her neck, opened the small supply cabinet, and took out two pairs of latex gloves and an extra large heavy-duty garbage bag, which she tossed to Jeff.

"Hey, how'd you like that line? 'I was born ready.'" Jeff tucked the bag under one arm.

"Not exactly original." Tahmina handed him a pair of gloves, and he thrust his fingers into the latex haphazardly.

"I'm telling you, we could put this shit on TV."

"There is no TV, Jeff."

"That's what I'm saying, partner. When it starts up again, they'll need talent and programming. We could be the new reality stars: *Zombie Cops!*"

"Uh-huh." Tahmina put on her own gloves.

"We should jump on that shit."

"You loaded?"

"Totally."

Tahmina cut the power to the fence, and they slid up the metal hatch that allowed them into the steel-plated walkway.

"You know tonight's prom night. 'S gonna get insane," Jeff said, sweeping his eyes along the thin slits in the metal, searching. "I hear the chess club went in for these crazy tuxes."

Tahmina gave a small laugh while also keeping a lookout. "Oh, my God. Not the powder blue seventies numbers?"

"Indeedy. With the ruffled shirts. Two words: hideously awesome. Too bad there's no yearbook. That would be a great picture."

"No doubt. Okay. Here we go—eyes up." Tahmina dropped into shooting position. Jeff flipped the four locks on the gate. He pushed it open and swept his rifle left and right. Nothing. He poked the decimated body with his gun. It didn't move.

"Anything?" Tahmina called. She had her rifle trained on Jeff, just in case.

"Nah. We're good. Let's go."

Moving quickly they manhandled Connor Jakes's graying corpse onto the bag. A loose finger fell off, and Tahmina tossed it onto the body. She secured the straps and helped Jeff lift the package onto a raised platform of stones just off to the right. It was hard work, and the desert was hot and windy. It blew soot from the sacred fire into Tahmina's eyes, and she blinked furiously against the pain.

"Let's take him up to the tower now," Jeff panted.

Tahmina shook her head. "In the daylight. Has to be daylight. Besides, there might be more tonight."

Tahmina surveyed the desert again. Nothing. Not a jackrabbit or even a tumbleweed. They stripped off their gloves, dropped them into the ash can for burning, and closed the gate, securing all four locks. Jeff electrified the fence. Tahmina took down the clipboard and noted the time. It was eight o'clock, the beginning of their ten-hour shift. In the morning, when the sun spread its angry wings over the land, they would throw the body of Connor Jakes into Coach Digger's Hummer, the one he used to take to away games to intimidate the other teams. They would drive the body the five miles to the Tower of Silence, a small, flat hill with a deep hole in the center, near the base of the mountain range. There, according to the customs of Tahmina's faith, they would lay him out and tie him down on the flat surface far enough away from their town so that his corpse could not defile the earth. The vultures would come. They would clean him down to bones, which the sun would bake clean of impurity. Whatever was left of the body would be pushed into the center hole for burial. Tahmina would say the prayers and hope. It was all they had left. Nothing else had curbed the infection.

Robin Watson emerged from the shadows. She was wrapped in her mother's too-big sweater over a white formal gown. Her hair had obviously been set with rollers; her face was wet with tears. "That was Connor, wasn't it?"

"Yeah," Jeff answered without looking at her.

"You shot him, didn't you?"

"Sorry. No choice."

The crying became sobbing. "He was my boyfriend!"

Tahmina disinfected her hands and checked her handgun. "Not anymore."

In the battered cruiser, Tahmina and Jeff drove streets pockmarked by light from the few unbroken streetlamps. The siren stayed silent. Using it might attract unwanted attention. Same for the cruiser's red-and-whites. As it was, they kept the electricity use to a minimum. Blackout was mandatory after nine. In the looted Wal-Mart a fire burned in a trash can. Somebody was wilding tonight. Somebody was always wilding.

At the intersection of Monroe and Main, they stopped at a red light. Observing traffic rules was silly—their blue-and-white was one of the few cars on the road, what with the gas rationing. But law was law, and order was necessary in a world of chaos. Somebody had to enforce that law now that the adults were all gone, dead or undead. Jeff and Tahmina had become cops by default. They'd been in student government together at Buzz Aldrin High School. He'd been treasurer; she'd been vice president. Over the summer, when the infection was a report on the Internet, a distant fear hitting places that were only thumbtacks on a school map, Tahmina and Jeff would get together and make plans for the coming school year: a rock musical to replace the tired Rodgers & Hammerstein bullshit, overhaul of the debate team, LARP nights, maybe even a battle of the bands. No lame bake sales or craft fairs. In July they organized a roller boogie car wash and made five hundred bucks for prom. It was going to be the best senior year ever. They didn't even feel worried when the infection moved westward, and the adults built the fence.

Across the overpass the cineplex loomed. The *C* and *P* had burned out, making the word look like a first-grader's snaggle-toothed mouth.

Jeff thumped his finger against his window. "Wonder what's playing."

"Same thing that was playing last week and the week before that and ten months ago."

Jeff chugged a warm Pepsi. "Couldn't this shit have waited until after we got the new X-Men movie?"

Tahmina thought about the last time she'd been to the cineplex. It had been in September. She'd gone with three of her friends. They'd shared a large popcorn. The movie had been about vampires; the lead actor had been incredibly hot, and they'd nudged each other and squealed during the kissing scenes. They'd had no homework that weekend. Their English teacher, Mrs. Hawley, hadn't been well. She'd missed the whole week. That Sunday she'd died. Monday, during the autopsy, she had come suddenly awake and driven her ragged teeth into the coroner's arm, severing it. Then, before the terrified assistant could stop her, she had torn open his skull and eaten his brain. It had taken a hail of bullets to tear Mrs. Hawley apart for good, but she'd already passed the sickness on to her oldest daughter, Sally, who had been Tahmina's babysitter once upon a time. Tahmina remembered her at the kitchen table, them playing Monopoly by their own rules, Sally slipping the kids secret hundred-dollar bills. They'd had to set Sally ablaze when she'd reanimated. Father O'Hanlon had splashed her with gasoline. Someone else had tossed the lit rag. Her hair had ignited first, a halo of fire that had quickly engulfed her entire body. Tahmina had had no idea how fast a person could burn. Sally Hawley had staggered and twirled, emitting a high-pitched scream that had died down in the end to something that had sounded almost human.

The sickness had then passed from house to house, always taking root in the grown-ups, who would go straight for their children. By the fourth week, the kids had had to quarantine the adults, pushing them out into the desert. Some families had decided it was better to die together than to be split apart. They'd packed up their cars and fled in the night, leaving their homes behind, silent accusers. On the drives to the tower, Tahmina had seen some of those same cars in the desert, sand-encrusted, bloodstained, doors open, a doll or shoe half-buried nearby. Some teens had run off to find their parents, but when those same teens had started coming back to the town, hungry for flesh, the survivors had had to put everyone on lockdown. Nobody in or out, except for the drive to the burial ground. It was the only way to stay safe. Tahmina thought at times like this that it was weird to have to play cop with your friends. Like some kind of mock trial experiment in social studies where each person played a role and somebody always broke character by giggling. Nobody was laughing these days.

The radio crackled with static, followed by the deep, garbled voice of the night's dispatcher, a Goth girl who had been in Jeff's geometry class. "Yo, Joe Law. Got a call. Possible unlawful shenanigans at the Gas 'Er Up out on Pima Boulevard. Somebody's handing out happy pills. You copy?"

Jeff picked up the handset and pressed the side button to speak. "Copy. We're on it."

"Over and out. May the force be with you."

"Over and out," Jeff said, laughing. He put the handset back. "See, that's what I mean about snappy one liners. We should use that for our show."

"Whatever, Holmes." The light turned green. Tahmina signaled, a reflex, and turned left onto Pima.

Since the infection, drugs were a prized commodity. Now that the banks were useless, the ATM had been bled dry, and all the best stuff had been looted from the stores, money was worthless; bartering happy pills was a means to power. Prospective dealers broke into the pharmacies or raided their parents' medicine cabinets, and traded drugs for car parts, food, sex, generators, whatever they needed or wanted. Tahmina had to keep an eye on the drugs. Strung out teens couldn't be counted on to mount a counterattack. They might do something stupid, like fry themselves on the fences or possibly become more vulnerable to infection. Those Percocet and OxyContin would be necessary if somebody broke a leg or had to have a tooth pulled. And if things got really bad, they would need enough to end it.

The gravel crunched under the cruiser's worn tires as it eased into the parking lot of the Gas 'Er Up. The headlights caught the ghostly images of several kids huddled near the rusted-out ice cooler. At the first sign of the lights, the kids scattered, except for the two dealers, who had fumbled their precious stash and were hurriedly retrieving their pills from the ground.

"Freeze!" Jeff yelled.

The two boys popped up, hands behind their backs. They were young, Tahmina thought. Maybe sophomores or freshmen. "What are you guys doing out here?"

"Nothing," the shorter one with the long brown hair said. His words had the frayed ends of a voice stretching from boy to adolescent. Not even high school. Middle school. The taller boy still had braces. He'd have those braces for as long as the infection held.

"Don't bullshit me," Jeff demanded. "Show me your hands."

When the boys didn't, Tahmina repeated the order.

The smaller boy smirked. "What are you, his bitch?"

Jeff whacked the kid's head with the palm of his hand. "Watch it, shithead."

"Hey, that's police brutality!"

"Fine. Make a report. If you can find somebody to take it."

"Partner," Tahmina warned, shaking her head. "What're you guys holding?"

The taller boy, the follower, held out his palm full of round white pills. "This shit's mine. I got it from when I had surgery last year. So why can't I do what I want with it?"

"Because it's called drug dealing and it's illegal," Tahmina said. "Besides, we don't know how long the infection will last. We might need those."

The smaller kid smirked. "What I need is cash. Then I'll own this fucking town."

Tahmina laughed. She gestured to the smashed windows of the ruined Gas 'Er Up, the burned-out streetlamps, the litter skittering across the parking lot, the half-starved cat skulking near the trash can. "Be my guest. Run for mayor."

"Whatever," the kid said. "Who died and made you God?"

"Everybody," Tahmina said quietly. She looked from one kid to the other. There was no remorse to be seen. No fear or hope. Just a relentless need, an angry want that would never be satisfied no matter how many pills they sold. "Just give me the drugs and get out of here."

"Repent! The end days are upon us and we must be purified by the holy fire!" The figure caught Tahmina and Jeff off guard.

"What the fuck!" Jeff gasped, fumbling for his gun.

The boys took their chance and sprinted across the open field, taking the cache of pills with them. "Hey!" Tahmina shouted after them, but it was no use and she knew it. "Dammit!"

"The fire of heaven will save us all," the figure said, stepping closer. He was a tall, skinny guy in shorts and an ASU cap, a poster-board sign hanging from a string around his neck.

"It's our old buddy Zeke. Gonna be a banner night," Jeff said, holstering his gun. He approached Zeke warily. "Hey, Zeke. Whassup, buddy?"

Tahmina could read Zeke's sign now: REPENT OF YUR SINS! GOD'S RATH IS JUDGEMINT UPON YOU! Zeke's spelling was no match for his zeal.

"The end days have come. We have to repent, repent." Zeke's eyes scanned the road constantly, unable to rest on any one spot. He looked like he hadn't slept in days, and Tahmina wondered if he had stopped taking his Risperdal for the schizophrenia that the shrink in Phoenix had diagnosed his junior year. Two red gasoline cans rested at his feet, though Tahmina knew the Gas 'Er Up's pumps were empty. There was only the one by the precinct, which was for the Hummer. These cans were probably left over from his family's lawn care service.

"Zeke, what's in the cans?"

"The fire of heaven. It will cleanse the earth. Not like what you're doing on the mountain. That's an abomination."

"It's . . . Whatever. Never mind." Explaining Zoroastrianism to Zeke would take more trouble than it was worth, and Tahmina needed to save her energy. It was prom night, after all. No telling what was ahead.

"Hey, buddy, you want to ride with us? Come on. We'll take a nice ride in the car," Jeff said, like he was talking down a grumpy toddler.

"No! I have to purify!" Zeke zigzagged in the empty parking lot. His foot caught a squished Twinkie pack, and he tracked fake cream filling across the asphalt in little white heel marks. "Don't you get it? This is a punishment on us. We have to be cleansed. Then it will stop. I've heard the voices. They tell me it's so."

"What's it a punishment for, then?" Tahmina asked sharply. "What did you or me or Jeff or anybody else in this town do to deserve this?"

"Our parents, all the grown-ups, they fought the wars and ruined the land and exploited each other."

"And what did we do?" Tahmina pressed.

"We turned them out into the desert to die!"

"It was them or us," Tahmina started. "I'm sure they would have wanted us to—"

Zeke raised his arms heavenward. "It was wrong! When Abraham offered Isaac on the mountain, God spared him. Maybe God was testing us. Parents give us protection, and we owe them our obedience."

"Not when they're trying to eat us. Just sayin'," Jeff spat back.

Tahmina shook the gasoline cans. They were mostly empty, but she could smell the gasoline, and even a little gas was dangerous. "Sorry, Zeke. You know you can't have this. We need it."

Zeke stood right in front of Tahmina, his eyes searching hers. "For what? What are we saving it for? There's no help coming. It's like the last month of school *all the time*."

Tahmina couldn't help but laugh. In some ways that was the worst part of the infection—the endless waiting, the absolute crushing boredom of it all.

"I'll save you," Zeke whispered, his eyes huge. "I'll save you all."

In a flash, he had one of the cans. He ran to the edge of the lot, unscrewed the cap, and poured the trickle of gas over his body.

"Holy shit!" Jeff yelled. He and Tahmina raced for Zeke, and shoved him to the ground. Tahmina secured Zeke's hands with the cuffs, and they hauled him, screaming, to the cruiser.

"I will die for you! Let me die for you!" he shouted.

"Not tonight," Jeff answered, and locked Zeke in the backseat. He sniffed his wet sleeve, made a face. "Fuck. Now I smell like gas."

"Let's drop him at the station, then check the perimeter," Tahmina said.

The last time Tahmina had gone to the Tower of Silence was Monday. She and Jeff had taken the body of an anonymous soldier Tahmina had shot as he'd tried to tunnel under the fence with his clawlike hands. They'd also taken a half-starved uninfected dog they couldn't afford to feed. Jeff had driven, and through the metal grate over the windshield (it had been fashioned by the automotive kids in the old shop classroom), Tahmina had kept watch, letting the sun-bleached sameness of the desert lull her into reverie. It was Tahmina's father who had built the tower, who'd taught her to say the prayers, who'd showed her how to keep the fire going for three days. "You must be the law now, Mina," he'd said, pressing his palms to her cheeks as if he'd wanted to memorize the geography of her face.

She'd tried to honor the traditions, but it was getting harder. While Tahmina performed the rites, Jeff would stand guard with the rifle and Molotov cocktails in case of ambush. Once, two undead were waiting at the base of the tower when they got there, and Jeff had to slice through their necks with his machete. Tahmina tended the sacred fire in a trash can just inside the fence, feeding it small bits of wood, the clothing of the dead, spent cereal boxes. The week before, when they'd found Leonard Smalls hanging from a rafter in his garage, his car radio still blaring Metallica (if it hadn't been for the noise, they might not have found him for days), they'd loaded up the house's furniture and picture frames, and even his suicide note, which read only, *I'm so tired of this bullshit.* The new kindling would last them a while, so there was that, at least. The smoke and soot was harsh, though, and Tahmina lived with an almost constant irritation in her eyes, nose, and throat, as if her body wanted to expel something but couldn't.

Now, as they drove Zeke to the station, they passed neighborhoods of darkened houses. On the left a sign boasted the future site of Bliss Valley, a gated community with a golf course. The half-built houses loomed like skeletons. About a dozen teens walked hand in hand down the side of the road, heading toward the high school stadium, where prom was taking place. Somebody sang a song that had been popular the summer before. In the backseat Zeke began a prayerful monologue.

Jeff started in again. "I'm just saying, like, this scene here— you, me, Zeke spouting the crazy in the backseat—this would be great fucking TV. I mean, the cruiser's already outfitted with a camera. We just upload."

"Remind me to get right on that," Tahmina muttered.

"Hey, don't be a hater," Jeff said. "Who's my partner, huh? Who's my copilot?"

"I am," Tahmina said. "I'm your partner."

"I promise, if you turn, I will pop a cap in your head, no questions asked."

"Gee, thanks. So sweet."

"I would do that for you. Would you do that for me?"

"You'll never turn," Tahmina said.

"Anybody can be turned," Jeff said.

Sometimes Jeff got like this, and Tahmina just had to ride it out. On all the shows and in the movies, partners supported each other, and she and Jeff were partners. In the past six months they'd been through a lot together. Jeff had been there when Tahmina had had to wrap her father's decapitated body in the tarp and drive him to the Tower of Silence. He'd kept a lookout while she read the prayers from the Avesta and waited for the birds to pick her father's bones clean and for the hot desert sun to purge those bones of impurity so that his soul could join Zoroaster. Tahmina had sat with Jeff the night he'd had to put a bullet through his mother's forehead and another two into his brother, who'd lain sick on the couch, insisting he would get better, and please, please, please, for the love of God, would Jeff put the gun away? Afterward, Jeff got so drunk he puked on the carpet twice and it smelled awful. Tahmina cleaned up the mess and burned the traces of his family. The next day she moved him into the old Sheraton, which had a really nice pool. Jeff liked to swim.

At the intersection the crowd of teens waited. From the

backseat Zeke shouted at them to repent of their sins, and they laughed. A tall guy in a ridiculous top hat flipped him the bird. Robin Watson hovered around the edge of the pack, her white dress fluttering in the hot wind. Two fat lines of mascara scarred her cheeks. Some of the other girls hugged her, and one of them held out a flask, refusing to take it back until Robin had drawn hard on the illicit liquid inside. Tahmina waved them on, waiting as they streamed past in streaks of color, tuxes and gowns probably looted from the mall. Prom night. There were no parents to take pictures, to fuss over the placement of a corsage. In fact, there were no corsages at all, since The Little Flower Shoppe was dark, the flowers inside long since dried up in their tall plastic buckets. Tansey Jacobsen bumped into the car as she wobbled across the street in tall heels. She had pinned an orange-red papier-mâché rose to her sparkly silver mini-dress. In the car's headlights the fake flower lit the night like a flare, before being swallowed by the dark again. Robin trailed after the others, her face eerie in the glare of the headlights.

The precinct was pretty quiet when they arrived—just a few teens helping out. Jeff took Zeke to a holding cell and went hunting for some Valium to help him sleep. Otherwise he'd spend the night yelling. At the front desk the Goth girl dispatcher looked up from her Sudoku puzzle. "Somebody's here to see you." Tahmina immediately thought of her mother, and her heartbeat quickened. But then she saw Steve Konig sitting on the other side of her desk, all taut energy, like a windup toy somebody had turned the screw on and was just waiting to let go.

"Crap," Tahmina muttered. "Hey, Steve. What can I help you with?"

"I want to make a report of suspicious activity, possible infected," he spat out. He wore his Mustangs varsity baseball shirt. If they'd had a season, he probably would have been named MVP and picked up a nice scholarship, too. He'd put on a little weight around the middle, Tahmina noted.

She took a seat and opened her notepad. "What's the complaint?"

"It's Javier Ramirez. He lives next door to me."

"Yeah, I know." Tahmina resisted the urge to roll her eyes. "What makes you think he's infected?" Since they'd turned out the adults, there'd been no new cases of infection among them.

"He's been acting kinda funny."

She snorted. "That describes Javier on a good day."

"I saw him sniffing around the trash cans. He told me he ate an armadillo. Those things could be crazy infected." He poked a finger at her notepad. "Aren't you supposed to be writing this down? Isn't this what you guys are supposed to do?"

Tahmina raised an eyebrow. "Steve. C'mon. Javier's just messing with you. That's what he does. That's what he's done since eighth grade. If you ask me, that's the most normal thing I've heard in, like, forever."

"Okay. How about this: He's stockpiling. I don't know what, but I've seen him hauling out boxes. Who knows what it is or what he's planning on doing with it?"

Tahmina tapped her pencil against her thigh, thinking. Steve and Javier had had a beef since eighth grade, when Steve had bullied Javier in gym class, and Javier had retaliated by making a fake website nominating Steve for douche of the year. Tahmina searched Steve's face and tried to determine whether this was payback or something more. Finally she said, "All right. We'll go talk to him after we check the perimeter."

"You should lock him up," Steve said.

"We're all locked up," she mumbled, and tossed the notepad aside.

Tahmina and Jeff followed Diné Road to the cutoff at Bald Eagle, a street of pickups and muscle cars and small, worn 1970s ranch-style houses. There used to be block parties here. Javier's dad played in Los Muchachos, a popular Tejano band, and the street would thrum with the bright, happy sound of horns and guitar. After his mom had died, Javier's family had tried to outrun the infection. His dad and two sisters had set out for Tucson and the home of some cousins, while Javier had stayed behind to get their call if they made it. The call never came.

"I'll poke around in the garage," Jeff said, and walked around the side of the house.

The doorbell was broken, so Tahmina knocked. A few minutes later Javier opened the door. His hair was slicked back into a ponytail. He wore cutoffs and had a towel draped across his bare shoulders. "Hey. Sorry. Just got out of the shower. What's up?"

"Can I come in?" Tahmina asked, even though they both knew it wasn't really a request.

Javier let her pass. He smelled of soap and spicy men's deodorant. Freshman year Tahmina had had a thing for Javier, but he'd gone out with Marcy Foster instead. Five weeks into the infection, Marcy's mom started feeling sick. That night she shot all three kids in their beds and then turned the gun on herself.

"So, what's up?" Javier asked, crossing his arms. The house glowed with candlelight. A tablecloth barely concealed three cardboard boxes stacked by a stereo cabinet in the corner.

"What's in the boxes?" Tahmina asked.

Javier held his ground. "Just some old shit. Been doing some housecleaning." He smiled. He'd always had great teeth. For a second Tahmina imagined herself in an ice blue gown, slow-dancing with Javier under the chandeliers of the Sheraton while a DJ spun songs into the early morning hours.

She cleared her throat, nodded. "Can you open one, please?"

Javier laughed and stroked her arm. "Come on, Mina. Give me a break."

Tahmina's eyes burned. "Excuse me," she said, and ripped open the top one. Inside were about two dozen bottle rockets. "What're you planning to do with these?"

Javier shoved his hands into his back pockets and rocked back on his heels. "I told you—housecleaning. Those are left over from last Fourth of July. Me and my uncles used to sell 'em by the side of the road out on I-10."

"You know you can't have these, Javier. Too dangerous."

"Come on, man. They're just firecrackers. You remember? Firecrackers? Summer? Good times?"

"Firecrackers attract attention. We don't want to attract attention. And if there's an accidental fire, we're screwed."

Javier's face fell. "Yeah, I know," he said softly. "I just . . . miss that shit. You know?"

They stood uncomfortably for a minute. Tahmina nodded at the Western suit hanging on the back of the door. "Yours?"

"It was my dad's. He used to wear it with his band. Prom's tonight."

"So they tell me."

"Not going?" He slipped an arm around her waist and tried to pull her into a twirl. She pushed him away. "I'm on duty."

"Any undead tonight?"

"One. Connor Jakes."

He whistled, low. "Sucks."

"Yeah."

"Anybody tell Robin?"

"She knows."

He winced. "Damn. And on prom, too. Still. That's the only one in two days. Last week we only had, what, three? Maybe it's stopping."

"Maybe." Tahmina smoothed the dry-cleaning bag over the suit. "Did you really eat an armadillo?"

"What? Oh, wait. Now I get it." The candle flickered with Javier's laugh. "Should have known douche of the year would call it in."

Tahmina was smiling in spite of herself. Steve Konig was, most definitely, a douche. It was a constant, and therefore a comfort. "Whatever. Do me a favor, okay? Try not to aggravate him?"

Javier spread his arms wide in affronted innocence. "Me?"

"Yeah. You."

He put his hands to his mouth and shouted in the direction of Steve's house, "Douche! You are the Douche-Man!"

Tahmina laughed out loud, and Javier joined her.

"You always did have the best laugh, girl." Javier slipped an arm around Tahmina's waist and drew her close, and for a second all she could smell was Javier and not the smoke from the constant fire for the dead. He sang one of his dad's songs, exaggerating the sexy parts to make her laugh, but then he sang it for real, soft and low in Spanish. He swayed his hips slowly from side to side, pulling her around gently in a slow dance. His mouth was warm and tasted slightly of peppermint.

"You sure you don't want to be my date tonight?" he whispered.

Tahmina thought about her mother's closet, the beautiful beaded gown hanging there. She wondered if she would ever see her mother again. "Sorry," she said, breaking away. "I'm on duty."

"Officer Hassani, keeping the world safe from the undead."

"Something like that. I'll be taking these." Tahmina confiscated the boxes of firecrackers.

"Harsh, Hassani."

"Just doing my job, Ramirez," she said, heading for the door. "Have fun at the prom."

Javier laughed bitterly. "Yeah. Fuck you, too."

Around midnight they checked the east side of town to make sure the fences hadn't sustained any damage. Tahmina slipped the night-vision goggles over her eyes, and the desert came into view in black and green.

"Anything?" Jeff asked after a few minutes.

"No. It's pretty quiet tonight."

"Nice of them to let us have prom without too much hassle. It's kind of funny. If they were here, there'd be chaperones checking for booze and breaking up the booty dancing."

"Yeah. Silver linings and all that."

"See? Now, that was some good cop talk right there. We have to remember that when we get our show, dude."

"Noted."

Tahmina took one last long look east in the direction of the Tower of Silence, following the trail that had been worn by the Hummer.

"Everything okay?" Jeff asked.

She watched the landscape for another minute, debating whether or not to tell him what she knew. He was her partner. Partners were not supposed to keep secrets.

"Tahmina? What's up?"

"Nothing," she said, tearing off the goggles. She hoped Jeff couldn't hear the worry in her voice. The breeze brought a fresh whiff of smoke till it was all she could smell. "I need some coffee."

The one diner that stayed open this late was the Denny's over by the high school. Roxie Swann's parents had owned it, and she kept it going. At the first sign of infection—a cluster of sores down her neck and a fever accompanied by the shakes—Roxie's mom had walked into the restaurant's giant freezer and asked

Roxie to lock the door, hoping the cold would either kill or cure her. It did neither. When Roxie opened the door three days later, her mom lunged, and Roxie emptied her gun as she had been told. But Roxie swore that just before her mother attacked, she paused as if she'd recognized her. As if she'd been trying to stop.

"Crazy night for you guys," Roxie said with a grin. She poured them weak coffee and cut two slivers of pie. The slices had gotten smaller. They were running out of flour. They were low on everything—medicine, gasoline, food. They still had water, which they boiled first just in case. But there was no telling how long that would last. They hadn't received a radio signal in ages. No planes flew overhead. There were no traffic noises. That's why they'd started sending volunteers outside, two a month in the past three months, south toward Tucson, east to New Mexico, west to California, north to Flagstaff. No one had come back until Connor Jakes tonight.

A group of prom goers sat in the corner booth, sharing some chips and salsa and arguing over which songs they would request once they made it to the Pima Panthers stadium. Somebody started singing "Rehab," and everybody joined in on the "No, no, no."

"Give it a rest," Tahmina muttered, playing with the pink plastic carnation stuck into a Coke bottle beside the empty napkin dispenser.

"Okay. Seriously. What's up with you? You're in, like, a fun-sucking mood tonight." Jeff took a bite of her untouched pie. "Did you want to go to prom? Is that it? 'Cause I'll totally take you, if you want. You can be my hag."

Tahmina rubbed at her eyes, but it was no use. They would just keep stinging. "Just thinking about something my mom said once about how she'd never leave me. I don't know. I was just wondering, what if there's some part of the human heart that can't be corrupted? There might be a cure in that."

Jeff snorted. "Reality check: I saw parents rip their kids the fuck apart and eat their fucking insides before we pushed them out. Parental love was no match for the power of that infection. Those things roaming the desert only see us as prey."

"What if you're wrong?"

"I'm not."

"But what if that part of them is still alive down deep and it can still be reached? My mom used to say that nothing, not my worst behavior, not even death, could stop a parent's love—"

Jeff brought his fist down on the table, rattling the grungy silverware. "Stop it, okay? Just stop." The diner got quiet, and Jeff took a shaky breath, waited for the prom kids to go back to singing and laughing. Finally he said, "Look. When I was little and we'd go to the store, my mom would tell me that if we got separated, just wait for her. That she'd always come back for me. Always. Well, guess what? She did—and it wasn't because she loved me. It was because she'd become some fucking animal who would have eaten my brain if I hadn't wasted her. There was nothing human left. I had to kill her before she killed me. So, you know, whatever concept you have of an unconditional love or God or law or humanity or meaning, you can fucking forget it." Jeff's eyes were red, and Tahmina knew it wasn't the soot or the desert dust. "You know what? I don't want to talk about this shit anymore. This is too much reality for our reality show. I gotta take a leak," he said, and walked away.

Tahmina stared at her reflection on the black surface of her coffee. It was her mother who had taught her to love coffee. In the mornings she would drink hers dark and strong from delicate cups that she had managed to smuggle out of the old country, escaping through a secret tunnel that stretched for miles under the city.

"Hmmm, I see your future," her mother would say playfully as she examined the coffee's remains like an ancient Persian fortune-teller.

"What is it?" Tahmina would ask, full of belief.

Her mother would tip the coffee-stained cup toward her. "Soon, very soon, you will be washing dishes."

Tahmina's mother used to teach at the university three days a week, commuting an hour each way. When the roads had become more dangerous, Tahmina had begged her mother to stay home. But her mother had said that it was important to keep the centers of learning open. To close the schools was to admit to hopelessness. She'd seen that happen in her homeland, and she would not see it happen here in the country of her choosing.

"But what if something happens to you?" Tahmina had asked tearfully as her mother had backed the car out of the driveway.

"I will never leave you," she'd promised, and Tahmina had watched her car growing smaller as she'd driven away. That night, her mother did not return. There were reports that the campus had been overrun with the undead. Infection was everywhere. Panicked, Tahmina had called her mother's phone, and it had gone to voice mail. She'd called through the night and the next day, but her mother never picked up.

"Accept the truth," her father had said, and he'd held her while she'd screamed and cried. But Tahmina couldn't accept it. If she had seen her mother die, that would have been one thing. What bothered Tahmina was the not knowing. Was her mother out there still, uninfected but maybe hurt or holed up in a safe house, unable to get home? At times these thoughts came down like a sudden hard rain, flooding her with such anxiety that she had to go to the firing range and discharge until her handgun spun with clicks. Some nights she still rang her mother's phone just to hear her voice.

Jeff plopped down in the booth again, an apologetic smile in place. "Sorry that took so long. But you know what they say—the longer it is, the longer it takes." He sipped his coffee. "You okay?"

"Yeah. Sure."

"Sure sure?"

"Sure sure." Tahmina worked up a fake smile. "Hey, how about that butt-ugly dress Tansey had on?"

"O-M-G," Jeff said, and laughed. "Did you see that shit? Like the unholy union of Hot Topic and mother-of-the-bride."

Tahmina had thought the dress was pretty, but she knew Jeff would go off on it.

"Too bad the infection couldn't have done something useful like wiping out her craptastic taste," Jeff said.

Roxie dropped the check. Under "Total" at the bottom, she had scribbled, *Whatever*. "Do y'all mind paying up? I'm thinking about closing early so I can go to prom."

"Sure. What do you need?" Tahmina asked.

Roxie laughed. "Everything. You could mop the back or fix the faucet or get me more coffee beans."

"I'll take a look at that faucet," Jeff said, and headed back to the kitchen.

Tahmina followed the conga line of prom goers out into the parking lot, and waited by the cruiser. Across the road the stadium lights were on dim, the best they could offer. Inside the diner Roxie hung the closed sign and carried her prom dress into the bathroom. A minute later Jeff came out singing an old R & B song his mom used to like.

"Did you fix the faucet?"

"Totally. Sort of. Okay, not really. I tried, though." He took the pink plastic carnation from his pocket and handed it to Tahmina.

"What's this for?" she asked.

"Prom. We're going."

"Right." Tahmina laughed. And then, a second later, she said, "You're serious."

"Indeed." Jeff opened the trunk, took out a straw fedora. He rolled up the sleeves of his uniform, exposing the muscular curves of his biceps.

"We can't go. We're the cops."

Jeff gestured to the empty parking lot. "Who is there to police? Everybody's at the stadium."

Tahmina looked down at her rumpled too-tight navy blue officer's uniform and bulky black sneakers. She wore no makeup, and her unwashed hair was tucked into a low ponytail. She smelled of smoke, spilled gasoline, and sweat. It was not the way she'd envisioned prom.

Jeff opened the passenger side door with a flourish. "Just for a while."

Tahmina got into the car and tucked the plastic flower behind her ear, and Jeff closed the door. For fun he turned on the lights, letting the kaleidoscopic red-and-white announce their arrival in style.

The football field swarmed with kids of all ages. Tahmina heard a group of senior guys complaining that lowly seventh graders had crashed the prom, but there was no one to stop them from coming, and the guys went back to passing a vodka bottle around the circle, since there was no one to stop that, either. On the fifty-yard line somebody had set up a battery-powered sound dock to play tunes. The speakers were too small, though, and the sound was mostly swallowed by the giant open space. Girls had taken off their shoes to dance, so that their heels wouldn't sink into the Astroturf. A line of obviously drunk dance team girls threw their arms across each other's shoulders for a high-kick routine that ended when they fell down on top of each other laughing hysterically. Up in the bleachers brightly clad teens sat in scattered clumps. They looked like one of those tile-strategy games abandoned midway.

Robin Watson had gotten drunker. Her dress was grass-stained and dotted with dirt. She moved unsteadily from person to person, taking their faces in her hands. "I'm sorry, so sorry," she'd say before moving on and repeating the gesture and apology. Most people laughed at her. A few girls hugged her. One of the guys copped a feel and high-fived his friends. Robin continued to thread her way through the crowd like an overzealous funeral director.

"Yo, partner!" Jeff shouted. He had found a cluster of dancers and was bouncing inside the circle of them. "Get your ass over here and dance."

"Sorry, partner!" Tahmina shouted back. "I can't compete with your promalicious moves. I'm gonna make the rounds."

"You want me to come with?"

"Nah. It's okay. You dance."

"You're all right, partner. This would be awesome cop-bonding shit for our TV show," Jeff yelled.

"You guys have a show?" a girl asked him.

"Not yet, but when things get back to normal . . ."

Tahmina walked away from the dancing, the music, the romance and small pockets of drama unfolding on the field, the sad ministrations of Robin Watson. Under the bleachers she passed the two drug dealers they'd busted earlier. They were back in business. The smaller one caught her eye and smirked. Tahmina let it go. She walked to the fence and stared out at the desert. The wind had changed direction, and the smoke was not as strong. The night air was clean and a little cool. She wondered if she should go back and bust up the drug trading. After all, she was the law. The law was a lie, she knew now, but it was a necessary lie, a construction that was needed so that everyone felt safe. Like having parents. Believing they would protect you no matter what, that they would bridge the unknowable distance between you and death for as long as possible. But there were no parents anymore, and everyone dancing on that football field had seen death up close. They had seen that it was not always the end, and that there were far worse things to fear than death, things that would not stop just because you said the prayers and fed the fire and kept the laws.

Tahmina took the night-vision goggles out of her pocket and slipped them on. She put her face to the metal cage and looked out toward the Tower of Silence, where the tunnels were. She had first noticed them three weeks ago, faint scars branching off from the burial site in different directions, all of them snaking toward the town. On subsequent visits she'd seen that they were moving, getting closer. In another two weeks, maybe less, the tunnels would reach them. She hadn't mentioned it to anyone, not even Jeff. What was the point? The law was an illusion. Tahmina would keep that illusion alive for as long as she could.

A loud bang startled Tahmina. She heard a girl's scream followed by a succession of hard pops like a hail of bullets. Gun in hand, Tahmina raced out onto the football field. Her breath caught as she looked up. The night sky was on fire with strange weeping flowers of colored light. The firecrackers zigzagged up into the dark with an audible hiss before exploding into tiny pinpricks of red, blue, green, and white that burst out yet again into rippling sparks. The crowd roared its approval.

"Hold on. We're just getting this party started!" Javier shouted over the din. Grinning, he caught Tahmina's eye.

"Sorry. I had an extra box under the bed. You gonna bust me, Officer Hassani?"

They all turned to look at her. Tahmina shook her head. "It's prom."

And then everyone was cheering, shouting "Fuck yeah!" Some of the football players nearby hugged her and offered her a beer, which she declined. Tansey Jacobsen threw her arms around Javier's neck and kissed him hard on the mouth, leaving a bright red smear of lipstick across his cheek when she pulled away.

"Get ready! This is the best one yet." Javier stood back and lit the tail on another firecracker. It shot straight up. For a split-second nothing happened. Tahmina craned her neck to the sky, anxious for the heat-quickening bang, for the moment of wonder. She couldn't stand the waiting.

"I'm sorry," Robin Watson said into the unbearable silence. "I'm sorry."

And the sky exploded with new light.

About the Authors

LIBBA BRAY is the author of the *New York Times* bestselling Gemma Doyle Trilogy and is the recipient of the 2010 Michael L. Printz Award for *Going Bovine*. She lives in Brooklyn with her husband, son, and two cats of questionable intelligence. She has always found zombies to be vastly entertaining dinner companions who will eat just about anything, whereas unicorns are vapid bores who complain a lot and never bring good wine. You can visit her online at LibbaBray.com.

MEG CABOT (her last name rhymes with "habit"—as in "her books are habit-forming") is the #1 *New York Times* bestselling author of over twenty-five series and books for both adults and tweens/teens, selling over fifteen million copies worldwide. Visit her website at MegCabot.com.

CASSANDRA CLARE is the *New York Times*, *Wall Street Journal*, and *USA Today* bestselling author of the young adult urban fantasy series The Mortal Instruments. She is also the author of the upcoming prequel trilogy The Infernal Devices. She lives in western Massachusetts with her fiancé and two cats. She was once suckered by a unicorn into a real estate scam in Florida and now she doesn't trust them. Visit her online at CassandraClare.com.

KATHLEEN DUEY grew up in the Colorado mountains and now lives in Southern California. Kathleen's young adult trilogy, A Resurrection of Magic, began with *Skin Hunger*, a 2007 National Book Award Finalist. The second book, *Sacred Scars*, was a 2009 Cybils finalist. Both books were honored as *Kirkus Reviews* "Best of YA" picks, featured in *Locus*, and are on state Teen Read lists. Kathleen is working on the third book now. You can learn more at KathleenDuey.com.

ALAYA DAWN JOHNSON lives and writes in New York City, whose many charms do not include its smells or its weather. She is the author of the Spirit Binders trilogy, the first two books of which are called *Racing* *the Dark* and *The Burning City*. (Book three is in the works.) She has also written the entirely unrelated 1920s vampire novel *Moonshine*. You can find out more about her on her website: AlayaDawnJohnson.com.

MAUREEN JOHNSON is the bestselling author of several young adult novels, including *Suite Scarlett*, *Scarlett Fever*, *Devilish*, *13 Little Blue Envelopes*, and its upcoming sequel, *The Last Little Blue Envelope*. She lives in New York City, where she eagerly awaits the zombie apocalypse. You can visit her online at MaureenJohnsonBooks.com.

MARGO LANAGAN has written three short story collections: *White Time*, *Black Juice*, and *Red Spikes*; a novel, *Tender Morsels*; and a novella, "Sea-Hearts," published in the anthology *X6*, edited by Keith Stevenson. She has won three World Fantasy Awards, two Printz Honors, four Aurealis Awards and four Ditmar Awards, and found herself on the shortlists of numerous other awards, including the Hugo, Nebula, Tiptree, and Shirley Jackson. Margo lives in Sydney, Australia, and is currently working on another novel and a fourth collection. She can be found online at AmongAmidWhile.blogspot.com.

GARTH NIX's novels include the award-winning fantasies *Sabriel*, *Lirael*, and *Abhorsen*, and the young adult science fiction novel *Shade's Children*. His fantasy books for children include *The Ragwitch*; the six books of the Seventh Tower sequence; and the seven books of the Keys to the Kingdom series. His books have appeared on the bestseller lists of the *New York Times*, *Publishers Weekly*, the *Guardian*, the *Sunday Times* and the *Australian*, and his work has been translated into thirty-eight languages. He lives in a Sydney beach suburb with his wife and two children. Learn more at GarthNix.com.

NAOMI NOVIK is the *New York Times* bestselling author of the Temeraire series and winner of the Campbell Award. She studied English literature and computer science and worked on computer games before writing *His Majesty's Dragon*, the first of the Temeraire novels. Her latest, *Tongues of*

Serpents, is the sixth. Naomi lives in New York City with her husband and ~~six eight~~ a large number of computers. Her website and LiveJournal are at Temeraire.org.

DIANA PETERFREUND is the author of the four books in the Ivy League series, as well as *Rampant* and *Ascendant*, two books about killer unicorns and the kick-ass girls who hunt them. She lives in Washington D.C., so she has first-hand knowledge that zombies aren't as scary as folks think they are. Visit her website: DianaPeterfreund.com.

CARRIE RYAN is the author of two novels set decades after the zombie apocalypse: *The Forest of Hands and Teeth* and *The Dead-Tossed Waves*. The third in the trilogy, *The Dark and Hollow Places*, will be released in Spring 2011. She lives with her husband in Charlotte, North Carolina, and they are not at all prepared for the inevitable zombie uprising. Visit her website: CarrieRyan.com.

SCOTT WESTERFELD is the author of many novels for both adults and teenagers, including the Uglies, Midnighters, and Leviathan series, and a vampire-zombie apocalypse duology, *Peeps* and *The Last Days*. He keeps well-stocked bunkers in both New York City and Sydney, Australia. Visit him online at ScottWesterfeld.com.